Soar Like

Eagles

For information contact;

Celebrate Lit Publishing

29078 Whitegate Lane

Highland, Ca, 92346

www.celebratelitpublishing.com

Book and Cover design by Roseanna White

ISBN: 978-1540779045

First Edition: January 2017

In Memory of

Carol Neuser Wangard
1933 – 2011

My mother had the gift of serving.
She would have made a fine Doughnut Girl.

Jesus! What a Guide and Keeper!
While the tempest still is high.
Storms about me, night o'er takes me,
He, my Pilot, hears my cry.
J. Wilbur Chapman

Chapter One

Dennison, Ohio
Wednesday, December 29, 1943

Carol Doucet unscrewed the bolt and wrestled the meat grinder off the table's edge. As she scraped the last of the ham sandwich spread out of the grinder, her friend Fran laid out slices of bread.

Fran blew a wisp of hair out of her eyes. "I still can't believe you gave up your job."

Carol pursed her lips. Why couldn't Fran understand her desire? They'd been over this countless times since she'd received notice from the Red Cross to report to Washington.

"Giving up my job as a society reporter can hardly be considered a sacrifice." She twirled her spoon in the air. "'Olive Sullivan wore a crimson gown trimmed with antique lace to last night's Rotary Christmas party.'" The spoon hit the table with a clank. "That is so frivolous. Who cares, with a war going on? I'm determined to do my part in the war effort, no matter how insignificant it seems."

"What do you call this?" Fran waved her hand around the train station's back room before grabbing the bowl of ham salad. She slopped the spread onto the slices of bread. "We're volunteering our time, our food, and our thanks to the servicemen coming through Ohio. Carol, you don't have to go overseas to serve coffee and doughnuts."

Carol added top slices of bread, cut the sandwiches in half diagonally, and stacked them on a platter. "No, but I want to go. The war is having a profound effect on our generation and I want to be part of it, to see it. I want to help. I'm sure I'll still have opportunities to write while overseas, maybe not as a reporter, but about my own experiences."

"Wars are deadly, Carol. You could be killed."

"The Red Cross won't send us to the front. I'll be safe."

"Are you sure you're not just running away from Sally and Mike?"

Fran's quiet question stopped Carol's hand from draping a tea towel over the sandwiches. "I can't believe you would think that."

Someone started a phonograph record, and the melancholy strains of "I'll Be Home for Christmas" flooded the train station. Carol winced. A song about a soldier dreaming of being home with his loved ones for the holiday was not going to cheer the soldiers and sailors crisscrossing the country in training and preparation for shipping out to the war zones.

Another canteen volunteer poked her head in the kitchen door. "A train arrives in five minutes, ladies."

Five minutes. Good. The song would be finished by then.

Carol hoisted the platter, careful not to topple the sandwiches, and headed out for the serving tables. If she was honest with herself, the opportunity to leave Sally behind was a joyful thought. She bit her lip. Someday, the events that had transpired last fall might be funny, but for now they were still too shocking to be believed.

After three dates, Mike had asked her to marry him before he reported for naval training. Carol didn't regret saying no. He possessed a wild streak that scared her. Wartime marriages might be patriotic, sending off a sailor happy in the knowledge he had someone at home waiting for him. What about when he came back to a stranger? How many of those quickie weddings would lead to lifelong love? Carol envisioned her parents laughing together as they washed the supper dishes and sighed. She couldn't imagine sharing intimate moments with Mike.

She'd been shocked when her good friend, Sally waltzed in four days after the rejection and announced she would marry Mike. What was Sally thinking? They'd had five days together before Mike shipped out, and now Sally was pregnant. Carol shuddered every time she thought of it.

Fran followed her out with a heaping basket of apples. "I know you're relieved not to be in Sally's shoes, but I heard someone ask if you wish you hadn't turned your back on a husband and baby. Busybodies can get annoying real fast, and the timing of your departure suggests a desire to avoid them."

Long tables groaned with goodies set out for the troops in transit. Carol shifted a bowl of someone's homemade divinity candy to make room for her sandwich platter. She accepted a rack of quart bottles of milk from a neighbor and began pouring the milk into glasses.

"A coincidence. You know I've wanted to join the Red Cross all year, but they have that minimum age requirement. Next month I'll be twenty-five and eligible. As it is, I'm surprised I'm allowed to report for training before my birthday."

The train whistled in with a squeal of brakes and a hiss of steam. A deluge of young soldiers and sailors raced into the station. Carol smiled. It was always the same. Some of the boys stepped right up while others stopped and stared at the abundance of food. She grabbed a knife to slice one of the cakes on her table.

"I hope you boys brought your appetites." Mrs. Wills served as president of the Dorcas Society at the church Carol attended. "Help yourself. We've got all kinds of sandwiches, hard-boiled eggs, fruit, cookies, cakes, pies, coffee." Her voice faded into the din of hundreds of voices.

A tall, quiet officer dressed in an airman's uniform stepped up to the table and hesitantly selected a sandwich he placed in an empty box marked with a "K." Carol scooped up a slice of cake and offered it "How about some delicious, prize-winning cherry cake?"

He smiled and accepted the dessert. With his first bite, his eyes brightened. "Mmm, I can see why it's a prize winner."

Carol grinned. "My neighbor made it. Another slice for the road, or should I say, the rail?"

"Don't mind if I do." Holding out his box, he plucked an apple from the basket and added it to his meal. "This is really great, what you're doing here. Do you use up your own ration stamps?"

"It's our way of thanking you for what you're doing. Communities from all around take turns providing food. Today it's a ladies group from a church in Canton." Carol removed an empty plate and helped Fran slide in a new tray of cupcakes.

The airman lingered nearby, sipping a glass of milk, watching the hubbub, and nodding in time to "Angels We Have Heard on High." After pointing out to a trio of sailors which sandwiches were ham, chicken, or egg salad, Carol came back to him. "Are you traveling cross country?"

He grimaced. "No, thank goodness. That's not a fancy Pullman car we're riding in. I can't tell you how good it feels to walk around."

He snatched an egg from a platter being carried to the table, and his jacket gaped open. Carol spotted navigator wings adorning his shirt. The only planes she knew of that employed a navigator were the big four-engine bombers. She shivered as though someone had allowed the winter breeze to sweep in.

The airman didn't seem to notice as he finished the slice of cake and wiped his fingers on a handkerchief. His eyebrows lifted. "What does the C stand for?"

"The C? Oh!" Carol touched the flowery initial embroidered on her blouse. "Carol. And you are?"

"Chet."

"All aboard!" The stationmaster's call echoed through the station.

Chet handed her his empty glass. "Sure doesn't take long to get the train watered when there's something worth getting off for." He dipped his head. "It's been nice talking to you, Carol."

"Godspeed, Chet." The farewell slid off her tongue as though she said it every day. She'd heard it explained in church as "May God prosper you." As she watched the handsome brown-eyed airman stride outside, the expression seemed most appropriate.

The canteen emptied as the servicemen ran back to their train. A moment of silence reigned as the ladies caught their breath.

"Whew. I don't know what they feed them in the military, but it must not be enough." Fran materialized beside Carol. "We'll be lucky if our food holds out until the next shift arrives."

"I've heard they subsist on K rations or C rations, or some little box of canned stuff they have to eat cold. This is a smorgasbord in comparison." Carol stared out the window as the train chugged away. Chet's box must have held K rations at one time.

"Carol? Come on, we have to get ready for the next train."

"Right." She looked at the glass in her hand. "I'll wash coffee cups and glasses this time." She turned toward the kitchen, but Fran stood in her way.

"You want to wash dishes? What's gotten into you?"

Carol leaned back against the table and grinned. "Did you see who I was talking to? Three dates with him and I might have to change my mind about saying no." She straightened up with another shiver. "Seriously, I wouldn't mind getting to know him, except he's on a bomber crew. In Europe, they're dropping faster than autumn leaves."

Chapter Two

Chet squeezed into his seat between the window and his pilot, Lowell Hendricks. "Sure was good to stand up for a little while." He opened his ration box and took out the sandwich. Smelled like ham, with flecks of green pickle mixed in. He took a bite and savored it.

"Didn't you eat anything back there?" Lowell eyed the box filled with canteen selections.

"Mm-hmm." He swallowed his bite and pointed in his box. "Ate a slice of this award-winning cherry cake. This one's seconds."

On Lowell's other side, co-pilot "Andy" Anderson watched Chet bite into his sandwich. "I wish I'd thought to take in a box to bring back food. I could have gotten something more substantial. All I had was dessert. A wedge of pie, some chocolate cake, and four different kinds of cookies. Hoo boy. I can hear my mother now. 'Oscar James Anderson, you call that a balanced meal?' All I brought back was this popcorn ball. Some girl tucked in a slip of paper with her name and address on it."

Across the aisle, the fourth officer in their crew, bombardier Harvey Bamberger, leaned over. "I got the names and addresses of six of the lovely young ladies. While you guys dream about your food, I'll be getting sweet-scented letters."

"How could you have gotten six addresses, Bomby?" Lowell's hands, lying flat on his thighs, clenched. "We were in there less than ten minutes. That's a minute and a half per girl. Did they all know what you were up to?"

"A couple, maybe. I worked the whole room." Bomby tucked the addresses into an envelope already bulging with potential pen pals. His suave good looks attracted girls like a picnic attracted ants, and he knew it. He assumed a hangdog expression. "May I write to you, miss?"

Chet gazed out the window. His crewmate's antics to wheedle addresses from girls were

nothing short of phenomenal. Wedding rings didn't stop him, or the married women. Chet rubbed his chin. The waitress at the diner last night had admitted her husband was overseas, and then wrote her address on the back of Bomby's bomb score tally sheet. Incredible.

Too bad he didn't think to ask Carol if she'd like to write. Had she worn a ring? He hadn't looked at her hands. But she sure had sparkling, wide-set brown eyes, shiny brown hair that curled across her forehead, straight white teeth framed by red lips in a perpetual smile, and a slightly low voice as soothing as hot chocolate. He wouldn't mind getting to know her. His appetite sated, he closed his box, saving the rest for later.

Someone started playing a harmonica. After a few discordant notes, the tune became "White Christmas." A light snow swirled down beyond the window, adding the proper touch, and he began singing along.

When the last note faded away, a moment of silence was followed by applause. Chet's eyebrows rose and he looked around. His crewmates stared at him, and men throughout the passenger car stood watching him. His face heated. Had he been singing so loud that everyone heard him over the clickety-clack of the train?

A soldier kneeling backwards on the seat ahead of him said, "You sing better than that Bing Crosby fellow."

"'N is lots better than that Frank Sinatry guy all the girls is swooning over," added a boy across the aisle. "You oughta make records and git famous."

Appreciation gleamed in Andy's eyes. "How about that? We've got us a singing navigator. You can lead the singing on those long, boring flights. That'd liven things up."

Lowell shook his head. "I can see the headline now." He waved a hand through the air. "B-17 crashes while crew distracted with song."

"Aw, Lowell, it'll keep us more alert instead of falling asleep."

The harmonica player started "Santa Claus Is Coming to Town." Chet relaxed and smiled. He didn't know all the words for this song, and the attention shifted away from him. The snowflakes lured his gaze back to the window.

"Where do you think we'll end up?" Andy's question pulled Chet's attention back inside the train. Their eventual destination brought endless speculation.

"It's gotta be Europe. That's where the majority of B-17s fly." Bomby stretched his legs out in the aisle.

Chet would almost have given up his window seat to do likewise. Almost. "I'd rather go to the European Theater of Operations than the Pacific. Reports of how the Japanese treat prisoners make it a very inhospitable place if shot down."

"Yeah, the Japs on land and the sharks in the water, don't forget." Bomby pulled his feet in after a soldier tripped over them.

"So it's the ETO for us." Andy nodded as though the matter was settled.

"That leaves the question of joining the Eighth Air Force in England or the Fifteenth Air Force in Italy." Lowell sat perfectly still in the hard, upright train seat. Good practice, he called it, for when they flew missions of nine or ten hours.

"The English will probably be happier to see us than the Italians. After all, the Italians sided with Germany until recently and the English were fighting alone," Chet mused. "On the other hand, how many crashes have occurred in the English fog?"

"Yeah, and I hear the English don't chill their beer." Bomby would think of that. "The Italians prefer wine, don't they?"

Lowell ignored the question. "I don't think I've heard horror stories out of Italy like those we've heard about the Eighth Air Force. I can't forget that mission in October when they lost sixty bombers. Six hundred men."

The crewmates fell silent. No matter where they went, someone would be trying to kill them.

One thing was sure. No matter where they ended up, they'd never get lost because of Chet. His father's oft-repeated mantra mocked him.

You'll never amount to anything, boy.

Chet would show him. He was a good navigator, the best in his class at the Pan American Airways Navigation School. They'd even invited him to work for them after the war. This crew wouldn't come to harm because of him.

Chapter Three

Tuesday, January 4, 1944
Canton, Ohio

Carol filed her last story at the *Repository*.

"I hope you know what you're doing, dear." Mrs. Brant hovered while Carol cleared out her desk. "You should be looking for a man to marry, not running overseas."

Carol hid a smile. "But Mrs. Brant, overseas is where the men are." She straightened up and looked her supervisor in the eye. "I'm so tired of men patronizing me. 'You'll just get married. Why bother with college?' Even my mother. She sort of understands my desire to do something with my life, but she's afraid I'll end up an old maid if I don't grab someone before all the good men are taken." She dropped her conch shell paperweight into her box. "I'd rather be an old maid than married to the wrong man."

"An admirable sentiment, dear, but lonely."

Carol sighed as she watched Mrs. Brant return to her desk. Mr. Brant had died after being gassed in the last war. Mrs. Brant had never remarried. Why? Had all the good men already married or been killed? Why did they have to keep getting involved in all these wars, anyway? She hefted her box and, after a last look around, strode from the room in a whiff of newsprint.

The next day, Fran hosted a bon voyage luncheon. Several friends offered advice. Take lots of toilet paper. Don't be out alone after dark with all those gal-starved men around. Cut your hair and get a perm before leaving. If you end up in Africa, watch out for bugs.

Jane twisted her birthstone ring around a finger. "I wish I was going, too. I don't know why the Red Cross turned me down."

Fran's eyes widened. "Did you apply?"

"Yes. Filled out the application. Interviewed the same day as Carol. And got a thanks, but no thanks." Jane's shoulders heaved with her sigh and she dropped her hands into her lap. She turned sad eyes on Carol. "You are so lucky."

Sally had been fiddling with her silverware. Tears glistened in her eyes when she looked up. "Are you sure you want to go?"

Carol set down her cup of tea without taking a sip. "Of course I want to go. You know I've been planning on this ever since the United States joined the war effort."

"I know, but..." A tear slipped down Sally's cheek. "I got a cable from the war department. Mike's been wounded in the Pacific. It said..." She pressed a hand to her mouth. "It said he lost both his legs. Stay and help me, Carol. Please? I hardly know him."

Carol gaped at Sally even as her stomach roiled at what must have happened to Mike. But help her? How? Hold Mike's hand when he returned? Soothe his inevitable anger? Babysit their child after it was born?

Fran saved her from the need to respond. "Why'd you marry him, girl?

Sally straightened, but didn't square her shoulders. Her hand trembled as she traced a finger through the condensation on her glass. "It was exciting. He was going off to war. Everyone was cheering. I might not have had another chance."

"Oh, Sally—" Anything Carol said would sound insensitive.

Fran had no qualms. "Did you give any thought to falling in love with the man instead of glorying in the image of weddings and presents and playing house? You're stuck now, Sally. You vowed 'for better or worse'."

Carol laid a hand on Fran's arm. No point in banging Sally over the head with recriminations. Her own resolve hardened. She would not commit her heart to any man during the war. As a Red Cross girl, she'd spend her time boosting the men's morale. She'd be in close proximity to lots of men lonely for home, but any relationships would all be casual. She would have no regrets.

Chapter Four

Washington, D.C.
Monday, January 24, 1944

Carol's new abode claimed an exclusive neighborhood. The White House stood a mere block and a half away from the Emery Hotel.

"Too bad we don't have time to sightsee." She looked out the window as she pulled on her coat. "With so many things we need to buy, we may not manage more than a glance at the monuments of Washington as we rush by with our shopping lists."

Midge, her roommate from Springfield, Missouri, stood at the mirror to put on her hat. "I'm afraid to see my final tally. So many blouses we need. Laundry facilities must be lacking. Two pairs of sensible oxford shoes with laces. Sensible, mind you. Girdles, of all things. Not to mention the equipment I'd think the military would supply us with. Duffle bags? Footlockers? Canteens? My goodness."

Midge grabbed her purse and the list of requirements, and followed Carol out the door. "My grandmother decided the Red Cross' stipulation that we be college-educated meant only the well-to-do who could afford college would apply. Now I understand why they appealed for the rich."

"Don't forget we'll receive a maintenance payment in addition to the $150 a month salary. I'm sure once we accumulate all this stuff, we won't need to do any shopping while we're overseas. With the war going on, what could be available anyway?"

Carol had better be right about that. Her family wasn't upper class. She'd gone to college on a scholarship, and her funds were limited. "My big concern is all those immunizations we need. Typhus, tetanus, smallpox, typhoid, cholera, yellow fever. Some of them multiple times. Did I leave any out? They're turning us into pin cushions. Although that new Pentagon building where we get them is amazing."

"Do you think these shots mean we'll be going to India or the Pacific? I'd rather go to Europe."

Carol glanced sidelong at Midge. They'd completed their first week of training at American University, where the Red Cross leased campus space. The quality of her fellow classmates was impressive. The girls came from all around the country, with a full range of accents. Most appeared to be outgoing, motivated, and gregarious, important qualities she'd

needed as a reporter. They were good sports, with the ability to laugh in difficult situations, a necessity according to one instructor. Midge, however, did not fit in.

"Everyone has to get all these shots, and everyone can't all go to the same place. Don't forget, the men in the military are required to get the works too."

"Yeeesss." Midge bit her lip. "But Mrs. Zastrow's lecture yesterday was all about what the Red Cross girls are doing in the China-Burma-India theater of war."

"True, but we also heard how the British demand we charge our men for the food we serve in our clubs in Britain, simply because they charge their men in their clubs, and ours are better paid." The little quibbles between allies had amused Carol until she heard how the GIs blamed the Red Cross for requiring payment.

They reached the department store and looked for the women's section. Carol searched through the cotton underpants for her size.

"You gals must be with the Red Cross." A saleslady hovered nearby with a knowing smile and nodded toward Midge's list. "We've had a continuous stream of girls armed with those requirements. Keeping everything in stock has been a challenge."

Carol pulled out the necessary underwear. "Do you have blouses in size six? I need three more."

They left the store laden down with packages. "I never cared for plain blouses." Midge shuffled her purchases for an easier hold. "I like bright colors."

"You said you taught first grade. Young children would appreciate colorful outfits." Carol studied her new friend. "Why did you volunteer for Red Cross service? I get the impression you'd rather be back in the classroom."

"I lost my position to a war widow. She's got three children and needs the job more than I do." Midge blew a strand of hair off her face. "A neighbor works with the Red Cross and suggested I apply. I don't have any brothers, only two sisters. My mother latched onto the idea of having one of her children serving overseas. I'll give her something to brag about at her ladies luncheons."

Carol stopped in the middle of the sidewalk. "This wasn't your idea? Who did your interview, the neighbor?" At her roommate's nod, she shook her head. "Oh, Midge, you shouldn't be here."

"You're not kidding." Midge hung her head as she scuffed her toes at the pavement. "But I can't go home. You can't imagine how my mother would react." She raised her packages. "And I've already got all this, besides the uniforms we'll pick up this afternoon."

Carol resumed walking. "You need to talk to one of the instructors. Maybe you could transfer into domestic service. You'd still need the uniforms and all these supplies. The Red Cross operates clubs here, or you could try hospital work."

"Mother would be furious."

Carol shook her head. "You've heard the lectures about how difficult some of our situations will be. Like Persia or North Africa, where the temperatures range from way below freezing at night to well over one hundred degrees during the day. Or how physically demanding clubmobile work can be. Midge, if your heart isn't in it, you'll fail. You'll let yourself down, the Red Cross, and the men we'll be serving."

A tremulous sigh slipped out of Midge. "I guess you're right." She squared her shoulders. "No, you are right. I won't be teaching children, of course, which is what I want to do. But I'll be away from home and serving in uniform, which should still please Mother. I think I'll ask about hospital work. She'll feel better if she can brag about me caring for the wounded rather than working at a club. By the time the Red Cross girls see the wounded, they're all cleaned up and bandaged, right? I shouldn't have to worry about fainting at the sight of blood."

"You'll do fine. You didn't faint when we got our first inoculations, but two Marines did, remember?"

A giggle turned into a belly laugh and Midge brightened for the first time. "That was pretty funny. Two big, tough Marines, laid out on the floor." She raised a shoulder to brush tears from her eyes. "When the one guy collapsed against the man behind him, I thought the whole line might fall down like dominoes."

Carol stared at her reflection in the mirror, and smiled. She looked good in uniform. The light blue summer outfit was beautiful, but for now, she wore the dark blue-gray winter suit. Regulations stipulated her white blouse must be pinned at the neck with a Red Cross emblem. Both a billed cap and an overseas cap also featured the emblem. A Red Cross patch rode high on the left sleeves of both uniforms and the winter overcoat. She turned to Harriet. "We're official now."

At five feet, two inches, Harriet appeared a less likely candidate than Midge, but her diminutive size concealed a gung-ho attitude. She hailed from Vermont and refused to believe the local weather qualified as winter. "Good thing I ordered the alterations. This is much more comfortable." She reached for her coat. "We have some extra time. Let's run by the Lincoln Memorial."

Carol pulled on her new white gloves. "Great idea. Maybe we can stop at the Jefferson Memorial, too. This may be our only opportunity to see them."

They were ascending the steps to visit Mr. Lincoln when a trio of sailors saluted them. Carol swallowed her surprise and returned the salute. The boys moved on, and Carol and Harriet stared after them.

"Well, how do you like that? They must think we're officers. These uniforms are swell." Harriet's smile stretched across her face. "I could get used to this."

"Once we graduate from the training program, we will be honorary officers." Carol shivered. Officer status was supposed to warrant them better treatment if captured by the enemy. Surely they wouldn't come so close to enemy lines as to make capture possible. She ran a hand through her shoulder-length hair. "Some of the girls were talking about getting permanents. I'm thinking of trying one."

"Not me. I'll keep putting up my hair in bobby pins every night. It's no big deal."

Back at the hotel, Carol found Midge paging through a stack of papers. She looked up with a new gleam in her eyes.

"I did it." Jumping up from her bed, the papers scattering, Midge grabbed her in a hug before twirling away. "I'm staying here in the States. Mrs. Schneider suggested I go into hospital recreation." She scooped up the papers. "I'll be taking classes in table games and crafts. Oh, Carol, this looks like fun."

Carol couldn't help laughing. Midge's new direction was right for her, but overseas remained Carol's goal, to serve where the fighting took place. And not just anywhere. She agreed with Midge's earlier desire. She wanted to go to Europe.

Chapter Five

Kearney, Nebraska
Tuesday, February 22, 1944

Their training came to an end. Chet and his crew reported to the Army Air Field in Kearney, Nebraska, where they found a field full of gleaming new B-17Gs. They'd been training in an older F model. As soon as they found their assigned airplane, Bomby jumped up to grab the edge of the forward escape hatch and swung his legs up to hoist himself aboard. He disappeared into the nose. Chet followed close behind.

The bombardier's station perched right at the edge of the Plexiglas bubble that capped the nose. Bomby grabbed the controller arm stowed to his right and swung it to the central position. Without switching on the power to the chin turret at his feet, he peered through the optical gun sight for the chin turret guns, lacking in the earlier models of B-17s. It had been added after too many planes were shot down in frontal attacks by enemy fighter planes.

"Have you figured out how to use that thing?"

"No pro-blame-oh." Bomby manipulated the control handles one way, then the other. "See that plane over there? It's a Focke Wulf 190. Ak-ak-ak-

ak-ak-ak." He spun back in the opposite direction. "See that? A Messerschmitt 110." He repeated his machine gun noise, breaking off when he whipped his head up. "Uh-oh, here comes a Stuka dive bomber with rockets." He stepped forward, but stumbled against the Norden bombsight.

"We're goners." Chet shook his head and seated himself at the navigator's table, located behind the bombardier's station on the left. His gaze lingered on the radio compass, the periodic compass, the drift meter. These were his responsibilities, and he knew how to use them.

Lowell poked his head into the nose. "Everything in order?" He watched Chet run his hand over the empty table and laughed. "You'll probably never see such a clean, uncluttered table again. Enjoy it."

Bomby spun around on his chair. "You can always tell a navigator by his pencils, maps, and such. You can always tell a pilot, but you cannot tell him much." He laughed as he spun back to face forward.

Lowell looked at Chet with a grimace. The oft-repeated ditty had worn thin. "We're going up for a check ride in the morning, for instrument calibration. Everything must be checked carefully. This is the plane we'll be flying overseas."

"Do you know our destination?" Chet didn't expect a definite answer. For security purposes, orders weren't issued until the last moment.

Lowell hesitated and glanced at Bomby, who turned around for his answer. "I've heard unofficially we'll leave in two days for Dow Field." He paused, building the tension. "Dow's in Maine."

Chet's breath left him in a whoosh. "So it's the ETO for us. I'll take that over the Pacific Theater of Operations."

"Yeah, Europe is better, but Maine suggests we'll be going north to England, not south to Italy." Bomby swore and pounded his fist on the bombing control panel.

Lowell frowned. "Careful with that, will you? We don't want to wreck anything before we even get this bird off the ground." He turned and eased up through the hatchway to the cockpit.

Outside the nose window, the six enlisted men assigned to their crew huddled with a maintenance man. Whatever he was telling them, he had their rapt attention. Chet stood to watch them. He smiled. He'd never seen them so intent. They sure were a mixed lot. Ken Cottrell, their engineer and top turret gunner, was the oldest man in their crew at thirty-one. He knew his business. If anything ever went wrong with their plane while they were in the air, Cottrell would figure out a way to fix it.

Dexter Small was their radioman, but he wasn't small. He bumped his head continually when moving about in the plane. Now he wore his steel infantry helmet all the time to avoid scrambling his brains.

On the other hand, their ball turret gunner bore the equally unlikely name of Homer Long. He barely cleared five feet, an advantage for his position. Chet had no desire to curl up in the ball, which hung suspended from the plane's underbelly.

Stan Price handled their left waist gun. Chet's gaze lingered on him. How in the world had Price survived basic training? His gullibility astonished them all, but no more so than his shooting ability. He said he'd hunted a lot in the hills around his Kentucky home. Any German fighter pilot who came within range of Price's gun would pay with his life.

Mike Zempel would join Price in the waist, manning the right gun. He was a hard drinking, scrappy guy from Boston whose temper concerned them. Chet knew of at least one instance when Lowell, as plane commander, had a talk with him. Now he stood calmly alongside their tail gunner.

John Lemke hailed from Alabama, and he wouldn't surprise Chet to suddenly proclaim, "The South will rise again." Good thing he worked in the tail, away from Zempel, who called him Johnny Reb. He glanced up now and, spotting Chet, grinned. Chet nodded. They were a good bunch.

With Lowell's blessing, Chet had plotted their route to pass over the southwest corner of Michigan. He'd called his grandparents to say goodbye before going overseas, but hoped to catch a glimpse of them on their way to Maine. Grandma had promised to wear her red coat.

"We should be coming up on Niles in three minutes," he reported as they flew over Lake Michigan. "It's twenty-five miles inland."

In response, Lowell took the bomber down to five hundred feet. They roared over the Michigan shoreline, Chet intently watching for landmarks. "Coming up, dead ahead. My grandparents live across from a park."

"I see a big flashing light." Andy reported from the cockpit. "And it's in an open space."

"That's the park." Chet swallowed hard. "Must be old Mr. Lauridsen signaling us." He strained to see through suddenly watery eyes. "There's the house. And there are my grandparents." He waved energetically from the bubble nose window.

Grandma had her hands clenched below her chin, but briefly raised one hand. Grandpa stood beside her, one arm around her, the other raised in salute. All around them, their neighbors stared upward. A few children jumped around, waving American flags. Jeepers creepers, they'd gotten the whole neighborhood out.

"So that's yer grandparents, but where's yer folks?" Price asked the question over the intercom.

"My mother's dead and I have no contact with my father. He's a drill sergeant somewhere. I lived with my grandparents after Mom died when I was eight."

Niles disappeared behind them and Lowell soared back up to a safer altitude. Chet slumped onto his chair and rubbed his eyes. Who knew when, or if, he might see them again?

#

After an overnight stay at Dow, the Hendricks crew flew on to Gander, Newfoundland. Chet learned they were to fly directly to Prestwick, Scotland, without a stop in Iceland. He took a deep breath. That meant one long haul and he bore the full responsibility to guide their course.

They took off in the evening, allowing him to use the stars in celestial navigation. Throughout the night, his constant companion was his circular slide-rule and a wind triangle called an E-6B computer. With it, he transformed his observations into true headings and airspeeds, and calculated their estimated time of arrival.

Most of the crewmen sacked out in the radio room, but Chet couldn't afford the luxury of a little sleep. During his star sightings through the overhead astrodome, he looked back at the cockpit. For a while, Lowell was missing, later Andy. Even the pilots could spell each other, but Chet had no one to relieve him.

By three o'clock, his eyelids threatened to stay closed every time he blinked. He stood up and stretched.

"You managin' to stay awake all night, sir?"

Chet started at Price's voice and nearly stumbled when the gunner eased through the hatchway. "Just barely."

Price crept forward to the Plexiglas nose. Ten thousand feet below, the North Atlantic glimmered in faint moonlight. "How do you know where to go?"

Chet smiled. "We have signposts in the heavens."

"Huh?"

"The stars. They're pointing the way."

Price's head tilted back. "Ya know exactly where we are by looking at them stars?" Disbelief colored his voice.

Chet snapped on his desk lamp and pointed to his map. "We're right about here."

Price stared at the map. "That there's Iceland?" His finger stabbed the island nation. "Most planes usually go there first, but that's way outta the way."

"Not really." Chet swallowed a yawn. Price gave him an opportunity to keep himself occupied. "We're flying the great circle route, which is the shortest distance between two points. Remember, the earth is rotating from west to east, so we have to fly faster than the earth's rotation to get to Scotland, because it's rotating away from us. But we fly a northerly route, so we'll catch up to Scotland faster."

Too bad he didn't have a globe to demonstrate, but maybe it didn't matter. Price looked at him in awe. "How do you know all that?"

"I've probably had a few more years of schooling than you."

Muffled laughter from the cockpit sounded in Chet's headphones, belatedly disguised by a cough. Chet popped his head into the astrodome. Andy greeted him with a grin and a thumbs up.

As dawn tinged the eastern horizon, Chet shot speed lines with his octant. They should make landfall over Donegal Bay in Ireland at 0700. As the hour approached, he strained his eyes searching for signs of land. A tailwind had pushed them speedily across the ocean, allowing them to bypass fog-shrouded Iceland, but if they didn't find land soon, they'd be out of gas.

You'll never amount to anything, boy.

His father's poisonous words taunted him. Chet stiffened his spine. *I'll show him. Wasn't I top student in my Pan Am class? Don't I possess a certificate for a job with the airline after the war?*

Ireland had to be close by. His watch read 0703. Three minutes beyond his estimated arrival time and nothing... There! He raised clenched fists. "Land ho."

"Can you identify it?" Lowell's question made sense. They'd heard of a crew who missed Ireland and landed in France, delivering a brand new B-17 to the Germans.

A shoreline wavered to the south, and more shore toward the north. Straight ahead was Donegal Bay. Bull's eye. Chet swallowed hard to dislodge the lump in his throat. For the rest of his life, he would cherish this moment. His voice quavered a bit as he gave Lowell the heading for Prestwick. All Lowell said was, "That's good work, Chet."

The gas gauges hovered at empty when they arrived over the Scottish air field. Fog had closed the field and a controller told them to divert to RAF Valley in Wales.

Chet grabbed his map and his euphoria vanished. "That won't do. Wales is over three hundred miles away. I'll try to find some other landing strip."

As Lowell circled Prestwick, one of the gunners screamed over the intercom. "There it is. A runway through a hole in the fog. Nine o'clock."

The bomber veered left. Lowell chopped the throttles and dove for the hole. Chet's maps and charts slid across his desk. The fog closed in again before they taxied to a stop at the end of the runway. A jeep bearing a Follow Me sign led them to a parking spot.

After flying over eleven hours, the crew tumbled wearily from the plane. The jeep driver greeted them. "You were lucky to find us. We've heard three planes have crashed."

Price hefted his duffle bag. "They didn't have ace navigators like us."

Chet permitted himself a small smile. Kissing the ground seemed like a fool thing to do, but he had an urge to do so. Strange sentiment, really. They'd arrived in the war zone.

Chapter Six

Liverpool, England
February, 1944

Carol wanted to go ashore. This was her first visit to a foreign country, after all. Formalities had to be observed, however, and that included assembling in the *Aquitania's* lounge for instructions. The last official to address the Red Cross girls was a gorgeous Royal Air Force group captain. Carol didn't mind sitting a little longer to listen to his mesmerizing elocution.

"Mm, hmm," Harriet agreed, her eyes dreamily following the group captain. "Too bad we won't be serving the likes of him."

Carol bumped her shoulder. "Watch it there, missy. The American military is well stocked with handsome young men."

"Yet not a single one of them was aboard ship with us. Believe me. In the twelve days it took to cross the ocean, I looked."

"His British accent caught your ear. Soon enough we'll be hearing it so much, we won't even notice."

A train ride brought the Red Cross contingent to London, where Carol, Harriet, and an Idaho gal named Audrey dropped their gear in their billet and headed out to explore. Audrey had a map and announced they were happily located near many of the famous landmarks. "We can see Buckingham Palace and Hyde Park. Down this street called the Mall, we'll come to the Houses of Parliament and Westminster Abbey."

"Where's London Bridge?" Harriet peered at the map, tracing a finger along the River Thames. "Goodness, the streets meander all over the place. What were they thinking when they laid out the city?"

"In medieval days, the streets were probably cow paths." Carol found their location on the map. "Since we have the time today, why don't we head for the parliament buildings and Westminster? They're at the river, so maybe we'll spot the bridge, too."

They set off, heads swiveling back and forth. Carol gaped at the extent of bomb damage. Everyone knew of the London Blitz in 1940 and further bombings inflicted upon the city by the German Luftwaffe. War-weary London displayed none of the brightness and energy of Washington. 'Dreary and gray' described the British capital. Boarded-up windows graced buildings all around them. They paused beside the shattered remnants of a building, none of them speaking. Had anyone died in the rubble? Carol hunched her shoulders. She'd wanted to be a part of the war. Now here she was, right smack dab in the war zone, seeing its destruction.

"There's Big Ben." Harriet took skipping steps in excitement. "What time is it? Will it toll the hours, do you think?"

An elderly man clad in a shabby coat with mismatched buttons spoke up. "Ben isn't the clock."

Harriet swung around. "He isn't?"

The man chuckled. "Ben is only the bell in St. Stephen's Tower." His shoes looked ready to fall to pieces, yet he stood erect as he tipped his hat to them. "May I show you around my city?" At their hesitation, he added, "It's the least I can do to show my appreciation for you coming across the pond to help."

He took them inside Westminster, offering the girls tidbits of insight they would never have gleaned on their own. "A bit of damage, unfortunately. The Germans left their calling cards."

As they wandered through the final resting places of famous Britons, Carol placed her hand on a railing. Here she was, in proximity to luminaries she'd read about in history books. Who, in centuries past, had clutched the handrail she now touched, and trod the well-worn steps?

She pivoted in a tight circle. England had hundreds of years of history. The people had repelled invasions, withstood assaults, and beaten back the

Luftwaffe. Yet they still thrived. Prime Minister Churchill had called it their finest hour. Now she got to share in the conquest of evil. An article wrote itself in her mind to send to the *Repository.*

Back outside, they circled around the Houses of Parliament to the Thames. Harriet looked up and down the river. "Which bridge is London Bridge?" When their guide raised his brows, she stammered. "You know, 'London Bridge is falling down, falling down.'"

Recognition dawned in the old man's eyes. "I suspect you're more interested in the Tower Bridge. It was designed to complement the Tower of London. That's the fortress begun by William the Conqueror in 1078, and the prison where Henry the Eighth had two wives executed."

"Oh, yes. Is it nearby?" Carol held her breath, waiting for his reply.

Audrey studied her map. "It's a bit of a distance."

"Not to worry. We'll be there in two shakes of a lamb's tail." Their guide flagged down a taxi and ushered the girls in.

Upon seeing the Tower Bridge, Harriet squealed. "This is great!"

They walked to the middle of the bridge and watched the river traffic before wandering the grounds of the Tower of London.

Their guide shared snippets of life during the blitz. "My granddaughter was married and widowed in the same week. Her husband died in the collapse of a building when he was trying to dig someone out."

The girls murmured their sympathy, but he shook his head. "Don't be sorry for her. She's actually relieved now to be free of that union. She rushed to the altar barely knowing the lad. Nice fellow, I'm sure, but they were caught up in war hysteria."

"I know someone who married like that. She's sorry now." Carol watched a double-decker bus ease around a corner. How were Sally and Mike getting along?

Their host nodded. "He was to report to the navy two days after he died. They didn't want to miss out on anything. I don't understand such reasoning. If he survived and came back, they'd still have opportunities. If he doesn't, what's the point? Just to say they had a wedding?"

Exactly. A wartime romance could be enjoyed only as long as serious commitments weren't indulged. No man would change her mind and bankrupt her future.

At Audrey's request, their guide deposited them at Harrods department store. Before bidding them goodbye, he gave them directions for finding their way back to their billet. "You cawn't miss it." They showered him with effusive thanks as he tipped his hat and headed on his way.

"What a nice old man." Harriet hugged herself as they entered the store. "I wonder if he spends all his time looking for Americans to take sightseeing."

A pair of American soldiers on their way out stopped at the sight of their Red Cross uniforms. One asked, "Do you have an aspirin?"

Audrey's face clouded. "We aren't nurses."

Carol dug in her purse. "I should have some."

She found her pill case and shook out an aspirin into the soldier's hand.

He gulped it down without water and sighed. "Thank you, ma'am."

A grin split Harriet's face. "Like the posters say, the Red Cross is at his side."

By late afternoon, a substantial fog hid the sights. It also obscured the directions back to their billet. "The old man said we can't miss it, but I think we missed it." Harriet took Audrey's map. Her finger circled an area that probably contained a square mile. "We're somewhere around here, aren't we?"

Three men wearing Royal Air Force uniforms stopped beside them. "We'd be more than pleased to help you ladies. You're Americans, are you not? How smashing. Your American brothers are all over here helping themselves to our English lassies. Now we've got a switcheroo. Blimey, that's rich."

Carol bit back a laugh at Harriet's wide-eyed wonder. "Can you help us find Princes Gate?"

"I flipping well hope so. That's a posh address in Kensington. Right this way, if you please." Carol found her hand tucked into the elbow of a tall, brown-eyed, blond who introduced himself as Nigel. The others paired off with Audrey and Harriet.

The fog thickened to the point of hiding everything beyond three feet of them. "I say, this will keep the streets clear. No need to huddle on the sidewalk."

Nigel tugged Carol off the curb. Snaking his left arm around her, he clasped her left hand in his right and waltzed her out to the middle of the street. The other men followed his example. They danced the girls to their billet in short order. Breathless from laughing, Carol curtsied to Nigel's bow.

Harriet sighed as their escorts disappear into the fog. "What a fabulous first day in England. Whoever imagined we'd be dancing in the streets of London? I'm going to like it here."

Monday morning, all the new arrivals met together at the Red Cross Headquarters on Grosvenor Square for orientation. A surprise awaited them. They were given a choice in how they wanted to serve. The Red Cross operated several branches: clubs, hospitals, field service, and clubmobiles. Carol raised her hand to work on clubmobiles.

The recreation clubs had been created as homes away from home where American servicemen could congregate while on leave. They offered American food, music, tickets to West End shows, maps of places to see, underground and bus routes, and American girls to talk to. With the servicemen disbursed throughout Great Britain, however, most lacked the opportunity to visit the clubs. The Red Cross' solution was to put miniature clubs on wheels and send them around the countryside to the men.

"The clubmobiles are the best way to serve the men in their day-to-day routines," Carol whispered to Harriet. "And while we serve coffee and doughnuts to the men at their far-flung posts, we'll see much more of England."

"I want to stay in London. I like it here."

Carol sighed when Harriet opted for clubs. Everyone not joining the clubmobiles left for training elsewhere. Harriet waved and was gone. Carol probably wouldn't see her friend again, but she had little time to mourn.

"Hi, I'm Irene. Who's Carol and who's Audrey?" An ebullient blonde with Team Captain embroidered onto her Red Cross patch bounced to a stop in front of them. Barely giving them time to introduce themselves, she continued. "You're assigned to my team. We'll travel around to air bases clustered in East Anglia."

Irene bore responsibility for their paperwork, operation, and coordination with the Army Air Force. Carol would have more free time. Time to do some writing. She fought the urge to do a little bouncing of her own. Until the army was ready to invade Europe, the air force carried the war to Germany on their shoulders. And she would be there, at their side. She couldn't wait.

Their training began immediately with an introduction stressing the hard work they would be doing. Based in a small town, they would have a list of surrounding airfields in a fifty-mile radius to visit. They reached those bases on narrow, muddy roads, rain or shine. Their labor would be physically demanding, hefting large coffee urns, hoisting barrels of the specially prepared doughnut mix, making up the doughnut batter, scrubbing the greasy doughnut machine and the clubmobile, and washing coffee cups. No one asked to transfer to a different branch.

Such hard work made skirts impractical. Carol lined up to be fitted for her trouser uniform, known as 'battle dress,' at Debenham and Freebody's. As befitting an English tailoring establishment, the new uniforms, with a short Eisenhower-type battle jacket and slacks, came in RAF blue with a billed cap. An authorization slip from the Red Cross office entitled her to a pair of fleece-lined boots from the quartermaster stores. For further comfort in the cold, damp English winter, she purchased warm woolen red mittens and a scarf. Carol laughed at her reflection in the mirror with Irene. "We're ready to work, or take part in a snowball fight."

Before they could serve doughnuts, they needed to learn how to make them. "I used to watch the doughnuts being made from the window of a doughnut shop. They'd flip out of that machine, ready to be gobbled up, like magic." Irene leaned forward on her chair, her fingers kneading her thighs as though she itched to get at the machine. "Who'd guess I'd someday be making doughnuts myself?"

"The flour contains the sugar, skim milk powder, egg powder, and salt. All you have to add is water. You need the right amount of water to get the right consistency. Weigh it carefully." The instructor wagged her finger at them in time with her words. "Transfer the dough into the doughnut machine. The machine will do all the work for you, shaping the doughnuts, cooking them in the hot fat, flipping them over, and flipping them out. Don't touch the doughnuts with your fingers. Use these prongs." She held one up. "And ladies, don't get the prong caught in the flipper."

The process sounded easy enough.

British Green Line buses had been converted for clubmobile work. They all received the names of American states, cities, or heroes. Carol and her crewmates were assigned to the *Texas*.

"Oh, yay! I'm from Texas." Irene hustled aboard. Carol and Audrey exchanged grins and

hastened after her.

The kitchen took up the front. Panels opened out on one side of the clubmobile over a large counter where they would serve the boys. Coffee urns flanked both sides of the counter, with four more below. A little table stood between a metal-plated sink and the doughnut machine. Here they'd mix the dough. Irene pulled open a drawer, revealing rows of enamel cups.

Carol found another drawer full. "Guess we'll spend as much time washing dishes as making doughnuts."

The back of the bus featured a comfortable room complete with bunks where they could rest on long drives, or even sleep overnight. A Victrola and phonograph records claimed a place beside the bunks. A built-in broadcasting system allowed the girls to entertain the troops with the latest American music.

The Green Liners came with a professional British driver. Once the invasion took place and the clubmobiles followed the army to France, however, the girls would be doing their own driving in two-and-a-half ton GMC trucks. Carol bit her lip. She may not be assigned to go to the continent. No point in worrying about something that might not happen.

Finally, the day came when they received their assignment. Carol and Audrey crowded next to Irene to read their orders. "We'll live with a widow in Saffron Walden and serve the 121st Station hospital in Braintree and air fields in Sudbury, Lavenham, Bassingbourn, Nuthampstead, and Ridgewell. This is it." Irene bounced on her toes. "This is what we're here for. To serve up a touch of home for our men who haven't seen American women for months, maybe years."

A huge smile crossed Audrey's face and she danced a little jig. "Look out, airmen. Here we come."

Carol laughed. She grabbed Audrey's hands and they twirled together. "Look out, boys. We're ready for business."

Chapter Seven

Ridgewell Air Base
Thursday, March 16, 1944

Chet lay on his new bed in his new home. The cot was well used. One of the three crews occupying this Quonset hut had gone missing last week. The words of one of the veterans rang in his ears. "That used to be Harry Cooper's sack. Nice guy. Had himself a real sweet piece of work waiting for him at home. Nobody saw what happened to 'em. Maybe they'll come back, but probably not."

Chet had turned away. Hearing about missions gone awry was like sticking a finger in a socket.

Too bad he couldn't tune him out now. The man's snores would give a hog caller a run for his money. How were they supposed to sleep through such an infernal racket? A glance to his left revealed Lowell with his pillow pressed over his head. Beyond him, Andy suddenly sat up, ready to whip his pillow at the offender.

"No, don't." Given the long, deep penetration mission the squadron had flown that day, it would be rude to disturb the man, no matter how obnoxious the noise.

Andy threw off his blanket and stalked across the hut. "How are we supposed to get any sleep around here?"

Chet rose from his warm cocoon as Lowell uncovered his head. "He's on his back. Maybe if we turn him over, he'll keep his mouth shut."

The three crewmates flipped the offender over, tucked him in, and stood back to watch. Chet drew a deep breath at the rhythmic rise and fall of the man's shoulder. Being arrested for causing a death by suffocation would be a lousy way to start their combat tours.

They punched each other's arms in congratulations as they headed back to their cots. The other men in the hut didn't appear to use ear plugs, but Chet had better invest in a pair. He plumped up his pillow and settled down for some sleep.

"Bandits at ten o'clock level!"

The cry brought Chet to his feet, his blanket twisted around his legs. He stared around, heart pounding. Lowell, Andy, and Bomby all sat wide-eyed.

"Struthers, why aren't you firing?"

Their night crier was a member of the snorer's crew. Chet responded, "Gun's jammed. Smithers will nail them."

He looked to his own crew for support. Bomby raised two fingers to his forehead in a lackadaisical salute.

"Bombs away!" The new holler caused Chet to back into his cot and abruptly sit down. That crew was determined to be disruptive. "We got a hung-up bomb."

Once again Chet offered commentary. "Jonesy kicked it free. We're good. Let's get back to Ridgewell or we'll be late for chow." When no further shouts were uttered, he sank down onto his pillow. Maybe now they'd get some sleep.

"Fighters at twelve o'clock high!"

"Oh, for crying out loud." Andy jumped up and marched over to the guy dreaming out loud. "Those are Spitfires, man. Don't shoot 'em. They're our friends." He stood over the cot, hands on hips. If the man said any more, Andy would likely throttle him.

Silence stretched out. Finally, a chance to sleep.

But sleep took a long time to come. Chet laced his fingers beneath his head and stared at the rounded ceiling. Would they become like that too, reliving their rough missions in their sleep?

The Hendricks crew didn't start flying missions immediately. The four replacement crews that arrived together endured orientation lectures on pertinent topics ranging from flying conditions over the continent to living conditions in England. Together with Paul Braedel, a classmate from navigation school, Chet practiced with the Ground Electronic Equipment Box, a splendid navigation system that allowed them to pinpoint their position within half a minute.

"This measures the difference in arrival times of radio signals transmitted by Allied radio stations." Their instructor eyeballed each of his students. "I don't have to tell you we don't have any such stations in enemy-occupied territory. And the Germans are learning how to jam our signals, so," he paused, "exercise caution."

From the corner of his eyes, Chet peered at Paul, who sat in a deflated slump, and smiled. All the exciting possibilities of the box's capabilities popped like a balloon.

"It'll work well when we're within reach of England," he told Paul as they left the meeting. "I wonder if the Germans got their hands on a box from a downed plane. I know we're supposed to destroy the Norden bombsight if we go down, but nothing's been said about the GEE Box."

Paul had already flown his first mission. Despite Berlin being the target, deep in enemy territory, and the long distance, no enemy fighters had attacked and the flak shot up by anti-aircraft gunners had been inaccurate. Chet's squadron had been stood down that day. Too bad.

A throaty rumble rolled over the air base.

"The planes from today's mission are coming back." What an exhilarating sight! Goose bumps jumped up on Chet's arms. A formation of B-17s looked so majestic in flight. The rumble of the engines transmitted through the ground to his feet and vibrated in his chest. And he was a part of this mighty force. "Let's get over to the flight line."

They jumped on their bikes.

"Did you hear the plane crash on takeoff this morning?" Paul steered close to avoid a jeep.

"Yeah, it was from my squadron, but I don't know who the men were. I heard seven bodies were recovered, but only parts of the other three." Chet shuddered. How horrible it must have been to search through the wreckage. A fully fueled plane, full of bombs and fragile bodies, didn't leave much recognizable debris.

A crowd gathered at the control tower to sweat out the mission. "Twenty-two were put up, but one crashed." Paul counted the planes breaking out of formation in three plane elements. "Three, six, nine, twelve. Uh, oh. We lost a couple more. Only nineteen are here."

Scuttlebutt spread through the crowd. Chet and Paul skulked close to a man who had emerged from the first plane to land. "Two planes from the 532nd Squadron were lost over Germany. One exploded and the other left the formation with a lot of damage. They were *Dazzle Gal* and *Four Leaf Clover*."

Chet turned away, his stomach churning. "Three planes lost today from my squadron. And *Dazzle Gal* was the usual ride for a crew in my hut. The snorer and the guys reliving their missions."

They'd have quiet now, but what a high price had been paid.

How were they supposed to keep getting up in the morning, knowing their existence was so precarious?

Chet had done well in practice, but what if fear disabled him during a mission? Would he be able to do his job while someone was shooting at him? What would it be like?

Chet rested on his cot, too tired to even raise his arms to link his fingers under his head. His first mission lay behind him, and it had been easy, a milk run.

An operations officer had roused them from bed at three in the morning. Breakfast consisted of ham and eggs, food chosen to avoid giving the men gas, which would cause the bends at altitude. The mission briefing followed. Chet wrinkled his nose. The room had stunk of cigarette smoke, leather jackets, and pungent sweat. Rumor had it that one bombardier refused to wash his flight clothes for fear of jinxing himself. Must have been a lot of superstitious guys in the briefing hut this morning.

They'd targeted an airfield at St. Jean D'Angely, deep in France, closer to Spain than to England. Beautifully clear weather over France made the country look like an easily read map. No Luftwaffe planes would be using that airfield for a long time to come. They'd experienced no enemy fighters. No flak touched them. A perfect first mission. They landed back at Ridgewell by six, in time for debriefing and a late supper.

He'd done it. One mission down, twenty-nine to go. They wouldn't all be so easy, or so long. To be honest, he'd done nothing but go along for the ride. He'd marked checkpoints in his log, but tucked into the formation, they'd simply followed the leader.

A schoolboy could have done your job. You'll never amount to anything, boy.

Chet thrust his hands over his ears, but his father's hateful words refused to be silenced. He'd show him. He was a good navigator. Someday, he might even get to be a lead navigator. He'd prove him wrong.

Chapter Eight

Saffron Walden, England
March 27, 1944

The toilet flushed. Again. Carol leaped from her bed and dashed to the bathroom. No one was there. No one ever was.

Irene joined her with her hair up in bobby pins. "Audrey didn't do it. She's still sound asleep, and Mrs. Lester certainly wouldn't come upstairs when she has her own water closet downstairs."

"There must be a quirk in the plumbing, the water pressure, something like that." Carol turned back to the bedroom, her arms held close to her body. "I threw off my covers. Now my bed will feel icy cold."

"And it's a sure bet the coal has burned down to a useless smoldering in the fireplace." Irene scurried on tiptoe down the hall. "Morning's going to come quickly. We'd better ignore any more flushings. We've got a busy day tomorrow."

As Carol suspected, her bed sheets were cold. She didn't bother removing her bathrobe, and added another pair of socks before bundling herself back into bed. She peered through her cocoon of blankets to read her clock in the moonlight. Half past one.

Tomorrow was already today. They would spend much of their time at Lavenham Air Base. She ticked off the various stops—the hangars and around the perimeter where the mechanics repaired damaged planes, the motor pool, maybe they'd even pop into the infirmary. If a mission was underway, they might get to see the planes return. What a thrill it was to watch those huge planes come in. Finally warm enough to relax, her thoughts trailed away.

"I didn't hear a thing." Audrey was slathering marmalade on her bread when Carol came downstairs. "Are you sure the toilet flushed?"

"Yes." Irene stood with hands on hips. "Both of us heard it, more than once."

"Where's Mrs. Lester?" Carol spooned porridge simmering on the stove into a bowl. "Did you ask her about the toilet?"

"She went next door to help the neighbor with the sprained wrist." Audrey talked around a mouthful. "And I didn't know I needed to ask about it."

Irene drained her cup of tea and checked the time. "We need to hurry. Our ride will be here in ten minutes. I guess we won't get any cleaning done this morning."

"We could ask your ghost to do it." Audrey's eyes gleamed with mischief. Clearly she didn't take the self-flushing toilet seriously.

"Oh, good idea. We'll leave a list of chores for him to do." Carol kept a straight face even though she wanted to laugh. "Jot this down: dust furniture, shake out rugs, iron blouses."

Irene's eyes bugged when Audrey grabbed a pencil and scribbled down the list. She narrowed her gaze on Carol.

Carol shrugged. "Why not? I hate to iron." She exhaled hard to maintain her composure and tapped Audrey's arm. "Leave your note tucked into the bathroom mirror frame where he'll be sure to see it."

They arrived at their clubmobile and set to work making the doughnuts. Carol poured water into the bowl of doughnut mix. "Whoever thought I'd use my college degree to make doughnuts?"

Audrey rolled up her sleeves and waited to begin mixing the dough by hand. "And whoever thought I'd be going through seventy-five pounds of doughnut mix in a day? Think it's true the Red Cross will have bakeries supply us with doughnuts?" She held up a doughy hand. "My fingers are freezing already. Imagine how chapped our hands will get."

"It's true." Irene measured coffee for the first urn. "The doughnut machines break down too often. Hardly surprising, considering the rough rides they get in the clubmobiles. We'll still keep the machines for those times we need more in a hurry. And for the entertainment value too. The boys like to watch us make the doughnuts."

"We'll have more time to serve and talk with the guys." Carol transferred the dough to the machine, adjusted the pressure gauge, and started the motor. She grinned at her teammates. "And the best thing of all? Maybe we won't smell so strongly of doughnuts."

"Ah, what's the matter, Carol? Don't you like eau de doughnut?" Audrey laughed while waving a hand in front of her nose. "It's the signature scent of the Red Cross."

The doughnuts began flipping out of the machine. Carol and Irene speared them through their holes with their prongs and lined them up on their trays. "I think we've got over a thousand here. Let's get everything cleaned up and head out." Irene locked the last tray into place for traveling. "We'll get to Lavenham in time for lunch."

They should have been there by noon. Lavenham lay less than twenty-five miles from Saffron Walden, but road and town signs had disappeared when England feared a German invasion. Finally, their driver eased to a stop beside a farmer clopping along in his horse-drawn wagon to ask directions.

"Lavenham? Turn left at the fork up ahead and drive about three kilometers. If ye wait long enough, just follow the aeroplanes when they come back. Ye cawn't miss it."

"'Ye cawn't miss it.'" Carol repeated. She glanced back at Irene and Audrey. "I've heard that before."

"Yeah, that's what they all say." Irene's head bounced in a decisive nod. "That means we'll miss it for sure."

The air base finally materialized before them. The sentry at the gate leapt out of his shack at the sight of them. "Holy Mackerel! Real, live American girls." When Irene's eyebrows disappeared under her cap, he stammered, "Beggin' yer pardon, ma'am. It's just been so long since I've seen any of you."

Audrey nudged Carol as she bestowed a sweet smile on the guard. "And have you seen many real *dead* American girls?"

The sentry's Adam's apple bobbed as he gulped. Carol took pity on him and held out a doughnut. "Care for a snack, soldier?"

"Yes, ma'am. Thank you, ma'am." She might have offered him a nugget of gold the way he lit up over the simple treat. He sat down in the guardhouse, gazing at the doughnut with reverence. As the clubmobile pulled away, he took a small nibble. At that rate, it might last him an hour.

Their arrival at the hangar was greeted with cries of, "Here come the doughnut girls." The mechanics abandoned the planes under maintenance to rush out to the clubmobile. Carol and Audrey stepped out with trays of doughnuts. Irene remained inside, dispensing cups of coffee to the men who eagerly helped raise and lock the side panels into place.

Carol smiled at the men clustered around her. Some readily took a doughnut. Others simply gazed at her. Time to get them talking with the standard icebreaker. She caught the eye of a bashful boy who looked too young to have finished high school. "Where are you from, soldier?"

They came from all over. Tulsa. Saint Joseph, Michigan. Spanish Fork, Utah. Cleveland.

"Cleveland? Hey, I'm from Canton."

"You are?" The sergeant's eyes bugged. "Say, you wouldn't be that lady reporter who joined up, would you? Carol something?"

Carol nearly dropped her tray. "Don't tell me you read the *Canton Repository* society page?"

"He—ck no." The soldier stammered. "My cousin wanted your job, but somebody else got it. She wrote me about it." He took a bite of doughnut and stuffed it in his cheek to keep talking. "Boy howdy, this is swell. Now I'll have something to write her about. She'll be so jealous I got to meet you."

Audrey passed behind her to fetch a new tray. "Wow, you're famous."

"Hmpf." Carol suppressed a smile. She'd rarely found such enthusiasm for her work back home. She extended her tray to the man hovering on her right, but he didn't look at the doughnuts.

"Would you like to see a picture of my son?" The grease-covered mechanic gingerly held out a photograph.

Juggling the tray into a one-handed grip, Carol took the photo. "What an adorable baby. Look how he's grasping, whose finger is that, his mother's? Babies have such amazing grips." She noted the mechanic's proud but sad smile. "You haven't seen him yet, have you?"

The man's eyes blinked rapidly. "He'll be all grown up by the time I get home." His voice sounded husky.

"Oh, I don't think he'll be *all* grown up. But he may be walking. No, not walking. Running. Babies go from crawling to running, getting into everything. You'll arrive home to a thoroughly trashed house, and your frazzled wife will hand you the baby and say, 'Here, he's all yours.'" Carol nodded. Had she sounded convincing? Her experience with babies wouldn't fill a newspaper article.

Her words had the desired effect. The mechanic chuckled. "Alice frazzled? I'd like to see that." He slipped the photo into a pocket. "Say, those doughnuts look good."

Carol returned to the clubmobile for another tray.

"I think everyone's been served here. We'll move on to the dispersal area." Busy replenishing the candy tray, Irene had managed to monitor the activity surrounding them.

"Not yet." A soldier scrambled out of the clubmobile's lounge as the strains of "Don't Sit Under the Apple Tree With Anyone Else But Me" issued from the loudspeaker. "I just put on my favorite record." He held out a hand to Carol. "Let's dance." His feet were already moving.

"You mean jitterbug? I...I'm not very good at that." Tripping over her own feet would not present a pretty picture.

"Hey, no problem. I'll teach ya." He grabbed her hand and spun her close.

How could he be so agile wearing GI boots? She tried to match his steps, but couldn't keep track of his feet. Or hers. Someone was likely to get hurt. Probably her.

"Faster." He pulled her around to his side, then jerked her back in front.

She shuffled along as best she could, but they made a pathetically uncoordinated pair. By the time the song finally ended, heat flushed Carol's whole body. She backed away. "Give Audrey a whirl. She's probably better than me."

The girls were quiet on the way home that evening. Audrey ran a handkerchief around her neck. "We need to find us someone who will give us jitterbugging lessons. It's the popular dance of the day, at least with the young GIs. Why didn't they teach us this during training?"

Irene nodded. "The boys expect us to dance. We'd better become proficient. I enjoyed dancing in college, but now we need to be hip if we're going to keep them happy."

At the house, Mrs. Lester greeted them with tea and tarts. They sat around the fireplace, visiting with their landlady about their day. Audrey rose first.

"I need a soak in the tub. Our eager beaver dancer doesn't realize we're old ladies who can't keep up with his moves. My right hip aches something fierce."

Irene described their new behavior to Mrs. Lester. "Before coming here, I wouldn't have gone up to strange men and started talking, but here, we're supposed to be forward. That's our job, to be friendly and outgoing."

From upstairs came Audrey's exclamation. "Oh. My. Goodness."

Irene stopped talking and looked at Carol. "What'd she do? Step through her trousers and rip out the seam?"

They hurried up the stairs to find Audrey standing in their bedroom, holding two blouses on hangers. "You really do have a ghost. Look. Our blouses are ironed."

Chapter Nine

Tuesday, March 28, 1944

No rest for the weary. The Hendricks crew appeared on the schedule to fly again. Yesterday an experienced copilot had flown with them to help Lowell gain combat experience before leading his own men on missions. Now Andy returned to the cockpit for a mission to Rheims, France.

The bomber ahead of them disappeared down the runway into dense haze, and soon the green light flashed for them to take off. Lowell piloted *Rotherhithe's Revenge*, their assigned aircraft for the day, gracefully into the air and circled into the prescribed climb over the English countryside.

Chet dug his nails into his palms. They were flying blind. Taking off at thirty second intervals left little room for error should one plane turn a little tighter, a little faster, or a little slower than prescribed. Mid-air collisions were usually fatal.

For now, he had nothing to do but sit and worry. Lowell relied on radio compass readings to guide their pattern of ascent until they climbed above the clouds. Once they had visual contact with the other bombers, Chet would monitor their course.

His foot jiggled nervously as the minutes ticked by. They'd taken off over half an hour ago. By now, they should be in sunlight with a blue sky overhead and dozens of glistening planes surrounding them.

Bomby swiveled around. "When do we get to see the awesome power of the 381st Bomb Group? Shouldn't we be out of this soup by now?"

Chet had no answer. A patch of color showed through the window. He leaned forward. The clouds parted and *Rotherhithe's Revenge* sailed into the clear. He jumped up, only to stumble. *Rotherhithe's Revenge* flew all alone.

"What…?" Someone else sounded as confused as he was.

Chet looked out the side windows while Bomby craned his neck in all directions peering through the Plexiglas nose. Nothing.

"Does anyone see anything?" A tinge of concern colored Lowell's voice.

A chorus of negative responses replied over the intercom, but Chet's attention snagged on a peculiar observation. He cut into the chatter. "We're going the wrong way."

Lowell protested. "I followed the radio compass precisely."

This was an inauspicious start to his combat career as plane commander. Chet cleared his throat. "We're supposed to be flying east southeast. Into the sun. But we're flying out of the sun. We've got a faulty radio compass."

Silence reigned for ten seconds. Then the bomber banked hard in a one eighty-degree turn. "As I see it, we've got two choices." Lowell's voice sounded grim and determined. "We can return to Ridgewell with our tails between our legs and be the laughingstock of the base. Or we try to catch up with the formation before they reach enemy territory."

"They're an hour ahead of us. Can we catch them?" Someone sounded dubious.

Lowell ignored the question. "Chet, calculate the most direct route to intercept them. We'll see how fast this baby can go."

"Let's put the pedal to the metal. Or whatever you do in a plane." Not everyone voiced concern. "Maybe we should get out and push."

Without the occasional course changes to confuse German trackers, Chet figured they could make up a half hour. Burning off their precious fuel at breakneck speed gave them an outside chance of catching up before enemy fighters found them. That left the question of whether they'd have enough fuel to make it back to England. He pushed the thought away.

Concentrate on one thing at a time. He grabbed his airspeed computer and twisted the inner dial to line up his numbers with the outer dial. "Okay,

Lowell, come left three degrees. New heading, one two one."

He stood behind Bomby, straining to glimpse sunlight glinting on planes. The minutes dragged by. Maybe his watch had stopped. He grabbed Bomby's arm and twisted it to see his watch. Nope. Time really was standing still.

"Aircraft at ten o'clock!"

Chet didn't recognize the herald, but he squinted into the sun. His heart skipped a beat at the sight of sunlight sparkling off planes, and lots of them. He'd done it. His plotting had been on the money.

"Another squadron, dead ahead." Bomby looked back at Chet. "Twelve o'clock high."

"Which one is ours? Or is either of 'em?"

"I'm not particular," Lowell told the gunner. "We'll tag onto whoever we can catch first."

Chet grabbed his mission flimsie sheet diagramming the mission formation. "My guess is the 381st is in front of us and that's the 91st to our left."

"Full speed ahead." Lowell drove the plane like a racecar. "By the way, that's good work, Chet."

Rotherhithe's Revenge eased up into the Tail-End Charlie position. After the excitement of starting off in the wrong direction and the rush to catch up, joining the squadron seemed anticlimactic. Not until they flew east of Paris did the flak start bursting around them. One burst showered the *Rotherhithe's Revenge* with deadly shrapnel.

One of the gunners whispered, "Lord, have mercy."

Chet swallowed hard. *Rotherhithe's Remorse* might be a better name for their plane. During the bomb run, they couldn't fight back or take evasive action until bombs away. Flying a straight line gave the German defenders an easy task of finding their altitude. Chet cringed as another close burst hurled shrapnel in their direction. A jagged piece pierced the thin aluminum fuselage, letting in a stream of sunlight.

"W-why do they call that *f-flak* anyway?" The wobbly voice belonged to Price.

"It's short for *fliegerabwehrkanonen*, meaning 'anti-aircraft guns.' In our case, it applies to the stuff that comes out of the guns." Chet tried to inject humor in his voice.

Bomby announced, "Bomb bay doors coming open."

From the radio room, Dexter Small responded, "Doors opening."

Twelve hundred pounds of bombs tumbled away and *Rotherhithe's Revenge* lifted as though pleased to be free of the deadly weight. Chet marked the drop in his log. He inhaled sharply. Now all they had to do was get back to England.

The flak faded away behind them and no Luftwaffe fighters appeared. After the peculiar start to the mission, they would hopefully have an easy ride home. No one was hurt. *Rotherhithe's Revenge* was in fine shape. He sighed in relief.

Lemke shattered his complacency as they neared the English Channel. "Chief that B-17 behind us is firing at us."

"Say again." Lowell's disbelief rang through the intercom.

"That B-17 is firing at us." The tail gunner enunciated each word loud and clear.

Andy responded. "Does it have identification on the tail?"

"There's something there, but it's not clear, like it was painted over."

"It's probably a captured plane the Germans are flying to infiltrate us."

This time Lowell's voice held no doubt. "Shoot it down."

Lemke's gun fired away. Curled up in the ball turret protruding from the bomber's underside, Long joined in firing a few shots.

Someone asked, "Can you see anything?"

"No, they're directly behind us. They'd be in a blind spot if Johnny Reb had left his post in the tail and come forward once we got over the channel."

"A message has come over the VHF." Small broke in from the radio room. "The squadron leader wants to know what's going on back here."

"Tell him we're trying to stay alive against a marauding B-17 that's gone over to the enemy."

Chet grinned. Bomby shared his sentiment when the bombardier turned around, pulled away his oxygen mask, and yelled over the engine noise, "Lowell doesn't like being questioned."

"Ha!" Lemke's gun fell silent as he whooped. "I gave 'em a bloody nose. Their Plexiglas nose shattered, one engine is smoking, and they're drifting away."

The rogue bomber dropped down and disappeared into a cloudbank. Chet slumped at his navigation table and rolled a pencil between his hands. He didn't claim to be superstitious, but a college buddy's oft-repeated adage came to mind. "Strike three and you're out." What could happen next, a crash landing?

"There's the white cliffs of Dover. Purely a sight for weary eyes. Just in time, too. Engine three's running hot and redlining." Besides operating the top turret gun behind the cockpit, Cottrell served as flight engineer and assisted the pilots in monitoring the gauges.

Chet marked their location. The engine could explode in flames, maybe tear off the wing. Lowell instructed Andy to shut it down. Chet blew out his breath. They'd had enough excitement on this mission.

Lowell executed a textbook landing at Ridgewell. Chet dropped out of the nose hatch as Lemke strode away from the rear door. The irrepressible gunner raised an arm and proclaimed, "Ah, England, this sceptered isle. This blessed England, bound in with the triumphant sea, whose rocky shore beats back the envious siege of the nasty Nazis."

"Shakespeare, slightly fractured."

Lemke grinned. "It's been a year since I played that part in a school play."

Chet bobbed his head. "You did better than I would have."

Irene wasted no time in finding them a dance instructor. While she and Audrey tended the doughnuts rolling out of the machine, Carol faced Sergeant Mike Thomason. He looked too relaxed to try to dance her off her feet like yesterday's mechanic. Maybe too relaxed to jitterbug at all.

He faced her and took her hands. "It's easy once you know the steps in six beats of music. First we step to my left, your right, for two beats." So far, so good. "Now we go back in two beats."

Carol breathed easier. This wasn't anything like what they'd done yesterday.

"Now step your right foot behind your left foot, almost on your heel, and keep your weight on your toes, in one beat. In the next beat, step in place with your left foot. Then we start over."

Carol bit her lip as they went through the sequence several times with a quickening tempo. After a while, the steps came naturally.

"Now we'll add more moves."

"Huh?"

Mike laughed. "These few steps would get boring, don't you think?" He didn't give her time to respond. "After the step sequence, I'll send you out to my side, like this, you do a left side turn under my arm." He gave her a little push to accomplish the turn. "Do the steps again, and then a right side turn back under my arm, and back into starting position for more steps."

After ten minutes of practice, Carol found her groove. "Irene! Audrey! Look at me! I'm jitterbugging!"

"That's not what you were doing yesterday," Irene called back.

"Now here's your test." Mike looked around. "Hank, let's see if Miss Carol dances as well with you."

They had an audience. A half dozen soldiers perked up, wanting a turn. The opening strains of "Pistol Packin' Mama" filled the air, and she and Hank were off. At the song's conclusion, another soldier claimed her for the next number.

By the time Irene traded places with her, Carol was winded. "What a workout. Who knew we'd be serving our country by learning to dance the jitterbug? War's not supposed to be fun."

Audrey's toes tapped on the floor. "We're keeping the men's morale up, helping them remember what they're fighting for. I can't wait for my turn with Mike."

Carol washed her hands and started mixing up another batch of doughnuts. A snicker escaped her, which quickly grew to a belly laugh. "We're not doing too badly in giving some of the English people a bit of merriment either. Mrs. Lester never expected to be called a ghost when she helped out by doing our ironing."

"Oh, goodness. All because the toilet flushes when the tank fills too much." Audrey used the back of her hand to brush hair away from her face. She laughed as hard as Carol. "At least she wasn't insulted. I don't think I'll ever forget hearing her go back downstairs. Ooooooooooo."

Carol had regained her composure only to lose it again when she spotted the soldier standing in the doorway to the lounge, records in hand. He stared wide-eyed at Audrey, probably wondering if he should run for a medic.

"Don't worry about us," she gasped. "Our landlady's a ghost."

Chapter Ten

Somewhere Over Germany
Wednesday, March 29, 1944

Germany's down there. Chet stared through the Plexiglas nose, but all he saw was cloud cover. The deteriorating weather wasn't all bad. Apparently, the Germans in Brunswick hadn't thought they would venture out, so opposition was lighter than anticipated.

He wasn't complaining. As a new crew, they'd been assigned to the Tail End Charlie position, the most vulnerable spot in the formation. Flying at the lowest, outside edge, they were the easiest target for German fighters.

The clouds prevented visual bombing. Bomby dropped their load when the other planes dropped, announcing, "All I can guarantee is that they'll hit the ground. Bombing by radar might work in theory, but I'll bet most of our babies miss that aircraft assembly factory we're supposed to wipe out. I doubt if our employers will be satisfied with the results."

At the periphery of the nose window, a black cloud mushroomed. Flak! High and outside for a ball. Not everyone was asleep down there. No matter. They were still going to score a home run on this mission.

They turned north-northwest to get out of Germany and over the North Sea. Heavy, dense clouds billowed up to their altitude. A huge explosion erupted ahead and to their right. Two bombers had collided. Chet swallowed hard. Twenty men had just perished. Bits and pieces disappeared into the clouds. It was unreal, like a movie. He slumped on his chair and recorded the time and location in his log. "Anyone know what positions they were in?"

"One may have been a wingman in the lead element and the other a wing on the left element." Lowell paused before adding, "Being Tail End Charlie back here in the Purple Heart Corner isn't all bad. We're not boxed in like they are up ahead." His voice sounded strained over the intercom. "Everybody keep a sharp eye out for other Forts. Sing out fast if we're about to collide and in what direction."

Dexter Small broke in. "I just heard on the radio. We're breaking formation because of the poor visibility."

A moment later, they started letting down. Lowell explained, "I'm going to head down to the deck, carefully. Keep your eyes peeled. With no idea where the others are, we'll continue north for a bit over the North Sea, but then Chet, get us home as quickly as possible. We're below ten thousand feet, so come off oxygen."

Chet yanked off his mask and expelled his breath. First time he really had to earn his salary and he needed to get them out of a fog thicker than Dutch pea soup. He started sweating in his heavy flight gear and quickly shed his parachute harness and shrugged out of his flight suit.

Lowell continued descending. Chet stared at his altimeter as it dropped down to two hundred feet, one hundred feet, fifty feet, below zero. His heartbeat accelerated and he jumped up to the window. "Say, what is this, a submarine? The altimeter has us underwater."

The plane leveled off.

Bomby shouted. "I see it! The surface is about twenty feet down."

From the nose's bay window, Chet and Bomby had a daunting view of white caps rolling on a black sea. Nothing but dense fog surrounded them above and on either side.

Over the intercom came a small voice. "Can I get out of the ball now?"

"Okay, Homer, climb out, but everyone else remain at your stations and stay alert." Lowell sounded calmer. They didn't know where everyone else was, but having a visual of the surface was reassuring, even if they couldn't land on it.

Chet busied himself calculating their position and course. The wind prediction for their flight to Brunswick had been accurate, but at sea level, the wind would be less and, from the direction of the white caps, slightly shifted. He altered his airplot and offered Lowell a heading that should take them to England where he could make a course correction using the Gee set to get an electronic line of position. For the time being, he could relax a bit.

Lemke's voice came over the intercom. "How likely are we to run into a ship?"

"Oh, great, Johnny Reb. Give us something else to worry about." Mike Zempel was on edge.

"Tell you what." Andy's voice rang with laughter. "We'll sound our fog horn every ten minutes."

"We got a foghorn?" Stan Price sounded incredulous, and Chet laughed.

Lowell pulled up to a more comfortable fifty feet, and told Andy to take a turn at the controls. Chet doodled on his map in between attempts to acquire Gee fixes.

"Hey, we got company." Lemke's shout brought everyone to alert.

"What do you see?" Lowell cut into the sudden chatter.

"Another Fort about thirty feet up and twenty feet to my right, your left, and closing in to fly off our wing. I've been flashing my Aldin lamp. They must have seen it and decided to join up. I can't read their numbers to know if they're in our squadron."

"Who cares? We're not alone in the world anymore."

They'd covered four hundred miles when, through the rising fog, the coast of England appeared. Chet sagged in relief. He got a Gee fix and had a ready answer when Lowell asked for a heading and ETA to Ridgewell.

Irene yawned as she stirred her porridge. "I swear I heard planes flying over all night long."

"You do realize there's a war going on, don't you?" Carol smiled as she raised her coffee cup for a sip. "The RAF flies all night, and then around six I think our own planes started taking off." She studied the clock on the wall. "Just after eight. They're not necessarily over enemy territory yet. What did that officer at the control tower tell us? It takes an hour or two for all the bombers to get into formation before they can even head out."

Audrey joined them, her hands scrubbing her eyes. "I wonder if the gunners use that time to take a cat nap so they'll be alert when they have to watch for enemy fighters. I could sure use a nap."

"Don't let the boys see you yawning." Irene shook her spoon at Audrey. "They comment immediately if we're not perky and happy." She assumed a hangdog expression. "'Aren't you glad to see us?' Their sleep must be disturbed as much as ours, but we can't show that it bothers us."

"Maybe you can find someone to jitterbug with you, Audrey." Carol laughed, clapping her hands. "That'll shake you awake."

"Oooh. Not if I trip over my feet."

"We're going to Ridgewell today." Irene hopped up and deposited her bowl in the sink. "Maybe we'll learn where today's mission is."

Carol hurried back to the clubmobile. Bing Crosby sang "Deep in the Heart of Texas" on the Victrola while two GIs read books and magazines in the lounge. Two more washed coffee cups, and Audrey scrubbed the doughnut machine in the kitchen. Irene stood outside, talking with their driver.

"We need to make more doughnuts." Carol's announcement brought everyone's heads up.

Irene came into the clubmobile. "What's going on?"

"The mess sergeant asked if we'd have doughnuts to go with the Spam sandwiches and coffee he's preparing for the combat crews when they return. The weather's deteriorating and according to a radio transmission, the formation broke up to avoid accidents. They're going to be really stressed when they get back." Carol pulled out a mixing bowl as she spoke. "We'll greet them with doughnuts."

With their GI helpers, they had four racks of doughnuts ready when the planes were expected to return, but no one heard the hum of bomber engines. One of the GIs hurried off on his bicycle for news. He soon returned.

"They're late. When they do come, they'll probably be arriving in ones and twos since they broke formation. What a mess."

His uniform was damp. Carol looked out the window. A heavy drizzle fell. "This is bad, isn't it?"

"It ain't good." The man sipped from the cup of coffee Audrey handed him. He raised his eyes to Carol's questioning gaze. "Weather can be a worse enemy than the Germans. You can't do a thing about it. Besides the risk of colliding with each other, the men have a tough time figuring out where they are. I wouldn't want to be a navigator in that muck."

An hour after their expected arrival, the first Flying Fortress materialized out of the fog and settled on the runway. Another plane could be heard circling, lining up to land. Trucks followed them to their hardstands to bring the men for debriefing. The Red Cross girls set up in the waiting room next to the briefing room. Irene stood behind the coffee pot and Carol manned the hot chocolate. Audrey continually rearranged the trays of doughnuts.

The mess sergeant waited with the Spam sandwiches. He cast an apologetic look at the girls. "They may not be too hungry. Days like this tend to kill the appetite."

Carol traced a finger through the condensation on the hot chocolate pot. Here was the war up close. These men were coming back from the front lines of combat. How should she treat them? Should she ask how their day was or did they want to forget? After a harrowing flight, would they want to joke?

She rubbed her hand up and down the pot handle until the mess sergeant asked, "What's the matter? You nervous? Don't be. Just smile. That'll be the best medicine for them."

The first crew came in. The men all looked exhausted, but their eyes lit up at the sight of the girls. Carol poured a cup of hot chocolate and held it out. "Hot chocolate or coffee, gentlemen? How about a doughnut?"

She smiled at the nearest man and he reached out with a shaky hand. Before drinking it, he cupped his hands around the cup and let out his breath, his eyes devouring Carol.

"Rough day, hmm?"

"You have no idea." He exhaled his words and raised the cup to his lips. "Oh, that's good."

Carol poured another cup for a captain wearing pilot's wings. His face was lined, his eyes strained. He accepted the cup with a nod and quiet "Thank you, miss."

The second crew arrived. A young enlisted man came to an abrupt stop. "Girls!"

Carol laughed. The men constantly reminded her and her Red Cross colleagues what a rarity they were among the male environment on the military bases. Her laughter proved contagious. Soon both crews were laughing and Carol smiled as their tension drained away.

Planes continued to come in and their crews delivered to the briefing room. As they waited their turn to debrief, the men talked. Carol heard disgust in many voices. Someone had screwed up. They should not have been sent out in such lousy weather.

"They want to end this war quick, but that's not going to happen by killing us off instead of the enemy."

"I bet those generals wouldn't have gone up with us."

"How we ever found England I'll never know."

One young boy's hand shook so badly he put down the cup before spilling the chocolate. "Sorry. This was my first mission. I hope they're not all like this."

Carol grabbed his icy hand and rubbed it briskly between hers before offering him a doughnut. "I'm sure you'll have easier days."

"You'll probably have lots of leftovers. A bunch of planes aren't coming back here. They landed at the first air field they could find rather than try to locate Ridgewell."

Even with the missing planes, the hastily prepared doughnuts disappeared from the trays. Carol removed an empty tray and brought out a full one.

"Excuse me, miss, have you any cherry pound cake?"

Carol looked up at the odd request. A tall, brown-eyed officer watched her. She'd seen him before, hadn't she?

"Chet? Oh my goodness. Chet?" The tray clunked onto the table as she flung her arms around the man from her last day at the train canteen.

Chapter Eleven

"You really are Carol, aren't you?" Chet had rubbed his eyes when he stepped inside. Three months had passed since he'd spoken with the lovely canteen worker who'd served him the cherry cake. Now she served doughnuts.

"I've wondered what became of you." She stepped back. A flush rose in her cheeks as she glanced around the suddenly quiet room. She waved a hand toward the other women. "These are my teammates, Irene and Audrey." To them, she said, "I chatted with Chet in Ohio last Christmastime."

His own crewmates watched with interest, but before he could introduce them, an Intelligence Officer called them into the debriefing room. He grabbed a doughnut and looked Carol in the eye. "Don't go away."

With the ten crewmen seated around a table, the interrogator asked for their version of the day's events. Chet had his logbook ready and offered times and locations for the comments made. "We were still over Germany when the two planes ahead of us collided."

The interrogator looked up from his copious notes. "Two planes collided? They weren't lost by enemy aircraft?"

The crewmen looked at each other in surprise. "Are you saying fighters were up?" Zempel leaned forward. "We were Tail End Charlie and we didn't see any fighters."

By the time the interrogator was satisfied he'd wrung every detail out of them, they left the debriefing room. One final crew took their place. Chet went back into the waiting room. The Red Cross girls were helping the mess sergeant clear away food. He snagged another doughnut and accepted a cup of hot chocolate from Carol.

"We heard some planes landed elsewhere?" She voiced her comment as a question.

He nodded. "Thirty-three planes took off from here this morning. Twenty returned. The others are scattered around. Most of them. Not everyone." The sudden fire, the debris swallowed up by the clouds. The doughnut stuck in his throat and he hurriedly gulped the chocolate. Stuff like that wouldn't fade from memory.

Carol didn't ask for details. That was good. He didn't have to rehash the hours just past, much less talk about them. She stacked the trays that had held the doughnuts, and he hurried forward to carry them out.

She opened the door and led him to the clubmobile. "This is our first visit to Ridgewell."

He eased the trays down on a kitchen table, looking around the compact little house on wheels. "Your first visit? You'll be back?"

"Oh, yes. This is our territory. We rotate around a half dozen air fields from our base in Saffron Walden."

"That's not far. When's your next visit?"

"Probably in a week. We're still settling into our routine, but we try to hit each place once a week with a seventh day off. I can't say for sure we'll be here next Wednesday because we're open to juggling our schedule if we're requested to be somewhere at a certain time."

They sat in the lounge. Chet flipped through the stack of records. "Quite the little home away from home you have here."

"We like it." Carol eased off her boots and tucked a foot under her. "The best part is having a driver. We've heard if we go to France after the invasion takes place, we'll have to drive the clubmobiles ourselves." She reached out to grip an imaginary steering wheel. "Carol Doucet, truck driver. Who would've thought?"

"Do you hope to go to France?" Chet's heart beat faster at the way her eyes sparkled. When was the last time he'd sat and talked with a girl?

"Yes, I do. It'd be a lot harder than here. We three live with a widow in Saffron Walden who makes our breakfast and irons our clothes."

Chet raised his brows when she laughed suddenly, but he wasn't going to interrupt.

"In France, we'll have to do everything ourselves in conditions that could likely be wretched, depending on whether battles were fought there. But I have a lot of French ancestry. I'd like to see my forefathers' country."

"You'll be living like the army."

"I guess so. Do you have a desire to see France?"

"Up close and personal? No, ma'am. If I end up in France, something's gone horribly wrong."

"Oh, of course." Color rose in Carol's cheeks. "I didn't think."

Chet laughed. "Maybe, after the invasion, we'll have forward bases where we can stop for fuel. That would be a huge advantage. Now, if we run out of gas, we end up as prisoners or maybe dead."

Irene and Audrey had been putting things away and tidying up. Now Irene hesitated in the doorway. "We're ready to head back to Saffron Walden."

Chet hopped up. "I'll get out of your way."

"Please stop by on our next visit." Irene gave him a smile and turned back to speak to their driver.

Chet stepped down from the clubmobile. "There's usually a monthly party here. The next one is Easter Sunday, in a week and a half. Keep that in mind."

Carol leaned against the doorway. "Will you have to fly on Easter?"

"Maybe. War doesn't stop for holy days. I'll tell you more next time you come."

The clubmobile engine started. Carol waved and closed the door.

Chet flagged down a passing jeep for a lift to the barracks. No one else was there. Maybe everyone was at the mess hall. The hot chocolate and doughnuts had assuaged his hunger, so he had no need to go there. Now would be a good time to write to his grandparents. He got out paper and sat on his cot. No, he didn't want to be alone. He changed into his Class A uniform and headed for the Officers' Club.

He'd ordered a soda at the bar and turned to look for a familiar face when Andy and Bomby walked in. They got drinks and joined him at a small table. Andy wasn't even seated before delivering his news.

"Rickman's crew went down. He was on his twenty-eighth mission. Two more to go and he would have been home free."

"Who was in the other plane?" Chet held his breath. Don't let it be a name he would recognize.

"Hessel. Never heard of him." Bomby straddled his chair. "Guys are saying one of the planes didn't explode."

Chet straightened up. "Really?"

"One plane left the formation but seemed to be under control. Enough so they could bail out anyway." Andy dug out a handkerchief to wipe his mouth and eyed Chet. "We were over Germany at the time?"

"I'm pretty sure, although we were getting close to Holland."

"That improves their chances of evading, if they weren't captured right away."

An officer wearing medical insignia approached their table. "Mind if I join you?"

Chet pushed out the fourth chair with his foot. "How are you doing, Doc?"

"Very well indeed, thank you." He sat down. "I'm Captain Bland. How are all of you after today's mission?"

"Wishing we weren't so expendable to the brass." Bomby grabbed his glass and tossed back a big gulp. "Not that I'm crying in my beer, but I think if they had sons flying with us, they wouldn't have sent us out in such stinko weather."

"All those men in the planes that collided aren't here now because of bad planning by our own side, not because of the Germans." Andy crossed his arms tight to his chest. "I gotta say, they don't inspire confidence."

The doc leaned in. "Are you scared you might be next?"

Andy looked up, his brow furrowing. His arms dropped to his lap. "No, I'm planning on the bad stuff always happening to the other guy."

Bomby bounced a fist on the table. "Today was a wasted effort. I seriously doubt we hit that aircraft assembly factory we were after. Those guys died for nothing."

"That's war." Leaning on his elbows, the doctor steepled his fingers. "And that's weather. Sometimes missions have been cancelled because of bad conditions and it turned out to be perfect over the continent. A wasted day, giving the Germans a break. Sometimes we have to gamble. Today we lost."

Andy's and Bomby's stiff shoulders relaxed. Chet rubbed his thumb up and down his soda bottle. The doctor must be probing for potential breakdowns. The day had been disturbing, but for his part, he'd gotten his job done, bringing them back to base. What really made the difference was meeting Carol again. He smiled. Today had been a good day after all. And maybe tonight he'd sleep as though dead.

Chapter Twelve

Saturday, April 1, 1944

"Arg, what a day." Audrey collapsed on her bed. "I feel like I've been in a wrestling match with that confounded doughnut machine. First billowing clouds of smoke and then a blown fuse. Ooo." She pounded her fists on the mattress.

"At least the electrician we found knew how to fix it." Irene sat slumped on her bed, one foot on her knee as she rubbed her insole.

"Yeah, he was swell. And cute, too. But only twenty years old. Seven whole years younger than me." Audrey's head rolled back and forth.

Carol stripped off her battle dress uniform. "What time are we being picked up for the dance?"

Irene swung her wrist in front of her face and blinked at her watch. "About an hour and a half, thereabouts."

"Good. I'm going to take a quick bath. I don't want to go smelling like a smoky doughnut."

The tepid water, no higher than five inches in the tub as mandated by English rationing, was luxurious, but Carol didn't loiter. She wanted to give the other girls time in the bathroom. Wrapped in a towel with her hair tucked under another, she plunged her clothes into the tub. Not the best way to do laundry, but time was short.

She hurried back to the bedroom. "Bathroom's free. I need to write to my sister to send me more shampoo…" She stopped and stared. "You're wearing civilian clothes?"

"You bet. I want to feel like a woman again instead of a soldier." Irene grabbed her make-up bag and disappeared out the door, her voice floating back. "Besides, the boys like seeing us out of uniform."

Carol hadn't moved.

"She's right, you know." Audrey looked up from brushing wrinkles out of her red dress. "The boys see uniforms all the time. They like seeing us look normal." She draped the dress over the room's lone chair. "And you're right, too. I need more shampoo, and nail polish. The English don't have a good shade of red. I haven't found a cold cream I like, either. On the other hand, hygiene products, which I brought a year's supply of, can be easily obtained."

Carol donned her slip before sitting on her bed, arms tightly crossed. The Red Cross required them to be in uniform, even at dances. The Army stipulated they must wear uniforms to ride in army vehicles.

"Facial tissue is what we need to stockpile. I use most of my tissues with the toilet since what is provided, if any is, resembles wrapping paper."

Carol sighed and reached for her summer uniform. It might not turn heads like Audrey's red dress, but she wouldn't be flaunting the rules.

"Carol." Audrey planted her hands on her hips. "Wear your blue dress. It's so pretty."

"After hours of dancing, I want to be sure I don't end up walking back from Bassingbourn."

"Oh, Carol, that's not going to happen."

"You've got a really good band at your base." Carol snuggled deeper into her coat when the brisk wind slapped her face as she exited the dance.

"Yeah, they are good, especially since we get new guys all the time." One of the lieutenants who brought them to Bassingbourn led them to the waiting jeep.

"You mean replacements for the men who finish and go home?"

"Yes." He hesitated. "And for those who don't come back from missions."

Audrey broke the awkward silence. "Too bad Mike Thomason isn't here to give dance lessons. My poor feet have been stepped on so often tonight they'll be black and blue and swollen tomorrow."

The lieutenant joined Irene and Carol in the back seat after helping Audrey hobble into the front. His friend wheeled the jeep around and took off for Saffron Walden. How he managed to find the country lanes in blackout conditions with the headlights severely masked was a mystery. Carol hung on to the jeep frame. Under these conditions, a slower speed would be a good idea.

They were passing the turnoff to Nuthampstead when a waving beam from a flashlight brought them to a stop. A military policeman approached, shining his light on them, lingering on Audrey and Irene.

"Civilians are not allowed to ride in army vehicles. You ladies will have to get out."

Irene stiffened beside Carol while Audrey protested. "We're Red Cross girls. We've been to the dance at Bassingbourn."

"You know the rules. You can't ride in army vehicles unless you're in uniform." The MP shook his head in time with the baton he bounced against his palm. "You two have to get out."

"Here? In the middle of nowhere?" Audrey's voice rose three octaves.

Carol kept an eye on the baton. He'd likely start hitting them if they didn't obey. Lots of men chided her at the dance for coming in uniform, but boy, it was a good thing she worn it.

No amount of arguing could change the MP's mind. The lieutenant seated next to Irene got out and helped Audrey and Irene step down. "We'll find a friend of mine at Nuthampstead. He'll help us get you to Saffron Walden." Carol moved to the front seat as he retrieved a flashlight from the jeep and flicked it on.

"That flashlight beam must be taped over to allow only a slit of light." The MP didn't get far with his latest admonishment before the lieutenant spun around and leaned close.

"I've had enough of your harassment tonight, corporal. Now make yourself scarce."

After he exchanged a few words with their driver, he led Irene and Audrey away. Carol watched as the trio disappeared into the darkness. She turned back to the driver. "I can't believe the MP wouldn't allow us to drive them to Nuthampstead. Stumbling around in the dark can be dangerous."

A long moment passed while the driver negotiated a curve in the road. "Those MPs, some of them like to throw their weight around. They're not doing anything to win the war. They're policing their own side. So they have a grudge against the flyboys who get all the attention. And if they can make life miserable for officers, so much the better. That's my opinion."

He must have had his own run-in with the MPs. Weariness settled over Carol like a cloak. It had been a long day. She rotated her ankles. Bed would feel heavenly tonight. How was Audrey faring with her well-trod toes? The seven miles from home must seem like seven hundred.

Chapter Thirteen

Ridgewell Air Base, England
Tuesday, April 4, 1944

"Too bad we didn't know the weather would be soupy all week." Chet swung the barrack's door shut but it bounced back, failing to latch. Before he could turn around, Andy closed it firmly. "We should have requested a pass and gone somewhere for a few days."

"Gone where? London?" Andy tossed a rock from hand to hand. "You know what I'd like to see? Those white cliffs of Dover up close."

"I don't know about that." Lowell rubbed a hand through his hair before donning his cap. "With all the security against a German invasion, I doubt the British military allows anyone in the beach areas."

Andy's rock hit the ground. "What in blue blazes is Zempel trying to do?"

Chet spotted their waist gunner and laughed. The gunner leaned over a large barrel out of which splashed a great deal of water. "I believe he's trying to give a dog a bath."

"Just so long as he doesn't try to take it up with us when we start flying again." Lowell stopped to watch, his arms crossed.

"Aren't you going to tell him it's time to get to ground school?"

Chet raised a brow at Bomby's question. As plane commander, Lowell expected a smoothly functioning crew in the air, but on the ground, he didn't attempt to order the men around.

"Nope." Lowell resumed walking. "If he's old enough to go to war, he's old enough to keep track of his obligations."

Without his rock to toss, Andy shoved his hands in his pockets. "At least if we were off on pass, we wouldn't have to go to class. We had first aid and oxygen equipment yesterday. What do you think this morning's topic will be?"

"Maybe an intelligence officer will lecture on why we're fighting." Bomby snickered. "Or let us in on what the Germans are up to."

"That sounds more interesting than care and use of protective clothing." Chet spotted a Red Cross clubmobile ease up to a hangar. Today he'd see Carol. Too bad he couldn't sneak out of class.

"Next, we'll go out around the perimeter and stop at the squadron areas." Irene read from her notebook. "Some of the ground crew chiefs and mechanics live right there on the line so they can keep on servicing the planes."

"Don't they have barracks?" Carol peered ahead, but couldn't make out any dwellings among the parked bombers.

"Yes, but they're so dedicated to keeping the aircraft flying, they don't take the time to trot back and forth."

Their driver pulled the clubmobile up to the first cluster of hardstands.

"Hmm." Audrey paused before turning on the Victrola to announce their arrival. "Looks like they're getting ready for a bonfire. Somebody ought to strike a match."

Carol studied the heap of crates and canvas. "That's not to be burned, Audrey. That's what they live in."

Audrey nearly dropped the record she held poised to add to the stack. "Are you kidding me?"

Irene laughed. "It's like camping."

"I do not want to know what they use for a toilet."

Carol stepped out with a tray of doughnuts to the opening strains of Glenn Miller's "In the Mood." Men spilled out of the planes, hopped off scaffolding, and popped up out of the ramshackle hovels. Eager faces surrounded her. She tried not to grimace as a mechanic with greasy fingers took a doughnut. All that grease couldn't add anything nutrition-wise or taste-wise, but he didn't seem to notice.

Irene joined her outside with another tray. She singled out a sergeant. "Did I see you come out of that, uh, structure?"

"Yes, ma'am. That's my home away from home." He looked so proud of it.

Up close, it was clear he'd constructed his shack out of shipping crates, plywood boards, and what appeared to be half of a tent. A bicycle leaned against the side. "Are you married, Sarge?"

His Adam's apple bobbed with his swallow. "Why, yes, ma'am."

She nodded. "Does your wife know you'll be more comfortable staying out in the doghouse when you return rather than in the house with her?"

The men roared with laughter and added their own kidding.

"Hey, that's a good name for your place. Sarge's Doghouse."

"Where's Sarge? Oh, he's in the doghouse."

The sergeant grinned. "At least that's better than being in the outhouse."

One of the mechanics clapped him on the back. "Sarge here has the best record on base. His planes have flown forty-six missions without an abort. Four more and he'll get a medal."

"How many planes do you service?" Carol shifted so the wind didn't blow her hair in her eyes. "I thought each plane had its own ground crew."

"Only one at a time, but this is my third. *Lil Miss Lu* and *Pistol Packing Mama* failed to return from their last missions." Sorrow etched his face. "But *Lucky Lady* here is a real good ship."

"Ship? That's a plane."

Another man shrugged. "Sure, but that's what we call 'em."

"Uh huh." Carol raised her brows. "Sounds like someone would have preferred the navy."

More hooting arose as the man stammered that the lingo hadn't been his idea. Carol grinned and offered him another doughnut.

The clubmobile moved on to the next squadron site.

"Boy, Carol, you sure enjoy ribbing the boys." Audrey hurried to ready a tray for her own chance to get out of the clubmobile.

"They love it. They may be embarrassed, but they enjoy the attention." Carol looked up from the dirty cups she was stacking. "That's what we're here for. Make them laugh."

By the time they reached the fourth squadron area, Carol directed two men to carry out a coffee urn and place it on the hood of a jeep. The men could fill their cups out in the brisk air while she tended to the doughnut machine and the fresh batch they'd decided they'd need.

Someone came into the clubmobile lounge. She heard the sound of fingers snapping. "Oh, miss, I'd like a doughnut, please."

She spun around. Chet leaned back on the sofa, an ankle crossed on his knee. He quirked a brow, and his lips twitched suspiciously like he was about to laugh. "A doughnut?"

"You'd like a doughnut, hmm?" Carol grinned and turned back to the machine. She skewered a hot, fresh one with the prongs. Gingerly sliding it off, she pivoted back. "Here is your doughnut, gallant sir." She slow pitched it toward him.

Chet jerked upright, his foot hitting the floor as he caught the doughnut in cupped hands. "Yow, that's hot." He bounced it from hand to hand as he came into the kitchen.

Two men came up to the window and looked over the candy tray. "The Baby Ruths are gone. Do you have any more?"

Busy with the doughnuts, Carol glanced back at Chet. "Would you check that box under the table there?"

"Mure," he mumbled before swallowing a mouthful. "Let's see. We've got Milky Ways and, yep, Baby Ruths." He scooped up a bunch and dumped them into the tray, handing one to the mechanic. "You're in luck, Corporal. That'll be five cents."

"What?" The man pulled his hand back and the candy bar dropped into the tray.

Carol slid a fresh tray of doughnuts into the rack. "Chet, play nice. You know there's no charge."

"How can I take you out for a nice dinner if I can't make any money?" He managed to pout and laugh at the same time.

The corporal chortled. "That's going to be some nice dinner on a nickel."

Another man stepped up. "I'd like a cup of java and a sinker on the double, sir."

"Coming right up, bud." Chet looked around. "Where are the clean cups?"

Carol gave him one, scanning the group mingling around Irene and Audrey. "We need to wash dishes. These are the last two clean cups."

With the doughnut supply assured, maybe she could get to that now. It looked like everyone had been served.

A woman's work was never done and that sure included the Red Cross gals. She locked the last of the trays into the rack and turned to the sink. There stood Chet, his sleeves rolled up, washing cups.

"That was nice of Irene to suggest you take a walk." Chet wanted to take Carol's hand. Or tuck it around his arm. He didn't have the right though. How much time had they spent together? An hour? Two at the most. And that was spread over three months. Still, Carol Doucet was special.

"She didn't expect to find a cleaned-up clubmobile. By moving around the perimeter, we didn't have the GI help we usually do." Carol bumped her shoulder against his. "Until you went to work on the dishes. That was so sweet of you, Chet."

"Washing dishes is easy. Grandma always expected me to help out at home. And did you notice? I didn't break any."

Her laughter sounded like bells tinkling, like the bell choir Grandma played in at church. Boy, he had it bad if he was waxing lyrical.

"Would you like to explore the innards of a bomber?"

Carol's eyes widened as she stared up at the nearest Flying Fortress. "That would be okay?"

"Sure, why not? You can't do any damage." He led her to the next plane in line. "This is the 532nd Squadron. My squadron. We've flown in this bird. The corporal who ordered a coffee on the double from me is part of the ground crew." He opened the side door and helped her step up.

A low, steady thrum filled the interior. Carol looked around. "Is the plane turned on?"

"That's the ground generator allowing the crew to work on the plane."

Carol turned around in the waist compartment, her eyes growing bigger and bigger. Two men worked in the narrow passageway to the tail, paying them no mind. "It's so, so spartan." She swung her gaze to him, as though she might have offended him. "I don't know what I expected, but it looks unfinished. Is it still under repair?" She reached out and touched a plywood ammunition box before jerking her hand back.

He looked around, trying to see it again for the first time. Bundles of cables were routed throughout the length of the plane. The frames of the fuselage remained exposed. Gauges and regulators for oxygen and machine guns would make little sense to someone uninformed of their purpose.

"Where do you sit?"

He grinned at her question. "Nobody sits in here. The gunners man their guns, watching for enemy fighters." He pointed to a gun mount over a window. "The guns are removed after each mission. When we're safe over England, the gunners congregate in the radio room." He prodded her forward.

Plywood floorboards provided easier walking in the radio room. He pointed to the swivel chair. "The radio operator gets to sit while he monitors all his equipment, the transmitters, the command radio set, the liaison receiver. Still nothing fancy, but this is a war machine. We're not supposed to feel at home."

He opened a door. "Watch your step on the catwalk."

Carol stepped over the riser and froze. Chet hid a smile. He balanced himself with one hand on the overhead fuselage and held out his other hand to assist her across. They entered the upper turret compartment behind the cockpit.

Carol turned back for another look. "What is that place?"

"The bomb bay."

"Oh." An inscrutable look crossed her face. "Does it bother you to carry bombs?"

"The whole point of having bombers is to carry bombs to drop on the enemy. The ordnance is the only part of the ensemble we hope we don't come back with."

"They could blow up while still in the plane, couldn't they? When you're under attack?"

"Sometimes they do." He closed the door on the bomb bay and turned her around. "Try sitting in the pilot's seat, on the left. Watch the hatchway, just step over it."

"Why is there a hole in the floor there?"

"That leads down to the nose, where I work." Chet eased into the copilot's seat.

"So many dials and switches. It must be hard to remember what each thing does." Carol put her hands on the semicircular control yoke very gently. "Do you know how to fly?"

"I learned to fly a Stearman, but that's a far cry from this baby. Let's go down to the nose and you can see where I'm at home."

Carol lost her balance when she tried to get her leg around the pilot's control column. She dropped back into the seat, her left hand connecting with a handle. A rumbling noise sounded behind them.

Carol yanked her hand away as Chet dove over her and shoved the handle back into position. He dashed around the top turret gun post, flung open the door, and leaned into the bomb bay.

He sagged back against the side and chuckled weakly. "Did I say you couldn't do any damage?"

She held her breath. "What did I do?"

He straightened and came back to the cockpit. "Started the bomb doors to open. No harm done. No one around and nothing fell out. Come on. Watch your step and your head." He dropped down the hatchway.

Watch her head? How about her shins and her elbows and everything else? Carol eased down through the hatchway.

Chet waited, hunched into a ball. He pointed to a square outline. "That's the forward escape hatch, where I'll go out if we need to leave in a hurry." He pivoted, crawled through a small opening, and stood up.

Inside were more plywood boxes, a plywood table to the left, and a plywood pedestal all the way forward at the edge of a big Plexiglas nose cup. More nonsensical equipment littered the small room.

Chet nudged a swivel seat at the table. "This is my station." Such pride filled his voice. He pointed to something on a plywood shelf over the windows. "That's the gyro-compass amplifier, and that's the radio-compass master-bearing indicator."

He may as well be speaking a foreign language.

"Come up to the window where you can get a full appreciation of the tremendous view Bomby and I have."

With the window starting at her feet, Carol looked straight down. Her stomach wrenched at the very thought of looking down from twenty thousand feet high. "Um, why do you call him Bomby? Because he's the bombardier?"

"His name's Harvey Bamberger. He didn't take too kindly to being called Bamby," Chet's mouth twisted to the side. "I can't blame him. Anyway, it was changed to Bomby, which matches his job."

"What do they call you?"

"Chet or Vogel. In Holland, it was Vogelzang. That means birdsong. My grandfather shortened it to Vogel, which means bird." His brows drew together and he glanced back to the entrance. "I wouldn't care to be called Birdman."

Carol zipped her lips. "I won't tell."

He laughed. "Ready to go? Watch your head." He hunched down and slid right out.

Bonk! The jarring vibrated all the way down Carol's spine. She dropped to the floor and raised a shaky hand to her head. Chet turned back, reaching out to her, and she held up her hand. "I know. I know. Which part of 'Watch your head' did I not understand?" Her hand went back to her head. "Oh, look at the pretty stars."

Alarm flashed in Chet's eyes.

She tried to laugh and waved him off. "I'm kidding. I'm fine. How do you scramble through there so fast during combat?"

"We stick to our guns during combat. In normal, unthreatened flight, we're careful. You learn after a couple months." He leaned back into the nose and checked her head. "No sign of blood."

"So, no Purple Heart?"

He grinned. "Not for a self-inflicted injury."

Chapter Fourteen

Braintree, England
Easter Sunday, April 9, 1944

Hospital visits had never been a favorite pastime. Carol's nose wrinkled at the medicinal odors. She rubbed it briskly. Couldn't let the bed-ridden men see any signs of distress. She pushed a borrowed serving cart laden with doughnuts into a ward. Too bad they didn't have any Easter eggs.

"Hey, it's the Red Cross girls. You wanna dance?"

Beside her, Audrey came to an abrupt stop. "Mike Thomason?" Her voice came out in a squeak. "What are you doing here? I thought you were a noncom."

Their dance instructor scowled. "I was until I did battle with a load of runaway bombs. The guy driving the tractor towing the dolly of bombs turned too sharp and the dolly tipped." His hands were in the air, demonstrating the maneuver. Then his fists slammed down on his bed. "Next thing I know, a five hundred pound bomb rolls into me, knocking me off my feet, and another one lands on my leg. Crunch."

"Ouch." Irene grimaced. "You lost the battle."

Carol snapped her fingers. "Say, now we can jitterbug better than Mike can."

The other patients laughed, but Mike whipped back his covers. "You want to see about that?"

Carol held up her hands. "No, no, no. You stay in bed, mister, before you do more damage." She shielded her eyes. "Ooh, look at the blinding white cast. You need some artwork on there."

Mike handed her a pen.

Art wasn't one of her talents, but she did well with caricatures. Accepting the pen, she sat on the edge of the bed and considered her options. She began sketching.

Around her, Irene and Audrey served coffee and doughnuts. They asked about the men's injuries. One man groused that he didn't have a million dollar wound. Irene asked what constituted such a wound.

"It would have gotten me a ticket home. Instead I have to go back and give the Germans another shot at me."

Carol shuddered. A war-ending wound must be permanent. She'd rather take a chance of not being wounded again rather than suffer lasting consequences. Finishing her drawing with a flourish, she grinned at Mike. "There. What do you think?"

Mike stretched to see his cast while ambulatory patients gathered around. She'd drawn a sad-eyed hound dog with floppy ears and a leg in a cast watching a cat prance in front of him.

"Hey, that's great. Will you draw a cartoon on my cast?" The kid looked like he should still be in high school. A heavy cast covered his arm from shoulder to wrist.

Carol spent the next half hour decorating casts.

When they got to the next ward, Audrey sat down on a vacant bed to rub her tired feet. Calls of sympathy rose when she told her tale of walking to Lavenham in the dark. Two men shuffled to the bed. One pressed her shoulder back while the other raised her feet and shifted her so she was lying on the bed. "We'll fix you up."

Audrey tried to get up when another convalescent snatched a tray from a nurse who came into the room. He picked up a syringe. "Here's what you need."

"I don't think so." Before Audrey could get away, the men adjusted her bed. Her feet rose while her head went down.

"If that shot's for me, I don't want it," a man in another bed called out. "She can have it."

"Irene? Carol? Nurse?" Audrey's head zoomed up, leaving her in a V configuration. "Get me out of here."

A doctor entered the ward. "What's going on here?"

The men came to attention. The nurse hurried to retrieve her tray. Audrey struggled off the bed.

"We were just curing the lovely lady of whatever ails her," a patient drawled.

"Yeah." Audrey staggered over to the serving cart. "Now I think I have vertigo."

The doctor's mouth twitched. "Is that so? I recommend a cup of coffee and a doughnut." He directed his gaze to the patients. "And since you all seem so chipper, I'll schedule extra physical therapy so you can return to your units more quickly."

The girls left to a chorus of groans. Irene consulted her list. "One ward left. These will be the more seriously wounded."

"Million dollar injuries?" Carol pressed a hand to her forehead. Feeling queasy was silly. The men had been cared for, their wounds bandaged. As Midge had said in January, she wouldn't see any blood. Why couldn't she control the fluttering in her stomach?

The ward was quieter. Those men who were awake brightened at their entrance. The girls took trays and walked around the beds. Carol stopped between two. She smiled brightly. "Think you can do justice to our doughnuts?"

One man reached out a hand and she held the tray close. Then she turned to the other man. He raised his bandaged hands. Her stomach lurched. His fingers were stubs. "Frostbite. I took off my gloves to get my gun working."

Swallowing hard, Carol set the tray down, selected a doughnut, and held it to his mouth.

"Mmm, that's good." He licked his lips. "Guess I won't be playing baseball anymore, will I?" A shoulder shrugged. "I'll have to find something else to do."

Carol nodded. She couldn't speak. Her throat was clogged. She hoped he didn't notice the tears brimming in her eyes. With his dark brown hair and brown eyes, he looked a lot like Chet. This time her heart clenched. Whatever made her think she wanted to be this close to the war?

Ridgewell Air Base, England
Same Day

The crew chief stood in front of *Uncle Sammy*, pointed a finger at the cockpit, and made a whirling motion with his other index finger. The high-pitched whine of the starter preceded a cough as engine one rumbled to life. Beyond Chet's window, the outboard propeller started to spin. The three other engines started in quick succession. The power of the twelve hundred horsepower in their Wright Cyclone engines vibrated the entire aircraft and throbbed deep in Chet's gut.

Around them, other planes taxied toward the runway. The ground crewmen pulled the chocks away from *Uncle Sammy's* wheels, allowing the bomber to lumber off its hardstand and join the parade. Blue exhaust flames issued from the engines of the plane ahead of them. The screech of hydraulics rose above the roar of the engines as the pilots wrestled their huge B-17s to stay centered on the taxi strip.

Poised at the edge of the runway, the plane in front of them raced down the narrow strip. In thirty seconds, the green light would flash for them. Chet took a deep breath. *Uncle Sammy* lurched forward and picked up speed. What a way to spend Easter. *The Lord is risen. He is risen indeed. Uncle Sammy* rose off the runway. They were on the way to Gdynia, Poland.

The briefing officer had told them this was their longest mission of the war to date. Over eleven hours would elapse before they saw Ridgewell again, if all went well. And tonight was the party. Carol was coming, and he'd be worn out. *The Lord is risen. He is risen indeed.* Forgive him, but the familiar words failed to cheer him.

Once the formation assembled, they headed out over the North Sea. Thursday's mission had been scrubbed. Friday's mission had been scrubbed. Yesterday logged the first mission of the month. Oldenburg, Germany, was now missing its airfield, and the Bomb Group had suffered no losses. Now they were headed for Poland and in a few hours, everyone back home in Niles, Michigan, would head to church in a sea of Easter bonnets. Grandma always opted for something in blue.

The enemy coast was in sight when the intercom crackled and Dexter Small broke into Chet's musings. "Recall. The mission's been scrubbed due to weather. Let's go home."

The formation banked in a wide turn. Bomby headed back to the bomb bay to put the cotter pins back in the bombs, rendering them harmless. Chet grabbed his logbook and scribbled down the time and location. He was grinning like a fool, but he couldn't help it. Today was a day for peace on Earth, goodwill toward men as much as Christmas. Yessirree. *The Lord is risen. He is risen indeed.*

A truck picked up the Red Cross crew along with several local girls. Correctly dressed in uniform, Audrey scowled at the colorful dresses they wore. "This is still an army vehicle, right? Why are they allowed to ride in those clothes while I, an American, was ordered out of a jeep?"

"Shh." Carol glanced around. No one else seemed to hear Audrey's complaint. The gears ground noisily, but Audrey would likely shout in her ear just as the gears fell silent. "The air force must have an agreement for special occasions. Be glad they included us in their pick-up."

Audrey settled back with a huff.

In the conversation taking place to Carol's right, an English girl hoped to find an American officer who'd give her food from the base stores. Carol stared at the girl. Had she heard correctly? She wanted an American boyfriend for what she could get out of him? When the girl had climbed aboard the truck, her navy skirt had been faded on one side, as though it were stored partially in the sun. One of her sandals had been repaired with twine. Maybe her father was away in the war, or had even died, and the family suffered hardship. And now she wanted a rich American boyfriend. All England knew the American fighting men were overpaid, oversexed, and over here.

Irene caught Carol's eye and shook her head. She'd remarked the other day how forward the English girls were.

The truck stopped and hands reached up to help them down. Carol hung back. The eager English girl didn't let go of the hands that assisted her. "I'm so excited to be here. Thank you so much for inviting us. I know we'll have a wonderful time. I just love to dance, don't you?"

Carol smothered a laugh, but the next voice snapped her head up. "Head right on into the hangar and you can dance your feet off."

Chet.

Carol hurried to the tailgate and was met with a smile. Chet tugged his hand free, grasped her waist, and swung her down almost before she got her hands on his shoulders. "I've been waiting for you."

The English girl's mouth pulled down, but she quickly turned to another man. His face lit up with interest in the girl. Someone ought to warn him of her ulterior motives.

"Looks like our live wire will get to dance."

Carol looked up at Chet. "She wants an American to provide her with food."

His sigh might have come from the depths of his soul as they walked to the hangar. "Life is tough for the English. They've been at war for five years. Most of the men have been away during that time. Then we arrive, and suddenly there are scads of young men around who are deprived of female companionship. Sounds like either a perfect solution or a blueprint for disaster."

The Red Cross girls were there to boost morale and remind the men of home and who they were fighting for, but three girls on a base of a few thousand men couldn't give them the attention they desired. Maybe the English girls' presence helped the American warriors after all.

Carol tucked her hand around Chet's arm. "I do wish none of them had a mercenary attitude, but I guess I shouldn't feel responsible for our men. I'm glad I'm not their mother. They should be old enough to handle their social life."

Chet hesitated before pulling open the hangar door. "My pilot would agree with you that they're old enough to take care of themselves. Unfortunately, many here have no experience with wily woman. They're exposed to all sorts of temptations and get in over their heads. Good morals were an early casualty of the war."

He guided her inside with a hand at her back. Half of the huge enclosure was brightly lit, and teemed with milling servicemen. Many danced while many more waited for a dance partner. A band played on a raised stage, the musicians all in uniform. In the far, darkened end of the hangar, two war-weary B-17s sat surrounded by scaffolding, engines resting on the floor below their wings.

Chet led her to an officer standing by the refreshment table, who smiled at their approach.

"Carol, meet Paul Braedcl. Paul and I go all the way back to navigation school in Miami."

Paul inclined his head. "Hello, Carol. Did you bring any doughnuts?"

She laughed. "No, I did not. Tonight I am free of the scent of our stock-in-trade."

Chet offered her a cup of hot chocolate. "Paul attempted to make himself look good during our training flights by trying to get the rest of us to navigate to the wrong cities."

Paul pulled back and pressed a hand to his chest. "I beg your pardon. I offered in-flight challenges to keep everyone on their toes." He chuckled. "I would like to know how Charlie Spencer is doing these days."

"Paul succeeded in diverting Charlie from his route to Fort Pierce to fly across state to Fort Myers instead." Chet raised his cup to Paul. "Captain Lunn was unamused."

Paul shrugged. "Of course, I could never get Chet off course. He was the boy wonder of our class. Did he tell you he has a job offer with Pan American Airways?"

Carol swung her gaze to Chet. "You do?"

He nodded. "My grandparents are safekeeping a certificate for me, good for a job after the war." He turned to Paul. "Can you imagine, flying anywhere in the world and nobody shooting at us?"

"Pure bliss."

"Come on, Paul." A red-haired officer with bombardier's insignia approached with two girls. He prodded forward a timid but hopeful-looking girl clad in a pretty floral-print dress. "Time to dance."

Paul's smile grew strained. He set his cup on the table, nodded to Carol, and escorted the girl to the dance floor.

Chet didn't suggest they join the dance. He frowned after the bombardier.

"What is it?" Carol moved into his view. "Do you know him?"

"He and Paul are crewmates and have been friends since kindergarten. I don't know if it's his familiarity with Paul that causes him to be insensitive or if he's naturally that way. They're not in our squadron, so I don't know him too well."

He led her to the dance floor. Compared to the jitterbug, their present dance resembled a handholding, foot shuffle. "Because he expected Paul to dance with that girl, you think he's insensitive?"

"Paul's wife died last year, just before we started navigation school."

Carol jerked her head up, narrowly missing Chet's jaw. "His wife died? How awful."

"I'll admit, I dragged Paul along to a country club dance in Miami and, uh, urged him to dance with a recent war widow." Chet grimaced. "Maybe I was a little heavy-handed, but I did it to get him out among people instead of holing up in his room all the time. Art wants him to dance because he feels it's time to forget Rachel."

"Oh, dear."

Across the dance floor, Paul's partner laid her head on his shoulder. He appeared to hold her as though she were glass. He might even be gritting his teeth. He caught Carol staring and gave her an ear-to-ear smile, as phony as a three-dollar bill. At least he didn't need to make conversation.

A young lady near the edge of the dance floor was questioning everyone in an increasingly frantic manner. They came within earshot. "Do you know where Cecil Webster is?"

"Uh, oh." Chet tried to turn away, but the woman accosted him.

"Excuse me. Have you seen Cecil Webster?"

"He may be in the infirmary." At her sharp gasp, he added, "His plane crash-landed after the landing gear didn't come down. No one was seriously hurt, but I heard the crew was sedated."

The woman rushed off, asking anyone who would listen where the infirmary was.

A shiver chased down Carol's spine, and the hot chocolate turned sour in her stomach. That could have been Chet's plane. How could they stand it, never knowing if they would be killed or wounded whenever they took off? How would she react if she was told Chet had been wounded? Killed?

Chapter Fifteen

Wednesday, April 19, 1944
Ridgewell Air Base

A hand shook Chet awake early. "Sir? You're to replace a navigator too sick to fly today. I've got a jeep waiting outside."

Chet fumbled into his flight clothes. Great. His crew wasn't scheduled to fly but now he would. He peered at his watch. After five. At least the later hour meant he could plan on a shorter mission. After double checking his navigation briefcase for all his equipment, he cast a last longing look at his cot and headed out.

The driver barreled for the flight line. Chet frowned. "What about breakfast?"

"Sorry, sir. No time. The other navigator made it out to the plane before he got sick."

That meant everyone else had been up for several hours. Today's mission could be a long haul after all. Too bad he didn't keep a couple candy bars in his briefcase for scenarios like this. Grandma would be horrified by such a breakfast, but it would be better than nothing.

When the jeep careened around the perimeter track to the 533rd Squadron dispersal area, it was clear something was amiss. Why didn't they call one of their own navigators to take over? They screeched to a halt in front of *Smashing Time*. "Here you go, sir."

Chet dragged himself and his gear out of the jeep, and the driver zoomed off.

Chet plodded around to the waist entrance. He clambered aboard as an officer headed aft, a machine gun cradled in his arms. "Welcome to the party," the officer said as he continued on to the tail gun position.

A bolt of lightning may as well have stabbed Chet. "Are you serving as a gunner today?"

"Yeah, aren't I lucky? Flying Control Officer."

Chet swallowed hard. The copilot served in the tail to keep watch over the formation when they had a command pilot onboard, which meant this was a lead crew. He headed up to the cockpit with leaden feet.

Captain Foster, the Group Navigator, met him in the radio room. "Oh, good. You're here. I'm sorry you didn't get to attend the briefing. I put the maps and charts on your desk with the course plotted and all the coordinates."

He moved around Chet to leave the aircraft, but Chet stopped him. "What position do we have in the formation?"

The captain looked him in the eye. "You're leading the formation."

Chet's blood ran cold. This squadron was leading the whole combat wing. That meant *he* was leading the whole combat wing.

"I'm not a lead navigator. The closest I've come to flying lead was when we were deputy lead for the squadron once, and the squadron hadn't been lead." No big deal. But this! He didn't belong here. Why didn't the Group Navigator take the flight himself?

"We've had our eyes on you. You're in line to become Squadron Navigator of the 532nd. This might not seem the likeliest mission to break you in on, but you'll do fine." He turned and left before Chet could ask where the target was.

In the cockpit, he stepped up to the hatchway and hesitated. He should probably announce his arrival. The pilot looked over his right shoulder and gave him a nod. Presence acknowledged. He dropped down the hatchway and crawled into the nose.

As promised, the maps awaited him. The first map bore a red line heading east. He flipped to the final map. The red line ended at Eschwege. He slumped over the desk. Midway into Germany. This was no milk run.

His father's voice sneered in his mind. "You'll never amount to anything, boy."

The hateful words had the effect of ramming a steel rod down his spine. He'd show dear old dad. He'd prove Captain Foster's faith well-placed. He upended his briefcase and dumped out his E-6B computer, triangles, pencils, eraser, plotter, and maps of England and Germany. He could do this.

For a navigator, the weather cooperated beautifully, presenting a CAVU day, with ceiling and visibility unlimited. He had no trouble marking their progress by viewing ground features. Of course, that meant the enemy had no trouble spotting them. German fighters nipped at the formation's edges, but the fighter escorts drove them off.

Chet marked their progress on his map. "Navigator to pilot. Initial Point coming up in six minutes. Prepare to turn left to one three four degrees."

"Roger that."

The minutes ticked by. "I.P. coming up in five, four, three, two, one. Turn." The plane banked slightly. They flew past the I.P. and onto the bomb run. Chet rotated his shoulders. Half his job was done. Flak bursts exploded below them. The Germans hadn't figured out their altitude yet. By the time they did, the lead squadron would be beyond them.

Or maybe not. *Smashing Time* buffeted in a blast on their right, then another on their left. The bombardier asked the pilot if the Automatic Flight Control Equipment was engaged, allowing him to take over control of the plane through the Norden bombsight's connection to the autopilot.

"All yours."

He never looked up as the flak increased. Staring through the bombsight, he announced, "I see the airfield."

Smashing Time banked hard left.

Chet's heart bumped into his throat. They'd been hit? No. He jumped up and looked out the window. The whole formation followed them in the turn. "We've gone off course."

The bombardier snapped the safety back over the bomb switch. "We can't hit the target now." Anger tinged his voice. "Why'd we turn away?"

A reply from the cockpit was long in coming. "Command here, we'll do a three sixty. Navigator, give us a good heading."

A good heading? Was he implying the previous one had been bad? The bombardier whirled around on his swivel chair and shook his head. Anger gleamed from his eyes.

Chet drew a shaky breath and calculated their position. Their turn had to be wide enough to accommodate the entire combat wing. This fiasco could add an hour to their time over the target.

Halfway through the counter clockwise turn, the copilot in the tail burst onto the intercom. "Our low squadron's getting plastered by fighters and flak. Two bombers are going down."

Chet took a moment to glance at his formation chart. Paul's squadron occupied the low position. He gritted his teeth.

Finally, the bombs fell and the copilot made his report. "Doesn't look like that airfield will be usable again for a long time to come."

Chet gave the pilot a return heading to fly west over France before turning north. The route had been planned to avoid known flak gun installations. Fortunately, the enemy fighters didn't follow them.

By the time Ridgewell hove into view, Chet needed a shower. Boy, did he stink. The Red Cross clubmobile better not be visiting today. Carol wouldn't want to come near him.

The formation circled the base. Ordinarily, the lead plane would land first, having been the first to takeoff. Three planes fired red flares, however, indicating wounded aboard. All three were from the low squadron. Chet swiped his arm across the desk, sweeping his tools into his briefcase. If they hadn't made that inexplicable detour, maybe no one would have been hurt or lost.

Saffron Walden, England
Wednesday, April 19, 1944

"Oooh, would you look at that?" Irene threw a letter down on Mrs. Lester's table.

Carol picked up the Red Cross letterhead and scanned the contents. Her jaw dropped. "A rebuke from headquarters for the muddy condition of our clubmobile? 'The coach was untidy, particularly the coffee urns... I know how busy you are and how hard it is to do drudgery work...'" Her voice trailed off and she stared at Irene. "Who inspected us? When? Did someone report us?"

Mrs. Lester set down bowls of steaming porridge and took a turn reading the letter. "Oh, dear. You've come a cropper with this."

Audrey frowned and opened her mouth, but Carol fluttered her hand on the table. Now was not the time to chatter about the meaning of British sayings.

Irene stood rigid at the window, arms crossed and jaw stiff.

"There was someone from London here last week," Audrey said. When Irene swung around with raised brows, she continued. "Remember when we got back late from Bassingbourn and had to hurry to get ready for the dance at Lavenham?"

Irene's breath swooshed out. "There wasn't time to clean the clubmobile that night. We cleaned it in the morning." She waved a hand at the letter and quoted in a sarcastic tone, "'I'm sure you will take the matter in hand immediately and it won't happen again.'"

Tears glittered in her eyes before she whirled back to the window.

Carol frowned. "Writing a rebuttal won't help. They'd think we're making excuses. We're expected to attend as many dances as possible. That's why we're here. And we're supposed to welcome the GIs into the clubmobile, muddy boots and all. We can't stay up into the wee hours and still be off early in the mornings. The men will be insulted if we're tired and yawning."

"So what do we do?" Audrey picked at her nail polish, then thrust her hands behind her back.

Carol snapped her fingers. "The boys like to help out. We'll put them to work on cleaning details. Each base's mud will stay on base."

Irene faced them, nodding slowly. "That could work. We'll have to have our own mop with us. Think the driver would hose off the outside when we return to Saffron Walden?"

"He should help out. He's got a pretty cushy job." Audrey twirled about the room, the reprimand apparently forgotten. "I can't wait to go back to

Lavenham. I met a swell guy in the photo lab. His name's Wally and he's from Vermont." She hugged herself as she twirled. "And he likes me."

Carol and Irene exchanged glances. A hint of a smile appeared as Irene brightened. "How is he with a mop?"

A knock at the door announced their ride to the clubmobile had arrived. Irene went to answer it while Carol scraped her spoon around her bowl to get every bit of porridge. "Either he's early or we're late."

She gulped down her coffee and rose to hurry upstairs, but Irene returned, looking more stricken than she had over the reprimand.

"We're asked to go to Braintree today instead of Nuthampstead." She took a deep breath. "The Germans bombed the hospital yesterday."

Carol sat back down. "The hospital? On purpose?"

"I heard a lot of planes during the night." Mrs. Lester wiped the counter with more force than necessary. "They've never dropped bombs on Saffron Walden, though they've come close. Bombing in the dark like that must be random, hoping to hit something big, but satisfied to simply terrorize us. Those barbarians don't realize the English will not cower."

"How bad is it?" Audrey pulled bobby pins from her hair.

"Two wards completely flattened and seven others badly damaged. But aside from minor injuries, no one was killed. It's quite a mess, of course. They're busy evacuating and rearranging. Lots of the wards were filled with patients."

Carol took a deep breath and straightened her collar. "Well, let's go. It'll be a long day, and we'll get our hands dirty." She winked at Irene. "Maybe even the clubmobile."

Chapter Sixteen

Ridgewell Air Base
Saturday, April 22, 1944

Chet skidded his bicycle to a stop outside the infirmary. Paul had been wounded. He was in the 534th Squadron. *Please, let him not have been wounded during the Eschwege fiasco.* Chet leaned his bike against the side of the Quonset hut and hurried to the door. He nearly bowled over Chaplain Kyle Hogan.

"Excuse me, Chaplain." He paused to catch his breath. "I heard Paul Braedel's here. Do you know where he was wounded?"

"Paul? A bullet grazed across his ribs. It didn't penetrate his body, but he lost a lot of blood. And he has a concussion." Chaplain Hogan possessed such a kindly smile, like he'd just come from the presence of God.

Tension eased from Chet's shoulders. "So he'll be okay. I figured he must not be too badly hurt since he's still here and not transferred to the hospital in Braintree." He blew out his breath. "But I meant, do you know what mission he was wounded on?"

The chaplain chuckled. "That late afternoon trip to France on Thursday."

Chet's head dropped back and he stared at the sky. "Thank you." He looked back at Chaplain Hogan and laughed at his elevated eyebrows. "I had nothing to do with that flight."

"Ah. That's good to know." Puzzlement etched on the chaplain's face, but he didn't probe. He pulled open the door. "Shall we go see him?"

Orderlies served lunch to the patients. Paul dozed propped up in bed, watched by another man sitting on the next bed. The man stood when they approached.

"Chet, have you met Rafe Martell? He and Paul share quarters." The chaplain turned to Rafe. "Paul and Chet were classmates in navigator school."

Rafe offered his hand and a smile. "Paul's mentioned you."

"And you." Chet took the bowl of steaming soup from the lunch tray delivered by an orderly, and waved back and forth in front of Paul's face. Paul's nose twitched. His eyelids fluttered and slowly opened.

Rafe grinned. "Just like in the funny papers! He even leaned forward to get a better whiff."

Chet returned the bowl to the tray now held by Chaplain Hogan and offered a spoon.

Paul reached for the spoon with a hand that shook. "What do you expect?" His voice sounded rusty. "I think they're trying to starve me here."

"That's not so," called an orderly serving lunch to another patient. "You simply haven't stayed awake long enough for us to get any food into you, sir."

"I'm awake now." Paul accepted the tray Kyle set before him and got a spoonful of soup into his mouth. His eyes closed. "Mmm." After another spoonful, he asked, "Did one of our gunners really lose his leg?"

At Rafe's nod, Paul's eating slowed. "Those milk run missions just across the English Channel can be deadlier than a deep penetration of Germany."

"Eschwege was deadlier for your squadron." Chet's eyes strayed down the clean white linen to the outline of Paul's healthy legs. "I'm glad you weren't wounded on that mission."

Paul paused with his mouth full before swallowing. "Would it have mattered?"

"To me it would have. I was the lead navigator."

Paul laid down his spoon, wiped his mouth, and carefully folded his hands on his lap. "Lead navigator of what?"

Chet hesitated before blurting out, "The combat wing."

His friend's reaction would have been comical if it wasn't painful. Paul jerked upright, jarring the lunch tray. He grabbed it with one hand and his side with the other before dropping back. His face paled as he panted. "Since...when?"

"Since Wednesday. I was a very last minute replacement, and I thought I did fine until we turned off course on the bomb run."

The words were barely out of his mouth when someone called his name. An enlisted man stood in the doorway. "You're wanted in Colonel Leber's office." His demeanor suggested pity and Chet tensed. "A couple of generals from the First Air Division are here asking questions."

Chet nodded and turned back. "Eschwege."

The chaplain moved Paul's lunch tray to a vacant bed, and Chet helped Rafe ease Paul down in his bed. His friend's eyes were closing even as he whispered, "We'll be praying."

With another nod, Chet headed out to face the inquisition.

He entered headquarters and spotted the bombardier, pilot, and copilot huddled in a corner. The bombardier nodded him over. "General Doolittle's here."

"Doo—" The commander of the Eighth Air Force was here? That was bad news.

The major who'd flown as command pilot entered with the squadron commander, laughing and joking.

They were called in to take seats before a long table. Chet scanned all the brass seated there. No one needed to point out General Doolittle. Maybe the

Group Navigator, also present, would plead Chet's case if he was in trouble.

Another general read a summary of the Eschwege mission. Chet grit his teeth to avoid squirming as the general eyed each of them. "What went wrong?"

"We were a few miles off course as we approached the target." No surprise that the major would speak up. He outranked the rest of the crew. "I ordered a go-around to avoid wasting our effort and necessitating a return mission."

What an innocuous answer. A few miles indeed. They hadn't been off course until something went wrong. That's what Doolittle was questioning.

"Why were you off course?" Chet almost smiled at the general's question. Cut right to the chase.

"We should have been on course. The conditions were perfect. Our navigation was just a little off."

Chet would have gnashed his teeth, but his jaw had dropped. Their navigation was off? *He* was off? He struggled to inflate his lungs. The major wanted to pin the fiasco on him.

"Our navigation was right on the money, sir." The bombardier nearly came out of his chair. Fists clenched, he looked Doolittle straight in the eye. "The bombsight was flying the plane, the target was in sight, and I was ready to release the bombs when we suddenly turned away."

"Did you initiate the turn?"

"No, sir, I did not. To that point, we had a textbook-perfect flight."

Chet breathed easy. The bombardier hadn't hesitated to contradict the major. He had someone on his side.

General Doolittle looked straight at him, and his heart rate sped up. "Lieutenant, as you neared the target, what was the maximum deflection of your compass heading?"

Chet blinked. The general knew something about navigation. "About twenty degrees, sir."

If the bombsight had been in control, corrections could not be more than a handful of degrees. Any more than that could only be caused by a pilot overriding the system.

The general turned his attention to the pilot. "Did you take over control of the aircraft?"

"No, sir."

Steely eyes focused on the major. "Chuck?"

A brief hesitation. "The anti-aircraft gunners had zeroed in on us."

Every one of the brass facing them sighed, it seemed. Chet tried not to smile. He had sighed, too.

Colonel Leber spoke up. "No evasive action. That's the rule. By trying to spare the formation, you ruined the bomb run."

Not to mention endangering the other planes. In a tight formation, sudden turns could easily lead to collisions. Chet stared down at his hands gripping his knees. The lost crews hadn't been his fault, and now it was official. He looked up, and his gaze tangled with the Group Navigator's. A smile and a nod. Chet squared his shoulders. Squadron navigator. The job would be his. *Stop right there.* In this business, take life one day at a time.

Chapter Seventeen

Saffron Walden, England
April 24, 1944

"Nine o'clock. That's not too bad. We'll get to bed before midnight." Irene stood with hands on hips, searching for the tiniest bit of untidiness in the clubmobile.

Audrey opened the door and inhaled the fresh air before stepping down. "We can head for home if our ride is here, and there's the jeep."

Carol followed Audrey out, but came to a halt when she spotted the jeep. Chet sat behind the wheel, not their usual driver. He climbed out and started toward her. Something was wrong. His steps seemed stiff and his smile, when he finally smiled, looked strained, even in the deepening twilight.

"Like a doughnut?" Either Audrey didn't notice or she thought a doughnut could cure whatever ailed him.

He barely glanced her way. "No, thanks. I'm not hungry." He stopped in front of Carol and devoured her with his eyes. "Ready to head for Mrs. ..." He snapped his fingers a couple times. "Starts with L."

"Mrs. Lester." Carol smiled as his mood lightened. "We spent a little extra time at Lavenham, getting the men to help clean the clubmobile." She lowered her voice as they walked to the jeep. "We got a rebuke from Red Cross headquarters about not keeping the *Texas* clean enough."

"Really?" Chet looked back at the clubmobile. "My grandmother always says she keeps the house clean enough to be healthy, but not so clean that no one will feel uncomfortable putting their feet up on the coffee table."

"I haven't even met her and I like her already." Irene still sounded dejected whenever she thought about the reprimand.

Carol climbed into the jeep. Something dropped to the floor with a clank. She felt around for it.

"Is the jeep falling apart?" Chet paused before starting the engine.

"Nope." Carol held out her hand. "We served the ground crews working on the Liberators at Lavenham, and one of the guys gave me this souvenir. A German bullet."

About to pick up the object she held, Chet reached for the ignition instead. "Really? How thoughtful of him." He wasn't sarcastic exactly, but obviously not impressed.

Carol clenched her fingers around the bullet. Goodness, why would he be? She and the ground crewman didn't have to worry about being on the receiving end of one of these bits of lead. For Chet and the combat crews though, they were lethal.

The ride back to Saffron Walden passed quietly as Chet concentrated on driving in the dark. When he parked at Mrs. Lester's, Carol twisted to face him. "You're not flying tomorrow?"

"Probably will. Had today off." He waited until Irene and Audrey disappeared into the house. "Anywhere we can walk around a bit?"

He held Carol's hand as they walked. She didn't object. Maybe he saw them as more than casual friends who hadn't dated. A tingly sensation swept through her. Oh, yeah. She wouldn't mind getting to know Chet Vogel better. He sighed heavily and his hand convulsed on hers. Okay, maybe he merely needed a human touch.

"Bad day?"

Another sigh, this one a bit shaky. "You remember Paul? You met him at the dance."

Uh, oh. She gripped his hand. "I remember. Your friend from navigation school whose wife died." Carol swallowed. The weak moonlight hid Chet's expression. "Is he, was he killed?"

"No, he was wounded last week. Not seriously." Chet stopped and faced her. "But he didn't fly today with his crew. Their plane exploded. They were killed."

"Oh, Chet. What must he be feeling now?" She reached for his other hand. "Is it right to say he was lucky to be wounded?"

His shrug traveled through her hands. "I doubt he would agree. He misses his wife something awful. Death would have reunited them. And the bombardier was the lifelong school friend. He's taking it pretty hard."

So was Chet. His emotions clearly seethed beneath the surface. If it weren't dark, she'd suggest a run to work off some of his angst. But something didn't add up right. Various combat crewmen had told her they didn't form close friendships with others outside their own crews. Why should the loss of Paul's crew affect Chet so deeply?

"Did someone else," how could she say this, "meet with misfortune?"

Chet's head dropped to his chest. Another sigh. "Another navigation school classmate and I planned on visiting Cambridge over the weekend. Vern's at Bassingbourn. I went to meet him there, but he didn't come back from the mission. They had to ditch in the North Sea."

He let go of her hand and turned to walk, but didn't make it more than one step. "I got word today. His body washed ashore overnight. Air-Sea Rescue never found them."

"Oh, Chet." Carol wrapped her arms around him and hugged him tight. Tears stung her eyes.

His words tumbled out. "I don't have a relationship with my three older brothers. They lived with their, our, father. I guess that's why my friendships are so important to me. And now one's dead and another's hurting so bad, I can't imagine."

Carol stroked one hand up and down his back, and swayed from side to side. Rocking him like a baby. No brilliant words of comfort came to mind. His arms around her waist clung to her like a lifeline. Words weren't necessary. Just her presence.

Minutes passed before he straightened. "I should get back to Ridgewell. Wake-up can come in a few hours."

They walked back to the jeep in silence. Not until he was ready to start the engine did she reach for his hand. "The Lord bless you and keep you, Chet."

There was more to that blessing, but she couldn't remember it.

His other hand covered hers, somewhere between a grip and a pat. Then he was gone. She stayed outside until the sound of the jeep faded.

"You and Chet are getting awfully cozy," Audrey greeted her when she entered their bedroom.

"He had a bad day at Ridgewell. Needed to get off base, find a bit of normalcy." Carol's heart was heavy. If only her roommate would leave her in silence.

Audrey's next words stopped her in her tracks. "Nothing normal with that clutch. I thought you weren't planning on marrying a serviceman."

Carol swung around so fast, she nearly fell. "We enjoy each other's company. We're not talking marriage."

Audrey shrugged as she continued putting her hair in bobby pins.

Carol planted her hands on her hips. "He and a friend planned to go to Cambridge, but he found out today his friend is dead. Another friend's crew was killed today. The war is wearing him down."

Interest bloomed on Audrey's face. She set aside her can of bobby pins and unfolded her legs from beneath her. "Oh, let's do go to Cambridge. I'll ask Wally. We can make it a foursome." She turned to Irene, who came in from the bathroom, toweling her hair. "Want to go too?"

"As a fifth wheel? No thanks. I need to go to London and check in with headquarters next week. Go then."

Carol pulled her pajamas from the bureau. Had Audrey heard anything she'd said besides Cambridge? A little sympathy for Chet was in order.

Carol grabbed her hairbrush from the top of the bureau. A day of sightseeing with Chet would be fun.

Maybe by next week he'd be ready for a diversion. She silently scoffed as she headed for the bathroom. They spend a little time together and Audrey thinks they're getting married? No sir. No wartime marriage for her.

Of course, after the war, when life returned to normal, who's to say what might happen?

Chapter Eighteen

Bassingbourn Air Base, England
Thursday, May 4, 1944

Eating in the mess halls with the boys—"men," Carol reminded herself; they hated being called boys—always resulted in delicious meals. She'd be lucky to get any food today, though. One of the mess sergeants was missing, so she'd filled in on the chow line, just until he returned. Except they wouldn't let her leave.

The line moved along and a young man—boy, she insisted—stopped in front of her. He turned beet red when their eyes met. Ignoring his embarrassment, she scooped up a serving of Brussels sprouts and ladled them into his mess kit. With a barely perceptible nod, he shifted to the next server. His buddy was bolder.

"Brussels sprouts? Again?"

Carol slopped a large dollop onto his kit. "These are in plentiful supply. Now eat them all up. They're good for you. Remember, if you don't finish your vegetables, you can't have dessert, and I happen to know the cooks have prepared a delectable butterscotch pie." She wagged a finger at him. "I'll be keeping an eye on you."

He grinned at her teasing even as his color rose. Even better, his bashful friend laughed.

After doling out at least ten gallons of the vegetable, she was allowed to have her own lunch. As she looked around the room, everyone appeared to be busy eating and paying no attention to her. But no sooner did she step around the serving line than the men stopped eating. Calls of "Sit here," and "I saved you a spot," rang out.

She chose a particular table. "I promised I'd keep an eye on someone."

The finicky eater grinned, until he saw her own meal. "Three measly Brussels sprouts. That's all? What gives? You gave me enough for everyone at the table."

Carol raised her nose. "You need to keep up your strength for the arduous missions you fly. I, on the other hand, have to watch my weight."

Oops. She shouldn't have phrased it like that.

A lanky fellow with greasy hair falling across his forehead half rose from his seat and ogled her. "I'll help you watch your weight."

"Put a lid on it, Kramer," Finicky said. He turned to her. "Don't mind him. He doesn't think before he talks."

She smiled and took a bite of her vegetable, trying not to show her distaste. He was right; they did have Brussels sprouts way too often. He was also at least five years younger than she. All of them were. This was the equivalent of eating with a bunch of seventh graders when she was a high school senior. She shoved the thought from her mind.

The boy at the end of the table sat stiffly, both hands resting on the table on either side of his mess kit. He stared ahead but probably wasn't noticing anything. A friend urged him to eat.

Finicky commented on her observation. "His crew ditched a couple weeks ago. He floated around in a raft on the North Sea with two dead buddies. He's the only survivor of his whole crew, and hasn't spoken a word."

The Brussels sprout she'd swallowed hovered over her windpipe and she began coughing. Chet's friend had been at Bassingbourn. Now she was at Bassingbourn. "What…" She swallowed hard to get that miserable sprout down her throat. "What was the navigator's name?"

Finicky lowered his fork and exchanged glances with Bashful. "Why do you ask?"

The Brussels sprout began to resemble a rock in her stomach. "A friend at Ridgewell lost a navigation school classmate who was based here. He was found washed ashore. His name was Vern."

"I think there was a Vern on his crew." Bashful eyed the survivor and kept his voice at a whisper. "They were joking on the radio as they went down.

Their gas tank had been hit and they lost too much fuel to make it back. They told everyone to leave them something for chow and not to grab all their gear for ourselves."

"What happened?" Carol watched the young man stare at his food.

Bashful shrugged. "The sea was rough that day. We think one of the two dinghies capsized and the other, well, there should have been four or five in it, but only three by the time Air-Sea Rescue found them. They were drenched, and two had died of hypothermia."

How traumatic to float on a cold, endless sea and helplessly watch two friends die. "What's his name?" Her voice quavered.

"Jerry," Finicky said. "Jerome C. Milhous the Third."

Taking a deep breath, Carol rose and slowly approached Jerry. The men's closest friends were the members of their own crews, Chet had told her. They didn't try to get to know many others because of the strong possibility of them being killed or shot down. Had anyone put an arm around this tortured soul? What he probably needed most was a hug from his mother, but she wasn't here.

She crouched down beside him and placed a hand on his arm. "Hi, Jerry. My name is Carol."

A long moment passed. Then his face turned in jerky movements. Pain-filled eyes beseeched her for absolution. She wrapped her arm around him, pulling him against her, stroking the side of his face with her other hand. Only the words of a Sunday School song came to mind and she whispered them through her clogged throat. "Jesus loves you, this I know. For the Bible tells me so."

Around them, the mess hall fell silent. The men averted their eyes, their Adam's apples bobbing. The stricken crew's misfortune could have been any of theirs. A chill swept Carol. It could happen to Chet.

Jerry shuddered in her arms. His anguish leaked out in tears and dampened her hand. An officer wearing chaplain's insignia approached and together they pulled Jerry to his feet and led him from the mess hall.

By the time Carol returned to the clubmobile, she wanted nothing more than to curl up in bed and pull the covers over her head. Irene pointed to a small box. "A couple of guys brought that for you."

Carol raised the cover, and tears stung her eyes. Finicky and Bashful had saved her a slice of butterscotch pie.

Friday, May 12, 1944

Chet's crew received a forty-eight-hour pass. While most of his crewmates planned a trip to London, he arranged a ride with a courier to deliver him to Cambridge. Carol and her teammates scrambled to rearrange their schedule, and Carol and Audrey would meet him with Audrey's friend Wally.

The thirty-mile ride to the northwest passed through quaint villages forgotten by time. How could the thick straw-thatched roofs covering most houses keep the occupants dry in torrential rainstorms? The residents went about their business unfazed by the constant rumble of bombers flying to and from battle.

From his drop-off point in the middle of town, Chet wandered cobblestone lanes too narrow for cars. The old buildings must have been constructed before the Pilgrims arrived at Plymouth Rock. Maybe even before Columbus discovered America.

He sat on a bench alongside an ancient church and watched the people. A bird with a blue head and yellow breast fluttered down to peck about near his feet, keeping an eye on him. A woman stopped to chat with an acquaintance. Her small daughter clung to her legs and peered around at Chet with big blue eyes and an impish grin. He winked and she giggled. With her mother ready to move along, she warbled a lilting, "Cheerio."

Terri Wangard

The acquaintance looked him over. "Are you lost, Yank?"

"No, ma'am. Just filling time until my friends arrive." His time alone was precious. Privacy was rare on base. While seeing Carol would be great, a bit of solitude was a gift. Of course, he couldn't tell the lady to leave him in peace.

"What sort of bird is this?" He nodded toward his feathered friend.

"That's a blue tit, it is. Quite the dapper little fellow. Doesn't mind if he's right side up or upside down." The woman wore a brown tweed coat too warm for the spring day and a hat with a flower that bobbed with every movement she made.

"Reminds me more of the chickadees back home than bluebirds."

"You'll not be finding any bluebirds in England." Her look censored him. "You Yanks wrote a song about peace when bluebirds fly over the cliffs of Dover, but that'll never happen. We don't have bluebirds here."

"That's too bad. They're beautiful birds." Before she could elaborate on her dispute, Chet looked at his watch and rose. "Would you point me in the direction of King's College?"

She preened at his appeal for her assistance and launched into complete instructions, ending with, "You cawn't miss it."

160

He arrived at the colleges making up Cambridge University at the same time as Carol and her friends. Audrey immediately brought over a bespectacled officer lacking wings on his uniform.

"Chet, meet Wally. He's in charge of photography at Lavenham." Audrey hugged the man's arm like she was afraid he'd get away.

"Photography? Do you develop the strike footage?" Chet's crewmate, Dexter Small, operated a camera from the radio room during their missions, but they never saw the resultant film.

"My men do the developing. I analyze the photos to determine how well the target was bombed. So often, if they could have only gotten a little better approach, they could have wiped out the target."

Typical of a noncombatant ground pounder. Of course, the combat crews required a lot of support personnel behind them, but these guys didn't understand what they endured. Wally bristled with pride, or maybe Chet imagined it. Either way, he couldn't resist responding to the perceived insult. "Yeah, there's no such thing as hitting the pickle barrel at twenty-five thousand feet while flying over one hundred miles an hour. But I can assure you, *they* don't enjoy risking their lives on wasted missions."

Wally reddened, as if just spotting Chet's navigator wings. "You combat crews do an amazing job, under the circumstances."

"Yeah." Chet linked his arm with Carol's. "Ready for some lunch before we see the sights? How about a traditional English meal of fish and chips?"

Carol gripped his hand. "Oh, yes, I've wanted to try that since I've been over here."

Soon they had their hands full of big hunks of fish and steak-fried potatoes wrapped in old newspaper. "Would it be all right if we walked around the campus while we eat? If we stay here, I'll be tempted to get more and eat too much." Carol licked her fingers. "What should we do first?"

Chet nodded toward the campus. "One of the guys in my barracks visited here. He recommended seeing the King's College Chapel."

The left side of Wally's lips turned down. "How about some punting?"

"As long as we're here, let's have a look. Then we can go to the river." Audrey bumped her arm against Wally's.

He sighed. "All right, but let's make it quick."

Students wearing flowing academic gowns walked or rode bicycles. Wally frowned. "Are they graduating today? Maybe we should go somewhere else."

"No." Chet wiped greasy fingers on his handkerchief. "I've heard they always dress like that."

"Like wearing uniforms," Audrey added. She stopped a student. "Which way to the chapel?"

Raised brows greeted her question. "Which one?"

"King's College Chapel." Chet stepped up. "I've heard it's not to be missed."

The student responded with lengthy directions that left the girls looking befuddled.

Carol grinned at Audrey after he left them. "You cawn't miss it."

"I didn't know I needed to take notes." Audrey's reply came out in a soft wail.

Carol turned to Chet. "You're the navigator. Navigate."

"Right this way, folks." He set off in the indicated direction. Too bad he didn't have a camera. He glanced at Wally's empty hands. "Do you enjoy taking pictures?"

"Yes, but I didn't bring a camera since there's nothing here to photograph." His failure to look at anything they passed confirmed his bored status.

"Oh, that looks like a church." Audrey pointed to the filigreed towers of a cathedral off to their left.

"That's not King's College." Chet pointed ahead. "That wide street should be King's Parade. The chapel should be close by."

"What difference does it make if we go to one or the other? Is one Catholic and one Lutheran?" Wally seemed to measure the distance.

Carol peered at him around Chet. "Cambridge University is made up of several colleges. Each college has its own buildings, including chapels."

"And they're probably all Church of England." Chet took Carol's empty newspaper, folded it with his, and deposited them in a trash can.

"Seems awfully extravagant. They likely don't fill any of them on Sundays." Wally chuckled.

Carol leaned close to whisper, "What does he find humorous about that?"

Upon entering the chapel, Chet's gaze was drawn upward by the soaring architecture. Stained glass windows sparkled in the sunlight. He and Carol began walking down the aisle.

"This place must have quite an echo." Wally's voice rang out behind them.

Chet spun around as other visitors turned to stare. "We're in a church." He kept his voice hushed. "A little reverence, please."

Wally shrugged.

"Seen enough, babe?" Wally tugged on Audrey's arm. Her face glowing red, Audrey scurried outside.

Carol expelled her breath. "I don't know what she sees in him."

Chet nudged her to continue down the aisle. "This must be much nicer in peacetime." He nodded up to the stained glass. "Apparently they don't expect any more bombing here. Or maybe that's newer glass. I was told the ancient glass was taken down and stored in cellars, and the tar paper on what's left doesn't do it justice."

"Ancient glass?"

"King's College dates back to the 1440s. This place could be five hundred years old. I'd say that's ancient."

"In fourteen hundred and ninety-two, Columbus sailed the ocean blue." Carol whispered the grade school ditty.

Chet stifled a snicker. She was echoing his earlier thoughts.

"When Columbus discovered America, he found a primitive culture." Carol tipped her head back to gaze at the ceiling high overhead. "He was used to places like this. In Spain, of course. Or was it Portugal? I'm forgetting my history lessons."

"And now places like this are being bombed into oblivion." He massaged his temple. "Some buildings took over a hundred years to build, but they crumble into rubble in seconds. Doesn't say much for modern civilization, does it?" He rotated his shoulders. "Care to try punting on the River Cam?"

They left the chapel and headed toward the river.

"I was surprised to hear you'd gotten a pass. The bases all seem to be so busy." Carol dropped her voice to a whisper, even though no one was within earshot as they walked down a neighborhood street. "Everyone believes the invasion to be imminent."

"Yes, it must be. It'll be nice to have the army involved. Of course, they are." Chet turned to her. Exhaustion bruised his eyes. "They've fought in Africa and Italy. Still are. But the air force has been alone in carrying the war to Germany."

He took a deep breath, his shoulders rising and falling with it. "The doctors are pressing for passes to be increased. They feel we've gotten stale and lost our drive. Guys are irritable from the day-to-day strain with no let-up. The docs are looking forward to the invasion too. They believe we'll have renewed interest in keeping at it. I'm looking forward to sleeping late in a silent room. But that won't happen until the war's over or we're dead."

Carol shivered. Must he talk like that? "So what do you know about punting?"

A lazy grin spread across his face. "I think we just sit in the boat and let someone else do the work."

She poked a finger at his middle. "Don't get so relaxed you fall asleep on me."

She grinned at his laughter.

"No, ma'am. While we're alive, we have to make the most of our time." His arm snaked around her waist. "I fully intend to."

Chapter Nineteen

Saffron Walden, England
Sunday, May 21, 1944

Carol burst out laughing as she sat at Mrs. Lester's table. She dropped her pen and brushed the moisture from her eyes.

"That article about jitterbugging must be awfully funny." Irene turned from the counter with a cup of tea.

"No, not really." Carol pressed a hand to her chest, striving to regain her composure. "I just remembered something with Chet in Cambridge." She gave up and let the giggles consume her.

Irene waited with raised brows.

"It was getting dark when we walked back to the inn where we had rooms. We were walking by a fenced-in yard. I noticed the flowers in the yard and thought they might be dahlias. It was too dark to be sure. A sign was posted on the fence and Chet asked, 'What's it say?' I couldn't make it out, and Chet leaned over the fence to reach a flower." A snicker escaped and Carol had to pause before continuing. "I said, 'Oh, I can read it now.' And Chet says, 'You can? What's it say?' 'Wet paint.'"

She convulsed with laughter as Irene's brows rose higher.

"It doesn't sound so funny in the telling, but you should have seen Chet. He shot upright and he looked down at himself with his fingers spread out." Carol held her own hands in front of her, as though afraid to touch her blouse. "Then he looked at me, real suspicious, and says, 'Wet paint?'" She exhaled hard. "So then I said, 'Oh, my mistake. It says West Pointe.'" She wiped her eyes on her sleeve. "Even little cottages get named here. I think if we had been on a bridge, Chet would have tossed me into the River Cam."

"You're falling for him, aren't you?" Still leaning against the counter, Irene hadn't budged from her spot.

"I suppose I am." If only Carol could keep to herself her feelings for the man who occupied so many of her thoughts. She shuffled her papers and pulled out another article. "I wish I had a typewriter. Chet recommended I submit the jitterbug article to *Stars & Stripes* or *Yank*. I'm going to ask if he'll look at it tomorrow. But would you read this one? I wrote it for the *Canton Repository*. Think the folks back home would be interested?"

Irene took the offered pages and read rapidly. She stopped and stared at Carol. "A bunch of grapes for five dollars? A scrawny little peach for a dollar twenty? This is what the British pay for food in Cambridge? Yes, send it. Maybe it will stop some people from griping about rationing."

Irene turned to head upstairs and spun back. "Here's something to think about. At Headquarters, we were told about going to the continent after the invasion. Think about whether you'd like to do that and let me know. I'll notify Headquarters."

Audrey entered the kitchen in time to hear Irene's announcement. "I'm staying right here. I wouldn't dream of leaving."

Carol studied Audrey, who poured herself a cup of tea. Several times in Cambridge Audrey had seemed embarrassed by Wally's behavior. Why was she so fascinated by him? Chet hadn't said a word against him, but she'd sensed his disapproval when Wally made disparaging remarks about England. At least Audrey wasn't talking about marrying the man. Sally's last letter had been full of woe. One friend suffering from a horrendous mistake was enough.

Sleep refused to come. The toilet flushed twice during the night, but it didn't bother Carol. She wanted to go to France. She wanted to see Chet. Pummeling her pillow didn't make it more comfortable or relieve her frustration. This is what came of getting involved with a man. She and Chet were involved, weren't they? *Arg.*

She rose in the morning more tired than when she'd gone to bed. As they waited for their ride, Mrs. Lester's neighbor presented the girls with a pot of red geraniums. Seeing this, a neighbor across the lane offered them a bunch of gorgeous blue irises. Not to be outdone, Mrs. Lester urged them to cut some of her lovely pink and white peonies.

"We'll be serving coffee and doughnuts in a garden all day." Carol handed a pot to their bewildered driver before passing irises to Audrey in the back seat. Climbing in, she took back the pot and secured it between her feet. "Drive carefully so our bouquets aren't wind damaged."

"Yes, ma'am." The poor man looked like he wanted to bolt from his flower-strewn jeep.

The clubmobile arrived at Ridgewell as the last of the Flying Fortresses took off, spiraling up into formation. Carol groaned inwardly. For security reasons, no one would tell them where the planes were going or how long the mission should last. Chet was likely flying today. If it was an all-day mission, she might not get to see him. After the long night, she really needed to see him.

They stopped by the control tower to serve the men who oversaw the mission get underway. "Be at the playing field later this morning." The man at the front of the line spoke around a mouthful of doughnut. "The ground officers are playing the enlisted men in a game of baseball."

"Oh good." Carol passed him a cup of coffee. "We'll referee."

Maybe, if she was lucky, the game would last until the planes came back.

The bombs tumbled toward the shipyards and naval base of Kiel in northern Germany. Right after they'd turned away from the target, *French Dressing* started vibrating violently. Chet lurched to the left window. Everything looked fine. He turned to the right.

Lowell came on the intercom. "We lost oil pressure on engine two. I've cut the power, but I can't feather the propeller. It's windmilling. If this keeps up, it could tear off the wing. Be ready to bail out."

Bail out? They were heading out over the North Sea. The Germans might send a boat for them, but they were more likely to die of hypothermia in the cold water, if they didn't drown first. Chet sat down hard at his desk and checked the parachute clips on his harness. Bomby did likewise, his eyes squinting and his movements rigid. Everything had gone so well. No enemy fighters had opposed them. The flak over Kiel was intense but inaccurate. Their plane betrayed them.

A loud clank rang out. From the ball turret, Homer Long yelled, "Engine four's on fire."

"We're on it." Andy's voice hinted at the strain the pilots must be feeling. "Activating fire extinguisher."

At the same time, the alarm bell rang, signaling "Get ready to bail out."

The noise level decreased as engine four was cut.

"It's working. The fire's out." If Long was smart, he'd get out of the ball in case they needed to bail.

The formation was pulling ahead of them. Chet watched it go. A vice squeezed his chest. Stragglers were favorite targets of the Luftwaffe. Once they were alone, German fighters would likely appear. "Small, have you called for a fighter escort?"

John Lemke answered from the tail. "There's a pair of 'em circling above us."

Chet hopped up and stuck his head in the astrodome. Sure enough. Sun glinted off a shiny Mustang. The fighters couldn't help them if they bailed out, but at least they didn't have to worry about being jumped by the enemy.

The noise level dropped again and the vibration ceased. Chet nearly lost his balance in the sudden stillness.

"The prop disconnected from the engine." Relief filled Lowell's voice. "It's still windmilling, but it's not turning the engine over. Crew check. Is everyone still with us?"

One by one, everyone called in.

"Boy howdy, I sure wasn't going to bail out if I didn't have to." Stan Price's voice sounded an octave higher than normal.

"The fighters want to know if we'll be okay on our own now. They think we're far enough away from the continent and we haven't seen any enemy fighters." As their radio operator, Dexter Small was the only one in contact with their escort. "What should I tell them?"

"Go ahead and release them with our thanks," Lowell replied.

"Wait." Chet hurried to interrupt. "Before you do, ask them to confirm our position. I want to be sure our instruments weren't damaged in all the vibration." From his view in the astrodome, he watched one of the Mustangs soar higher to get direct line-of-sight communication with his base in England. A minute later, he had his answer.

"He says we should reach England in about three hours on a QDM compass heading of two-five-zero."

"Three hours?" Zempel broke in.

"Are you happy with that?" Small continued as if there'd been no interruption.

"I'm happy. Tell him thanks." Chet marked his log and plotted their position and time on his map.

"I'm not happy." Zempel wouldn't let up. "The rest of the group will be back long before us."

"At least we'll be joining them there. Remember, we came close to bailing out. Now let's keep a sharp lookout for other planes. Either a German hoping to jump us or another straggler we can join up with." And quit griping on the intercom, Lowell should have added.

Chet put on his American Optical sunglasses and stepped up behind Bomby to scan the skies. Zempel was right about being unhappy. The delay meant the Red Cross clubmobile would no longer be at the base by the time they returned. He'd miss seeing Carol.

"We got company," Ken Cottrell called from the top turret. "It's one of ours, a P-47 Thunderbolt."

"Does he think we need help?" Always count on Zempel to have something to say.

Lemke made a guess. "Maybe he's lost."

The fighter came alongside and crept closer and closer. Chet watched in consternation as the Thunderbolt snuggled up to their wing. Way too close to engine one's propeller. He looked into the cockpit and his heart sank.

"He wants our protection. He's badly wounded. Blood's all over his face, and he's having a hard time holding his head up."

Such a head injury must be fatal. If he bailed out over England, if he got to England, hitting the ground would kill him. If he tried to land in his condition, he'd crash. A fighter pilot had no one to help out in emergencies. Chet appreciated his crewmates more than ever.

Not everyone shared his sentiments.

"I wanted to be a fighter pilot." Andy's voice sounded like he still did. "I was put in as a copilot as punishment for not volunteering for the heavies."

"What are you talking about?" Bomby glanced back at Chet. "There's no shame in being a copilot."

"Ask any copilot if he requested fighters or heavy bombers. I'll bet most of 'em wanted fighters. Instead, we got assigned to bombers as second fiddle."

"What'd you request, Lowell?" Chet didn't think their pilot had the devil-may-care attitude common to fighter pilots.

"Heavy bombers. I figured aviation is going to be a big business after the war, and bomber experience would be better than fighters." Lowell didn't give anyone a chance to continue the conversation. "Small, can you raise this guy on the radio?"

"I think so, unless it's a German trying to fool us. Someone's slurring his words badly. I can't understand him."

"Call the base. Request a pair of Thunderbolts to rendezvous with us who can guide our friend to a fighter base and talk him down. We can't help him with that."

Chet updated his log and stood to watch the fighter pilot. The wounded man's head bobbed up. Chet waved, and offered a thumbs up. The bobbing head tilted to the side and a hand briefly appeared. He had determination. Maybe he'd make it after all.

Fragments of the navy hymn circled Chet's mind. "Eternal Father, strong to save." Too bad he couldn't remember the new air force stanza. Something about beseeching God to save those who dared to fly like eagles. "O hear us when we cry to Thee for those in peril on the sea." And in the air.

"The planes should be coming back from the mission soon. Let's head for the control tower."

Carol's ears perked up as she offered doughnuts to the cluster of men. She angled back toward the clubmobile with her tray. If the men planned to head for the field and watch the planes land, so could they. "How's our supply for the combat crews?"

"We've been keeping back nearly two hundred and fifty. I was told twenty-eight aircraft are on the mission." Irene grabbed a pen and did the math.

"Most have nine men, but some still have ten. Say two hundred sixty men. We'll be short." She grimaced. "I hate to start up the machine to make just a dozen more."

Carol shoved her tray up onto the window ledge. "Here's seven more. And don't forget, the mess sergeant will probably have something. Let's go." She waved for Audrey and climbed inside.

Audrey hurried in after her. "I didn't get rid of all my doughnuts."

"Good." Irene relieved her of her tray. "Now we have enough for each airman to have one."

They parked the clubmobile alongside the crowd gathering at the control tower. Men gravitated toward them with hungry looks. Carol glanced at Irene with a raised brow.

"Sorry, boys. We have only enough doughnuts for the returning airmen. We're here for the show, too." Irene marched out among them and herded them away from the clubmobile. "Where's the best seat in the house?"

A distant rumble grew into a roar and the base's formation thundered overhead. None of the planes shot off flares indicating wounded aboard. They'd had a good day. Carol bounced on her toes. No matter how many times she watched the bombers take off or land, the sight still sent shivers through her. She looked to the man next to her. "You wouldn't happen to know which plane is Chet Vogel's, would you?"

He stared at her for a moment and seemed to deflate with a sigh. "Do you know which squadron he's in?"

"The 532nd."

He nodded. "That's the low squadron today. The last to take off and the last to land. He'll be down in about an hour."

"An hour? An hour? They're right here, overhead. Why so long?"

The guy smiled slowly. She'd asked a stupid question. "They can't all land at the same time, you know. There's at least thirty seconds between planes."

"Fifty-six minutes." Her shoulders slumped.

"At least. Usually more."

He was laughing at her.

She wandered away from him as the first plane touched the runway, tires emitting a squeal, kicking up a puff of dust. She clasped her hands together before raising an arm to wave as it turned and taxied past.

Audrey tugged on her sleeve twenty minutes later. "Time to move over to the interrogation hall. The first crews will be arriving shortly for debriefing."

Carol nodded, watching the planes still circling overhead. Which was Chet in? Could he see her?

After they'd been serving coffee and doughnuts for half an hour, the roar of planes ceased. Chet would arrive soon. She forced herself to concentrate on the men before her.

An officer arrived and spoke to Colonel Leber, the commanding officer of the 381st Bomb Group. "They've all landed except the Hendricks crew."

Hendricks? Wasn't Chet's pilot Lowell Hendricks? A hot flush swept across Carol and curled in her stomach. An airman was reaching for the cup of coffee she held, but she didn't notice him. "Do you mean Lowell Hendricks, sir? From the 532nd?"

The men looked at her. "Yes, I do."

The coffee cup landed on the table with a thud. "Why...?" Carol couldn't bring herself to ask if they'd been shot down. "Why haven't they landed?"

The officer quirked his brows at her interest. "They'll be late. They had to drop out of formation after they lost two engines."

"They lost two engines? Where'd they lose them?" She wasn't handling this well, but she needed to get her words out fast so he could answer her. Men waiting to debrief began gathering around.

"Oh, they still have the engines, I'm sure." He swiped a hand across his face. Wiping away a smile? "But the engines aren't working, and with the loss of half their power, they couldn't keep up. They're tootling along close to England, but they're also shepherding a wounded fighter pilot." He turned to Colonel Leber. "They requested Thunderbolts to meet them and take over with the Little Friend. We have no idea when they'll be coming in."

Carol's heart sank. She and her teammates had promised to attend a dance at Lavenham. No way would Audrey allow them to be late. Not when she planned on spending the whole evening with her Wally.

The last of the crews arrived and polished off the doughnuts. Irene beamed with pleasure. "No leftovers, and we didn't run short." She began stacking trays and thrust a bunch into Carol's arms. "If you'll take these, I'll grab the coffee urn."

As they crossed to the clubmobile, Carol stopped and gazed into the distance beyond the end of the runway. No sight or sound of the missing plane. Her shoulders sagged and the armload of trays shifted.

Chet could look at her article next week. Or she could ask that friendly copilot at Nuthampstead to read it on Wednesday.

Forget the article. Who was she kidding? She wanted to see Chet.

"Come on, Carol. Look lively."

Audrey had been prattling incessantly about Wally. If only Carol could beg off going to the dance and enjoy a quiet evening at Mrs. Lester's house, but that would be wrong. She'd come to England to serve their military men and that included dancing with them. She needed to write her sister and ask her to send a new pair of shoes. All this dancing was wearing hers out.

Chet packed his navigating tools into his briefcase. Another mission successfully behind them. Longer than it should have been, but they'd made it back safely to England and their wounded friend had survived his landing. Yes, it was a good day after all. He'd head to the radio room for their own landing.

Just before he unplugged his communication cable, Price yelled, "Fire on engine one."

Chet sprang to the window. From here, the engine looked fine. He scrambled up to the cockpit and plugged into an outlet in time to hear Andy say, "Feathering number one."

Chet grabbed the back of Lowell's seat. The two remaining engines had been run at maximum power for hours and had nothing left to give. At least they were over England if the last engine should fail. Bomby squeezed in beside Chet. The plane sank lower, struggling on one engine.

"Everyone get to the radio room and assume crash positions." Lowell didn't look around to be sure they responded. He and Andy were too busy trying to keep them in the air.

Ridgewell's triangle of runways appeared in the distance. Chet prodded Bomby and Cottrell back toward the radio room. He shut the door behind him and, before dropping down to brace himself against it, looked out the window. Smoke still billowed from the outboard engine one. If there was a fire...

He amended the hymn playing in his mind again. "O hear us when we cry to Thee for those in peril on the land."

Chapter Twenty

Saffron Walden, England
Friday, May 26, 1944

"Wally and I are getting married on the Fourth of July." Audrey twirled into the house. A long day at Lavenham hadn't diminished her energy.

"So you're officially engaged?" Irene lifted the lid off the pot on the stove and sniffed. "Mmm, smells good, whatever it is."

"What about your friends and family back home?" Carol frowned. Another letter from Sally had arrived yesterday. Her old friend had practically blamed her for the mess she found herself in. Mike spent his days on the couch with the radio blaring and a beer bottle in his hand. He expended no effort in rehabilitation or job hunting. What would happen when the baby arrived? That could be any day now.

"Your backgrounds are so different. What do you have in common, besides the emotional attachment? The war makes you think you're in love, but it's an artificial environment. Wait until after and see if it carries over into civilian life."

"Don't you believe in love at first sight? My grandparents knew the day they met they'd marry. They did, and they're still married. The war has nothing to do with it." Audrey folded her arms and raised her chin.

Carol looked to Irene for support. Irene shrugged. "My folks married six weeks after they met."

"But what's the rush? It's not like Wally's going to be killed in combat, since he's in a noncombatant role. And he's already shipped out, so it's not like he's going to be leaving you behind for months or years." Carol raked her fingers through her hair. "Making major commitments during wartime isn't a good idea. Look how many married men have taken off their rings and act like they're single. The war has caused a breakdown in normal conduct. Live for today; forget about yesterday and tomorrow."

"You think I'm so fickle? You think Wally has a wife back home?" Audrey's face flared bright red. "What about you and Chet? You two are sure cozy."

"We enjoy each other's company. We're not pledging our lives."

"Well, good for you. Just quit being so sanctimonious." Audrey stomped out of the room and up the stairs. The bedroom door slammed, rattling the windows.

Carol heaved a sigh.

Irene leveled her gaze at her, arms crossed. "She's right, you know. If she wants to marry for better or for worse, it's really none of your business."

"Fine." Carol hopped up and headed out to the garden before she said anything she'd regret. A trio of birds interrupted their singing to inspect her before returning to song. A breeze fanned her flushed face.

No, Audrey's life wasn't her concern. But didn't she have an obligation to urge caution when a friend was treading down an unwise path? Or was her opposition pushing Audrey to do it?

Back home, her minister insisted on a few meetings before the wedding to discuss relevant topics like handling finances, a wife's need or desire to work, raising children, free-time preferences. Who was counseling everyone here? Did Audrey know if Wally would spend weekends with her or go out with the boys?

Instead of taking time for counseling, Sally and Mike had rushed to the courthouse to marry, and look where they were now.

Of course, some wartime marriages did succeed. Maybe Audrey would be one of the lucky ones. If not, at least Carol would be spared seeing her crash and burn. Going home and seeing Sally so miserable would be bad enough.

She'd better go mend fences with Audrey. A lot of good they'd do trying to raise morale if they couldn't get along with each other. She trudged up the stairs and tried the knob. Unlocked. She eased the door open. Audrey sat with her back to the door, pinning up her hair without the help of a mirror.

Carol took a deep breath and crossed to the dresser. "You're absolutely right, Audrey. What you and Wally do is none of my business." She pulled out her pajamas. "I'll even host a hen party for you."

"You really mean that?" Audrey turned around, a lock of hair spilling out of the curl before she had it pinned. "We'll be happy together. You'll see."

"Hmm." Carol headed to the bathroom. There was a time to say something and a time to stay silent. Speaking up hadn't helped. She wouldn't say another word.

Chapter Twenty-One

Monday, May 29, 1944

Chet brooded all the way to their target. Paul's plane was shot down over Germany on Saturday. Several parachutes had been seen. Not enough for the whole crew, but maybe had Paul survived. If not, he was reunited with his wife. Either way, Paul's absence left a gaping hole in Chet's life. He tossed his pencil onto his desk.

Sunlight sparkled through the Plexiglas nose on a beautiful, clear morning. This would likely be the longest mission of the war for them, all the way to the railroad shops in Posen, Poland. Seventeen-hundred miles presented a lot of territory if something went wrong. Their route took them over the North Sea and Denmark, where they might encounter enemy fighters. Chet fingered his map of Sweden. He'd be ready if they needed to seek sanctuary in the neutral country.

From twenty-two thousand feet, Posen resembled a miniature model village. Train tracks pointed to the target, just like on the reconnaissance photos they'd studied.

"Take a good look, gentlemen, because those choo-choo shops are about to disappear." Bomby released the bombs. "Keep an eye on those babies. They're right on the money."

So was the flak.

"Engine three's smoking." Homer Long's yell erased the satisfaction of a job well done. "And we're leaking fuel. They got a gas tank. There's holes all over the wing."

"Fuel transfer, Ken." Lowell didn't waste time. "Feathering three, and hit the fire extinguisher, Andy."

"Let me know our fuel status as soon as you can, Ken." Chet grabbed his E-6B calculator and began computing their wind velocity, heading, and airspeed. Over eight hundred miles to go, and they were in trouble. "Can we maintain our position in the formation?"

"We're sure going to try." Lowell didn't sound concerned. "At least it's just one engine and not two like last week. We saved most of the fuel."

Time ticked by. Sweden shimmered in the distance, a beacon of safety surrounded by Nazi-occupied territory. Chet turned his attention to plotting their position and recalculated the distance. If nothing else went wrong, they might make it to England. Sweden disappeared from view. Bypassing the neutral country better not be a mistake. They passed over Denmark. Moderate but inaccurate flak greeted them. The North Sea stretched before them. Still a long way to go.

Chet continuously monitored his instruments. His conclusions weren't cheery. "We're getting an increasing headwind. We should start jettisoning as much extra weight as we can."

"Does that include my ball turret?" Homer always welcomed a chance to crawl out of the ball and unwind.

"Yes, get out of there." Lowell would want that weight eliminated. "We're in the lead formation. We can drop out and slide back to the lower squadron."

"Don't jettison the ball." Chet calculated the time, distance, speed, and wind from his latest instrument readings on his E-6B. They weren't going to make it. He took a deep breath, held it, and exhaled. "If we have to ditch, and that's looking more and more likely, we don't want a hole in the bottom of the plane."

"Are you sure about that, Chet?" Lowell's voice was higher than normal. "We'll have to ditch?"

Chet pulled off his oxygen mask and dragged a hand across his mouth. "Unless we pick up a tremendous tail wind that blows us to England, yeah, I'm sure. You can try letting down five thousand feet for a weaker wind. We might gain a couple miles."

Flak suits, machine guns, ammo, and radio equipment went out the windows and rear entrance door. Bomby pulled free the top-secret Norden bombsight and heaved it out the escape hatch.

Chet spotted a fighter plane hovering nearby. Good. Their escorts knew they were in duress. Still, he continued to determine their coordinates and made sure Dexter Small radioed them to the British Air-Sea Rescue Service.

"Engine one is running hot." Cottrell's warning sealed their fate.

"Everyone go to the radio room." Now Lowell sounded resigned. They couldn't save the plane. Saving their lives was priority number one. "We need to go down while we still have control." He rang six short rings on the ditching signal, "Prepare for ditching."

Chet swallowed hard. Ditching came with no guarantees. As he came up through the hatchway into the cockpit, he paused and put his hands on Lowell's and Andy's shoulders. Andy's eyes twitched, but he nodded. He probably didn't mind having a bunch of crewmates around him now.

Chet joined the rest of the crew in the radio room and closed the door. No loose objects remained in sight. The emergency equipment they'd need waited: raft accessories, emergency radio and signaling equipment, his navigation kit, water and rations. They'd drilled often enough to do everything in their sleep.

He looked at the men. "Everyone got your collar open? Neckties off if you're wearing 'em? Parachutes off and life vests on?" They sat down facing aft, knees drawn up, backs against the bulkhead or each others' legs, fingers clasped behind their necks. They were as ready as they'd ever be.

One long ring on the ditching alarm sounded. "Brace for ditching." The nose eased up. Chet fought the urge to tense. *Stay relaxed.*

The tail hit first. Then the nose went down. The plane bucked through the water as though it was a road full of potholes before coming to an abrupt stop, like hitting a brick wall. The momentum drove Stan Price hard into Chet's legs. Water sprayed across the overhead hatch.

Chet pushed Stan back. "Everybody up. Time's wasting."

Homer Long pulled the handles for the life raft storage doors. Zempel gave Lemke a boost that sent him flying out through the overhead, hopefully not into the water. Chet followed with the emergency radio. Lowell and Andy had already exited through their side windows, and were perched on top of the fuselage. In less than a minute, everyone was out, the dinghies launched, and equipment stowed. Chet and Lowell joined Small, Lemke, and Price in the left dinghy.

Chet blew out his breath. His heart beat like a tom-tom, but they'd done it. Everyone was safe. Of course, it helped that the wind at the surface was slight. Mild swells rocked the raft like a lullaby. They paddled clear before the bomber nosed down, the tail rose, and the plane disappeared below the surface. Chet scanned the horizon in all directions. Water. Nothing but water.

Chapter Twenty-Two

Ridgewell Air Base

The clubmobile pulled up next to the mess hall, and the girls hurried into the kitchen.

A mess sergeant with a Cheshire cat grin turned from the huge galvanized pans he was scrubbing. "If you're looking for breakfast, you're too late."

Irene studied the remains encrusted on the pan. "Hmm, scrambled eggs, likely the powdered kind."

"You bet, sweetheart. Only the combat crews get the real thing."

"I didn't see many planes around the perimeter." Carol helped fill steam boilers with water to be ready for coffee refills later on. "Did they leave early?"

"Takeoff started at eight. We're never told where they go, of course, but scuttlebutt says they'll be gone all day."

Another week without seeing Chet. Carol's eyes slid shut for a moment. What did she expect? This was war. She smiled at the cook. He was probably in his thirties, his stomach straining his white tee shirt. His service cap was the only suggestion he was military. "We'll be back before you know it for the water."

How the men could drink hot coffee on such a warm day was a mystery. Her mouth watered for an ice-cold soda. With the doughnut machine heating up to 375 degrees, the clubmobile turned into a sauna, even with the doors open. Audrey came in with an empty tray, and Carol didn't waste time to take a turn outside.

An engineer loaned her his bicycle and she eagerly mounted it to take a spin. Oh, how wonderful to have a breeze cool her face. She looped around and headed back. A jeep approached, crossing her path. She backpedaled to yield the right-of-way, but didn't slow.

"Hand brakes! Hand brakes!" Someone saw her trouble.

She fumbled for the lever below the hand grip. The bike jerked to a halt, nearly catapulting her over the handlebars. She got her feet on the ground, her lungs heaving for air.

The engineer ran to her side. "Forgot to ask if you'd ever ridden an English bicycle. They take a while to get used to."

"No problem. All's well." She managed to get her words out in gasps. "Just glad I don't have to visit the hospital today." She staggered back to the clubmobile. Enough excitement for one day.

They returned to the mess for their hot water. Cletus, a talkative young enlistee, was on duty.

Audrey backtracked. "I'll clean out the doughnut machine while you two tend to the water. I don't care to hear about his mother's surgery or his latest conquest in London."

Irene winked at Carol. "We can regale her with his tales tonight and she won't miss a thing."

Carol smothered a laugh as she approached the corporal. "Hi, Cletus. What's new?"

She expertly flipped the lid off the first boiler, staying clear of the swoosh of hot steam.

"Got a letter from Ma. My sister was plannin' on marrying her boyfriend last month. He was a gunner on a Liberator and finished his tour and was all set to go home. They were goin' to meet in New York." He spoke in a monotone, unlike his usual devil-may-care attitude. A shivered zipped through Carol. "Trixie had already left to join him there when a telegram came. He'd volunteered for another mission and got killed. Ain't gonna be a wedding now."

"Oh, no. Did anyone meet her in New York to tell her what happened?" Carol looked away from the second boiler as she uncovered it. She failed to move away in time and scalding steam scorched her arm. "Oh!"

She dropped the lid and grabbed her arm. Tears stung her eyes. How could she have been so thoughtless? Pay attention in the kitchen.

Around her, men scrambled for butter and soda, slathering them on Carol's arm. The fiery sting barely diminished.

"Wounded in action." A burly sergeant swept her up in his arms and headed for the door.

"I can walk." Carol's protest went unheeded. A jeep whisked her to the base hospital.

Three patients conversing among themselves looked up and stared when the sergeant carried her in.

"She can have the bed next to mine." An enlisted man with his arm bandaged from shoulder to finger tips hopped up and pointed to an unoccupied cot.

"Nothing doing, McPherson. She'll never get any rest around you." This man lay unmoving. Bandages wrapped around his head and under his chin made speaking difficult. Carol's stomach started spinning. This was no time to be sick.

McPherson snorted, but before he could retort, a doctor stepped into the room. "What have we here?"

"Kitchen accident." The sergeant looked around. "Where do you want her?"

"Bring her into the surgery." The doctor led the way to a door at the back of the Quonset hut.

"S...surgery? I don't need surgery." Beyond the door stood a stretcher mounted on a metal frame under bright lights and an oxygen canister. Carol started squirming.

The doctor looked back with a smile. "The treatment room. Come on into the treatment room." He indicated a chair alongside a table, and the sergeant lowered her onto it. The doctor redirected a bright light and unwound the cloth covering her arm. He wiped away the butter and soda. "Hmm, looks to me like the boys were preparing you for lunch."

His joke wasn't funny. Really it wasn't, but Carol started giggling and couldn't stop. Hospitals made her stomach churn. The *smell* of hospitals made her vision waver. Her arm stung. Chet wasn't here. She shouldn't have gotten up this morning. It was so hot in here. She couldn't stop giggling.

The doctor looked at her sharply, but didn't say anything. He cleaned her arm, applied salve, and bandaged it. "Keep it dry and you shouldn't have much, if any, scarring." He gave an order to someone behind her and a tray bearing a cup of water and a pill was delivered shortly. "Here," he told her, "take this."

Something for the pain. Wonderful. She gulped down the pill and leaned back in the chair, lowering her arm gingerly to her lap. She really needed to get back to the clubmobile, but, oh, just a few minutes to sit would be good. Being injured really took the starch out of her.

The doctor pulled her to her feet and led her to the operating stretcher. "Lie down and rest for a while."

He stepped aside, and the burly sergeant picked her up and laid her out. Had he stayed in the room all along?

She twisted her head to the side and her gaze collided with a tray of instruments. She squeezed her eyes shut. Someone covered her with a blanket. The temperature was too warm for a blanket, but it sure did feel cozy. A little rest sounded lovely.

Someone laughed. Carol stirred. Her bed was awfully uncomfortable. Since when did it have a rail along the edge? Her eyes popped open. This wasn't her bed. A light fixture hung over her. She lay in the base hospital at Ridgewell. Sunlight angled in from the window. Not from high overhead at noon, but low in the sky. She must have slept the whole afternoon.

Voices laughed again, and one of them was Irene's voice. Audrey, too. They must want to leave. She maneuvered herself off the operating cot. Her arm still stung, but compared to the injuries the boys suffered, it was nothing. She opened the door and the conversation stopped.

"Look who's ready to rejoin the land of the living?" The guy with the head injury was right; McPherson wouldn't have given her any rest.

Irene approached her, a strange look on her face. "How do you feel?"

"Fine. A little sore. I didn't mean to sleep the day away." Why was everyone staring at her? She would have checked a mirror, if she had one. A familiar rumbling penetrated her thoughts. "The planes are back from the mission?"

"Ye-ah." Usually articulate, Irene drawled her answer. "Some of them, anyway." She looked at Audrey, who shrugged.

An officer she had never seen before spoke up. "A couple planes landed at Coltishall. They ran into some flak near the German coast." He hesitated and glanced at Irene. "The Hendricks crew didn't make it back at all. They had to ditch in the North Sea."

The *Hendricks* crew? Chet's crew? Just like Jerome C. Milhous the Third. The sole survivor of the crew from Bassingbourn who ditched. The silent, traumatized young man locked in his pain. *Chet? Chet?*

The scene before her wavered. Her fingers started tingling again. She looked for a chair, but blackness closed in. The rumbling turned into buzzing. Someone picked her up again as she descended into darkness.

Chapter Twenty-Three

Chet and Dexter set up the emergency radio. "There's not enough wind to fly the kite with the antenna. We'll have to use the balloon." Chet directed Lemke to inflate it with hydrogen. The hydrogen generator had to be immersed in water, and Price shifted around to help. "A lot of heat is produced by the chemical reaction that produces the hydrogen, so be careful."

"You sure you know what you're doing with that?"

Zempel. Even in an emergency, the querulous waist gunner couldn't stop heckling Lemke. He was assigned to the other raft, but procedures recommended lashing the two together so they wouldn't drift apart.

"Blow it out of your bag, Zempel," Lowell growled as he wrapped their flares, the Very flare pistol, and cartridges in a parachute to keep them dry. "No more talking than necessary. Anyone. It dries out your mouth, and we have limited water."

Chet looked up from the radio. Lowell had never used slang before to tell someone to shut up. He glanced across at Andy. Busy inventorying their life raft kit, the copilot snapped off a two-fingered salute, his shoulders shaking with suppressed laughter.

"We've got seven cans of drinking water here, and you should have the same over there. We have three cans of sea marker. If anyone sees or hears a plane, sing out. We're supposed to quickly pour a can out on the water and stir it with an oar." Andy pulled something out of the kit and thrust it at Zempel. "Here's a survival booklet. Read it and be ready with answers if we have any questions."

Lemke got the balloon inflated to its four-foot diameter. Dexter attached the antenna and began reeling it out. Chet positioned the curvy Gibson Girl radio between his knees and started working the hand crank to operate the internal generator. So far, everything worked as it was supposed to.

Price watched Chet work the crank. "How long before that starts working?"

"It's working now." Chet smiled at the doubt on Price's face. "It's emitting a signal, pre-tuned to the international distress frequency of five hundred kilocycles. A rescue boat can home in on the signal."

"How do you know if someone hears it?"

"We don't. There's no receiver. We just wait for someone to show up."

In the other raft, Cottrell frowned. "The Germans can pick up the signal too, can't they?"

"Yep." Andy continued to rummage through their supplies. "If you see a boat coming from the south or east, or a submarine surfacing from those directions, we're in trouble." He held up a folded blue and yellow tarpaulin. "Here's the emergency signal panel we can use as camouflage if we spot a German plane before they spot us. It should be ten feet square and we drape it over us, blue side up. Don't know if it'd work with a boat though." He pulled something else out of the kit. "Ocean charts. Here, Long, pass this over to the navigator. Anyone want any sun protective ointment?"

Chet accepted the charts. What good were they, except for possible use as a paddle? He located the general area of their last known position. Closer to England than Belgium or Holland. As long as they didn't drift the wrong way, they were in good shape. The lack of wind was a real blessing. The rolling swells sported no white crests, making the wind speed less than ten miles per hour. They needn't worry about capsizing.

Dexter took over with the hand crank, and Chet stretched out, pillowing his head on the edge of the raft. Lowell questioned Dexter if Air-Sea Rescue had told him whether they had any boats in their area. Chet rubbed the back of his neck. Rescue would come when it did, or didn't. Nothing he could do would change that. However, knowing if they had a short or long wait would help Lowell decide when to dole out a ration of water or food.

Moving only his eyes, he scanned the sky. Nothing but blue infinity and a few dirty white clouds. No birds. No formation of planes. Nothing. What might be below them in the dark water, didn't bear thinking about.

His left hand itched. It was gritty with white...salt? When had he gotten wet during the ditching? He tried brushing it off, but the residue proved sticky. Using his water ration to wash up wouldn't be wise. The itching continued and a rash appeared. An allergenic reaction? Or sunburn? "Price, can you find the sun ointment from our kit that Andy talked about?"

Price fished around and found the first aid kit. Chet smeared on a cream that sounded promising.

With nothing else to do, Lemke also pawed through the kit and pulled out their signal panel. "Here, why don't you cover up with this? That's the trouble with Northerners. They don't know how to tolerate the sun."

Chet caught the gleam in the tail gunner's eyes. "Careful there, Lemke, or you may find yourself swimming."

He shrugged. "Good activity for a goldfish."

Chet raised his head. Had he heard correctly? Must have. Everyone else stared at Lemke, too.

Busy investigating their supplies, it took Lemke a moment to look up. "We're members of the Goldfish Club now. We survived a ditching."

"Better hold that thought until we're picked up." Bomby was a bundle of cheer in the other raft now floating behind Chet. "The longer it takes for them to find us, the less likely they will."

Lowell scanned the horizon in all directions before reaching for the radio to take a turn at cranking. "Make sure the Very pistol is ready to shoot off a flare if we spot any Allies."

After passing the radio to Lowell to crank, Dexter leaned back against the raft's edge. "Too bad the warring nations can't settle their differences with a game of cards. It'd be a lot healthier for us."

Lowell's lips quirked. "Think that would work?"

"Probably not. The loser would accuse the winner of cheating and come to blows."

Silence settled over the crew. Chet closed his eyes. Water lapped against the raft. The sea smelled kind of salty, kind of fishy. The sun angled down in the western sky. He raised an arm over his eyes to block the glare.

This experience didn't match anything in the recruitment film made by actor Jimmy Stewart. Join the air force and learn about courage, leading men, pride in your work. A second lieutenant earns two hundred forty-five dollars a month, plus a five-hundred-dollar bonus every year. *Yeah, right.*

Chet snorted. "Did anyone see *Winning Your Wings* a couple years ago? Jimmy Stewart described the positions available in a bomber. A photographer, two engineers, two radiomen. Nothing about a bombardier or gunners. Nothing about fighting and dying and being lost at sea."

Lowell pulled the tarpaulin up to Chet's chin. "Go to sleep, Vogel. You'll take the midnight-to-four watch."

Carol's roiling stomach pulled her from sleep. The smell of doughnuts made her gag. She stumbled to her feet, intent on hurrying to the toilet. Wait a minute. She was in their bedroom at Mrs. Lester's house. And the doughnuts? The smell was on her clothes, in her hair. Why hadn't she undressed for bed? She grabbed a robe and headed to the bathroom.

She flicked on the light, and caught her breath. Ditched! Chet was somewhere on the North Sea. How many crews had died because they couldn't be located? Would Chet wash ashore like his friend Vern?

Avoiding a wartime marriage had been her credo. How stupid could she be? She should have avoided a wartime romance that led her to think of marriage. If only she'd never met Chet Vogel. If only he had a noncombatant job.

With her hair shampooed and her battle dress left in the tub to soak, she sank to the floor, knees drawn up to her chest. She rested her head on her knees. *Chet's missing, but someone said their location is known. Maybe he's already back at Ridgewell, sound asleep in his own bed.*

Hadn't Vern's position been known as well?

What did Chet mean to her? Why was she taking his ditching so hard?

Because she could easily imagine a future with him. Marriage, family, growing old together. They hadn't discussed such possibilities, but Chet Vogel was her soulmate. And he was missing.

Tears sneaked past tightly closed eyelids. Her breathing became labored as her nasal passages clogged. Somewhere in her bathrobe pocket, she had a handkerchief.

"I love you, Chet Vogel. I never told you, but I love you." She blew her nose and wiped her tears. "God, take care of him. Please." Tears continued to flow.

A tap sounded at the door. "Carol?" Another tap and the door eased open. Irene stepped in. "Oh,

Carol. Chet will be back. They went down under control and Air-Sea Rescue knows where they are."

"Just like his friend, and only Jerome Milhaus the Third survived, a shattered soul."

Irene rubbed Carol's shoulder. For a long time she said nothing. Good. Meaningless assurances wouldn't help.

"The chaplain will notify us tomorrow when…" Irene hesitated. She knew as well as Carol there was still a chance the Hendricks crew may have been lost. She cleared her throat. "When they have news."

Carol nodded and blew her nose again. "Would you send my name in to Headquarters for duty in France?"

Irene pulled back. "Carol, there's a very good possibility Chet's still alive and…"

Carol waved away the protest. "I know, I know. But I've wanted to go to France, remember? It's my ancestral homeland. Chet and I talked about it." Not recently, but Irene didn't need to know that. "With the invasion coming soon, I need to get assigned." She mopped her face and looked up. "I also need to get away from Audrey. I'm sorry, but her prattle about Wally..."

Irene patted her shoulder. Humor laced her voice. "I know. It is a bit much."

"Why don't you apply for France, too?"

"No thanks. I'm happy here." Irene stood and offered Carol a hand up. "Actually, I probably won't be here long either. Red Cross policy is to move girls around. We're all due for reassignments."

"Audrey will not like that." If they were split up in reassignments, she'd no longer have a problem with her crewmate. Of course, she could get a worse problem. No, she wouldn't be swayed. This was her opportunity to see France. Now, before she got tied down with postwar responsibilities, hopefully with Chet. She was so close. She'd always regret her decision if she didn't go.

"So you're going to say *adieu* to Chet and that's it?"

Carol squared her shoulders. "Not quite. If we're supposed to be together, we'll meet again. With God, nothing is impossible. I'm going to hold Him to that promise. I'll give Him my burden of grief and love and hope, and take His rest." She nodded. "That's what I'm going to do."

Her brave words didn't help her sleep. When Mrs. Lester began moving about the kitchen early Tuesday morning, Carol dragged herself out of bed and down the stairs. The phone rang and she froze in the doorway. Mrs. Lester answered with a cheery hello. Carol gripped the back of a chair until Mrs. Lester said, "Oh, that's jolly good news."

She dropped into the chair. Chet's alive. *Chet's alive.*

Mrs. Lester hung up the phone. "Your young man and his friends were picked up not two hours ago. A bit chilled they were, but not a hair harmed among them."

Two hours ago. They'd spent the night on the sea.

"Their base will send a plane to bring them back to Ridgewell in a day or two."

She'd see him again. To say good-bye.

Chapter Twenty-Four

Ridgewell Air Base, England
June 5, 1944

First Lieutenant Chet Vogel. Sounded pretty good. The promotion came because the Table of Organization required a lead navigator to be at least a First Lieutenant, not a Second Lieutenant. A yawn marred his image in the mirror. The down side of his promotion meant he had to get up an hour earlier to attend a pre-briefing, giving him extra time to study the target and battle order.

Upon finally getting back to Ridgewell after their night on the sea, he'd been told to report to squadron headquarters. The order hadn't been a surprise. Captain Foster had told him he could expect to be appointed lead. Still, being taken off a well-oiled crew and put in with a bunch of strangers was unsettling. Today's mission better go like clockwork or he could change his name to Mudd. He hurried to the jeep for his ride to the briefing.

In the briefing room, lead bombardier Max Withers looked up from the maps spread on a table. "Coastal defenses near Caen, two and a half miles in from the French coast. We'll be carrying five-

hundred-pound armor piercing bombs. That's new.
D-Day's got to be very close."

Max's sloping forehead ending in heavy eyebrows
gave him a forbidding look, but he had a wry sense
of humor that could defuse tense situations. Better
yet, he lacked Bomby's constant flirting with the
ladies.

Chet studied the map. Almost due south from
London, near the port of LeHavre. "Far from Calais,
where the Germans must expect the invasion." He
traced a finger along the coast. "This looks like it
may be a nice beach to go ashore."

The infantrymen who would shoulder the burden
of getting a toehold in France had an unenviable
task. Give him an airplane any day.

"Lieutenant Colonel Fitzgerald is flying with us."

Chet paused. Brass. *Get used to it.* Squadron lead
usually had a top ranking officer aboard.

By the time he arrived at the plane, Chet was
raring to go. He couldn't have asked for an easier
target for his debut as squadron lead. Missions didn't
come any shorter. Just cross the English Channel and
they'd be there. A fifty-minute delay while the
munitions crew finished loading the bombs gave him
more time to study and memorize the course. He'd
be able to fly this mission in his sleep.

The air temperature was minus thirty-two degrees
centigrade at twenty-five thousand feet. Chet didn't

break a sweat as they arrived at the initial point of the bomb run near Le Havre and Max took control of the bomber through his bombsight. Watching over his shoulder, Chet spotted a convoy of twenty-five German trucks headed south. Odd. If they anticipated an invasion, they should be bulking up defenses, not moving out. No enemy fighters or flak opposed them either. Really odd.

The bombs fell away and looked to be on target. The strike photos would verify his observation. The formation turned away with no battle scars and Chet gave the pilot his heading for home. Sitting back down, he relaxed and crossed his ankles. He couldn't have done anything any better. Wouldn't his father be surprised?

Late that evening, he was called to Group Headquarters for a meeting with all the lead pilots, navigators, and bombardiers. Unusual. Something was up.

Colonel Leber looked over the assembly in the briefing room. "Well, men, this is it."

He pulled back the curtain covering the map and pointed to the Normandy coast.

D-Day! Shivers chased through Chet. In a matter of hours, the great invasion of France would begin and he would play a part. He leaned forward, intent on not missing a word.

"You have a six-mile wide corridor in which to form up and fly over. Maintain precise clockwork. Once you drop your bombs, men will be storming the beaches. They'll likely have a hot enough reception without worrying about us."

The navigators verified and double-checked their work. At one point, Captain Foster upset a pencil holder, spilling pencils all over the table. Chet grinned. It was nice to know the seasoned leaders were antsy, too.

Before they headed out for an early breakfast, pistols were issued. "Should you be forced down, you will join the men fighting on the ground." Colonel Leber leveled a steely gaze on them. "I don't need to remind you of the absolute need for secrecy. Share this information with no one. Not your crew members, not the ground crew. No one."

Flying in their corridor, Chet frowned. A nearly complete cloud cover blanketed the whole region. He stood behind Max Withers, searching for a hole in the clouds. Was the invasion proceeding? Cloud cover probably didn't affect infantry like it did airmen. Still, bombing by radar couldn't compare with bombing visually.

Max suddenly jerked. "Look there. Ten o'clock low. The whole doggone navy is in the channel."

Chet stared through the hole. Big ships and little ships, all with wakes indicating they steamed for France. So crowded were they, a man could jump from ship to ship with no problem. Flying at a low fourteen thousand feet gave them exquisite detail before the clouds filled in the hole.

"Landon, did you get a picture of that?" Pilot Fred McQuaid asked the ball turret gunner.

"I sure did. I was beginning to think I was lugging this camera along for nothing. I didn't know we had so many ships over here. Where were they hiding 'em all?"

Back at his desk, Chet reviewed all his instruments. He looked at his watch, synchronized with everyone else's. "We're coming up on the I.P. in three, two, one."

"It's all yours, Withers." McQuaid turned over control of the aircraft to the bombardier.

Releasing the bombs seemed anti-climactic. Flying back, the cloud cover remained total. What was going on down there? The army should be landing on the beaches now. With so much fire power behind them, how could they fail? The bigger question was, how much firepower were they running into? Were any of Chet's brothers involved? He had no idea where they were. Men must be dying down there. In spite of that, they had to establish a beachhead. They had to.

Chet bowed his head. *Keep them in your care, Lord.*

The phone rang. Carol groaned. Morning already? Planes had been flying overhead all night long. Mrs. Lester tapped on their door and opened it. "Irene? A call from your headquarters, dearie."

Irene raised her head and stared around through half-open eyes. "We must not have a driver today. Carol, would you go talk to 'em?" Her head dropped back to the pillow.

Carol fumbled with her robe on the way down. Oh, for crying out loud, she was holding it upside down. She barely said hello before an excited voice rattled off an announcement. She turned her robe around. "Okay, I'll tell Irene." She hung up and continued wrestling with the robe. What was wrong with it now? Oh, it was inside out. She pulled out her arm, bringing the sleeve with it.

The phone message finally registered. Her head snapped up.

"The invasion! The invasion!" Dropping her robe to the floor, she danced across the room and grabbed

Mrs. Lester's hands. "This is it. The invasion has started."

Footsteps pounded down the stairs, and Irene and Audrey barged into the kitchen. "The invasion is underway? Really?"

"Oh, let's go to Lavenham today instead of Bassingbourn." Audrey twirled around.

"No, we're not going anywhere." Carol sobered as she recalled the message. "All the bases were locked down yesterday. No one in or out except for the planes flying missions. We have the day off."

"But I want to share the day with Wally. Why are they shutting us out?"

"Something about an anticipated counter invasion. I don't understand that. If the Germans couldn't manage an invasion during the Battle of Britain, why should they be able to pull it off now?"

Mrs. Lester was already warming up her radio. "The BBC will tell us what's going on."

Carol grabbed her robe and ran upstairs to dress. Civilian clothes today since they weren't going to work. Maybe they could at least visit the hospital. How were the bomb groups spending the day? With their troops swarming ashore, heavy bombers didn't seem a likely participant, unless they flew further inland to stop reinforcements.

The invasion. Next week she'd head for London to train for duty in France. Soon she'd be there, too.

She'd get to see Chet one more time. That is, if he wasn't on a mission. She checked her appearance in the mirror. One chance to say good-bye. Maybe for the last time. She headed back downstairs at a much slower pace.

Chapter Twenty-Five

June 14, 1944

The invasion had succeeded. The Allies held the beaches at Normandy, but the Germans wanted desperately to contain them. The air force, consequently, was tasked with knocking out German airfields to hinder them.

Chet yawned as they flew over France. He needed to find a rhythm. While regular crews flew every time their squadron flew, three out of every four missions, lead crews might fly three missions a month. He'd have to anticipate being roused at midnight and get to bed extra early when they were scheduled.

Plenty of flak rose to greet them over Melun, southeast of Paris. *Lovely Lily* shuddered as shrapnel punctured her fuselage. A piece ricocheted off the bulkhead behind Chet and dropped onto his desk. He swept the jagged metal off his map.

"These here sightseeing flights are hazardous to our health."

Chet grinned, and copied the gunner's words on his log.

With good visibility, they watched their bombs tumble down on the airport. The Luftwaffe wouldn't be able to utilize that field to impede their ground forces.

Today's route didn't take them over the invasion beaches. Getting a good look at all those D-Day ships in the clear skies would have been welcome. The beaches had been hard won, a real bloodbath. Whole squads had been mowed down without even stepping foot on the beach. How could the men find the courage to go forward in that carnage? One report said the waves washed the beaches red with blood. Impossible to comprehend.

Easier to understand was Carol's news that she would soon transfer to the continent. She'd wanted to see her ancestors' homeland. This might be her only chance, she said. True, but what about the mess sergeant's report that she'd fainted when told he'd ditched? Surely, she felt something for him.

Yes, he led a dangerous life, fighting a war. Maybe she wanted to distance herself from him as much as see France. He released his breath in a deep sigh. He couldn't be wrong; together they had something special. Maybe his job scared her or maybe he'd only imagined her interest. Not that it mattered. Either way, she was leaving.

All planes returned to base despite the flak hits. One gunner in another squadron had been killed. Chet looked around the field. No newsmen waited to quiz them about their mission. With the invasion underway, the public preferred to hear about the infantry now instead of the air war and the men who flew. The army got the clubmobiles now, too.

That thought was unfair. Lots of clubmobiles still visited the air bases. Just not with his favorite brunette.

The crew took seats around the debriefing table. Chet slid his logbook to the interrogation officer, who began his usual questions. "Any fighters? Any new areas of flak?"

He referred to Chet's logbook as the crewmembers described the action. At one point, he twisted the book sideways to read a note in the margin. "'These here sightseeing flights are hazardous to our health.'" He looked at Chet askance. "Ya think, Vogel?"

Chet scrunched down in his seat as a gunner snickered. The comment didn't seem so funny now.

London, England
Tuesday, June 20, 1944

Carol had learned to drive her father's car in Canton. Once she'd even driven fifty miles to Cleveland. That did not prepare her for driving the narrow, busy London streets in an eight-ton truck. Nor was the British army tank course any easier. The steep hills offered good practice in learning to double clutch, a necessary skill for shifting gears. Carol wrestled the gearshift. The truck emitted loud grinding noises, suggesting it was about to cough up the engine. Carol's mechanic instructor turned purple.

The truck lurched and settled down to a purr. "Ha. I knew first gear had to be there."

The instructor didn't release his white-knuckled grip on the window frame. She shrugged. Saturday's drive had been a lot jerkier. She was getting the hang of this.

Her new teammate, Louise, waited for her as she braked to a stop. A farm girl who'd grown up around tractors and trucks, Louise had transitioned to the GMC truck without breaking a sweat. She smiled as Carol climbed down from the cab. "You did great. Looks like you'll be able to spell me behind the wheel." She stepped closer and lowered her voice. "Just between you and me, I don't think Gloria will ever take a turn."

Carol laughed. "That's the advantage of being team captain. She can order us peons to wrestle with the beast. Maybe she'll be better at the mechanical aspect. All that talk yesterday about velocity joints, and the pillar box, and the thirty-six points for greasing the chassis has me so confused."

"On the farm if things went wrong, my dad or one of the hands took care of it. We'll have to hope if we have problems with our clubmobile, there'll be GIs around who are eager to help us."

"Louise! Carol!" Gloria ran toward them. "Come see our clubmobile. We've been assigned to the *President Washington*."

London, England
Friday, June 23, 1944

Chet stood at the window of the St. James Court Hotel, watching Londoners hurry about their business. He had joined Lowell and Andy on a forty-eight-hour pass. Their sleep had been continually interrupted by sirens alerting them to the presence of the pilotless planes the Germans had begun sending over after the invasion.

The hotel clerk who checked them in had told them, "You'll find the buzz bombs a bit of a nuisance."

Right. When the motor cut off, the flying bomb would either drift a bit or fall straight down. And explode. They had ten to fifteen seconds to get out of its way. For combat airmen accustomed to flak exploding with no warning and nowhere to hide, ten seconds sounded leisurely.

The first buzz bomb had shattered their complacency. The noise of a single engine putt-putting along didn't sound threatening. It sounded almost like a Piper Cub reconnaissance plane that needed a tune-up. Then the engine had quit. Chet raised his head from his pillow. *Boom!* The hotel shook violently. All three men were on their feet.

"Do we need to find a bomb shelter?" Andy had grabbed his pants and shoved one leg into them.

Lowell had pulled back the blackout curtain. "Looks like it hit a couple blocks over."

Chet and Andy had joined him at the window in time to watch a building crumple. Throughout the night, further putt-putt motors woke them, but none came close.

From the window now, Chet couldn't spot any smoke evidencing the night's destruction. London didn't look so foreboding now. Even better, he was with his former crewmates. He could almost wish he hadn't been promoted.

"Be glad you missed the Berlin mission on Wednesday. Lots of Messerschmitt 420s firing rockets attacked at the Initial Point of the bomb run. Talk about persistent. I thought our luck had run out." Lowell shrugged into his shirt and joined Chet at the window. "The 533rd Squadron, meanwhile, met up with a bunch of Junkers Ju 88 fighter/bombers and shot most of them down."

"You'd think the Luftwaffe would have transferred more of their planes to France to attack the invasion forces. That's where most of our missions have been." Chet watched an elderly woman walking her dog. The little fellow barked a greeting at each passerby. He smiled and called toward the bathroom door. "Hey, Andy. Do you plan on spending the whole day in the bath?"

"Do I need to remind you we don't have luxuries like this back at Ridgewell?" Andy called back.

A distant wailing rose. Chet and Lowell turned back to the window and searched the sky. Another siren, closer by, joined the first. People on the street hesitated and looked up.

"There!" Lowell stabbed a finger at the window. "Look at that. It really does look like a plane."

The motor cut out while it soared directly overhead. Chet dove across the bed and lunged for the hallway door, Lowell right behind him. The bomb exploded. Chet wrapped his arms around his head as shards of glass and wood blew into the hall from their room. The hotel quaked worse than during the night's explosion, but remained standing.

From their bathroom, Andy emitted a yell. Chet and Lowell rushed back in. Andy stood in the tub, blood trickling down his chest. The high window behind him had shattered, and light glinted off a glass fragment embedded in his flesh.

Chet crunched onto the glass-strewn floor. Good thing he had his shoes on. He plucked the glass from Andy's wound and a drop of blood fell to the floor. "You've been wounded by the enemy. Something to tell your grandchildren about."

Lowell shook out a towel and handed it to Andy. "Lean over the tub and shake. Your hair glitters."

Andy wrapped himself in the towel. "We're close to Buckingham Palace. Maybe the Germans were hoping to get the king."

Chet headed back into the room. From the window, now stripped of most of its glass, came the wail of sirens as emergency vehicles rushed to the latest scene of devastation. As he was about to turn away, Chet stilled. A covered figure lay in the street. Beside it sat the old woman's little dog, resting its chin on its mistress.

The hour was late by the time the men returned to Ridgewell. The ancient village looked especially appealing after the chaotic energy of London.

"How about stopping in here?" Lowell waved a hand at the King's Head. "By the time we get to the mess, all the food will probably be gone."

Low beamed ceilings suggested people had been shorter centuries ago. The paneled walls were blackened from smoke. Linen cloths draped tables set with silver for four. Fortunately, the airmen were required to wear their Class A uniforms off base.

Flight clothes would have seemed out of place in this ancient elegance.

The waitress suggested pheasant. "You Yanks seem to feel it's a rich man's supper, but here the hunters and their dogs make it plentiful for everyone."

Chet enjoyed the meal. So did Andy, to a point. He suddenly spit out a mouthful. "Man-a-living." He clutched his jaw. "First a buzz bomb, then this. Now I've got to go to the dentist."

Mixed in with his bite of pheasant was a shotgun pellet.

Chapter Twenty-Six

Southampton, England
July 17, 1944

Excitement crackled in the air. This was it. They were headed for France. Carol watched a GI back their clubmobile up a ramp onto a Landing Ship, Tank. Today the LST could be called a Landing Ship, Clubmobile.

Beside her, Louise fidgeted. "I don't see why they didn't let me take *President Washington* aboard. He better not sideswipe him on anything. They probably don't care if tanks get scuffed."

From her other side, Gloria patted her arm. "Don't worry, Louise. I'm sure this man's well experienced with heavy vehicles."

With the last clubmobile loaded and immobilized, the ship got underway. Carol and the rest of the Red Cross girls lined the deck. Warships filled the harbor. Wolf whistles resounded as men on other ships watched them steam away. Carol grinned. Clad in their battle dress, they couldn't compete with Betty Grable and other pin-up girls, but the men didn't care.

The sound of music drifted over from another LST hauling clubmobiles. "Hey, they've got one of their record players going." Louise zeroed in on the nearest sailor. "Wanna dance?"

The sailor's eyes lit up. In short order, the girls had one of their own record players hooked up and blaring "Boogie Woogie Bugle Boy." Carol didn't hesitate to join in when a sailor reached for her hand. Jitterbugging had never been such fun.

She was up early and back on deck to watch the French coast loom into view. Crossing the channel had taken all night due to the cluttered remnants of war in the water. They passed unidentifiable debris bobbing on the surface. Broken pieces of ships and planes, gear from soldiers' backpacks. As they waited for the tide to come in so they could land, she studied Utah Beach with borrowed binoculars.

The mood of all the Red Cross girls grew pensive at the signs of the battle six weeks earlier. Closer to shore, the waves lapped over four round, black objects, the wheels of an overturned jeep. Wrecked ship hulls poked out of the water at odd angles. In spite of the beautiful weather, Carol shivered. D-Day must have been a scene out of Dante's Inferno.

Overhead, the sky rumbled with fighters and bombers headed for their day's mission.

"St. Lô," a sailor commented when she shaded her eyes to watch them. "The Germans are determined not to surrender the place, but by the time we're done pounding away at it, there ain't going to be nothing left to liberate." Artillery fire added to the cacophony.

"Come on, Carol. We're ready to go." Louise sat behind the wheel, cleared to drive *George* off the LST. Carol hastened to join them.

Once ashore, a whole new vista of war opened up to them. Cleanup had started, but the beach was still an obviously recent battlefield. Various destroyed military vehicles had been shoved aside. No blood remained, but it must have been gruesome.

Mortar shell craters gave the impression of an obstacle course. *George's* right front tire dropped into a crater and the steering wheel nearly jerked out of Louise's grasp.

"Oh, my goodness." Louise tightened her grip. "We'll be lucky if our teeth aren't loosened and start falling out."

"Not to mention what this is doing to our doughnut machine," Gloria added.

"Or the record player." Carol cranked the window closed against the dust stirred up by traffic. "We may not have any records left intact and unscratched. Imagine how the wounded feel, being brought back to the beach for evacuation."

All across the beach, vehicles loaded up with cargo and headed off in all directions. A military policeman pointed them to their road leading off the beach.

"Would you look at that?" Gloria pointed to their right. "Men in cages."

"German prisoners." Carol studied them as they passed. Some looked sullen. Others stared about them, looking awestruck. "They probably never saw so much equipment in one place."

Away from the beach, Carol cranked the window back down. Her nose twitched. "Odd smell here."

"War smells?" Gloria asked. "Like gunpowder?"

Louise rolled down her window. "Death. It smells like death and decay. One of the sailors told me that while the bodies of our dead servicemen have been removed, you can still find dead Germans away from the beach. And animals. Cows with their legs sticking up."

Carol had smelled dead deer along the roadside back home. "Maybe it's a combination of odors. What grows around here? Didn't someone say we'll see lots of apple orchards?"

The narrow lane hadn't been intended for large vehicles. Louise hugged the side of the road when a jeep whipped around a bend. She moved back into the middle after negotiating the curve. "All these signs saying 'Mines Cleared to Hedges' make me nervous."

High, dense hedges hemmed in the sunken lanes. Here and there, gaping holes through the hedgerows offered brief looks inside the small fields enclosed by the growth. Carol estimated the height at four feet. "These hedgerows are as wide as they are high. All these holes must be where tanks plowed through. No wonder so many infantrymen lost their lives here. They had no idea what they'd find beyond the hedge."

Around the next bend, they found themselves in a small village. The houses had been demolished. Here, a chimney remained standing. Across the lane, a corner of a house lay shattered. Not a window remained unbroken. Bullet holes pockmarked walls still erect. Rubble that had fallen into the road had been pushed back to allow traffic to pass. Trees that should have been in full foliage were bereft of leaves. The people were still there. They lined the road, waving and yelling, *"Vive la France!"*

"They look so excited." Tears welled in Carol's eyes at the sight of an elderly couple shuffling along with a handcart filled with their possessions. Probably all they had left after a lifetime of hard work.

When their convoy slowed to a crawl, the girls in the clubmobile ahead of them stopped to change drivers. The locals besieged them, offering cups of refreshment. "What are they giving them? Wine?"

Before Carol could hazard a guess to Gloria's question, a little girl ran up to her window. She held out a fistful of wildflowers.

Carol accepted them. "*Bonjour, mademoiselle. Merci.*"

Ducking her head with a shy smile, the child scurried back to her mother.

Louise peered around Gloria. "You speak French."

"Not really. A few polite phrases. In fact, I just about used up my whole vocabulary with her." Carol touched a purple blossom. Somehow, she'd find a way to press these flowers. They'd be a favorite keepsake of France.

In the late afternoon, the group of eight clubmobiles pulled into an apple orchard. Gloria joined the other team captains clustered around Doris, their leader. She returned with an update. "We're staying here tonight. We can pitch our tent or sleep in the barn. This has been used by different army units, so there's already a latrine. Supper will be K-rations."

Carol and Louise groaned in unison. "K-rats. Nutritious, but not delicious."

Carol laughed at Louise's lament. "I'm not sure they are nutritious. Not without fruits and vegetables." She surveyed the sky. "Doesn't look like rain. I vote for the tent."

"Me, too." Louise nodded. "I equate barns with mice, and I don't care to share my sleeping bag."

"All right then." With hands on hips, Gloria looked to her left, then to her right. "How about to the side of the first line of apple trees?"

They'd practiced setting up their pyramidal tent in England with no problems. Now it kept sagging first one way, then another. Maybe the barn wouldn't be so bad after all. Carol tripped over an exposed root and nearly fell. A truck ground to a halt. "Say, ladies, could you use a hand?"

A half dozen GIs spilled out of the truck and swarmed around them. The tent stood straight and taut in seconds. Before they moved on, they erected three more tents in front of the orchard.

"Too bad we don't have any doughnuts for them." Carol watched them tip their caps and vault back onto their truck. She turned to Gloria. "Where's the latrine? In back of the barn where those other girls are heading?"

"Yes, let's check it out."

Carol expected an outhouse, but the latrine was a slit trench. No privacy.

"Okay," one of the other girls said. "How about we form a line to be on guard duty while someone, uh, uses it."

Carol and Gloria joined her in turning their backs. "Most of the trees here look healthy. As long as the servicemen don't filch all the..."

"Aagh!"

They whirled around. One of the girls had fallen in. They rushed forward to help her up. The ditch was too narrow for her to have hit bottom and the filth it contained. She'd scraped against the side though. The brown smears on her hip could be dirt or... Carol swallowed hard.

The girl was nearly hysterical. She yanked her clothes back into place. "I need a bath." She looked around wildly. "Where can I find a bath?" She brushed her filthy hands together. They had likely hit bottom. "Oooh. I didn't sign up for this."

Her teammate tugged on her arm, leading her away. "Come on. We'll find some water and get it heated."

That would take time. The poor girl wouldn't feel clean any too soon. The remaining girls looked at each other. Carol studied the trench. "You know, I think we're supposed to straddle it, not try to balance with both feet on one side." She fished in her pocket for the bit of toilet paper she'd saved from a K-ration box. After a hurried look around, she added, "Excuse me, but I gotta go."

Before they settled down for the night, Doris called them all together. "We can expect to hear from Bed Check Charlie. Every night we'll have to be back in camp by 10 p.m. because the German Luftwaffe sends bombers over at eleven o'clock, like clockwork. We'll hear them and we'll hear our own anti-aircraft guns. Keep your flashlights off."

She paused, her gaze settling on the girls individually. "The darkness is our best protection. The beaches are their favorite targets, but as the army moves inland, I'm told they drop their bombs anywhere, hoping to get lucky. Should they sound like they're coming directly overhead, don't hesitate to use any of the foxholes you see around here. In fact, select one now, before bedding down."

Carol bit her lip. She'd wanted to experience the war up close. Boy, she sure was now. Her sleeping bag wasn't anything like her safe, comfortable bed at Mrs. Lester's. At least the airmen coming back from their missions each day got to sleep on clean sheets and eat delicious meals in their mess halls. What would Chet say if he could see her here?

She'd barely gotten to sleep when a shrill whine bolted her upright, her heart pounding. The artillery guns were firing. Engine noise provided a steady rumble, but at a distance. The plane wasn't coming overhead.

"Do we need to find our foxhole?" Louise whispered, and Carol wanted to laugh. No German pilot could possibly hear her.

Gloria took her seriously. "No, the guns are off to the north. And the shells are going from west to east."

Carol listened. Gloria was right. Like the change in a train whistle coming close, passing, and fading away. A light illuminated the tent canvas. "A searchlight looking for the plane?"

"Maybe." Gloria paused for a moment. "Or the Germans are dropping luminary flares, hoping to spot a nice, juicy target."

"It really is going to be a long, noisy night." Louise sighed. "I'll need to find ear plugs."

The guns quieted at daybreak. Paradoxically, the silence woke Carol. She stumbled out of the tent. Now would be a good time to visit the slit trench. Louise followed her out, and tripped over a root.

"Wait a minute." She bent over and poked it. "This isn't a tree root. It's the toe of a boot." Gripping it, she gave it a hard yank. A leg and more burst out of the ground. With a shriek, Louise backpedaled and fell over a tent rope.

Gloria rushed out, wide-eyed. "What's going on?"

On a dirt-encrusted belt buckle, Carol made out *Gott mit uns*. Looking around, she spotted other boots protruding from shallow graves. "Oh my word. We slept in a German cemetery."

Chapter Twenty-Seven

Over Germany
Thursday, July 20, 1944

The factory hid beneath six-tenths cloud cover. The bomber formation had penetrated deep into Germany to bomb the new jet-propelled aircraft assembly plant in Dessau, southwest of Berlin. And they couldn't find it.

Chet stood behind Max Withers, trying to make out features in the intermittent ground sightings. They led the low squadron only, not the whole shebang. As a group leader, they shouldered responsibility for eighteen planes, not the fifty-four of the entire wing. Being the navigator out front in the lead squadron would be pure frustration. Pretty soon they'd have to abandon Dessau and look for the secondary target. Someone else would have to come back to hit that plant. The production of those jet fighters had to stop. The Allies had nothing comparable in their arsenal.

"Radio to pilot. Starting a ninety degree turn north to find the secondary target."

"Roger." Resignation laced Captain McQuaid's voice. At least no enemy aircraft had been sighted, and flak was meager and inaccurate while they wandered around.

If only they could get the job done here before heading back to England. As the formation turned, Chet's gaze swept back and forth, scanning each tiny break in the clouds. Off to his right, he glimpsed something that looked like...

"There it is." Yelling on the intercom wasn't necessary, but he couldn't help himself. The high and lead squadrons ahead of them wouldn't be able to make the turn, but they still could. "Two o'clock position."

"I see it." Max nearly fell off his chair when he swiveled around. "Major, should we bomb it?"

Major Weston occupied the copilot's seat for this mission as command pilot. "Yes! We're going for it." The plane banked sharply to the right.

Their regular copilot, Clancy Elroy, was consigned to the tail gunner's post to keep watch over the squadron. He came on the intercom, laughter in his voice. "We caught the squadron by surprise with that sudden turn. They're hopping all over the place, but they're following us. We don't have a parade ground formation, but at least nobody collided."

"Engineer, fire our identifying green-yellow flares so they know to form up." Excitement infused the major's voice.

During Chet's first effort as lead navigator, a sudden evasive maneuver had scattered the formation then, too. This time they had a good excuse. He searched the sky. A single squadron of eighteen bombers would be more vulnerable under enemy attack, but enemy fighters were wondrously absent.

Less than a minute passed. "Bombs away." *Lovely Lily* lurched upward in time to Max's announcement.

"Hoo-wee. Plastered it." The ball gunner certainly enjoyed his view.

Elroy concurred. "Our strike film should have some mighty fine pictures. And the cloud cover's drifting back. We really caught a break."

"Okay, Vogel," Major Weston brought Chet's attention back inside the aircraft. "We're on our own. What's our heading?"

Chet sucked in his breath. Here's where he earned his keep. Rejoining the rest of the wing offered them the best protection. That meant finding them at the secondary target, east of Berlin. He directed them north. "We should converge with the others within twenty minutes."

Soon the flight engineer sang out. "There they are at one o'clock high and they're taking flak. They're dropping their bombs."

Streaks of light shot upward. Those would be the flak guns. Other billowing bursts of flame were the exploding bombs. Chet grabbed a camera and started filming. He'd been asked to film the lead squadron's bomb drop, but this should satisfy the request. They rarely witnessed a strike from this perspective.

Their squadron tucked back into place with the wing for the trip home. The radio operator said, "Major, the colonel sends his regards. Glad we could join them."

Chet located the lead plane out in front. He chuckled to himself. They must have had a bit of consternation aboard that aircraft when the copilot watching over the formation announced the disappearance of an entire squadron, deep in enemy territory. The colonel would forgive their unheard of departure when he learned they'd hit the primary.

Back at Ridgewell, the crew dropped out of *Lovely Lily* and piled onto a waiting jeep for the ride to debriefing. Chet's step faltered when he spotted the Red Cross clubmobile. He sighed. Carol wasn't with the clubmobile anymore. He continued into the building.

Irene waved to him when he came back out. She'd been a good friend to Carol. The replacement girl attracted a lot of attention because she was new. A note was pinned to her blouse. "My name is Mary and I'm from Virginia."

He joined Irene and pointed with his doughnut at Mary. "Carol said you're most frequently asked where you're from."

Irene laughed. "I'm thinking I'll have to try that." She turned serious eyes on Chet. "This is my last visit to Ridgewell. Next week I'm transferring to Southampton. With all the traffic funneling through there for France, they need more girls."

"So you volunteered?"

"No, but I knew my time here was limited. The Red Cross likes to move us around."

Chet paused in chewing. He swallowed the doughnut. "So Carol would have been leaving anyway."

"Yes." Irene watched him. "You know she wanted to see France." Her statement sounded like a question and he nodded. "She didn't want to leave you, but I think she was afraid to stay."

"Why? Because we ditched?"

Irene twisted her lips as she stacked away doughnut trays. "Carol was adamant about avoiding a romance. Civilian life is completely different. She's convinced it's not possible to really get to know a person's true self during wartime. Not well enough to commit to marriage. You might not love each other if you knew each other better." She grabbed a rag and wiped up spills around the coffee urn. "Did she tell you about a friend back home?"

"You mean the guy who proposed after three dates and then married her friend?"

Irene nodded so vigorously, a lock of her hair fell forward. She shoved it back. "That friend is in a pretty bad spot now. The guy lost his legs and is taking his frustration out on the poor girl." She tossed aside the rag. "The whole situation only made Carol more determined. Problem was, she'd already fallen for you, and that scared her silly."

Carol had fallen for him? Chet backed up a step. Carol had fallen for him, so she left?

"So that's it? Did she think I was about to propose? Insist on marrying while we're in England?"

They'd rarely seen each other more than once a week. They'd never made any plans. He'd only allowed himself to dream.

His father's face loomed in his memory. "What do you expect? You'll never amount to anything." Chet shook his head. He was worthy of a girl like Carol.

Irene sighed. "You're in a very dangerous job, you know. Every time you go out," she pointed skyward, "you're flirting with death. Watching the planes come back, wondering if yours is coming, that's stressful."

"So she left."

"She saw your friend's crewmate who survived a ditching. I think in him she saw you. But the main reason she left now is to see France. If she gave up this opportunity, she'd kick herself for the rest of her life." Irene patted his arm. "And she hasn't given up on you. She believes if God wants you two together, He'll reunite you."

Well, there was something to look forward to. But how much had Carol confided in Irene and how much was Irene surmising?

Audrey hoisted a coffee urn, and a rock on her finger glistening in the sun. Wally must have put it there. Interesting. The weekend in Cambridge made it obvious those two were not well-matched. At least Carol was spared witnessing any more of their shenanigans while she trod in her ancestors' footsteps.

Back in his barracks, his mail had been tossed on his cot. A letter from Grandma lay on top. He started reading it as he divested himself of his flight clothes. Her first words stopped him. *Len stopped by for a quick visit.* Len? Why was his oldest brother in the States?

Sitting down in his long underwear, he read on. Len had been wounded in the Pacific and sent home to recuperate. By now he should be headed back. So it wasn't a serious wound. He stared across the room. Len was the most like Dad. A gung-ho Marine, he'd tangle with anyone; the enemy, his squad mates, the officers. He hadn't thought twice about beating up his little brother.

Chet looked back at the letter. *He was quite surprised to hear you're a combat officer in the air corps.* "I'll bet he was." Chet's head dropped back as he laughed. Too bad he hadn't been able to see Len's expression. It was a sure thing Len wouldn't salute him if they came face to face.

That night we received a telephone call from your father. What? Why? *Len had contacted him and Hank couldn't believe your status. Your grandpa didn't mind ribbing him, asking what he thought you'd be doing, serving as a guard at an internment camp or some other noncombat position? He also didn't mind bragging about the job waiting for you with Pan American Airways. We've never known Hank to be so speechless.*

His father's expression would have been priceless to see. His youngest son, who wasn't supposed to amount to anything, now outranked him. That would gall him. He wouldn't be impressed though, because he didn't like officers. Chet just couldn't win.

A weary sigh slipped out. Maybe he should see if a softball game was in progress. A little exercise, cracking that ball out of the park. Or maybe not. He wanted to talk to someone. But who? Paul was gone. Carol was gone. Lowell and Andy were off base. He didn't know Max that well. The chaplain? He'd been a good friend to Paul. Before he could change his mind, he dressed in his Class A uniform and headed for the chapel.

"Describe your father in one word." Chaplain Hogan paced four steps in one direction, pivoted, and walked four steps back while Chet explained his quandary. Now he perched on a corner of his desk and waited.

"Tyrant." Chet crossed his arms, his fists clenched under his elbows. "He's a drill sergeant." He forced himself to relax, and pressed his lips together to be sure he couldn't be accused of pouting.

The chaplain hopped up and paced again. "A drill sergeant." He nodded. "His job is to belittle, humiliate, and criticize new recruits. He'll either break them or toughen them." He paused and faced Chet. "And he brought his work home with him, hmm?"

"He probably would have broken me if my grandparents hadn't asked to take me. He thought that was a great idea. Glad to see the last of me." His words ended on a sigh. All because he wasn't rough and tumble like his brothers. Being different hadn't been acceptable.

"Would you say you're most likely to think of him when you come up against a challenge? You hear him saying you'll never amount to anything?" Chet barely had time to nod before he continued. "But now he knows you've amounted to something. You outrank him. You have a prestigious job awaiting you." He snapped his fingers. "Now when you meet a challenge, instead of hearing him sneer, picture him flummoxed."

Chet laughed and spread out his hands. "I have no idea what that looks like. I've never seen him mystified." He stared at the floor. "But it sure would be nice to see a little respect in his expression."

Chaplain Hogan sat on his desk again. "Pray for him, for his happiness, contentment, salvation. Anything that promotes his well-being." He grabbed the Bible from his desktop and flipped through the pages. "Matthew chapter five, verse forty-four says, 'Love your enemies, bless them that curse you, do good to them that hate you, and pray for them which despitefully use you, and persecute you.' Every time a bad memory pops up, forgive him again. He's probably unaware of the harm he's done to you. I'm guessing the hurt he caused you is festering in your heart." He rose and put a hand on Chet's shoulder. "Don't give him the power to cripple your spirit."

Chapter Twenty-Eight

Somewhere in France
Tuesday, August 8, 1944

Three weeks without a bath. Carol ran her hand around her collar. Any bit of breeze would be welcome as the clubmobile jounced along. Along with the air came dust. Dust saturated her clothes, her hair, even her teeth felt gritty. "Tonight I absolutely have to have a sponge bath and wash my blouses. I don't think I have any more clean ones."

"You and me both." Gloria traced a design in the dirt coating the door frame. "I'm surprised nothing has started growing in my hair. We've got to find us a bucket though. Washing up out of a helmet is no good when it keeps rolling over and spilling the water."

Back in England, a lot of the airmen would have done well to visit their showers more often. Now she must smell as ripe as they did. So did the infantry men they served. It had to be expected when they all camped out in orchards and among hedgerows.

Being malodorous seemed to be taken for granted by the French civilians. She hoped the elderly man she'd tried to converse with this morning hadn't noticed when she'd involuntarily stepped back after getting a whiff of him. Frequent bathing seemed to be an American predilection that she, for one, missed.

They arrived back at their bivouac early, but found the *West Virginia* already there. Before tending to themselves, they set to work cleaning *George*. Carol scrubbed the greasy field range. Louise washed coffee cups and the urns. Gloria mopped the floor before hustling over to the supply tent to replenish their doughnut mix.

"Now we can boil water on the field range and get cleaned up." Gloria hoisted a sack of mix up to Carol.

"You want to get cleaned up?" Hazel from *West Virginia* paused beside her. "We passed a stream on our route not far from here. Jean went to find a GI guide. Wouldn't that be great to sink into water up to our chin?"

"That would be heavenly." Louise pressed her hands together in supplication. "We brought bathing suits for such an opportunity, but I was beginning to think we'd never get a chance to wear them."

Carol already pawed through her musette bag. Her suit must be at the very bottom. Her hand shook as she pulled it out. Oh, to be clean again.

"Let's bring soap and our laundry." Excitement made Gloria's voice quaver. "It won't be the cleanest wash without hot water, but we'll feel clean."

A jeep skidded to a stop in front of the clubmobiles. Jean jumped out and raced to the *West Virginia*. "Ted says there's an actual swimming hole the guys have found."

Ted guided four of the clubmobiles to reach the units they'd been assigned to serve. The army engineers were doing a tremendous job clearing out mines and filling in bomb craters, but travel remained perilous.

With six Red Cross girls crammed into his jeep, Ted stepped on the gas. "It's just over that hill there." He sped past a vineyard bursting with grapes and careened around a curve. Up ahead, several Frenchwomen lined a small bridge spanning the creek. Male voices spoke English, but no men could be seen.

The jeep halted at the edge of the bridge, and Carol gasped. Frolicking in the stream was a squad of buck-naked soldiers. Beside her, Louise slapped a hand over her eyes. The men caught sight of the jeep, and them. A cry arose, "American women."

Instantly, the GIs dove beneath the surface and swam under the bridge. The Frenchwomen turned to the jeep in bewilderment.

Ted threw the jeep into reverse and backed far enough away to get them out of sight. "I'll, uh, go see how long they plan to be here."

He hurried back to the bridge where the Frenchwomen had resumed their entertainment.

Hazel hadn't glimpsed the bathers. "What was that all about?"

Jean patted her knee. "Our gallant soldiers don't want to scandalize us in their nakedness."

Hazel waved toward the Frenchwomen. "What about them?"

"Americans are supposed to be Puritanical, dear. The French don't have our scruples."

Carol frowned. What did that say about American men's scruples? They didn't mind being ogled by the Frenchwomen, but were embarrassed to be seen by American women? Would Chet have been willing to display himself? She heaved a sigh.

Those men better leave soon. She'd strip in front of those Frenchwomen too, to get into that water.

Chapter Twenty-Nine

Over Cologne, Germany
Tuesday, August 15, 1944

"We should be on the bomb run in less than a minute." Chet recorded his calculations and the time on his log before hopping up to stand behind Max. Visibility was good. Finding the targeted airfield should not be a problem. Unfortunately, the clear sky left them exposed, and flak peppered the sky.

"We're at the I.P.," Max spoke into his headphones.

Captain McQuaid responded, "It's your airplane."

Max finessed their course via the bombsight controls with such a deft touch, no alteration could be felt in *Lovely Lily's* flight. He looked up through the Plexiglas nose. "We'll have bombs away in fifteen, fourteen, thirteen, twelve…" He looked back into the bombsight. "What the…? Abort. Abort the drop. We've got a flock of B-24s below us in the drop zone."

Chet leaned over Max's shoulder to look straight down. The twin-tailed Liberators disappeared off to their left. He took a deep breath and blew it out. Now they faced a time-consuming go-around and the flak was murderous. He dropped back onto his chair to record the snafu as the pilot began circling back.

Colonel Hall, flying as commanding officer from the copilot's seat, asked Elroy in the tail how the wing was responding to the go-around.

"Formation's loosened up quite a bit. The high squadron's trying to catch up and the low squadron got scrambled. Whoa! Fletcher, leading the element behind us, just took a hit on engine three. The prop flew into the fuselage. They're dropping back."

Chet added the comments to his log. A flash of light, followed by a bang that drowned out the engines, caused him to duck. *Lily* shuttered, but kept flying. He raised his head. A freezing wind numbed his face. Max sprawled on the floor between his chair and the bombsight controls. Chet jumped up and reached for him. He was alive.

"Max, are you all right?" Chet helped him sit up against the controls, then move to his chair.

Max tested his jaw. "Yeah. I'll probably be sore in the morning."

"What's the situation down there?" Captain McQuaid's voice sounded hollow over the interphone.

Chet looked around. "We could use a broom. The place is a mess, but I don't think any vitals were damaged."

"The Plexiglas has more holes than a golf course and it's gotten windy in here." Max flicked his fingers, indicating Chet could get back to his own work.

Chet hesitated before turning back. A piece of flak, or maybe Plexiglas, had sliced into Max's parachute pack. Chet tugged it out. The chute didn't spill out. Maybe it hadn't been compromised. Parachutes could still perform their tasks with a small hole or two. Plenty of guys had landed safely after the enemy had fired on them.

The second attempt at their target proceeded without further incident. Elroy yelled over the intercom that the Luftwaffe wouldn't be using that airfield anymore. Corroborating his statement, no enemy fighters waited for them outside the flak zone. Better yet, despite the battle damage inflicted on the bombers, none of them had gone down, not even Fletcher, lagging at the rear.

Chet sat back as they flew west over Belgium. The worst was behind them. He donned his goggles to protect his eyes from the icy blast, packed away as much as possible into his briefcase, and stood to the side of the nose to watch their progress. There lay Liege to the south and, further on, Brussels to the north. Their route threaded them around areas known to bristle with anti-aircraft guns.

They overflew the border into France. Chet gave Captain McQuaid a new heading to start their turn northward to England.

"Flak coming up." The call must have come from the ball turret gunner. "There shouldn't be any flak here. There's nothing down there."

"Probably a mobile gun. Looks like a main road and also a railroad." If Elroy was seeing that from the tail, they must be past the danger.

Bam! *Lovely Lily* flipped over. Yanked off his feet, Chet slammed against the fuselage. Pain seared through his left shoulder and his vision darkened while his head throbbed. *Lily* plummeted downward, out of control. Chet was flung forward into the Plexiglas nose, but much of it was gone. Before he could grasp the frame, Chet plunged right through.

"Vogel!"

Chet winced. His head throbbed so badly. Something was wrong. Just leave him alone in the darkness of oblivion.

The voice yelled again. "Vogel, pull your ripcord!"

He pried open an eye. Max. What did he want?

"Your ripcord, Vogel. Open your parachute."

Chet opened his other eye. How peculiar. Max was falling through space a few yards away from him. His gaze drifted down and he jerked. *He* was falling through space, a childhood nightmare come to life. He dragged his gaze back to Max. The bombardier held out his own ripcord. Of course. Open his parachute.

He tried to raise his left arm. It didn't move. Hot pain radiated from his shoulder. That's right. *Lovely Lily* had gone into a spin. While he grasped for the ripcord with his right hand, he tilted his face heavenward. High overhead, a widening distance grew between them and the bomber formation. A single Flying Fortress struggled to regain altitude and catch up. *Lily*. McQuaid and Hall had wrestled the plane back under control. They were heading back to England, leaving him and Max behind.

He pulled his ripcord. His parachute spilled out above him. Whoop. The chute snapped open, nearly yanking him out of his clothes. One flying boot popped off his foot. He cried out against the pain in his head and shoulder, and hung limp in his harness.

Max deployed his own chute. Chet tried to concentrate on watching it open. Anything to distract him from his agony. The canopy snapped open, jerking Max nearly horizontal. But then the parachute ripped from edge to center. The canopy folded and collapsed. Max continued in a free fall to the Earth.

Chet's stomach churned. The chard from the blast that took out their window. It must have sliced up a seam. Now Max was doomed. Chet couldn't look away. They'd been flying at twenty-five thousand feet, dropping maybe a thousand feet or more during *Lily's* wild gyrations before they'd been tossed out. Max didn't have a chance. He'd slam into the ground and there probably wouldn't be much left to mop up.

Max had waited to pull his ripcord. Waited to make sure Chet pulled his.

Chet's goggles fogged. Or maybe he had tears in his eyes. Tears of pain. Tears of despair. Tears of helplessness. He and Max hadn't gotten to know each other beyond superficialities; Chet still bunked with his old crewmates. But Max was a fine man.

How long did it take to fall twenty-four thousand feet? More than a minute. What did a man think about, knowing he was about to die? Utter a prayer? Picture coming face to face with God? Did Max know God?

He must have hit by now. Chet blinked hard, but couldn't see him. Too many trees. He should be concerned about his own landing. He needed to face the direction of his drift. That meant a turn to the right. The parachute could be manipulated by pulling the risers, but hc needed two hands for that. Nope, his left arm was useless.

A tree reached up to him. He crossed his right arm in front of his head and buried his face in the crook of his elbow. With his legs and feet pressed together, he let his head droop against the parachute riser. He slammed into the branches.

"Vers la gauche maintenant. Dépêchez-vous."

Gibberish roused Chet. He'd slept for five minutes or five hours. Didn't matter. Pain still seized him in its grip. A disturbance in the tree caused him to drop two inches, wrenching a groan past his lips. The leg straps of his parachute harness, uncomfortably tight under normal circumstances, cut into him.

A moment of stillness surrounded him. Then, *"Monsieur?"* French for mister. He knew that much. So the Germans hadn't found him yet. He fought off a wave of dizziness as he opened his eyes. A man dressed in rough workman's clothes stared up at him. *"Monsieur, pouvez-vous détacher votre parachute?"* More gibberish. Chet could only stare back.

The man gestured to someone else in the tree. *"Il faut couper les cordes du parachute pour le libérer."*

A voice answered behind him. Branches swayed, buffeting him. An arm reached around him, feeling his harness. The hand located the clasp and tugged. The clasp released and Chet dropped. The man on the ground caught his useless arm. A cry ripped from his throat. Stars danced before his eyes, and darkness closed in.

Water trickled in Chet's ear. A towel dabbed at him. Something pressed at his lips. A woman's voice. *"Buvez monsieur."*

This time water dribbled through his lips. Boy, did that feel good going down his parched throat.

"Thank, uh, mercy." No, that wasn't right. Accent the second syllable, like ballet or Doucet, Carol's surname. *"Merci."*

Her voice sounded pleased as she rattled off more French. *"C'est mieux, n'est-ce pas?"*

He butchered one simple word and she thought he was fluent.

Chet forced his eyelids open. He lay in a gloomy room. It smelled musty, a little smoky. An oil lamp burned on a table beside the bed. The room appeared to lack windows. He rolled his head the other way, slowly, to avoid setting off the tom-tom beating on his skull. A woman hovered next to him. At first glance, she looked as old as Grandma, but she was probably in her fifties. She held the wooden cup to his mouth again, and he drained it.

Setting the cup aside, she placed a towel into a pan of water. Her graying brown hair was pulled back into a ball at her neck. Her dress sported a threadbare elbow and a frayed, mended collar. Grandma would call her pleasantly plump.

The woman wrung out her towel and patted his face and neck. Chet closed his eyes with a sigh. *Oh, yeah.* The towel moved to his damaged shoulder and he tensed. She made a clucking sound, moving the towel to his chest. His eyes snapped open. His chest? Where was his shirt? His good hand probed around. He no longer wore a single stitch of clothing. Consternation drove his hand to feel around the bed for a sheet. Nothing.

A low chuckle came from the woman. *"Un américain modeste."*

She proceeded with his sponge bath, moving over his hip. "Hmm hmm hmm." Finally she finished and produced a knit blanket to cover him. *"Ma fille est partie chercher le médecin. Reposez-vous maintenant."*

Why had he spent years in school struggling over a dead language like Latin? They should have learned practical languages, like French. Hopefully, *médecin* meant medicine. Maybe someone had been sent to fetch some. A doctor, too, would be nice. The pain in his shoulder had settled down to a steady pulsing heat. His head continued to throb, and something was wrong with that hip she hummed over.

The woman patted his good shoulder, murmuring more senseless words. She took the lamp and left. In the dark, Chet relaxed one muscle at a time. Let go of the pain, float, it'll ease.

Lovely Lily. What happened there? A mobile flak gun had found them. A shot must have exploded right under one of *Lily's* wings. That caused *Lily* to flip over, out of control. She'd nosed down into a dive. He and Max had been thrown against the shattered Plexiglas. It couldn't hold them and they'd crashed right through. Then the pilots had wrestled her out of her dive. He and Max were lucky they hadn't been hit by a propeller.

Max. Chet's chest squeezed so tight, tears pushed out from under his eyelids. He should have said something that shard. A spare parachute should have been aboard. One of the gunners could have brought it forward. Max's death was his fault.

The door opened, revealing the woman with her lamp and two men. The woman uncovered him, pointing at his useless arm, and jabbering away. One of the men lifted his arm and probed his shoulder. Chet tried to roll away, but the other man held him in place. The first man, presumably a doctor, had a lot to say, directing his words first to Chet, then to the others. He nodded at the other man. While that man tightened his grip on Chet, the doctor gripped Chet's useless arm and shoved hard.

Chet's shoulder popped. Red-hot pain scorched him. He gasped for breath as stars once again danced in his vision. Darkness swallowed him again.

Chapter Thirty

Somewhere in France
Monday, August 21, 1944

A blinding flash of light penetrated Carol's eyelids and woke her a moment before a horrendous boom shattered the night's tranquility. The earth rocked hard, tossing her off her cot and collapsing the tent on top of her.

A bombing raid. What else could it be? Among the cacophony of noises now filling the air, she picked out the fading sound of an aircraft engine. Bed Check Charlie. It must be indicative of how tired she was that it hadn't awakened her earlier. A flickering light pierced her cocoon of sleeping bag and tent canvas. Something must be on fire. She had to get out of here.

"Oh, my word!"

In spite of their situation, Carol smiled at Louise's exclamation. She didn't sound like she was having much luck at freeing herself.

"Are you ladies all right?" Ted's voice filtered to them as the canvas lifted up at one end, then the other. A flashlight probed for them. "Ladies?"

"If that's the end of tonight's entertainment, that's fine with me." Gloria's reply was punctuated with a sneezing fit.

"Carol? Where are you?" Ted rolled back the canvas with help from someone on the opposite side of the tent. "Carol?"

"Snug as a bug in the proverbial rug." She pushed at the weight pinning her down. "I think a tent post is holding me down."

Suddenly, she was free and Ted pulled her to her feet. Before she could think of a witty remark, he pulled her into a bear hug. Her breath swooshed out of her. He released her and, still tucked into her sleeping bag, she lost her balance. She hopped back and bumped into her cot. Ted grabbed her again before she fell. He guided her to sit on the cot.

"I'm sorry, Carol. I'm just so glad you're all right."

Carol pulled the zipper from his grasp and worked it down. Good thing she slept in regular clothes instead of a nightgown. She stepped out of her sleeping bag. "I didn't wake up when the German plane flew overhead. Maybe I'm getting used to the nightly racket."

"They dropped parachute bombs. One of them nailed my jeep. It is no more. Just a big smoldering hole in the ground."

Another GI helped Gloria and Louise step away from the canvas. "We'll get your tent back up in no time, ladies. It ought to be quiet for the rest of the night and you can get back to bed. Can't have you dozing off while making doughnuts tomorrow."

The tent stood erect again in no time. Still Ted lingered. "Need anything else?" His words could be directed to all of them, but his gaze belonged solely to Carol.

She picked up his flashlight from a stack of boxes filled with clubmobile supplies. Handing it to him with the beam pointed downward, she smiled. "I guess all we need is a little sleep so we don't doze off in the doughnuts, as your friend said. Tomorrow is already today."

"Ted's in love with you." Gloria added a bit more water to the second batch of doughnuts she was mixing.

Carol looked up from the doughnut machine about to spit out the first batch of doughnuts. She waited with the prong to capture them. "He's nice. Interesting to talk to. Did you know he's from Colorado? The way he describes skiing down mountains, I don't know if I'm ready to join him or declare him insane." She skewered the first doughnut, then the second. "He doesn't make me tingle."

Not the way Chet did.

"That's good, isn't it? Because you don't want to get serious?" Gloria had the next batch of dough ready. She set the bowl aside to steady Carol's tray. "You can relax and enjoy his friendship without worrying about love complicating matters."

"From my side, yes, but what if he wants to get more serious? He'll think I'm leading him on." The machine ground to a halt. "Oh, no. Not again. This poor machine's been rattled too much on the rough roads."

Gloria headed to the door. "That's where Ted's infatuation with you comes in handy. He's always ready to do something for you, like fix that thing." She dashed out of the clubmobile, only to hop back in. "What am I doing? Did I not just hear what I said? You go get him."

Chuckling, Carol headed out. She paused beside the wreckage of a jeep next to the deep crater made by one of the parachute bombs. Four men had ventured down into the pit. One of them noticed her. "Thousand kilogram bombs make quite a dent. Want to help us fill it in?"

"Now, why would you want to do that? If you level out a ramp down into there, it would make a nice foxhole for a couple of clubmobiles."

"Heh, heh, heh. Make a ramp, she says." The GI took off his cap and scratched his head. "It'll be easier to fill it in."

Carol surveyed the scene. A lot of ground had to come out of the earth to result in such a big crater, but where was it now? Very little loose dirt and rock surrounded the area. She inspected the jeep. They could salvage a couple tires and shove the rest back into the hole, along with another burned-out hulk on the other side, but they'd need about a dozen more.

If that bomb had landed a hundred yards to the west, she'd have been vaporized. A shiver convulsed her. Next time she wrote home, she wouldn't say a word about this.

She found Ted, and he immediately left the jeep he was tuning to walk back with her. Carol stopped when her foot kicked something in the tall grass. She picked it up. Click. "A little noise maker toy."

Ted took it from her. "Hey, this is a swell find. It's a cricket."

He clicked it several times.

"It doesn't look like a cricket."

"The airborne troops used these when they were dropped into Normandy. To identify themselves in the dark." He clicked it once. "One click was to be answered with two clicks." He demonstrated the answer. "A group must have passed through here."

When he started to slip the toy into a pocket, Carol held out her hand. "My find, please."

She smiled as he reluctantly gave it back. She clicked it once in her left hand, then answered with two clicks in her right hand. Chet would find this a much better souvenir than the German bullet she'd been given in England.

By noon, they were ready to pull out with over sixteen hundred fresh doughnuts. Carol filled their canteens with water and obtained three boxes of K-rations. She sighed. More crackers, cold meat, and cheese. Meals at an army mess tasted so much better.

The day's scheduled stops featured units of an Anti-Aircraft Brigade. Like the airmen in England, the artillerymen appreciated visits from the Red Cross. One big difference marked the clubmobile's arrival. No music played from the loud speaker.

"You know, we could have left our record player behind, and saved it from all the jostling." Louise pulled out an Andrews Sisters record and inspected it for scratches. "Are we really so close to the front line that the Germans might hear our music?"

"They didn't issue us helmets for the sole purpose of washing up in them." Gloria opened the record player's case. "Looks fine to me. Go ahead and play a record at very low volume. I'm going to see about filling *George's* gas tank or we won't make it back to base tonight. I'll stop by that tree over there and signal you if it's too loud."

"Boogie Woogie Bugle Boy" wafted out of *President Washington* with the aroma of coffee and doughnuts. A line of men materialized at their serving counters. Carol grabbed a doughnut tray and went out to mingle. "Who's from Ohio?"

"I'm from Michigan," called out a soldier with a moustache. "That makes me a near neighbor."

"You qualify for a doughnut." She held out the tray. Reading the name stenciled on his buddy's shirt, she asked, "How about you, Simmons?"

"Vermont."

A man of few words. "Have a doughnut, Simmons from Vermont."

"He's nowhere near Ohio."

Carol turned to the objector. From the side of her mouth, she said, "He looks hungry. How about you?"

As she roamed among them, she asked how their experience in France had been so far.

"Wouldn't care to be a Frenchie living here." Michigan appeared at her side. Crumbs decorated his moustache. "Have you seen the farmers working out in their fields with the shells screaming over their heads? They must be nuts."

"This is their land. They have to eat." Vermont defended the local people.

"Do you think they stayed here through the worst of the fighting?"

"They probably sat it out in their cellars. Where could they go to be safe? So much of France is being destroyed. Besides, their natural inclination would be to protect their homes."

The state of Vermont bordered the province of Quebec. On a hunch, Carol asked, "Do you have French ancestry?"

Vermont's head jerked toward her. "I do."

"So do I. Coming here fulfilled a dream for me. The perfect opportunity to see how my ancestors lived." Carol's gaze swept across the landscape. "I hadn't counted on the destruction."

Abandoned German vehicles littered the countryside. The stench of death frequently nauseated her while they traveled to the different batteries. Broken carts surrounded gun placements that so recently had spit death. The desire to poke around scattered piles of personal belongings could be lethal. Many burned-out tanks, discarded equipment, and corpses hid mines. Carol suppressed a shudder. "We've heard the Germans even hide explosives on their severely wounded they leave behind."

Men around her nodded. "We saw a jeep yesterday." The crumbs dropped from Michigan's moustache while he talked. "Looked to be in perfect shape. Sure was tempting to take it for a spin. Too tempting for a new guy, fresh from the States. He opened the door and ka-boom! No more raw recruit."

As they traveled to their next stop, Carol watched the edges of the road, where the Germans usually planted their mines. Pulling onto the shoulder could be fatal. Why hadn't she considered the close proximity to death when she volunteered for France?

They'd seen death in England, but there the wounded men came back from the war in the sky over the continent. Here, they were on the edge of the war. They heard the screech of shells lobbed back and forth. German planes flew over them at night and dropped bombs. Step on a mine and be ripped into the hereafter.

More men flocked around as soon as they pulled up at their next stop. Instead of mingling in her morose mood, Carol stationed herself at the coffee urn, pouring cup after cup. Gloria and Louise disappeared out the door with trays of doughnuts.

"Ahh, all the comforts of home."

Carol spun around. She hadn't heard the brawny GI come in. He sat on the sofa, legs outstretched, arms across the back of the sofa, head tilted against the wall, doughnut clutched in one hand. "Oh, dearie, I'll take my coffee here in the salon."

Carol laughed despite his audacity. So he wanted to play house, did he? Splashing a cup of water in his face would be more fun, but she would play along. "Here you are, sir. One cup of coffee."

She hid a smile at his look of male satisfaction in being served by the little woman. "Be sure to wash out the cup when you're done."

"Huh?" His feet came under him as he sat up. "Wash the cup? You expect me to wash the cup?"

"Who else?" Carol waved a hand at the bin full of used cups from their last stop. "We're busy serving and, as you can see, clean cups are getting low." No need to mention the drawers they hadn't opened yet. She offered a sweet smile. "Don't you know that when you come inside *President Washington*, you score KP duty?"

Three minutes later, he invaded the kitchen. Maybe Carol shouldn't have assigned him cleanup duty. They'd had men in here before. Friendly men, eager to help. Like Chet, with his sleeves rolled up and his hands plunged into the soapy water.

This man's arms came around her, pulling her against him. Carol caught her breath. First rule around a dangerous predator, do not show fear. Pressing her elbow into his abdomen, she sought to keep her voice steady and pleasant. "Unhand me, mister. You're interfering with my work."

His grip tightened. "Don't I get a reward, baby?"

"A reward? You've done nothing that deserves a reward." She refused to raise her face to him. He'd take advantage of her, for sure.

Standing at the counter with the side of the clubmobile lowered for service, they stood in full view of the congregated men. A red-faced GI stepped up to the counter, attracting more attention. "Reynolds, what the devil do you think you're doing?"

"I'm here for a sweet treat, but she's not being very friendly." Reynolds no longer sounded friendly himself. One hand kept her shoulder pinned to him while the other slid down to her hip.

Carol glimpsed Gloria thrust her tray into a GI's hand and run for the clubmobile. Other men yelled at Reynolds to leave her alone. From her shoulder, his hand moved up and grabbed her hair, trying to jerk her face around to his. "Come on, baby. Give me a kiss."

Tears sprang to Carol's eyes as he pulled her hair. Blood pounded through her veins. He reeked of sweat and cigarette smoke. She might disgrace herself by throwing up. Maybe that was a good idea. He'd get away from her then.

The clubmobile door wrenched open and two men burst inside. "Reynolds, let go of her this instant."

Reynolds straightened to attention, letting go of her. Carol got as far away as she could, which was not very far, in the tiny kitchen. She pressed a hand to her heaving chest. Leaning against the wall, she kept her back to the service counter.

"Get out of here and report to the major." The lieutenant marched the snarling Reynolds out of the clubmobile.

"What are they doing in a man's world if they're not going to pleasure us?"

Carol's blood ran cold. She rubbed her mouth. He hadn't kissed her, but she still felt dirty. A damp towel appeared in front of her. Gloria. Carol nodded her thanks and sponged her face and neck.

While Gloria took over pouring coffee, Carol sat down in the lounge, though not in the same place where Reynolds had sat. The lieutenant returned.

"I want to apologize, ma'am, for Reynolds' behavior. They're not all like him." The lieutenant was definitely the youngest of the three of them in the clubmobile. Maybe he was one of those ninety day wonders, given a three-month course in leadership and expected, no matter how green, to lead seasoned men. "He'll be disciplined. A reprimand at the least. I'm not sure what the penalty is for manhandling a woman."

A blush rose in his cheeks and he fiddled with his cap.

Carol smiled at him, though her lips wobbled. "One rotten egg doesn't spoil them all. I know that. This was the first trouble I've had in five months overseas."

"Yes, well," the lieutenant replaced his cap, "as you know, our ack-ack units—the anti-aircraft guns—support the army as it advances toward Paris. We'll be test-firing a few of our ninety millimeter guns. If you ladies would like to join us, we'll let you fire a gun. Be sure to wear your helmets."

Gloria stood in the doorway. "Only if you let us aim the gun at Reynolds."

Chapter Thirty-One

Elsewhere in France
Same Day

Rain spattered on the roof. Ducks quacked. Ducks slept at night, didn't they? Therefore, it must be daytime. Chet must be out in the country. On his navigation maps, what was in northeast France?

He would go insane if he had to stay cooped up in this pitch-black cave. He needed a window. He needed to see the sun. He needed fresh air.

The room still smelled musty. At least he didn't stink. His hostess seemed bemused by his need to wash every day. Just because soap wasn't available didn't mean he couldn't scrub well with water.

He flexed his arm. The pain lessened every day. That doctor had known what he was doing. His arm must have come out of its socket, and the doc had pushed it back in. Seemed kind of primitive, but surgery hadn't been necessary.

Too bad he couldn't say the same for his hip. Only x-rays would reveal the problem there. Massive black bruising remained, but now contained all the colors of a rainbow. He couldn't put any weight on it and remained bedridden.

If he could walk around, he could get out of this prison. The first sign of Germans, and he'd return to his hiding place. Better yet, if he were mobile, he could head for allied lines. Since these folks hadn't turned him over, they must not favor the Germans. They must be eager to see him go, though. The penalty for being caught hiding an Allied airman was likely execution.

The door squeaked open. A woman he'd never seen before entered. She set down her lamp and studied him. He stared back. Younger than the woman who'd been caring for him, but older than himself, she wore snazzy clothes, a thin black sweater with a red scarf tied at the neckline to match her slim red skirt. Her hair reached her shoulders in a smooth, puffy style with the ends flipped under.

"Hello soldier."

Her greeting expelled his breath. "You speak English."

Her laughter flowed over him like music. "Madame Chotar says they have a guest who knows little beyond *bonjour* and *merci*. Your politeness pleases her, but she also says you grow impatient as you heal."

"Heal? I can't walk." Chet bit back further words. Now that he had someone to talk to, he didn't want to waste time whining. "What's the situation? Where am I and where are the Germans?"

She opened her mouth, but he held up his hand. "I'm sorry. My name is Chet Vogel. And you are?"

Another musical laugh. "I am Suzette Lefebvre." She inclined her head. "I am pleased to meet you. My home is in Cambria, which is south of here. Do you know of Cambria?"

Cambria was on the last map he'd looked at before being ejected from *Lovely Lily*. "Not far from the Belgian border. In the Forbidden Zone, right?"

"Oui, monsieur." Her smile lit up her face. "You know French geography?"

"Reading maps is my job. I'm a navigator. Please, um, *s'il vous plait*, sit down." He pointed to the chair beside the bed. *Please stay awhile.* "I doubt I would recognize the name of this little hamlet."

"What makes you think you are in a little hamlet?"

"Listen. What do you hear?"

Suzette cocked her head, her eyes straying to the ceiling. Then she shrugged. "Rain on the roof. Madame Chotar working in her kitchen."

Chet grinned, and offered a hint. "Quack, quack."

His guest riveted her eyes on him, her brow furrowing as she listened. Her mouth dropped open and she clapped her hands. "Ducks are outside enjoying the rain."

"Know of any ducks that live in a city?" Chet laughed before saying, "All I remember seeing while parachuting was woods. Are any Germans quartered around here?"

"No, this is little more than a crossroads, yes?" Chet nodded when she paused. "The people are fortunate, almost ignored. But if the Boche get suspicious, they will be ruthless. So, the Chotars keep you a secret. Their nephew helped bring you here. Only the doctor, the priest, and the mayor also know, and now me."

Suzette pressed her lips together and looked down at her hands. "I was engaged to the Chotars' oldest son, Antoine. He has been a prisoner of war more than four years, since France fell. Their younger son, Michel, was taken to Germany as a forced laborer almost immediately afterward. He was only seventeen. We have not heard from either of them in a very long time."

Chet reached out to her. "We're in France now. We're pressing on to Germany. The war can't go on much longer."

Suzette clasped his hand. Her eyes glittered in the lamplight with unshed tears. "I pray it ends soon." She inhaled sharply, sitting straight and moistening her lips. "The war comes our way. The Boche are retreating, and the British and Americans are indeed close behind. Cambria will likely become a battleground."

"And here?" Chet's invalid status loomed as a menace. He couldn't run from danger. He couldn't expect his hosts to endanger themselves any more than they already were.

"We might get run over, but no one should stop. Monsieur Chotar talked of moving you down to the cellar in case the bullets start to fly."

Chet rolled up on his elbow. "And on the way down, we can stop to look out a window." He eased back on the pillow. "I'll see the sun, the sky, grass, the ducks, flowers. I thought I caught the scent of roses the other night."

Suzette leaned forward and patted his arm. Before she could say anything, a streak of orange launched itself onto his bed with a high-pitched yowl. A kitten stuck its cold nose in Chet's ear. He snapped his fingers, and the tiny creature pounced on them. Then it sank its sharp little teeth into the bandage keeping his upper arm immobile and pulled with a growl.

Chet grabbed the kitten before Suzette could reach it. He lifted it by the scruff of its neck. Paws waved in the air with needle-like claws extended.

"Yow."

"Hello to you, too." Chet flipped the cat onto his abdomen and turned its ears back. "How do you like that? A real spittin' kitten." He let go and it leapt to the bedside table, knocking off Chet's cup.

"Sisi, bad girl." The kitten jumped down before Suzette could capture it. When it dashed to the door, she picked up the cup. "You may be seeing a lot more of Sisi. She's a house cat, and I don't want to banish her to the barn."

"Great." A little playmate to brighten his dreary days. "But you might want to rethink the name. Sassy is a better fit."

"Yow." Sisi raced back into the room and jumped on the bed. She crouched at Chet's feet and began to stalk toward his head. He ignored her until she came within reach. Then he tackled her. "Yow."

"Back for more punishment, huh?" He roughed her up before holding her down and gently stroking the soft fur into place. Sisi relaxed and her purrs echoed off the ceiling.

"Got her motor running."

Suzette crossed her arms, shaking her head. "I have never seen her settle down like this. You have a way with animals. Have you pets at home?"

"No. My grandmother does not believe animals should be in the house." Petting Sisi brightened his heart as much as it soothed the kitten. "Suzette, one of my crewmates was tossed out of our plane with me. His parachute failed." He took a deep breath, raising Sisi to his shoulder to cuddle her. "Do you know what happened to him? Was he buried?"

Suzette patted his arm again. "I heard Monsieur le Curé buried him in the church yard. The Germans saw your parachute. When they came here, Monsieur le Maire told them you did not survive your injuries, and they were shown the grave. They took the identification necklace."

If they took Max's dog tags, maybe they notified the Red Cross. The base would hear of his death. Chet squeezed his eyes shut. "His name was Max Withers. A good man. And I could have saved him."

Once again, he saw the parachute snap open. The yank as it caught Max's weight. The canopy ripping and collapsing. Max flailing as he plunged four miles down.

Chet squeezed his eyes shut and shuddered.

"How could you save him?" Suzette jiggled his arm. "When you are falling in a parachute, you cannot help another person."

"Mew, mew." Sisi had squirmed from his hold and nosed his chin. "Mew."

The kitten's concern pushed tears past his eyelids. Opening his eyes, his watery gaze attempted to focus on her big green eyes.

"Mew." She batted at his nose. He pulled her back to his shoulder and looked up at Suzette.

"I didn't tell him his chute had been pierced by flak. I didn't request someone to bring the spare for him. I thought the danger was behind us."

"War brings many regrets, Monsieur Chet." She stroked his arm like he stroked the cat. "We must ask God's forgiveness and put our lost battles behind us, because we need all our energy to carry on in this war. Doing what is right and avoiding Nazi wrath is like walking a circus tightrope. Concentrate on surviving what is still to come. And the coming days will most certainly be full of challenge."

Chapter Thirty-Two

Paris, France
Tuesday, August 29, 1944

Units of the American army had entered Paris four days earlier, when the city was liberated. French military forces with General de Gaulle had paraded through the streets on Saturday, amid wild celebration. Now the Red Cross girls came into town and joined in the American parade. They found a scene of chaotic joy. The air pulsed with electricity.

"They're still having a party." From the back seat of Ted's jeep, Gloria waved back at the French civilians crowding the streets, waving their flag, and shouting a welcome.

Carol hesitated to return their waves. She hadn't done anything to secure their liberty. The troops should be treated like conquerors, not the clubmobile crews.

A little girl jumping up and down in the street, swinging her arms to and fro, locked gazes with her. Wide eyes and a big smile filled her face. She couldn't have any idea why everyone was so excited. The people's exhilaration had infected her though, and she couldn't keep still.

Tears glistened in some eyes, streaming down cheeks of others. For four long years, the Germans had occupied France. Now they'd been pushed out of Paris. That was reason to celebrate. And the locals wanted to include them in the celebration.

Carol put more enthusiasm into her wave. She reached out to an elderly woman as the jeep passed close by. The woman grasped her hand with gnarled fingers. Her smile revealed missing teeth.

The party continued all the way to the university where the army billeted them. There another, more welcome, delight greeted them. A private room awaited each woman. Clean beds with sheets and pillowcases, running water in the bathroom, sheer bliss. Carol collapsed on her bed. When was the last time she'd felt such comfort?

"Come on, Carol." Louise skidded to a stop at her door. "We're going out to explore the big city."

Carol sighed and heaved herself up. Later. She'd rest later.

Arm in arm to avoid being separated, Carol, Gloria, and Louise negotiated the congested streets. The tower that, more than anything, represented France to Carol drew her attention. "Can we go up in the Eiffel Tower, do you think? Or would everyone have that idea?"

"Maybe if we go first thing in the morning." Gloria pulled them to a halt in front of a store window. "I hoped to find some small souvenir of Paris, but look at the prices. Four dollars for that comb."

Louise's shrug tugged Carol's arm. "It's not like we've been able to spend money for a while. You can afford it."

They found Champs Élysées and started up the famous avenue. Ahead stood the Arc de Triomphe. "Pictures. I've forgotten to take any pictures." Carol stopped and pulled her camera out of her bag. "I'm slipping as a journalist. The perfect opportunity to report for the *Canton Repository*, complete with photographs, dangles right in front of me, and I hadn't even thought of it."

She stepped into the street and framed a shot of the crowds with the Arc in the background. She spotted something else in her viewfinder. "Gloria, how about French perfume for a souvenir?"

They squeezed into the shop. "Mmm, smells divine in here." Louise picked up a bottle. "Chanel 22. How much is a hundred and eighty-seven francs?"

Gloria squinted as she did the calculations. "About three seventy-five, I think."

"Splurge." Carol nudged her and added in an undertone, "That's cheaper than the comb." She sniffed a bottle of Ciro Gardenia. "I'm getting this one." She found other floral fragrances: rose, jasmine, hyacinth, bergamot. These would be lovely gifts for her mother, sister, and friends like Fran. She wouldn't trust the mail with them, but if she packed them amongst her clothes, she could present them herself when she returned home.

"Don't forget, once we leave Paris, bathing opportunities will be few and far between again." Louise couldn't decide between Fleurs de Rocaille and Bellodgia Scandal. She took them both. "These will help mask the aroma."

Back on the street, Louise looked around. "What a difference between Paris and London. Here they have well-stocked stores, nicely dressed people, and undamaged buildings. London was so drab and dull in comparison."

"Notice how thin the Parisians are." Gloria kept her voice down. "I heard the city was on the brink of starvation when the Allies marched in. That's one reason we're so welcome. We're bringing food."

Carol gestured to a bullet hole in the stone façade of a corner building. "And don't forget, London's enduring a shooting war from the Luftwaffe and V-1 rockets. By giving up in 1940, the French avoided that, but they may have scars we don't see. If they didn't behave the way the Germans wanted them to, I imagine life got most uncomfortable."

"So the moral to that is, the English should have surrendered, too."

"Bite your tongue, Louise." Gloria frowned at her. "The only reason Paris is liberated is because of the Allies throwing the Germans back since the invasion. The French have nothing to be proud of while the British can stand tall. Who would have rescued England had they surrendered? We were an ocean away, not wanting to become involved in a European war."

Louise shrugged. "I still like Paris better than London."

In the early evening, Carol walked along the Seine River with Ted. She had to agree with Louise. "Paris is beautiful. I love the architecture. So many mansard roofs, and have you noticed all the statues everywhere?"

When she admired a colorful scarf in a Frenchwoman's impromptu sidewalk sale, Ted bought it for her. She looped it around her neck with a casual knot.

"I like the river banks, all neatly walled. And that wall across the river," Ted pointed her in the other direction, "has a walkway down below, with stairs leading to the water if you want to hop a boat."

Carol watched a rowboat's slow progress. "Lots of trees all over." She pointed to the roofs. "Several chimneys have lots of flues, but they're not as obvious as in England. That was one of my first impressions of England. All the chimneys, which would need chimney sweeps, just like in the *Mary Poppins* books."

He laughed. "You read *Mary Poppins*?"

Carol raised her nose. "I most certainly did. I volunteered to read aloud during the library's story hour back home. Part of an effort to attract older children to reading."

"Very noble of you." Ted draped an arm around Carol's shoulders as they strolled. "Somehow, I can't see the chic French sweeping their chimneys."

She squirmed under the heavy weight of his arm. How could she politely get him to remove it? Had Chet ever put his arm around her? If he had, she hadn't minded.

They passed a poorly dressed man sprawled on a bench snoring, an empty wine bottle on the ground. His fumes assaulted Carol's nose. "You were saying something about chic, Ted?"

"Hmpf. He ought to go over there for some help." He nodded across the river.

"The Cathedral of Notre Dame." The name slipped reverently from Carol's lips. She aimed for the bridge. "I've heard the front façade features lots of statues. And don't those flying buttresses give it so much character?"

"I remember hearing something about that. They had to be added to keep the place from collapsing."

"And besides support, they gave the cathedral added grace and style. Otherwise it'd be just another big church. They give it a satisfying sense of symmetry, like wings about to take flight."

Ted laughed. "Aren't you waxing poetic?" His eyes gleamed as he looked at her. "I know real beauty when I see it."

Uneasiness skittered down her spine. She pulled away and headed for the street corner to cross. "Chet would appreciate the symbolism of wings."

A frown pushed away Ted's gleam. Carol bit back a smile. She couldn't let him forget she was interested in someone else. Maybe walking with him hadn't been a wise decision.

An antiaircraft gun sat surrounded by sandbags, a reminder that the war, now seemingly so far away, had recently been here. Snipers still fired potshots from windows. A German air raid had killed and wounded hundreds the night after the French parade. Yet here the world seemed at peace. Illusionary, of course.

Cooing directed her attention downward. A pigeon strutted about at her feet, its head tilted to fix its eye on her. She spread her fingers wide. "Sorry, bird. No handouts."

Overhead, swallows wheeled in place of German planes.

"I suppose you want to go in the church."

Carol looked up at Ted before checking for traffic, and back at Ted. She shrugged her right shoulder as she crossed the street. "We don't have to go inside. I'm guessing from your tone you don't care to."

"Donna would want to." Ted stared straight ahead.

"Who's Donna?"

"My wife."

Carol's feet stuck to the sidewalk. "Your *wife*?"

"Mm-hmm." He could be discussing the weather. His arm pressured her to keep moving.

She pulled away from him. "You're *married*?"

"Yeah." Now he looked back at her. "You coming?"

Birds still flew overhead. People still meandered along the river walkway. The sun still shone as it sank in the sky. And she was keeping company with a married man. Carol swallowed hard and resumed walking to the cathedral, but kept distance between them.

"What's the big deal?" Ted's brows bunched together over his nose. "We're in a different world here. It's not normal and the same rules don't apply. Besides, you've got some guy in the air force."

"Chet and I made no promises, no vows." Her chest hurt when she sucked in a breath. What had Gloria said? She could enjoy a friendship without getting serious. No complications. But Ted had crossed a line, putting his arm around her. Next he might want to kiss her. And all this time he had a wife waiting for him back home. Donna.

The dozens of statues scowled down at her in censure. Hard to tell, the way tears blurred her vision. She blinked them away. She had no reason to feel guilty, did she? This was supposed to be a casual friendship. She hadn't known she was spending time with another woman's husband. What was Donna like? Were they to meet in other circumstances, would they be friends?

"I need to get back to my quarters." What was the shortest route back to the Cite Universitaire? She'd hail a taxi if one was available, but lack of gasoline had the Parisians riding bicycles. She started off in what she hoped was the right direction.

Ted kept pace with her. "Why are you acting like this, Carol? We've done nothing wrong."

"I've done nothing wrong, but I feel like the 'other woman,' and that's not a good feeling." The university was north of here, right? She needed Chet's navigational skills. No, she needed Chet. She'd left England primarily because of her desire to experience her ancestral homeland, but also because of her fear of a wartime romance. A lot of good leaving England did in those respects. Admit it. She loved Chet Vogel.

Her brisk pace caused a stitch in her side, but she wouldn't slow down. Ted's grumbling spurred her on. Only her sense of decorum kept her from running when the university came within sight. At the door, she yanked the scarf from her neck and shoved it into Ted's hands. "Here, send this to Donna."

She found Gloria and Louise together in Gloria's room. "Did you know Ted's married?"

Their heads jerked up at her sudden appearance. "Married?" Gloria echoed. She stared for a moment, and then thrust her hands on her hips. "Men ought to be required to wear wedding rings, too."

For the first time since Ted's admittance, Carol's lips quirked upward. "Rings aren't required of women."

"And we've heard of plenty of men who have taken off their rings so they can fool around." Louise tucked a foot under her other leg. "They feel war entitles them to have fun over here."

"That's what Ted said." Carol looked at the Paris map spread out on Gloria's bed. "Planning something?"

Gloria clasped her hands together. "Tomorrow we'll go see the Eiffel Tower. We're expected to serve coffee and doughnuts to the brigade in the afternoon, but we'll have time to go up to the observation platform."

Thoughts of Ted evaporated as they planned their excursion. Before going to bed that night in her wonderfully private room, Carol started a letter to Chet. She stalled after "Dear Chet." I miss you? Having a great time? How are you? I've been such a fool? She stared at the blank page.

Writing was no use. She tucked the paper back into her musette bag and crawled into bed. He was probably settling in for the night, too, anticipating an early wake-up call. Where would the bombers be flying tomorrow?

Lord, keep him safe.

Chapter Thirty-Three

Near Cambria, France
Thursday, August 31, 1944

Chet stood perfectly still, one hand pressed against the wall, the other gripping the bedside table. Sweat beaded above his lip. He couldn't wipe it away without losing his balance. His shoulders sagged in defeat as he lowered himself to sit on the edge of the bed.

His hip wasn't the problem. That gained mobility every day. No, his thigh bone, the doctor decided, must be cracked. Crutches would enable him to move around if his arm wasn't in a sling. None were to be had anyway. The dark room remained his prison. At least Suzette left his door open, and the door opposite his room. Faint sunlight filtered in. A link to the outside world. And a conduit for the mouth-watering aroma of baking bread.

Skittering on the stairs announced Sisi's imminent arrival. He'd never been a cat fancier. Give him a dog any day. He'd wanted a Dalmatian as a boy. This little feline, though, proved to be a blessing. An orange streak rocketed into the room and zoomed up beside him on the bed. The frisky critter kept him sane through the long days of healing.

She jumped up on his wounded leg, causing him to wince. Placing her paws on his chest, she stretched up to get nose to nose with him. "Yow."

"Hello to you, too, Sassy." He ruffled her fur and tweaked her tail. "Have you been rearranging the furniture downstairs? I heard quite a clatter not too long ago."

"Yes, that was me, monsieur." A high-pitched voice preceded Suzette into his room. She placed a lunch tray on the table before turning a stern eye on the kitten. She resumed her normal voice. "Sisi knocked two full bowls of apples onto the floor." She nodded toward his lunch. "We made the bruised apples into a cobbler." She turned her disapproval to him. "And why are you sitting up instead of lying down?"

Chet raised his hands. "Don't fuss, Mother, don't fuss." Ignoring the crusty bread, he reached for the cobbler dish. "I am so tired of lying down. I'd hoped to get to the window, but that's not going to happen on my own."

"Certainly not." Suzette scooped up Sisi before she could get her whiskers in the cobbler. "You know what the doctor said. Any stress on the leg can worsen the break. You should be in traction." She sat down to visit while he ate, stroking the cat. "The battle line comes ever closer. Paris has been liberated. Soon all of France will be free again. By next week, surely. Everyone in Cambria tries to act unconcerned around the Boche, but inside we have much nervous energy. We could be caught in a crossfire or the Boche might destroy everything as they leave."

Next week. Chet lowered his spoon into the bowl. In just a few more days he'd be back with Americans. He'd be evacuated to England where he'd get good medical care. Maybe it wasn't too late to be sure his bones were healing properly. He could be spared a permanent limp or stiff shoulder.

"Is anything being done to make yourself safer?" What was diplomatic to ask? How had the French prepared for a hostile army to sweep across their land four years ago? Or had they even had time? Back home, Michigan touched the border with Canada. What a blessing to have a friendly neighbor.

"All the valuables are buried. Radios are hidden, as are rifles. So are young men who have come of age these past four years. Otherwise the Boche will send them to Germany to work, like Michel and a million others. Even when France is free, the prisoners will not be coming home. Not until Germany is overrun. Over a million and a half men from the army are prisoners, like Antoine." Lowering her head, she blinked rapidly. "They cannot be safe. Many are probably dead. I am so afraid for Antoine."

Chet couldn't reassure her. She was probably right. All their bombing missions targeting German industry put the French workers at risk. The Germans weren't likely concerned about providing foreigners with bomb shelters.

That afternoon, he awoke from a nap to find Sisi snoozing on his chest. As he petted her, loud purrs filled the room. She began kneading her paws. "Hey, wake up, Sassy. Your sharp little needles are drawing blood." He dumped her beside him and proceeded to torment her with a length of string. Every time she came close to snaring it, he yanked it away.

Downstairs, a door slammed. Loud voices called back and forth. Soon, heavy steps bounded up the stairs. A young man burst into Chet's room. The Chotars' nephew. Albert? Alphonse? Alain!

"*Excuses moi.*" He slid aside a panel, exposing a previously unseen closet. He pushed away a pile of clothing—Chet's uniform—and retrieved the gun Chet had worn in a shoulder holster. After sealing up the closet once again, he turned to Chet as he strode back to the door. He held up a hand. Quiet.

Chet didn't need the warning. Sisi had lain still like a miniature Sphinx while the nephew had been in the room. Now she stood up. Chet grabbed hold of her. "Yow."

"Shh, Sassy, we must be silent. Danger's nearby."

Rumbling filled her throat.

"Sassy, don't you know that little girls are made of sugar and spice and everything nice?" Alain had disappeared, but hadn't gone downstairs. Was he across the hall? Chet kept his voice at a whisper. "Settle down, Sassy. You're acting like a little boy who's made of snips and snails and kitty cat tails." He flicked her tail in her face and she batted at it, but stayed quiet.

Someone pounded on the door downstairs, and Chet tensed. That wasn't a friendly neighbor's knock. Next, an imperious voice made demands in a strident tone. Chet slowly inhaled. A German was in the house. He was trapped.

Sounds of a ruckus floated up. Someone was searching the house. Any minute they'd be coming upstairs. Chet turned down the wick on his lamp. What would they do if they found him? Drag him off to a prison camp when he couldn't even stand? Or shoot him in the bed? Kill the Chotars? Burn down their house? *Lord, help us.*

A new sound rang out. Hobnail boots on wooden steps. The door across from his slammed against the wall. Feet stomped around, but no angry words. Alain must not have stayed there, unless he'd hidden in another secret closet.

His door opened. With eyes nearly closed, Chet watched the man silhouetted in the dim light from the other room. The intruder snapped on a flashlight and waved the beam around. Naturally, it stopped on him.

"Aha."

That was the only word Chet recognized in the torrent that followed. The beam illuminated the lamp, and the man approached to turn up the wick. The dim light lit up the bright red armband sporting a crooked black cross. A skull ornament glinted off the band of the man's visor cap.

Monsieur Chotar appeared in the doorway just as the German reached across to strike Chet's injured arm with the flashlight. Another furious diatribe spewed out. Monsieur Chotar advanced into the room with a quiet rebuttal, his hands behind his back.

The German pulled out his gun and aimed it at Chet. "*Amerikaner?*"

The nephew had to be close by. Chet tossed Sisi into the German's face. The German yelled. Sisi yowled, her claws outstretched. Monsieur Chotar stepped forward, raised a cast iron skillet, and slammed it down on the German's head. The German collapsed in a heap. Sisi streaked out of the room and down the stairs, yowling all the way.

Alain stepped out of the opposite room. He gestured to someone below. More hobnail boots mounted the steps. Monsieur Chotar backed up alongside the door. A younger German entered the room. Behind him, Alain knocked off his helmet and hit him with the butt of Chet's gun. Down he went.

French two, Germans zero. No shots fired. Chet's lungs heaved as if he had run a mile.

Monsieur Chotar also breathed heavily. He nodded at Chet. "We make good team."

He moved to the doorway and called instructions to his wife. Then he and the nephew set about dressing Chet in his clothes. He might have been a ragdoll as they removed his left arm from the sling and eased it into his sleeve, followed by his right arm.

They stood him on his feet, one on either side, and shuffled to the door. The staircase was too narrow for three abreast. His hip throbbed with each jolt of their awkward descent, and he broke out in a sweat. They finally emerged into a sunlit room that caused Chet's eyes to tear up. The Chotars lowered him onto a chintz sofa before disappearing outside.

A low table held a pitcher and glasses filled with amber-colored liquid. Apple cider! He could use a drink. He pointed to the pitcher and raised his brows at Mrs. Chotar. She offered him a glass.

Chet knocked back a large swallow. The cider sizzled all the way down. His eyes flew wide open and tears trickled out. His throat had to be on fire. Steam probably escaped through his ears.

What was this stuff? It'd work just dandy as drain cleaner. Muffled laughter came from Mrs. Chotar. No wonder. His mouth drooped open and his tongue hung out.

Mr. Chotar and the nephew returned, Suzette right behind them. They hoisted him back on his feet and started for the door.

Suzette fluttered about. "Are you in pain? Your face is bright red."

"My throat's scorched from their rot gut." Chet's voice squeaked. His vocal cords must have been damaged, but at least he no longer felt pain in his leg. It was all in his throat.

They got through the doorway, and Chet was outside again for the first time in over two weeks. A light breeze caressed his flushed face. The scent of freshly mown grass tickled his nose. Familiar quacking drew his attention across the yard. A stout brick building stood in place of the red barns back home. Beyond that, an apple orchard boasted a bumper crop. No wonder the Chotars had served him so many apples.

A Mercedes convertible waited in front of the house. If only such luxury was for him, but the Chotars hustled him to a farm wagon. After a brief discussion, the nephew leaped onto the wagon bed and grasped Chet's upper right arm. With Mr. Chotar boosting him, Chet was dragged aboard like a sack of spuds.

While he lay panting, the nephew jumped down and helped Suzette up onto the wagon seat. This was goodbye. Mrs. Chotar had followed them out and stood now alongside her husband. Chet rose up on his elbow. He brought up his left hand as Suzette clucked to the horse. "Merci. Merci, Madame, Monsieur Chotar. Merci."

Mr. Chotar raised an arm in farewell before striding back to the house with his nephew. Mrs. Chotar remained in place, waving until the wagon rounded a bend and she disappeared from view.

Chet lay back and stared at the sky. Such a beautiful shade of blue. Danger may still surround him, but he was out of that stale, black attic room. Three birds wheeled in carefree circles through the azure sky. Oh, to do likewise.

"Suzette, what will the Chotars do with the Germans?"

She glanced back at him. "If possible, they will hide the auto. It would be a nice prize if they can keep it. They will ask the mayor for help with the Germans. They may decide to put them in their automobile and have them in an accident."

Though she didn't say so, it was a good bet the captives wouldn't survive the day. They wouldn't have hesitated to kill the Chotars and him. They were

Nazis, the cause of this war, guilty of all sorts of atrocities. Better they die than the Chotars.

"What was that apple drink Mrs. Chotar gave me?"

Suzette's shoulders shook in silent laughter. "Calvados." A laugh escaped. Her eyes gleamed when she turned to face him. "A very strong apple brandy. You are not used to powerful drink, hmm?"

Powerful drink indeed. Maybe they could use it for fuel.

Chet flinched at the distant boom of artillery guns. Using a bushel basket full of apples for leverage, he pulled himself upright and strained to see ahead. "Where are we going?"

"To find the American army. They are near Lille, northwest of here." Suzette grinned at him. "They will know what to do with you." Her smile faded. "We may meet Germans first. We will say you are going to see a specialist in Lille while we deliver apples. Your gun is in that basket. You may need to use it if there is only one, or maybe two, Boche, and they discover you."

The wisdom of wearing his uniform didn't seem very wise. Without it, he could be considered a spy and shot. Wearing it made him obvious as an American and endangered Suzette. He pawed through the basket. Locating his gun, he examined it. Ready to fire. Could he shoot a human being? He laid it aside. He found a work jacket and slipped into it. It was a poor disguise at best, but might pass a first glance inspection. An old hat with a sweat-stained band covered his military haircut. What rotten luck that he'd gotten a trim just before his last mission.

Suzette suddenly turned the horse off the road and under a tree.

"What's wrong?" Even as Chet spoke, the distinctive sound of airplane engines drew near. They came from behind, from German territory. Soon they roared over at treetop level, buffeting the wagon in their wake. "FW-190s. I saw enough of them on bombing missions."

Suzette guided the horse back to the road. "They will strafe anyone. Children playing, women driving wagons. They know their days here are numbered and they are taking revenge."

Like them, the planes headed for Lille. Trying to harass the Allied liberators, no doubt. Guns boomed again, from the same direction. They couldn't be far away. Chet leaned forward. Maybe even today he'd be in American care.

Another boom wafted through the air, different from the artillery bursts. Black smoke rolled skyward. Scratch one German fighter.

"That's the way. Show 'em who's boss." He swung a fist. He'd cheer, too, but that might be a tad ridiculous.

Suzette laughed at him. "You are bloodthirsty now, hmm? You must be in less pain."

Her words gave him pause. Bloodthirsty? Him? In the heat of an air battle, they tended to forget about the men in the fighters attacking them. Knock down the aircraft. If the pilot got out, fine. If not, oh well. Nothing personal. They had two goals on a mission. Deliver the bombs, and get back to base. That was war. Never seeing the enemy was fine with him.

Despite his desire to see everything around him, Chet's eyes grew heavy as the wagon rocked along. Suzette looked back to catch him in a jaw-popping yawn.

"Why don't you sleep? You have had a busy day after no activity, and the day is not over yet."

A busy day?

"Getting dressed, going downstairs and out to the wagon, being chauffeured to American lines, none of that on my own." His father would scorn him. Exhaustion pressed him down, and he pillowed his head on a blanket that smelled like it came from the barn. Not even the possibility of fleas could keep his eyes open. "Wake me if anything's about to happen."

"I have your countryman in my wagon."

Chet stirred. Did someone say something? Someone jiggled his left foot, causing pain to ricochet up to his hip. Wakefulness surged through him, and he found his gun in his hand, aimed at his new tormentor. Two soldiers in American uniforms stepped back and pulled their own guns, even as Suzette chastised them.

"Do not touch him like that. He is badly wounded." She scrambled down from the wagon and hurried around. She laid a light hand on his right leg. "Are you all right?"

He sucked in his lips to prevent a smile. After all the activity at the Chotars' house, this was nothing. Putting herself between the guns was gallant, but unnecessary. He laid his gun down.

The soldier who hadn't shaken him eased forward. "Who are you?"

"Lieutenant Chet Vogel, navigator with the 381st Heavy Bombardment Group, Ridgewell, England. I've been sheltered by this lady's future in-laws since the middle of August." He fished his dog tags out from under his shirt. "Do you have a doctor here?"

"He needs to be in traction." Suzette pointed to his hip. "Our doctor believes his thigh bone is broken near the hip, but Chet couldn't be taken anywhere for X-rays. He put Chet's shoulder back into place. He needs to keep it in the sling. Tell this to your doctor."

This time, Chet didn't try to hide his grin. "You heard the lady." He rolled himself upright and the soldier offered a helping hand until he sat against the wagon side. "Where's the front? Do we have a field hospital nearby?"

Not for the world would he admit in front of Suzette how much he ached.

"There's an aid station close by. We'll take you there." The soldier slung his rifle behind his back and nodded to his companion. Together they made a sling seat with their hands and carried him to their jeep.

Chet couldn't stop a groan as they hoisted him into the front seat. Too much jostling today. He'd almost welcome another swig of the Chotars' apple concoction burning a hole in his throat to numb his injuries.

"Suzette, will you take this jacket back to the Chotars? And give these guys the exact location where Max is buried?" He focused his wavering gaze on the soldier getting in behind the wheel. "Max Withers, the lead bombardier, didn't make it. Will you be sure Graves Registration knows where to find him?"

The other soldier wrote down Suzette's directions before leaping over the jeep's side into the back seat. Suzette leaned down to kiss him on both cheeks. She pressed a slip of paper into his hand. "The Chotars' address. Let us know how you do."

Thank goodness, someone was thinking clearly. Grandma would have been disappointed not to be able to write to the woman who had cared for him, even if she couldn't read English. He waved goodbye, his throat too clogged to speak. He'd likely never see Suzette again. What a strange acquaintance they'd shared. In the midst of a savage war, they'd taken him in at great risk to themselves. Not everyone would have had their courage. They could have turned him over to the Germans. He'd been blessed to fall into the Chotars' hands.

"We'll be at the aid station in about five minutes." The driver took his eyes off the road to study him. "You doing all right, sir? You've lost a lot of color."

Chet nodded. "Be good to lie down, have some morphine, stop the pain."

Soon, very soon. His ordeal was nearing an end. He'd be evacuated from France to the station hospital in Braintree. The doctors would make sure his leg healed properly and he'd walk again. His shoulder would regain its function. Grandma and Grandpa would be informed he was safe.

Carol was somewhere here in France. Be nice to see her again, but that wasn't likely. Her ancestors were probably a lot like the Chotars, extending hospitality to strangers. He'd have to write her about his French holiday.

He turned to the driver. "You can't imagine how good it is to be back in American hands."

Chapter Thirty-Four

Somewhere in France
September 2, 1944

Their Paris interlude ended, and the Red Cross girls followed the army back into the field.

"After all the hoopla over liberation, do you think the men will have a hard time returning to combat?" Carol would miss the bathroom facilities and clean sheets on a mattress.

"I don't think so." Louise paused as she negotiated potholes in the narrow road. "Some of the boys I talked with appreciated the cheers, but think the Parisians have the wrong idea. They act like the war is over."

"For them it is. V-Day will be anticlimactic." Carol adjusted the rearview mirror to watch Gloria struggle with the scarf she tried to cover her hair with. Riding in a jeep might be more comfortable than the clubmobile, but it offered no protection from the dust kicked up by the convoy. "Folks back home seem to think the invasion signaled an imminent end to the war, but the Germans certainly aren't ready to play dead."

"Euw. That guy is." Louise took a hand off the steering wheel long enough to point out the window.

A dead German lay sprawled on his back three yards from the road. One stiff hand reached upward. Flies appeared to be buzzing around the gaping mouth. Carol averted her gaze.

The convoy creaked to a halt. Another flat tire somewhere in the line, no doubt. Carol grabbed the chance to get out and stretch.

Gloria joined her, walking stiffly. "I've got dust in my hair, between my teeth, and seeped through my clothes. We're not far from where we'll be stopping for the night, and a river's supposed to be close by. I'm telling you right now, I've got first dibs on a dunking." She stalked ahead. "I'll see what's holding us up."

Carol clapped a hand over her mouth to keep from laughing while Gloria remained in earshot. They would all miss the luxury of a bathtub.

They stopped by the Oise River in the Compiegne Forest. Towering fir trees offered a fragrant respite from the smells of war and death. With a little imagination, Carol could pretend they were camping back home. Only the sound of distant shelling disrupted the peaceful tableau.

Their company of eight clubmobiles parted ways here. The *President Washington* and three others were assigned to serve an engineering brigade bound for Belgium. Their arrival delighted the engineers already encamped, and the men eagerly helped pitch their tents and build a latrine.

Carol, Gloria, and Louise made quick work of straightening up and cleaning the dust out of *George*. One doughnut rack had been jarred loose in the bumpy ride, and they couldn't get it to latch securely back into place.

Lionel, their GI guide, poked his head in. "Everything shipshape with *President Wash*?"

"No, everything isn't." Gloria shoved the tray into its slot and watched it bounce back. "How are you at fixing the tray rack?"

Lionel ambled in and poked around the malcontent tray. "Beats the, uh, heck out of me, ma'am, but you know what? We're surrounded by engineers. One of them boys oughta know how to fix this."

"Well, duh, why didn't we think of that?" Louise hurried out to find a fix-it man.

After the fiasco with Ted, Gloria had demanded he switch places with Lionel, assigned to the other half of their company. She and Louise also made sure Carol was never left alone with a man. The situation amused Carol, but it could likely become annoying.

Gloria turned to Lionel now. "So tell us, are you married?"

Carol cringed as a dull flush crept up Lionel's neck.

"No, ma'am, I am not. My girl didn't want a long-distance marriage. She writes now and again, but I think she's found some fellow at that factory she works at."

Carol's first thought of "Smart girl" faded at his last remark. "You're lucky to be free of her if she's so fickle." She put a hand on her hip, determined to avoid giving him the impression they were interested. "But I guess this means we can't plan on your receiving a box of brownies from home."

A slow grin filled his face. "No, ma'am, but I'll be glad to share my ma's chocolate prune cake with you."

Gloria's mouth twisted. "Prune?" She swallowed hard. "Quite alright, sergeant. I'm really not hungry anyway. Lots to do getting everything into place." She strode off toward the tent.

Lionel chuckled. "Ma's a great one for getting us to eat our vegetables and stuff we didn't like. She'd mix 'em in with dessert." He nodded to two men approaching with Louise. "Looks like your engineers are coming to the rescue. See you around, ma'am."

Carol hummed as she plunged a rag into a pail of water and began washing down what she could reach of *George's* exterior. Unlike in England, they weren't likely to be faulted for dirty clubmobiles. Not when everything else was dirty, including themselves. She'd barely gotten the windshield cleaned when five GIs stepped up.

"We can help you with that." A freckled redhead grabbed another old towel from the cleaning supply box and started drying the window. "By the way, I'm Tom, that's Gary, Smithy, Lance, and Dennis."

Carol had no idea who was who, but it didn't matter. His buddies brought up more buckets of water from the river and in short order, *President Washington* gleamed from roof to tires.

"Well, I'll be," one of the men said, bringing his bucket over to Carol. "How would you like fish for supper?" A small fish hardly bigger than a minnow swam in jerky movements in the few inches of remaining water.

Carol clapped her hands. "Oh, wonderful. We'll fry him up and have a feast." She reached in and plucked the guppy out by its tail between her thumb and index finger. Handling a large fish held no appeal, but the little miniature was too cute to bother her. "What a tasty-looking morsel."

She swung around to show the catch to the others. Tom stood directly behind her. She smacked him in the face with it. He swatted her hand away. The fish flew down into the tall grass.

"Hey, Tom, you didn't swallow it, did you? It was still alive." One of his pals clutched his own throat.

"What was that?" His words sounded strangled as his color continued to heighten. A hacking cough failed to produce the guppy.

"There went our chance to have fried fish for supper." The man who discovered the occupant in his bucket slapped Tom's back. "Don't worry, old boy. My cousin swallowed a goldfish and lived to tell the tale."

Another man handed him a canteen. "Here, drink up. Give the little fishy something to swim in."

Whether to provide a swimming pool or wash away the sensation of a slippery fish, Tom guzzled the water in big gulps.

Arms crossed, Carol watched the color recede from his face. "You didn't swallow the fish. You knocked it to the ground."

"Hey, miss, you're bleeding." One of the men pointed to her hand. He whirled to face Tom. "Look at that, Akers. You bit her."

Sure enough. Blood trickled from a small cut on the back of her index finger. As she wiped it off on a clean spot of her rag, it began to sting.

"Red Cross girl awarded Purple Heart after being bitten by GI." The man waved a hand through the air as though reading a headline.

"Come off it, Smithy. You only get the Purple Heart when you've been wounded by the enemy." The fisherman punched his buddy's arm.

"He bit her, didn't he? I'd say that makes him her enemy."

"More likely his fingernail got me." Carol hunched her shoulders. These soldiers acted like boys on a playground. "I think I'd better go see what my teammates are doing."

Before she could make her exit, the girls from the *West Virginia* joined them. "Whoa, look at *President Washington*." Hazel parked her hands on her hips. She leveled her gaze on Smithy. "It puts our clubmobile to shame."

He looked around and shrugged. "Come on, fellas. Three more beasts need a bath."

Carol hurried to her tent. Gloria jumped up from her cot at Carol's entrance. Shredded wrapping paper fluttered around her feet. "Mail found us. Just look at it all. We each got at least two packages and lots of letters. I don't know where to start."

Mail! Their first since arriving in France. Carol's packages came from her mother and sister Joanne. She ripped open her mother's box. "Mmm, I smell roses." She picked up two cakes of very fragrant soap. "Better than any French perfume." Next, she pulled out a pair of sheer stockings. She rubbed them against her cheek and sighed. "I doubt we'll have a need to dress up now."

Gloria upended one of her packages, oohing and aahing as the contents spilled on her cot. "A new comb, deodorant. Oh, a new lipstick." She immediately applied some and smacked her lips. Then she laughed. "I never would have thought I'd get so excited about Five & Dime stuff. Even writing paper. I think my folks are hinting I don't write often enough."

"All we can say is we're fine and having a wonderful time. The censors would delete everything else." Carol untied a paper-wrapped bundle. "Brownies. Yum." She bit into a piece and offered one to Gloria. Her mouth puckered. "Soap. It tastes like soap."

"Those fragrant fumes did them in." Gloria gave back the brownie she'd nibbled. "Maybe Lionel would like them. He eats cake with prunes."

Louise burst into the tent. "Guess what?" She stopped short at the sight of her mail-strewn cot. "Well, joy in the morning. My friends and family haven't forgotten me."

She pounced on her letters, spreading them out to read return addresses.

"Louise, what's your big news?" Carol paused in opening her sister's package. "Did the Germans surrender after all?"

Puzzlement furrowed Louise's brow when she looked up from sorting her mail. "What? Oh! No K rations tonight, girls. We'll be eating at the brigade's mess and they're making spaghetti. And for breakfast tomorrow, we might even have flapjacks with the porridge."

Carol's mouth started watering.

Several camouflage tarps covered the open air mess. The mass-produced spaghetti had an institutional flavor rather than seasoned with her mother's special Italian sauce, but Carol didn't mind. Sitting in a grassy field, she balanced her mess kit on her knees and savored the meal. "Much better than canned meat and dog biscuits."

"Dog biscuits. That's good. The whole K meal is like dog food." Gloria scooped up a forkful of canned peas, only to watch half of them fall off. "Well, no, I can't include the ration of four cigarettes and toilet paper that come in a K box. I've never seen a dog smoke a cig."

"Did you say this is like dog food?" A corporal plopped down near them and proceeded to devour his meal. "It's not bad for army grub."

His buddy joined him. "The ladies don't like our supper?"

"They're saying this tastes like dog food."

The newcomer puffed up like a rooster. Before he could vent his indignation, Gloria shook her fork at the corporal. "That is not what I said. The K rations are like dog food."

"You don't like Spam?" The newcomer dug into his spaghetti and spoke around a mouthful. "I think it's great. We never had that at home."

No loss there. Carol took her empty mess kit to a barrel of steaming, sudsy water and plunged it in, swishing it around. Then she dunked it in the barrel of rinse water. How satisfactorily the cleanup sanitized her kit she didn't know, but she hadn't gotten sick yet.

A heavy explosion brought heads up around the mess. Everyone rushed up a knoll to locate the action. In a distant valley, a pair of American fighter-bombers flew around a towering column of black smoke. One commenced a steep dive, and Carol saw a bomb fall away as the plane soared back up. His mate nosed down in turn. More smoke billowed upward. More planes joined the fracas.

"Whooee." The Spam-lover stood beside her. "Betcha a bunch of Jerries had their last meal of kraut."

Carol jumped at another boom. Their big anti-aircraft guns were firing. Hands started pointing south. Sure enough. A German plane had come to investigate the action. Two of the American planes peeled off to challenge the intruder, their machine guns firing. The German turned their way. Carol looked around wildly. Watching the show had left them all exposed.

Suddenly, the German plane burst into flame and spiraled down. One man bailed out. Too low. His chute wouldn't open in time. The plane slammed into the ground close enough that the earth shook beneath Carol's feet.

Some men raced for jeeps. Others sprinted for the plane. Carol turned away.

The next morning, the *President Washington* passed the wreckage on the way to serve the men. Twisted, blackened metal bore no resemblance to the plane they had seen fall from the sky. Louise idled the clubmobile. "I heard there were four bodies burnt to a crisp in the plane, and the one who jumped didn't survive either."

At their first stop, Carol spotted the men who had washed the clubmobiles. The fisherman joined her and took one of the doughnuts. "I've got something for you to replace the fish Akers lost." He dug something out of a pocket and dropped it onto her tray. "I got it from the Kraut who jumped out of the burning plane. He's dead and won't miss it."

He moved on to get a cup of coffee.

Shifting her load, Carol picked up a wedding ring. Yesterday, this had adorned the hand of a German flier. Somewhere in Germany, a woman now waited in vain for him to come home. The ring bore an inscription, a date. 15-6-1944. Newlyweds.

Chapter Thirty-Five

Somewhere in France
Sunday, September 3, 1944

How peaceful Chet's dark attic room had been compared to a military installation. The tent that housed the collecting station never quieted. The guy in the next cot never stopped moaning in his semi-conscious condition. A nurse insisted on waking Chet to stick a thermometer in his mouth every time he finally got to sleep.

"I'm not sick." He spoke through clenched teeth, turning his head to get away from the poking thermometer. "I was wounded a long time ago. Right now I'd just like a little rest."

The nurse glared at him. Apparently the freshly wounded didn't thwart her efforts like he did. "I need to record your temperature."

Keeping his lips firmly pressed together, he glared back.

A doctor rose from the patient he'd been tending across the tent. "Leave him be, Mavis. He's been in French care for a while and is here only until we can get him into the pipeline to go to a hospital."

"Braintree Station Hospital. I'm based at Ridgewell in England." Chet's nightmares included being kept in an army hospital and shuffled into an infantry outfit upon recovery. He was an airman.

The doctor pulled up a stool and settled down for a visit. "You arrived just a few minutes too late for the last transport to the clearing station. We'll put you on the first one in the morning. Your casualty ticket lists Braintree as your final destination. I suspect after you arrive at the field hospital and are X-rayed, you'll be evacuated right away. Field hospitals move around too much to keep anyone in traction, if that's what you require." He stood and patted Chet's shoulder. "By the end of the week, you should be back near your base."

If Chet's memory was correct, Suzette had delivered him to the GIs who delivered him here on Saturday. That meant today was Sunday. Back in England by the end of the week? Six more days? His chest rose and fell with his sigh. Distant rumbling moved closer. Rain spattered on the tent. A thunderstorm, not artillery fire at least, but still something to keep him awake.

The doctor stopped by again as Chet ate his breakfast, augmented by an apple from the Chotars' orchard. "The battle line is moving steadily eastward, and we need to follow the combat units. We've got an ambulance heading for the field hospital for supplies. We'll send you with it since you're not our usual battlefield casualty. You can bypass the clearing station."

Chet nodded, looking at his apple. The Chotars could be having a rough time today.

Lying on a litter in the back of an ambulance proved much more comfortable than sitting in a jeep. Chet dozed on and off until the ambulance creaked to a stop. Leaning up on his elbow, he saw an undamaged building that looked deserted.

"I don't understand it." The driver got out, took off his cap, and scratched his head. He leaned back in. "The hospital must have moved forward already. I'll go see if anyone's still around."

Chet lay back. His head started to throb. Moving only his eyes, he searched for a first aid kit. Nothing.

The driver came back and opened the back door. "A Frenchie pointed that way. We'll have to chase 'em down."

"Do you have any aspirin?" The very idea of chasing across rough roads ratcheted up the tempo of Chet's headache.

"Well, no, I don't." The driver stepped back. "Are ya sick?"

"No, I've got a headache. I need some aspirin."

"Sorry. This is transportation only, not an aid station. We'll find that hospital as quick as possible." The driver slammed the door shut.

Chet closed his eyes. He missed sassy Sisi, missed her motor purring loudly on his chest, her little needle claws kneading through his shirt. Petting her soft, silky fur would be a better cure than any painkiller.

The road suddenly got bumpier with a rhythmic thump, thump, thump. "Ah, man." The driver banged his hand against the steering wheel. He hopped out and, a moment later, flung open the back door. "We've got a flat tire."

Chet shaded his eyes against the sudden brightness. "Do you have a spare?"

"No, I don't." The man crossed his arms and glowered at him like it was his fault.

"Flag down the next vehicle and get help."

The defiance slipped. "We don't seem to be on a main road. I haven't seen anyone in a long time."

Chet massaged his temples. "Find some help, Sergeant. Walk back to the main road if you have to. We cannot stay here for the rest of the war." He felt around beyond his head and located his Colt .45. He allowed a small smile when the sergeant jumped back, his eyes widening.

"You can leave that door open so I get a bit of air." And be less likely to be taken by surprise. No Germans should be around, but Frenchmen unhappy with the war destroying their homes might feel vengeful. Or deserters eager for transportation.

The sergeant looked up and down the road before he headed back the way they'd come, shoulders sagging. His pace rivaled a turtle's. This was going to be a long day.

Staring at the roof, Chet calculated the number of missions his old crew likely had. He'd been gone three weeks. Good chance they'd still be at Ridgewell. Captain McQuaid should also still be there, but he'd have a new navigator. Didn't matter. Chet struggled to sit up in the confines of the ambulance. It'd be a long time before he could fly again.

The ambulance was devoid of anything to occupy his time. Stripped clean to load up with supplies. He should have asked the driver if he had a book or writing paper, something, before sending him off. His first order of business when he finally got to a hospital would be to write to Grandma and Grandpa.

What had they thought when they got word he was missing? Grandma probably cried. Grandpa would have stared out the window at the evergreen growing across the street. Once again, Chet felt Grandpa's hand on his shoulder. Did Grandpa remember his words as he stared at the tree? "That tree's been on God's green earth longer than I have, son. It's seen children grow up and move away. It has survived thunderstorms and freezing winters. It'll last longer than any of us."

They would have called Pastor Mitleiter, and he would have dropped everything to come and spend time with them. It being summer, they would have walked through the neighborhood streets, talking about God's promises, reminiscing about Chet's growing-up years, praying for him. The telegram would have said he was missing, not dead. They would pray that he was safe and uninjured. If he was injured, they'd have asked for someone to care for him. If he was dead, they would take comfort knowing he was with Jesus and Mom, and they would one day join them.

A tear trickled down Chet's cheek. "Your prayers were answered, Grandma and Grandpa. You prayed for the Chotars, for Suzette, and even for Sisi, a little kitten with a big heart. I'm all right, and you'll get another telegram real soon, telling you that."

The sun beamed down from directly overhead. The temperature couldn't be much over seventy degrees, but the ambulance heated up like an oven, even with the door open. Chet munched on the last of the Chotars' apples and pitched out the core. The driver should have found someone by now. Sure would be nice if they brought back a canteen of water. His stomach growled. Food would be appreciated, too.

He must have dozed. He dreamt an old man peered down at him. Lethargy pinned his head to the litter. When he opened his eyes again, no one was around. Too bad. He would have been glad for even a sip of rotgut cider to get rid of the gummy feeling in his mouth. Where was that driver anyway?

A fly buzzed in and bounced around on the roof. Buzz, bump, buzz, bump.

"Get out of here." Chet waved his hand, trying to shoo it out the door. The fly buzzed his head. Gritting his teeth, he wrapped his fingers around his gun. He aimed at the pest, and laughed. No doubt the army had a few rules about putting unnecessary holes in the roofs of its ambulances, not to mention damaging his hearing. "You're lucky, fly, I'm so conscientious."

A new sound challenged the buzzing. Raising his head, Chet spotted a jeep barreling down the road. Finally. It skidded to a stop ten feet away, and two enlisted men hopped out. They approached cautiously, one with his rifle ready. Chet lowered his Colt to the floor before they came around to the door.

"Do you have water?" His voice croaked like he hadn't spoken for days.

The men exchanged glances and stepped up to the rear. Their eyes scanned the interior. "Are you alone?" The corporal pointed his rifle down, but kept a finger on the trigger. "Who are you?"

Chet sighed. Formalities. Of course. "Lieutenant Chet Vogel, 381st Bomb Group of the Eighth Air Force, England."

"Vogel?" The private wanted to say more, but the corporal flicked his hand.

"What are you doing here?" Suspicion colored the corporal's tone. The air force was supposedly lax in military formality, but the army was worse. These enlisted clowns had yet to show any respect for an officer.

"What am I doing here?" Chet bit back a grimace as he hoisted himself up on his elbow. "I am waiting for the driver to bring back help and get the flat tire changed. Didn't he tell you?"

"We didn't see no driver. An old Frenchman told us this here ambulance was abandoned with a half dead soldier in it." The private put his hand on the door, causing the corporal to jump back. The private showed impatience. "He moved and nothing happened."

The corporal looked around again. "There ain't any booby traps here?"

"There's only a hot, hungry, hurting navigator here who would like a drink of water." Chet would have picked up his gun, but that corporal looked a little too eager for an excuse to fire his rifle.

The private ran back to the jeep and retrieved a canteen. He offered it to Chet like a puppy wanting to please. "We hafta be careful with equipment left lying around. The Krauts like to booby trap everything. You find a nice staff car, open the door, and kablooey. Last thing you ever do. They even booby trap their dead soldiers they leave behind. Even the wounded ones." He eyed the corporal. "We can't be too careful."

The water was warm and somewhat stale, but sure felt good sliding down Chet's throat. He drained all but one last swallow. "Got any aspirin?" The private shook his head, so Chet gulped the last drops. He could stand anything for another hour on that bit of refreshment.

The clowns stared at him. Apparently, the corporal had decided the only thing likely to go kablooey was Chet's temper, and waited for him to take the lead. He handed back the empty canteen. "I was on my way to the evacuation hospital, which seems to have relocated. Know where it is?"

The clowns shook their heads in unison. With the corporal struck mute, the private offered a suggestion. "We can take you back to our position. We're part of a 90-mm gun battery. Our jeep has litter brackets, so you can stay lying down, sir."

At least he'd get a breeze on his hot face. Chet tried not to cringe when the private bounced into the ambulance and grabbed the head of the litter. With the corporal pulling from the foot, they slid the gurney out and marched to their jeep. Hoisting him up across the back seat to lock into the brackets proved to be a simple exercise. Either they were stronger than they looked or he'd lost a lot of weight since joining the service. The past three weeks of inactivity must have reduced his muscles to jelly.

The private hopped in behind the wheel. "I'll take it kinda slow, so you don't have to worry none about falling off." The jeep jerked into gear and jumped forward. The kid made a tight U-turn that had Chet clutching the edge of his litter.

"I thought you just said you'd go slow." The corporal kept his rifle in hand and his head swiveling, watching for any threat. He glanced at Chet. "Our battery is dug in about a mile and a half from here. The battery commander will find someone to get you back on your way. Do you know the name of your driver?"

"Michaels or Michaelson." Chet closed his eyes against the sun. He failed to picture the missing man. The only features he dredged up were brown hair and ears that stuck out. He turned his head to the side. "Tell me about this gun battery of yours."

"We got four of the big guns, all planted about fifty yards apart. Each gun has a thirteen man crew. Carter here brings up shells from the storage pit. I'm the gunner. We work at night. That's when the Krauts like to come over to bomb and strafe because our own planes aren't going to find them in the dark. The guns need constant attention, so half of us work on them in the morning while the other half sleeps, and then we switch places in the afternoon."

The corporal yawned wide enough to crack his jaw. Must have been time for him to turn in. Instead, he'd been sent out to investigate an abandoned ambulance. No wonder he hadn't been chummy. Chet closed his eyes again, hoping they'd have some chow to share.

"Heh, heh, heh. Won't they be surprised when we come in with Lieutenant Vogel? Heh, heh." The private's cackle popped Chet's eyes open. What was so funny about his name?

The passing field snagged his attention. Vines laden with grapes stretched back a hundred yards. Women harvested purple-blue clusters. Must be part of a vineyard for some of that famous French wine.

The corporal interrupted his musing. "There's our field."

At first, Chet saw nothing but a lumpy meadow of trampled brown grass. Closer examination revealed the lumps to be camouflage netting. One net covered pup tents. From the smells emanating around another, it covered a field kitchen. His stomach growled as they passed by.

"Where ya going? We need to deliver him to the exec." When the private pointed one way, the corporal pointed the other. "First find O'Dell. You can tell the sergeant later."

The private veered away from the gun on the far side of the field and headed for a larger tent erected between two towering fir trees. The corporal climbed out and saluted a lieutenant sitting in front of the tent at a makeshift table made of crates. The driver hopped out and raced off in the direction he'd wanted to go.

"So, Barkley, you found the abandoned ambulance?" The lieutenant rose and sauntered over to stare down at Chet.

"It has a flat tire and the driver went to find help, but we didn't pass him. He was taking Lieutenant Vogel here to the field hospital to get back to England, but the hospital moved." Corporal Barkley continued his report, but Chet stopped listening.

The lieutenant's brows had bounced upward upon hearing the Vogel name. Maybe they'd been briefed to be on the lookout for him. Seemed highly unlikely an artillery unit would hear about a missing ambulance and its patient, but no other explanation came to mind.

"Do you need medical aid?" The lieutenant searched his face as though looking for answers without asking questions.

"Just food. I could really use some chow."

As Chet answered, another jeep from the far side of the field pulled up alongside. He didn't pay attention until he heard an incredulous voice. "*Chet?*"

He turned to the newcomer and a jolt rocked him to the tips of his toes. He looked up into a face from his past. His brother Nate.

Chapter Thirty-Six

Somewhere in France
Sunday, September 3, 1944

The combat chaplain created an altar by placing candleholders and a brass cross on the hood of his jeep. The large attendance at his service included soldiers who couldn't speak a complete sentence without swearing, men who had wives back home and girlfriends here, and GIs who bragged about how many of the enemy they had killed. Now they sat quietly at a religious service, guns across their laps. Maybe their experiences during the last three months since the invasion had shaken vague notions of God into stark reality that death could indeed be a heartbeat away.

Tears pressed against Carol's eyes during their *a cappella* rendering of "When I Survey the Wondrous Cross." The cross on the hood wavered as her vision blurred. It took little imagination to picture the Savior hanging there, dying for a world intent on killing everyone.

In the not-too-far distance, artillery guns boomed, adding discordant notes to their song. At that very moment, people were being ripped into eternity. Into either everlasting joy or everlasting torment. Carol looked at the sea of faces surrounding her. Many of these young men wouldn't live to the end of the year.

She focused on the chaplain, trying to make his words drown out the thoughts of gloom. "'Consider the lilies of the field, how they grow.' Our Lord spoke these words in the middle of a sermon on trusting God for the things we need. In times of trouble, we're tempted to run somewhere, do something. Stop, Jesus says. Look at a flower, listen to a bird, watch a cloud redesign itself in the sky. And remember, God is with us always, and He loves us." His gaze roved amongst his congregation. "He loves you."

Overhead, a bird chirped. Carol looked up into the tree. Why wasn't the bird frightened away by the shelling? Too distant maybe. But the tiny creature illustrated the chaplain's homily. While not exactly the same as keeping soldiers alive in wartime, God fed the birds though they didn't sow or reap.

The service over, she took her time returning to the clubmobile encampment, carrying that thought further. God was with her. She dared to dream of a future with Chet Vogel, but if that didn't happen, God had a different life in mind for her. The thought didn't appeal to her, but a long-ago Sunday school teacher's favorite saying promised that God knows better than you do.

She paused before ducking into her tent. Holding Chet at arm's length wasn't keeping her heart safe. Staying in touch would be difficult, but necessary. That's what people who cared about each other did. How glib she'd been, telling Irene if they were meant to be together, God would make it happen. Chet probably thought France meant more to her than he did. *Well, it did when I ran away, didn't it?* She'd write him tonight and post her letter at the next mail drop they found.

Carol entered the tent to find mayhem. Gloria had all the boxes of supplies they'd been using as tables lined up at the door. Her bedroll was tied up at one end of the cot while she stuffed belongings into her musette bag.

"Let me guess. We're moving on."

Gloria nodded. "The brigade's been ordered to advance, right after lunch." Her hands stilled from rolling up stockings. "Kind of funny, really. Stop the war, it's time to eat."

Carol got busy packing her own gear. She took her bedroll outside for a vigorous shaking. It appeared clean, but she'd been feeling itchy all day. Something must have been sharing it with her. She rummaged through her toiletry bag. "Nice of the army to provide us with this powder for body crawling insects." She sprinkled a liberal dose on her calves. "Some cooties have been making a meal out of me."

"Yeah, I'm afraid to ask what they are. Remind me of the chiggers back home. Never see 'em, but you sure do feel the results." Gloria started scratching her lower back. "I hope they bother the Germans as much as us."

Louise waltzed into the tent. "Guess what I heard?" She didn't give them time to guess. "We'll be staying in a house tonight. Ooo-la-la. I hope it has running water. Hot running water. Electricity. And warmth. That would be swell."

"And a butler who serves breakfast in bed." Carol smiled as she rolled up her clean trousers in her bedroll.

"Oh, that won't be necessary." Louise hooked her mess kit to her belt and grinned back. "Wouldn't be bad though. Come on, grub's ready and it's likely to go fast with everyone rushing to get ready to pull out. We can drop off some of this with *George* on the way." She hoisted a supply box and disappeared.

Carol tied up her bedroll. "More likely grub will go fast because we'll be on K rations for a while if the mess kitchen doesn't have time to set up."

Like Louise, she and Gloria grabbed boxes to load up.

A picnic atmosphere prevailed over the field where they ate. Sitting on a cleaning rag to protect her clothes from grass stains, Carol hoped no crawling insects joined her. Yellow jackets descended on them, eager to share their food. She speared carrots on her fork, shooed away a pest, and popped the bite into her mouth before it could return.

"Spotter planes are dropping flares to the east." A GI stood, pointing in the distance. "That must be where the German army is."

An arc of artillery fire flashed toward the lingering flares. Soon smoke billowed up.

"We're going to find a mess when we get to that spot."

Carol turned to the speaker. A lanky technical sergeant bit into his bread and chewed. A rumble rolled over the field. The sergeant smiled. "Took a long time for the sound to reach us. Reckon it's three, four miles away. The Krauts are retreating, and we're sure to find carnage. They take their time as they run away. They're rigging explosives now to slow us down."

Another screech filled the air, much closer, and everyone instinctively ducked. Someone had said, "You never hear the one that kills you." How did anyone know that? If everyone died from shells they didn't hear, how did they tell the living they hadn't heard it?

The screeching continued, and heads rose. That wasn't the usual sound of incoming shells. To

Carol's right, Hazel of the *West Virginia* bounced on her knees. "A ye-ow shacket shung me." Her hands fluttered about her mouth.

Beside her, her teammate Jean wrung her hands. "She didn't see a yellow jacket on her food. She bit it and it stung her tongue."

Men jumped up, offering solutions.

"Drink some coffee. The heat will melt away the pain."

"No, she needs ice."

"Where we gonna find ice?"

When Carol burned her arm at Ridgewell, the boys had frosted her with butter.

The lanky GI chuckled. "I'm sorry she got hurt, but I sure am glad we didn't come under attack. That'd be a fine howdy-doo. We clobber the Krauts and they strike back." Laying aside his mess kit, he pulled a small notebook and pencil from a pocket. Swatting away a yellow jacket buzzing about his lunch, he made rapid strokes. He ripped out the page and handed it to her. "Give this to your friend, will you? Someday she'll be able to laugh about this."

Carol grinned. He'd sketched a yellow jacket wearing a devilish grin and a tiny German uniform.

Carol's lunch companion was right. Disabled German equipment cluttered an abandoned campsite. A knocked-out truck alongside the road still smoldered, its heat reaching out as the clubmobile passed. Interspersed among the artillery pieces, the horses that had pulled the Germans' wagons lay dead.

The carnage did slow them down. Before the bulldozer leading the convoy could shove wreckage off the road, the engineers had to neutralize booby-traps. From their position at the end of the column, the clubmobilers heard explosions as some detonated.

They kept their windows rolled up because of the cooler weather, but the stench of cordite seeped in. Gunpowder and…blood. Lying in a dark red pool, a grizzled German stared unseeing, an expression of vague surprise frozen on his face. Except for the blood he lay in, he bore no evidence of wounds. His back must tell a different story.

Gloria's face paled. "I wish we hadn't eaten before pulling out."

"Don't look." Easy for Louise to say. She had to keep her eyes on the road.

"I can't not look." Carol's hands ached from clenching them so tight. "It's like the morbid curiosity that makes you twist your head to see everything at the scene of a car accident. It's gruesome, but you're powerless to look away." She swallowed hard at the sight of a dismembered body, tendons trailing from the severed arm. Her stomach started to spin.

The jeep in front of them stopped. When Louise opened her door, the driver called, "Stay inside, all of you."

The clubmobile girl riding with him turned to them. "That man lying by the road up ahead is still alive. He needs help."

Carol squinted at another bloody body. Sure enough, the fingers feebly waved.

The jeep driver hopped out, telling the girl to get out and duck behind the jeep. He strode back along the road. "Ah, this will do." He hefted a large stone. "You watch. The Jerries leave behind their critically wounded who are sure to die and set them up to take a few Americans with them. The best thing to do is put them out of their misery. Here's for a strike."

Holding the stone up, he swung it back and then bowled it toward the German.

The stone hit the man's foot. His leg jerked, and he exploded.

Gasps filled the clubmobile. Nothing remained on the smoldering ground that bore resemblance to a human being. The driver raised his hands in victory, sporting a satisfied smirk as he headed back for his jeep.

"It ought to be raining, because heaven is surely weeping." Carol clutched her throat, trying not to gag. She reached up to brush back a lock of hair. Her hand fluttered like a leaf on a windy day. "He killed him."

"Yeah." Gloria stared straight ahead.

"He had no choice." Louise drummed her fingers on the steering wheel. "The Kraut was dying. He put him out of his misery. Think of it as mercy."

"We don't know his wounds were fatal." Gloria's fingers kneaded her legs. "Maybe the Germans were simply in too much of a hurry to retreat and left behind their wounded."

"They…" Carol had to clear her throat. "They had time to booby trap him."

Louise nodded. "Exactly. That guy knew he was dying and he aimed to take as many Americans with him as possible."

Late in the day, a subdued group of girls arrived at what had once been a beautiful chateau. Until recently, it had been occupied by Germans and they'd made a shambles of it. A tapestry had been torn down from the wall and placed on the floor as a rug, now covered by muddy boot prints. Cognac bottles lay strewn about, most of them empty, but from the stains and smells in their vicinity, they'd recently been full. One door remained shut. The odor emanating from behind it suggested the Germans used the room for their latrine.

The girls brought in their bedrolls, but before they could sleep, they had work to do. "We'll be expected to serve coffee and doughnuts tomorrow, so let's get *George* cleaned up now and make sure the doughnut machine is in working order." Gloria stared out the window at the clubmobile. She gave herself a shake. "Right now."

Lionel pumped several buckets of water for them, which they boiled. From the four clubmobiles dispersed in the estate's yard, the lilting strains of "This Is My Father's World" rose. Carol joined in, singing halfheartedly. As much as she loved the song, she hadn't heard much music of the spheres today. She concentrated on dismantling the field range, using a small brush to whisk away every last trace of dust.

The birds their carols raise. Well yes, during the chaplain's service, the birds did provide a soothing counterpoint to the shelling. A yawn turned into a sigh. Her letter to Chet would have to wait.

Though the wrong seems oft so strong, God is the ruler yet. Carol sat back on her heels, rubbing gritty fingers together. Yes, God still reigns. The day had been full of horror, but no one in their convoy had been hurt. She put the range back together and admired its gleam. What they needed now was fresh water to boil for shampoos, sponge baths, and laundry.

Cold winds blew the temperature down. Carol dressed hurriedly Monday morning. On her way to the kitchen, she passed an office, probably the landowner's den. This room appeared less ransacked, and she tiptoed in. The desk had been hurriedly cleared. Scraps of paper, a pencil, and an overflowing ashtray remained. She pulled open a drawer, assuming the German officer who used the room had taken anything of value. She sucked in her breath. The second drawer down held a stack of Nazi letterhead. The boys often needed paper for writing home. What a kick for their folks to get letters decorated with swastikas. She pulled out the stationery and rushed back to her cot before going to the kitchen.

Her jest about a butler to serve breakfast failed to materialize. Instead, she cranked back the lid on a can of chopped ham and eggs, and sniffed. The smell didn't tantalize her. She fished around the K ration box, and found the fruit bar and compressed cereal bar. The slim box of four Chesterfield cigarettes got tossed into their kitty. "Maybe today we'll find a

French farmer who'll trade some real eggs for these cigs."

"Or fresh milk. I never realized how much I like milk until I got to England and rarely saw it." Gloria dropped a water purification tablet into a kettle she'd scrounged in the chateau's kitchen. "Now collecting everyone's powdered coffee for this morning's brew."

Carol offered her packet. "If we served this stuff to the men with their doughnuts..."

"They'd riot, that's what they'd do." A girl from another clubmobile slumped at the table, her eyes at half mast. "We really ought to treat ourselves to some of our good coffee first thing in the morning to get ourselves going. Oh, look." She perked up. "There's a cat."

Carol spied the creature, and yanked her feet up from the floor. "That's not a cat. It's a gigantic rat."

Squeals echoed through the room as half a dozen grown women hopped up on the table or stood on their chairs. Carol tucked her feet under her, Indian style. She wanted to laugh at the ludicrous sight, but didn't want anyone suggesting she do something about the intruder.

From her perch by the window, Gloria rapped on the glass and shrilled, "Lionel, get in here."

Their stalwart GI hustled in and stopped short, staring at them.

"The rat. Get the rat." Six voices snapped him out of his bafflement. His eyes bugged at the rodent twitching its nose at him. He unslung his rifle. Carol clapped a hand over her eyes. She heard a scuffle and a couple thuds.

"Okay, ladies. Anyone care for some fresh meat for breakfast?"

"Euw, get it out of here." Just coming into the kitchen, Louise jumped out of the way. "If there's one, there must be more."

Breakfast became a hurried affair. Before heading out to the clubmobile, Carol retrieved her bedroll and other belongings. No point in tempting any friends of the rat. Everyone else followed her lead.

The morning hours passed quickly as they made the day's supply of doughnuts. Gloria pulled out a list. "Here's our assignment for today. Mostly engineering units working at clearing out mines and filling in bomb craters but, for our last stop, we're also to serve an artillery unit."

At every stop, the first question Red Cross girls heard was invariably, "Where ya from?" As *President Washington* arrived at its third stop, Louise announced, "I'm so tired of saying I'm from Bakersfield. Next time we're asked, I'll say I'm from Belgium."

The first fellow to step up asked the question. Louise didn't miss a beat. "I'm from Belgium. Where are you from?"

Her ploy backfired when the fellow's buddy lit up. "You're from Belgium, Wisconsin? Say, that's great. I'm from Fredonia. I meet a lot of guys from around Milwaukee, but I've never found anyone so close to home."

Louise's smug smile dissolved. She cast a frantic glance at Carol. Carol shrugged. Her friend would have to find her own way out of this quandary. She held out two steaming cups. "Who'd like some hot coffee on this chilly day?"

A wrong turn delayed their finding the artillery unit. Riding in the jeep with their guide, Gloria started fretting. "We need to be back before dark. Maybe we should give up on this one."

Carol studied the map across her knees. "It should be just ahead on the left."

"So it is." Relief filled the driver's voice as he steered into an open field.

A large tent stood between two trees at one side. Various vehicles hid under camouflage nets. No one seemed to be around. Carol and Gloria got out of the jeep when Louise pulled up alongside them in *George*.

A cry rang out. "American girls."

Suddenly dozens of men materialized and stared.

"Anyone interested in doughnuts and coffee?" Gloria winked at Carol and they hurried into the clubmobile to raise the side into a serving window, and lower the counter. A line quickly formed.

Carol set the first tray of doughnuts on the counter, looking out across the field. She froze and blinked. Surely she was seeing an apparition.

Chapter Thirty-Seven

Somewhere in France
September, 1944

"Nate?" Chet rubbed his eyes and looked again. "Nate? What are you doing here?" More than a dozen years had passed since he'd seen his second oldest brother. Maturity hadn't erased the devil-may-care aura of the boy who'd delighted in scaling a ladder up to the roof and surveying the neighborhood from the peak. For years, Chet had believed a neighbor's words to be prophetic. Nate had frightened their mother into an early grave.

"What am I doing here? This is where I belong. Better question is, what are you doing here, little brother?" Nate Vogel reflected Chet's shock. He touched tentative fingers to Chet's shoulder, as though needing to verify he was real. His gaze worked downward, pausing at Chet's insignia. "You're an officer. Dad would spit nails if he knew."

"He does know." Pleasure again tickled Chet's soul. "Len stopped to see Grandma and Grandpa when he was stateside on convalescent leave. That night, Dad called and Grandpa confirmed Len's big news. He was speechless."

A bark of laughter erupted from Nate. "I'll bet." He nodded to the arm sling and the splint securing Chet's leg. "What happened?"

Chet dragged in a deep breath. "I'm lead navigator on a B-17 crew." A low whistle alerted him to his audience of artillerymen. "We bombed Cologne on August 15th. The Germans like to go after the lead plane, so they came after us."

The day rushed back to him. "We must have gotten a burst of flak under a wing. The plane flipped over. Captain McQuaid regained control, but not before the bombardier and I were tossed out through the nose window. It had already been shattered in an earlier burst. I think being thrown against the edge of the nose before falling out is when I was injured."

One man tilted his head back and stared up at the sky. "How high up were you?"

"Around twenty-four thousand feet. Four and a half miles." Chet smiled when they all looked up.

The questioner gazed off to the west. "That'd be like from here to where we ran that old biddy off the road."

Chet swung his attention back to Nate, but his brother wouldn't meet his eyes. His mouth twisted to the side, lips firmly pressed. There must be quite a story here. Chet preferred to hear it, but another question came his way.

"How long does it take to fall that far?"

The kid asking should have joined the paratroopers. He radiated excitement as he leaned forward.

"Ten minutes. Probably less." Chet could have explained he had fallen several thousand feet before releasing his chute. And all because Max Withers had yelled at him to wake up and pull his ripcord. "The bombardier's parachute had been damaged by flak and failed. He likely hit the ground in two minutes."

The kid gulped, his Adam's apple surging up and down. "That's what happens to the Krauts we fire at? When they bail out?"

"Yeah, Jeffers, it's called war. If we don't knock them down, they bomb and strafe us." The artillery lieutenant shooed everyone away. "Back to work. Back to your guns. Vogel, take charge of your brother." He looked down at Chet. "We'll send out word that you're here, but it may take a while for someone to come if they're all in transit."

Nate hopped into the jeep beside the driver who'd summoned him. "Take us to my gun."

The kid delivered them to the furthest gun. He helped Nate unhook the stretcher and lower one end so Chet stood upright. A wave of dizziness swept over Chet after being horizontal for so long. He leaned heavily on Nate.

"Come on, you gold-brickers," Nate yelled at the four men who stood around the gun to watch their approach. "If you're not going to work, find a chair to make my brother comfortable."

A folding canvas chair was set up, and Chet eased onto it. It sat too low to be comfortable, and getting out of it would be a problem, but he couldn't complain. He saw little in the way of furniture. A private ran over with a sandbag for him to use as a footstool, and he nodded his thanks. Here he would find out how the army lived.

The gun in front of him had been dug into a deep, round pit. All he could see of a man standing in it were his head and shoulders. Dozens of sandbags rimmed the pit. Surely the army didn't haul full bags around. The men must have filled them while digging the hole.

The jeep driver returned and presented him with a meal. "They don't have anything ready now at the kitchen, but they heated up a C ration for you."

The chicken and vegetables wouldn't hold a candle to Grandma's cooking, but to Chet's starved taste buds, the meal was ambrosia. He gulped it down, barely noticing the mushiness of the vegetables or the tinny taste of the chicken. Only Nate's raised brow slowed his fork.

"Excuse me. It's been a long time since breakfast at the collecting station. After three weeks on a

French farm, I've gotten used to regularly scheduled meals."

"Whatever rings your bell, kid." Nate snitched one of the crackers. "We had to eat a lot of these the first weeks we were in France, until our field kitchens and service units caught up with us. Try heating that stuff over a fire. I usually got mine too hot or not hot enough."

Chet returned his attention to the gun. "I would have thought more men would be needed on one of these."

"You're not even seeing half of them." Nate tilted back on the rear legs of his chair, but straightened when it wobbled on the uneven ground. "We work at night. These babies need a lot of attention, so during the day, half of us sleep while the other half maintains the gun."

Chet nodded. The corporal had said as much. His powdered lemonade hadn't quite dissolved. He swirled it in his cup. "You like working at night?"

"No choice. That's when the Jerries like to harass us. During the day, our own flyboys keep them away." Nate stood and grinned down at him. "Although, not you bomber boys." He moved to the pit. "Komansky, check that the equilibrator is in the proper adjustment."

"On it, boss."

"Boss?" Chet stared at his brother as he returned to his chair.

Nate offered a playful salute. "You're looking at the gun commander. I've got a swell crew that makes me look good."

A head popped up in the pit. "And the gun's looking good, too, boss. The oil reserve in the rear of the floating piston and the gas pressure in the recuperator are sufficient."

"I didn't understand a word of that."

"Don't worry, little brother." Nate landed a hand on Chet's shoulder. "I did."

The gun barrel poking up from the pit held a morbid fascination for Chet. A gun like that was responsible for him being in France instead of back in England. He had an intimate acquaintance with the deadly flak spewed out by the shells fired from these monsters. Germany possessed way too many antiaircraft guns.

"What does everyone do?"

"In action, I'm on the telephone with the director and relay the orders to my crew. One man sets the azimuth dial to control the gun's horizontal position while another works the vertical elevation. I've got a gunner, a loader, the fuse range setter, cannoneers, and the ammunition squad. You'll see everyone in action tonight. Don't plan on getting any sleep while the guns are firing."

One of his men asked Nate to check something. In his absence, another came to sit with Chet. "You ever wonder what your crewmates thought when you disappeared out of your plane?"

The image prompted a smile. "When we didn't answer any calls on the intercom, the pilot probably sent the flight engineer down to the nose." Chet couldn't remember the man's name, but he tended to be smart-alecky. "I can hear him say, 'They must have stepped out for a breath of fresh air.' We hardly needed to with the broken nose window. Quite a wind was whistling in, and the temperature was minus twenty-four degrees."

The artilleryman shivered. "Hoo-wee. I thought it got cold here. Even in July we were freezing. For sure, France ain't nothing like Oklahoma." He drummed his fingers on one knee. "I don't wonder the navy's any better. My wife's cousin is in the North Atlantic, and the sea spray froze on his face in winter."

"All right, Hillers." Nate returned and sent Chet's company back to work.

"Do you know he's married?"

Nate nodded. "Got his draft notice just before finishing school. He worked at a filling station, pumping gas. Married his girlfriend before reporting. She wanted his allotment. They're all of nineteen. Can you imagine?"

No, Chet couldn't. Straight out of high school he hadn't been ready to take on a wife. Of course, he'd had no one in mind. He could imagine what Carol would say, especially about a girl marrying a guy for his military pay. He sighed.

Nate heard him. "Maybe you should try to get some sleep. Like I said, nights aren't restful here. I don't think any ambulance is going to be too quick to come for you."

Settled in Nate's tent, Chet stared at the canvas walls. *So this is the army, Mr. Jones.* The Bing Crosby song prompted a one-sided smile. The fictitious Mr. Jones might not have gotten good service, but Chet sure was. Nate's crew's fascination with his officer brother from the air corps brought a full smile.

Sleep proved elusive, and he shifted around, trying to get comfortable. All he'd been doing for three weeks was lying around and dozing. His leg ached. The day hadn't been conducive for healing. Or the day before. Anxiety over possible long-term damage being caused by delayed treatment hovered over him like crows over road kill.

He cast about for a diversion. What *had* the crew thought when they discovered he and Max were missing? If they'd been over England when they were ejected, it might have been funny, as long as their parachutes worked. *Thanks a lot for dropping us off, McQuaid. You know how much it cost to have a taxi bring us back to base?*

Words they'd never utter.

Who replaced him on the crew? Stovall? Duggan? Overton? Whose crew would he be reassigned to? He didn't have a clue. One of Grandma's favorite Bible verses echoed down through the years. *Take no thought for the morrow, for the morrow shall take thought for the things of itself. Sufficient unto the day is the evil thereof.* Wasn't that the truth?

A slim, little book caught his eye. He latched onto it. Maybe some light reading would put him to sleep. *A Pocket Guide to France.* He flipped through the pages and paused. The Germans had stripped France bare after taking inventory of the nation's possessions and shipping everything they didn't need to wage war in France to Germany. Chet huffed. Unfortunately, the French badly needed their possessions. Like their men. Like the Chotars' younger son.

He thumbed forward. France is the size of Utah and Nevada. What did that make Germany, the size of Montana and Wyoming? Hard to imagine those states going to war with each other. Yet Germany had the audacity to take on the world.

He yawned, letting the book slip from his fingers as sleep crept up on him.

Chapter Thirty-Eight

The sky grew dark and quiet by eleven o'clock. Silence replaced all the airborne traffic. Chet sat on a pile of sandbags against the wall of the gun pit, wrapped in a blanket. Across the pit, one of the gunners puffed on a cigarette, his blanket draped over him to hide the tiny glow.

Wooden boxes of reserve shells were dug into the pit wall. They were similar to the boxes filled with machine gun ammunition on the Flying Fortresses. Just like a bomber crew, each man here specialized in a job and waited to perform it.

Most of them loafed around, waiting for the Germans to arrive. This equated to the time when the bombers took off from England and flew across the Channel. No danger yet, but it was sure to come.

The young married man squatted nearby.

"How much danger is there here?" Chet asked. "Do they bomb or strafe you?"

"Nah, we don't see the blood and guts part of war. Here in the pit, the only thing that can get us is a direct hit, and since they can't see us at night, that's like spitting in the dark. We never even had a close call on the beaches right after the invasion. Here we're outside the reach of their field artillery."

Nate stood with a telephone pressed to his ear. "Stand by," he yelled.

Everyone jumped into position. A distant drone of motors rode the cold night air. Nate repeated the target destination he received.

The gun barrel began weaving through the air while a buzzing noise filled the pit. Chet wrapped himself tighter in the blanket, never taking his eyes off the barrel whining and grinding into position. The gun stopped. Chet grabbed a quick glance in the direction it pointed. Nothing but dark sky.

Nate glanced down at him. "You might want to cover your ears."

Chet pulled up the blanket and pressed it to his head.

"Three rounds," Nate called out. "Commence firing."

Even knowing what was to come, the blast of the gun jolted Chet. A spurt of flame burst from the muzzle, and smoke filled the pit. He would have jumped off his sandbag chair if something wasn't pressing him down. The pressure lifted from his head. Nate had held him in place.

The empty shell case clattered to the ground, and the shadowy figures of the artillerymen reloaded. The second salvo fired. This time the blast pressed Chet back against the wall. The vibration passed through the sandbags to resonate in his heart. He brought the blanket over his nose to filter the stench.

The smoke wafted away after the third round. Chet shook his head, trying to clear the ringing.

"Care to join the artillery?"

Chet stared up at his brother. "What's that doing to your hearing?"

Nate turned to face him fully. "We didn't have herring for supper."

Chet blinked. "I asked what…" In the darkness, he spotted Nate's shoulders shake. "Ha. Right. You had me going for a minute."

"Seems to take my hearing longer to return to normal than when I first started with the guns. A doctor told me the noise won't matter, but I'll probably end up a deaf old man. I'm sacrificing my ability to hear birds sing or babies laugh on the altar of freedom. That's the price of war." Nate spun around, the phone still pressed to his right ear. "Stand by!"

During a lull just after midnight, Nate sat down beside Chet. "Does Grandma still bake those cinnamon cookies?"

"Snickerdoodles?" Chet pulled back the blanket he'd drawn over his head to guard against the bitter chill of night. "You bet. Not often enough though. She doesn't want me to get fat. She sent a couple boxes to England. They tend to break up, but I ate them with a spoon. Still tasted good."

His brother sighed. "You were lucky to live with them."

Chet wondered if his own hearing had been damaged. "Did you want to live with us?"

Nate didn't answer directly. "I always admired how you stood up to Dad."

"Stood up? Me?" Chet stared at him. Where did he get such an idea? "I was afraid of him."

"You didn't give in when Dad expected us to play ball outside. I still remember it so clearly." Nate's eyes swept the sky, ostensibly looking for German intruders, but reliving a day Chet didn't care to revisit. "You'd gotten water paints from Grandma and Grandpa, and you wanted to finish your painting. Dad told you to get outside, but no, you had to finish before your paint dried. You had the guts to refuse him."

"More like I didn't have the guts to play ball." Chet bit his lip, trying to picture Nate in those long-ago days. Hadn't he been eager for those rough and tumble games? "I always ended up on the bottom of the pile. Didn't matter if we were supposed to be playing baseball or football. It ended up being a cross between wrestling and boxing, and I was the punching bag. I didn't dare cry. You know what Dad would have said."

"'Take it like a man.' Yeah, we weren't allowed to be boys." Nate crossed his arms, leaning back against the pit wall. "And then Grandpa came and told Dad they were taking you to live with them. Boy, I envied you."

"And Dad didn't object. Said good riddance of the little sissy pants." The words still rankled.

Nate pushed off the wall. "You heard that?"

"Of course." Chet grinned. "I hadn't been deafened by your gun yet." He got a swat on his blanket-covered head for his wisecrack.

"We heard what you were doing. You got to go to church with friends, stuff like Vacation Bible School. Sounded like fun, but the rest of us couldn't go." Nate leaned back against the pit's sandbagged wall. "Did you know we attended the Christmas pageant when you sang a solo? You sang 'O Come, All Ye Faithful.' I remember afterwards, the lady ahead of us saying children usually sang 'Away in a Manger,' that you had real talent. The look on Dad's face, like he wondered who that kid was and what happened to his—"

"Little sissy pants." Chet massaged his shoulder, moving it in small circles. "How'd Mom hook up with him anyway?"

"He used to be a nice guy, according to our high school principal who knew him back then. He got picked on at an assembly line job." Nate laughed when Chet dropped his blanket. "Yes, Dad. Picture him as a runt. He joined the army, but busted his arm in a brawl, and didn't get to come to France during the last war."

"A brawl?" This night was full of surprises. "It didn't happen on the job? What about that story he likes to tell about the ordnance pile spilling and him trying to save something?"

"Pure fiction." Nate stepped aside, his phone pressed tight to his ear. "Stand by!"

The crewmen hustled up from their catnaps and the barrel began its weaving dance into position. The sound of a motor came closer, but though he strained his eyes searching for a plane, Chet could not spot it.

Boom!

That gun was going to give him heart failure yet. The second salvo fired. Chet watched its trajectory. Suddenly a burst of orange light blossomed in the sky. The throb of engine noise turned rackety. The ball of orange flame began spiraling down. Around him, the men cheered.

"We got us a flamer!" The azimuth setter leapt up from his perch at the side of the gun and pumped a fist in the air. He returned to his position before Nate could chastise him.

Chills swept through Chet. Had someone cheered when *Lovely Lily* was hit and flung out of control? When he and Max were flung into space?

He expelled a shaky breath as two parachutes blossomed in the flickering light of the doomed plane. The darkness made bailing out more hazardous. Of course, he'd bailed out in daylight and still ended up in a tree.

Quietness settled over the area like a quilt. Chet waited for the crash of the plane, but only the hum of crickets serenaded him. In the distance, a dog howled. He wrapped his blanket more tightly about him. Empty shell cases clanked together as a man from the ammunition squad gathered them up.

Nate eased down on a stack of sandbags, the phone still stuck to his ear. He picked up their conversation as though the last momentous minutes that had turned a German air crew's lives upside down hadn't taken place.

"See, everyone else was going to France and being lauded back home. The officer who wrote up the incident assigned plenty of blame to Dad. I don't know the circumstances, whether he deserved any blame, but he also had to make restitution to the bar that got trashed. He was not going to advance with a black mark like that on his record, so he got snarly. Made up a big, heroic story to explain away his lack of combat. 'Course then, people asked why he didn't get a medal for his bravery."

"He always said he doesn't believe every little good deed should merit an award. He was just doing his job." The heat of anger warmed Chet, and he pushed back the blanket. "What about Mom? Did she know the true story?"

"I suspect she did. I can't remember one instance of her repeating Dad's version whenever the subject came up. She never offered a word of praise when Dad played up his heroics. She always looked," Nate expelled a breath. "Sad? Disappointed? Ever since the principal told me what really happened, I've thought of her a lot. I think she lived with a load of regret over that one day that ruined all our lives."

"I'm surprised Dad stayed in the army."

"Well, think about it." Nate leaned back, stretched out his legs, and linked his hands behind his head, still keeping the phone close by. "If he'd gone back to the factory, he'd always have to defend his story. In the army, there was enough change over that no one was familiar with him. And being a drill sergeant allowed him to boss people around. Who was going to challenge him?"

A bar brawler. The hypocrite. Comments Chet had heard at Mom's funeral took on new meaning.

Illness? Bah. She died of a broken heart is more like it.

She's leaving those four young boys defenseless.

Life never turns out the way you hope it will.

Deep in thought, he barely noticed when Nate leapt to his feet and his crew sprang into action. The boom of the gun failed to distract him. Mom's image filled his mind, praising his drawings, encouraging him to read, hugging him close. The antithesis of Dad.

He chuckled when Nate once again stepped away from the gun. "I sure would have liked to have seen Dad's face when Len told him I'm an officer. Think he'll ever salute me?"

Nate's teeth gleamed in the gloom of night. "Don't bet on it."

Chapter Thirty-Nine

Two new guests were brought to the gun battery while breakfast was served. A pair of military policemen prodded two German airmen out of their jeep. One had a wrapped ankle and leaned heavily on his compatriot, who helped him hobble to a small tree and sit.

One of the MPs reported to the artillery lieutenant. "I understand one of your guns shot these Krauts down. They're on their way to a prison camp in the states."

"Lucky stiffs," a private muttered. "Wish I could go home, too."

"They're not going home, doofus." His buddy elbowed him. "They're going to prison."

"Yeah. Back home."

Several men gathered around, staring at the Germans like they were a zoo exhibit. The uninjured prisoner stared back boldly. Chet was again thankful he'd been rescued by the Chotars and not discovered by the Germans. These men were likely the first enemies to be seen by the gun crews. Serving behind the front lines, they didn't see the action of battles or take aim on a foe directly before them.

One of the GIs tossed a slice of bread to the wounded airman. "Breakfast is served."

"Hey, we're the good guys in this war." Chet sat up straighter. "Show 'em a little respect."

The soldier bristled. "They're murdering helpless folk and bullying the whole world."

"I didn't say be his bosom buddy. Just treat them like you'd want to be treated. Demonstrate how they should act." Considering how the enlisted man talked back to him, that might be asking too much. Dad's mocking voice sneered in his mind. *Some officer you are. Can't even make a lousy private obey you.*

Nate stepped forward. "Mind the officer, Carstedt."

Surprise filled Carstedt's face. He took another look at Chet and stiffened to attention. "Yes, sir. Sorry, sir."

He beat a hasty retreat back to the mess line.

Chet knew he didn't look officer-like. No doubt nights of poor sleep had etched haggard lines into his face, bruised his eyes. If she could see him, Grandma would ache to strip him bare to wash and iron the clothes he'd been living in. His broken leg made him helpless. He couldn't wait to be back on his feet. In the meantime, he unzipped his jacket enough so his insignia showed.

The sight of his navigator's wings stirred the Germans. Foreign gibberish passed between them. Then the uninjured one inched forward. He held up four fingers. *"Fliegen Sie vier Motoren?"*

Four motors. Did he fly four motors? Chet nodded. "B-17s. Flying Fortresses."

More gibberish from the wounded man, his eyes bright with excitement? Awe? *"Fliegende Festung."* He clenched a hard fist. *"Starke Flugzeug."*

Chet grinned. "Yeah, they are tough birds." A stab of pain lanced his leg when he shifted, and he grimaced. "Most of the time."

He couldn't blame his misfortune on *Lovely Lily*. If her nose window hadn't been shattered, she would have sheltered him and Max when she spun out of control. The old girl had responded to Captain McQuaid's commands. Yes, sir, B-17s could take a lot of punishment and keep on flying. The Germans should be impressed.

They were eyeing his leg. Without the language barrier, they'd probably be discussing how they'd all ended up on the ground when they belonged in the air. He pointed at them. "Your airplane?"

The one on his feet stood taller. *"Nachtjäger* Messerschmitt Bf 110."

Chet recognized the name Messerschmitt. His face must have betrayed his distaste for the enemy aircraft. The man smiled, kind of sad and wistful. *"Eines Tages werden wir Fruender sein."*

Someday we will be friends. Chet nodded. "I look forward to that day."

The MPs returned with breakfast for their prisoners. They waved them to get back in the jeep. Again the uninjured man helped his companion. Before climbing in himself, he turned, stood at attention, and saluted Chet. Chet returned the salute.

As they watched the jeep drive away, a gunner asked, "Why'd you salute him, sir?"

"The brotherhood of fliers."

Even though Nate turned to stare at him, Chet kept his eyes on the jeep until it disappeared around a bend. Only then did he look at his brother. "Nice guys. Too bad we didn't have a translator."

"The brotherhood of fliers? Is that some sort of fraternal order?" Nate clearly didn't know what to make of him. When Grandma and Grandpa had removed Chet from Dad's house, he'd been a fearful kid, afraid to speak up among acquaintances. Now he might need big brother's help to command the respect of lower military ranks, but he engaged in conversation with the enemy.

He massaged his aching leg. "We hate seeing enemy fighters when we're on missions. These days our own fighters go all the way to our targets with us, and do a good job of keeping the enemy away from us. The German antiaircraft guns are our worst nightmare. But we have to respect the German airmen. They're good. As they tangle with our fighters, more and more of them are shot down, and they're hard to replace. The Luftwaffe's probably sending up new pilots with inadequate training. But the veterans, we still admire them. And I guess they respect us, too." He grinned. "Or at least our airplanes."

Nate slowly shook his head, his eyes never leaving Chet. "You fight a strange war."

"What made you choose to go into the air force, sir?" the gunner asked.

Chet grinned. "Why walk when you can ride?"

A bark of laughter escaped his brother.

Lieutenant O'Dell ambled over. "Sorry we couldn't send you on with them, but they didn't exactly have room, and they weren't going to any medical units. We've told people you're here, but since you don't belong to anyone in France and you're not an emergency, you've got no priority. The front line's pretty fluid right now."

Chet twisted his mouth to one side. Then he laughed. "I don't belong to anyone in France, huh? I think I'll go home."

Nate messed his hair. "Not so fast there, kid. Lieutenant, I'll claim him." He started ticking off chores on his fingers. "We could use some help greasing the gun. The camouflage netting has a rip that needs to be mended. The empty shell cases need to be boxed up for shipment home."

His commanding officer walked away laughing, but Chet smirked at him. "I think I'll just borrow your pup tent and grab a nap, now that it's quiet."

He slept the day away. By late afternoon, he perched on an uncomfortable stool, groggily helping Nate with his records. A cry rang out. "American girls."

Chapter Forty

The men crowding around the clubmobile faded from Carol's awareness. She squeezed her eyes shut, then looked again. Lightheadedness caused her focus to waver.

"Carol? Are you okay? You look like you've seen a ghost." Gloria jiggled her arm. "Carol?"

She had to clear her throat before she could speak. "He looks exactly like Chet."

The man in front craned his neck to see who interested her. "The hurt guy? He's the sergeant's brother. An officer. Sorta got himself shot down last month."

An officer? Shot down? Great merciful heavens, could it be? She gave her informant a doughnut, unmindful that he already had one. "I have to see."

The words came from her throat but didn't sound like her voice. Gloria touched her arm, pressing her forward.

The men quieted. They cleared a path for her, watching, waiting. The man she aimed for had struggled to his feet with the help of an enlisted man who supported him. He leaned forward as though that would help him see her better.

She stopped four feet away. They stared at each other, surrounded by silence. Carol licked her lips.

"You said you'd only come to France as the result of a catastrophe."

Chet grimaced. "And so it was."

That voice, clear and deep and smooth as hot chocolate. His eyes gleamed green in the late afternoon sun instead of their normal hazel brown. Weariness etched his face.

"We still don't have any cherry cake."

His sudden grin transformed him. "Your lady wouldn't share her recipe? Guess I'll have to settle for a doughnut."

Carol flung herself at him, hugging him for all her worth. She was scarcely aware of the man who braced him until Chet's strangled voice said, "Careful, honey. I'm damaged goods."

She would have jumped back, but his right arm had snaked around her waist, holding her in place. "My right side's fine. My left side's had it."

So he said, but his left arm came around her too. His right hand tilted her head, and his lips found hers.

Wolf whistles and cheers split the air. Carol barely noticed as the kiss ended and she stared into Chet's eyes. She should never have left England.

A glance to her left revealed three men shoulder to shoulder, coffee in one hand, doughnut in the other. More behind them. All watching wide-eyed, like they were at a movie with popcorn and sodas. On her right, more men clustered.

"All right, you grubbers." A lieutenant shooed them away. "Give them some privacy." He herded them back toward the clubmobile.

One man remained, the one who kept Chet on his feet. He kept his eyes locked on her as he asked, "Anything you care to be telling me, Chet?"

Carol swallowed as her eyebrows rose. Why was an enlisted man being so familiar with an officer?

His impertinence didn't faze Chet. He laughed and spared the man a glance. "This is Carol. She used to visit my air base before she came to explore the land of her ancestors." His gaze swung back to her. "Meet my brother Nate. He's one of the gun bosses in this battery."

"Your brother?" What had Chet told her about his family? He didn't get along with his father and brothers. It sure looked like he got along with this one. Were Nate to walk away, Chet would collapse in a heap.

A knowing look entered Nate's eyes, as if he could imagine what Chet must have told her. Now that she really looked at him, she saw he had the same cheekbones, the same straight nose, the same height.

"Let's park you here." Nate helped Chet sit down before grabbing another canvas chair for Carol. He headed for the clubmobile, leaving them alone.

Chet reached for her hand. "So here you are in France. Has it been everything you hoped it would be?"

Images flittered through her mind like a kaleidoscope. The latrines, the sometimes abhorrent sleeping accommodations, shampoos in a helmet, unwashed clothes, being just as grungy as the soldiers. The squalor the French civilians were reduced to in their bombed-out villages, the exorbitant prices. She didn't want to waste what little time they had with gripes.

"I wanted to see the war up close. I sure have." She interlaced their fingers. "If my great-great-grandparents lived in any of the towns I've been through, they wouldn't recognize it now. I was in Paris in the days after it was liberated. Life looks normal there, but they don't have food. In the country, they might have food from their gardens, but the houses, Chet."

She looked around the field. Except for the camouflage nets and the military vehicles, it was a peaceful tableau. "We're hearing of damage still being repaired from the last war. Sometimes we trade the cigarettes from our rations for fresh vegetables. I feel guilty. We're getting something of value, but cigarettes aren't going to help them rebuild their lives."

His thumb brushed back and forth across hers. "Sorry you came?"

"I frequently ask myself that." Carol leaned forward and placed her other hand on top of their joined hands. "When I'm back home after the war, I think then I'll really appreciate everything I'm experiencing. I write articles in my head, and hope I'll remember it all later. I've jotted down snippets in a notebook. I don't dare mail it home. The censors would have a field day with it."

Chet's mouth smiled, but his eyes didn't. "I stayed with a French family until they got me through the lines two days ago. Everything they did had to be done with the possibility of a sudden, unwelcome visit from the Germans. Their radio stayed hidden behind a wall panel. I stayed hidden in a dark attic room."

Carol gripped his hand. "What happened, Chet? Where's the rest of your crew?"

His gaze drifted down to their hands. "Our airplane wasn't shot down." He shrugged a shoulder. "You could say it cartwheeled across the sky, and the bombardier and I fell out. He didn't survive."

His last words came out in a sigh.

"Bomby? Bomby's dead?" Chet's cocky crewmate fancied himself a ladies' man. Carol hadn't appreciated his attitude.

Chet shook his head. "No, not Bomby. I moved into a lead crew. Max Withers was the bombardier."

Try as she might, Carol couldn't remember any Max. Funny how the losses didn't hurt as much when the names didn't have faces. And yet someone, somewhere, was mourning him. "Your grandparents. All they know is you're missing, right?"

"Yeah." His mouth tightened. "That's another reason I need to get back to England, besides making sure my leg's healing properly." His eyes lit up. "But I can write a letter now. I don't know what Nate's mail service is like, but at the rate I'm moving, a letter might reach them before an official telegram."

Gloria approached them. "Carol? I hate to interrupt, but we need to leave now so we get back to base before dark."

Her hand convulsed on Chet's. They'd only just reunited. So much remained to be said, to be asked. She didn't want to say goodbye. Not now. Not again.

Chet didn't let go of her either.

His brother and a lieutenant joined them. The lieutenant addressed Gloria, waving a hand toward Chet. "Our guest seems to have been misplaced and overlooked by the army. Will you pass by any evacuation units where you can get him back into the pipeline?"

Carol caught her breath. They wouldn't have to say their goodbyes just yet.

"Everything passes by us." Gloria looked at Chet. "A supply truck can take you if we don't see a medical vehicle, although it may not be too comfortable."

"And we've got a post office unit nearby." Carol thought of the letter he wanted to write.   Chet laughed. "Great. You can mail me back to England."

A flush heated Carol's face when everyone else laughed. "I don't know about that, Chet. You might require too much postage."

Nate helped Chet to his feet and over to the clubmobile. After getting him up inside, he tucked a scrap of paper into Chet's pocket. "Let me know when you get to England, little brother."

Nate pulled him into a careful embrace, patting his right shoulder.

Tears stung Carol's eyes, but she blinked them away. Nate must have mellowed with age. From the way Chet's mouth worked, his brother's hug meant the world to him.

She got him ensconced sideways on the sofa, leaning against the wall with his legs stretched out. "Unfortunately, we don't have the roomy living area that our clubmobiles in England have. You can't stretch out on this sofa. Those days in England seem downright leisurely compared to our schedule here."

"How close to the front do you get?" After bouncing along the bad road, Chet shoved a rolled-up blanket behind his back.

"We've been within a few miles." Carol pulled off her shoes and sat Indian-style on the floor. "Once, we were told in no uncertain terms to get out of there. We moved back a couple miles. Our supervisor thinks the brass got all uptight because women were ahead of them, blazing the trail." She laughed when Chet wagged his head and hummed disapproving notes. "The guns are always audible. Occasionally, a stray shell comes close. Watching out for mines, though, is our biggest hazard. We don't dare pull off onto the side of the road. It may not have been cleared."

"Have any problem with buzz bombs here?"

"Buzz bombs?"

"The unmanned rockets the Germans are lobbing at England. Most are aimed at London, it seems. Forget the military targets. Kill the civilians and demoralize them. They started them after the invasion. It's a dirty war, Carol, not that I've ever heard of a clean one."

He rubbed a hand across his face and grimaced. He must have shaved that morning, although he would have had to borrow…

"You know what? Men in combat often lose their personal belongings, and we try to have a few supplies for them. Do you need any tooth powder or razor blades?"

His eyes brightened. "You have extras? That'd be great."

She pulled out a box from the compartment housing their phonograph player and flipped open the top flap. "Remember how we always played music at the air base? Here we have to be careful we don't play too loud when we're near the front."

Chet poked her with a toe. "What's the matter? Don't you think the German soldiers might like to jitterbug?"

"Ha, ha, ha. Let's declare a truce and everybody dance. Ah, here we are." She scooted next to Chet with the box of supplies. "Here's a toothbrush."

He took it with reverence and pulled out a box of tooth powder. "The Chotars didn't have any spare brushes. They can't simply go to the store and buy a new one. Nothing's available. I always tried to swish water around my mouth, but figured I'd go back to base needing a lot of dental work. Are you sure I can have these? I'll be back in England soon enough, but the guys here don't have a PX store to run to."

"But in the meantime, you have the need. Will your gear still be at Ridgewell?"

"

Highly unlikely." He balanced a bar of soap on his hand. "Everything would have been packed up and sent home. Now Grandma and Grandpa will have to send it all back." He grinned. "Efficient, our army."

"Oh, I don't know." Carol laughed. "We heard a story about the boy who lost his shoes in an air attack. His commanding officer gave him permission to go the supply depot for another pair, and told him to ride back with an ambulance. You think you had trouble with your ambulance? Well, this poor guy got a casualty ticket slapped on him at the clearing station. He ended up going clear back to the port and was about to be loaded onto a hospital ship. There was nothing wrong with him. He just needed a new pair of shoes, but he had that casualty ticket, so the army was determined to evacuate him to England."

Somewhere in the telling, Chet's hand came to rest on her shoulder. His laughter proved contagious. Tears rolled down her cheeks. She hadn't laughed as much when she first heard the story.

"I'm sorry your bombardier died, but I'm glad you came to France."

He nodded, and took a moment before he could respond. "I had to. You never wrote, never called."

"Oh." She gripped his hand. "I have something else for you." She scrambled up and pulled open a drawer. "You need to write to your grandparents and here's some stationary for you." She held out two sheets of the German letterhead she'd found at the chateau.

Surprise crossed his face before he chuckled. "They'll take one look at this and think I'm in a German prison camp."

"Close. Tonight you'll sleep on a cot recently vacated by a German soldier."

Chapter Forty-One

Somewhere in France
Monday, September 4, 1944

The chateau's interior rivaled the outdoor temperature. Chet pulled his collar tighter. The exertion of climbing the stairs and hobbling to the kitchen left him drained, even after Carol and their man Lionel practically carried him into the building.

"We've set up a cot for you in a little room just down the hall, sir," Lionel told him as he headed back out the door. "It's got doors to close it off from the rest of this shack, so you won't have to worry about rats."

"Rats?" What kind of place did the Red Cross ladies have to live in?

"The Germans left their pets behind." A perky gal with a head full of tight blonde curls dumped K-ration boxes into a crate. "No dull-as-dishwater supper tonight. A tank buster unit moved into the field out back, and we get to eat at their mess. It'll almost be like having a home-cooked meal."

That meant hiking over there. Chet sighed. If only his injured shoulder didn't prevent him from using crutches. Miss Perky would drop her jaw if he announced he'd stay here and dine on K-rations.

Carol came back downstairs from dropping off her bedroll. She carried a thick white coat. "Where did these come from?"

"Spoils of war." Perky grinned. "Try it on. They'll keep us warm in arctic gales."

"Fleece lining. Nice and toasty." Carol disappeared in the coat that had to be at least three sizes too big. "The Germans left these behind?"

Perky jerked a thumb toward the back of the chateau. "The guys who brought them over believe the Germans captured them from Russian ski troops. Now we've got 'em."

"They're so bulky, we'll have a hard time fitting them in with all our baggage." Carol ran a hand along the sleeve. "They'll sure keep us warm, though, as the days and nights get colder. We should be able to sleep now without our teeth chattering so loud from shivering." She peered out at Chet from the collar she held up to her face. "We take so much for granted back home. We don't realize how good we have it."

The conditions these ladies had to endure, both in France and in England, had to be much harder than they experienced back home. Yet Chet hadn't heard any whining. The Red Cross must have done a good job of weeding out possible belly-achers. The military couldn't provide a home-like atmosphere, especially in wartime, but for the women to voluntarily come overseas to serve them under wretched circumstances said a lot about their character. About Carol.

Even this chateau, which he would have expected to be an elegant abode of upper-class French folk, showed signs of wear. The floors sported scuffs and gouges that looked old, not recent ravaging by German occupiers. A tapestry he spied hanging in a room across the hall looked so threadbare and washed-out, he wasn't surprised no German soldier had rolled it up and sent it home. At least here in the kitchen, cooking was done on a stove and not in the fireplace at the far end. His gaze stalled at the sink.

"There's a hand pump for water? Does this place have plumbing?"

Carol grinned as she folded her new coat and laid it over a chair back. "If you're asking about a water closet, there's an official one out back. The Germans designated their own necessary room." She wrinkled her nose. "None of us has dared open that door."

She pulled a tarnished serving tray from a cupboard. "I'll go get some supper and bring it back here." She vanished out the door. The rest of the Red Cross girls disappeared after her, leaving Chet alone in the gloomy house illuminated by flickering lights. He shook his head. Electricity, but no plumbing.

The constant rumble of distant guns grew louder. No, it was thunder. He hoisted himself to his feet and, gripping the table, inched his way to the counter and then to the door. A wind had picked up. Flashes in the sky to the west marked the progress of the coming storm. A figure hunched over a tray took careful steps across the yard. He opened the door and Carol burst inside. Rain began spattering down behind her.

"Whew. Made it just in time, or we'd be dining on soggy chow. Look what we've got." She slid the tray onto the table. "Steak and eggs. We're wondering where they came up with the steak, whether someone butchered one of the dead cows lying around with its legs sticking up in the air. The eggs are courtesy of a local farmer, and being served only to the Red Cross and the officers."

Chet's mouth watered at the aroma wafting up from their meal. "Even in England we rarely had fresh meat." The light flickered and dimmed. "Maybe we should dine by candlelight."

"Oh, good idea." Carol set plates on the table and turned back for the candles. "We found a good supply here. Probably a necessity." She brought them, along with a cigarette lighter with German words on it. Then she scrounged in a box. "I'll make some real Red Cross coffee to go with our meal and we'll think we're dining in a fine Parisian restaurant, although the way Paris was starving when we were there, I don't think we'd find a meal this good."

They could have been in a nice restaurant in Niles. Chet smiled and raised his coffee cup in salute. "*Bon appétit.*"

Being wounded was almost worth it. He was back with Carol. He'd seen his brother and parted as friends. Seeing the ravages and hardships caused by war was disheartening, but enlightening. "What are your impressions of France?"

Carol tilted her head as she cut her meat. "I've seen and smelled things I wish I hadn't. It's been uncomfortably cold, even in summer. But, Chet, it's been so interesting to see how people live. Like in England, where they don't have central heating because they say it's unhealthy. So they have gas fireplaces in every room and still shiver in bed with four layers of blankets."

She shivered and wrapped her hands around her coffee cup.

"Here in France, I haven't been able to tell how my ancestors lived. The war has been so destructive. Or maybe life's more like it was a century ago, more primitive. You have to admire the French. They're so resilient. Twice, this area been torn apart by wars, twenty-five years apart. Shells can be flying overhead, but the farmers are still out plowing their fields."

A loud crash of thunder had Chet searching the ceiling for a leak. "Do they have an open air mess here?"

"No, fortunately. They're in what must have been a carriage house at one time. The men have to sleep in tents though. The army has been so good to us. We get to sleep in this nice, dry house while they bed down in muddy fields. When we stop to beg a couple gallons of gas from different units while making our rounds, they fill up our tanks even when gasoline is scarce, and those clubmobiles are guzzlers."

The eggs had grown cold during Carol's trek from the mess kitchen, but she ate hers as though they were a feast. Chet didn't have the heart to mention the Chotars kept chickens, and eggs had been a staple of his diet with them. "You'll follow the army into Germany, won't you?"

"Yes, and I'll bet our reception there will be a lot different than it's been here. The French cheered us like they did the army, but they've had a hard time figuring out our role. One of the girls who speaks good French explained we're a mobile bakery, but a lot of them think we're, uh..." Carol's cheeks turned a rosy hue. She kept her eyes on her plate as she mumbled, "Bed warmers."

Chet bit his lip to keep from laughing. "Hmm, does that mean their soldiers never got doughnut breaks?"

Carol laughed. "I guess not."

The rain had let up, and pounding feet approached the chateau. Several Red Cross girls poured through the door. They stopped short at the cozy scene before them.

"A candlelight dinner for two," Louise, the driver of Carol's clubmobile, grinned. "How romantic."

Carol flushed again.

Chet snapped his fingers in the air. "Oh, miss, we're ready for dessert."

"Are you now?" Gloria looked around. "Coming right up." She whispered to another girl, who disappeared out the door. Then she moved the coffee pot from the stove and started cooking something else.

Louise pulled up a chair and joined them. So much for the romantic meal for two. "Rumor has it we'll be pulling out tomorrow."

"Already?" Carol shrugged. "That's good, because it means the front is moving eastward. But it means we might find ourselves sleeping in another muddy field. We do have cot frames with no mattresses, so at least we're off the ground."

"Or a smelly barn with our bedrolls laid out in hay that likely houses mice." Louise shuddered before turning to Chet. "You should have seen that rat this morning. It was as big as a cat." Her fingernails tapped on the table, not quite as offensive as scratching a blackboard. "So, you two met in England?"

This gal wasn't going to leave them alone. He couldn't be a rarity. All day, every day, they were vastly outnumbered by men. Maybe because he singled out Carol, and whatever one woman has, another wants.

"We met in Ohio." Carol's reply sounded abrupt. She didn't care for the interruption either.

"At a train canteen, where Carol got experience for her Red Cross service." He raised his glass to her and was rewarded with a smile.

"And you remember each other from that brief encounter?" Louise wasn't giving up. "She must have made an impression on you."

"She wore a blue blouse with a white collar that had red and white lace around it and her initial was sewn on the blouse with the same red and white thread. And she served delicious cherry pound cake."

Giggling came from the stove. Gloria came to the table and placed small dishes in front of Carol and Chet. "We don't have cherry cake, but, ta da." Each plate held a doughnut with chocolate drizzled on it.

"Chocolate-covered doughnuts." Chet took a bite. "Yum. You're going to have to serve chocolate covered doughnuts all the time. Plain doughnuts will never hold much appeal again."

Groans and laughter filled the kitchen. "Now look what you've done, Gloria," said a girl scraping melted chocolate out of a pot and licking her finger. "Our work load's been doubled."

"No, it hasn't." Gloria took the pot and began scrubbing it with a rag. "Chet's going back to England, and we'll get rid of all the evidence before the men arrive."

"What men?" Carol licked her own fingers after finishing her dessert.

"The piano in the music room is in pretty good tune." Perky twirled around. "We invited a bunch over to sing." She turned to Chet. "Do you play piano?"

Chet bounced his forefingers on the table. "I used to be able to pick out Chopsticks."

Perky waved a dismissive hand at him. "Nobody knows the words to that, if it even has any."

Louise leaned back in her chair, her gaze going from Carol to Chet and back again. "Good thing Ted's no longer here."

Carol stiffened as she frowned at her crewmate.

She wouldn't appreciate further comment, but Chet had to know. "Who's Ted?"

"Lionel's predecessor. He," Carol exhaled hard, "liked me."

"Easy to understand." Something went wrong with the mysterious Ted. Chet's hand clenched under the table as he waited for the full story.

"We walked around Paris together. Having a male escort makes us safer. And he knew I wasn't interested." Carol's eyes narrowed at her plate. Her back was ramrod straight.

"He knew about you." Louise grinned at him. Whatever happened couldn't be too bad if she was amused.

Carol continued as though Louise hadn't interrupted. "He started getting chummy, and then he says he's married." She looked up at him. Anger, distress, shame flickered across her face. "I was the other woman."

"Now, Carol," Gloria stepped away from the stove, her hands fisted on her hips, "how many times do I have to tell you? What happened is not your fault. If his wife finds out and blames you, that's her problem. He led you, all of us, to believe he was single, and you never had any feelings for him. Don't feel guilty when you're innocent."

Steam coming out of her ears wouldn't have surprised Chet. He leaned back, crossing his arms. Carol nodded in acknowledgement of Gloria's words, but kept her eyes cast down, her fingers worrying a groove in the tabletop.

When their guests arrived, they adjourned to the music room, leaving Chet and Carol alone. She heaved a sigh. "Men and women can't be friends, can they? Not a platonic friendship, anyway. I mean, you and Gloria can be friends and no one would think anything about it because…"

Her voice trailed off as she twisted a lock of hair around her finger.

"Because we're not buddies. We're no more than friendly acquaintances. You and I, however, have hope for something more in the future, do we not?" He slid his hand across the table.

Her lips quirked, and then her smile bloomed. "Yeah." Her hand met his. "When this cruel war is over."

Outside, the boom of artillery guns shattered the peace. Carol squeezed his hand. "Our nightly serenade begins."

"And my brother Nate is a contributor. Man, I can't believe we met up in a French field. We weren't close as boys, but now we're friends. That's a friendship I'll gladly take." He laughed. "He'll be deaf by middle age. You have a brother and a sister, right? Are you close?"

"My sister Joanne sends me packages of goodies not to be found in stores over here." She interlocked their fingers, palm to palm. "She and her two little ones moved back in with our folks while her husband's overseas. My brother Ron is six years younger than me. He was such a pest growing up. He's nineteen now, and got his draft notice. Our folks hoped the war would be over before he had to join up. He likes boats, and in Mom's last letter, she wrote he requested the navy. She hopes he'll get into maintenance somewhere, because he works as a grease monkey at a filling station during the summers."

Chet ran his thumb back and forth between Carol's thumb and forefinger. "He can still be a grease monkey in the navy. All those ships need lots of upkeep."

"Well, don't tell my mom. She'll be happy if he's assigned to the motorboat in Pearl Harbor that takes admirals and other bigwigs out to their ships."

Chet cocked his head at the sounds of furniture being scraped across the music room floor. "More scars on the hardwood. This poor house gets no relief. Too bad I can't ask you to dance."

"We don't need to dance." Carol scooted her chair around the table next to his. "We'll be heading out tomorrow to serve doughnuts. You'll probably be gone when we get back. In fact, you may leave before we even finish making the doughnuts."

"Write to me, Carol." Chet picked up Gloria's list of their stops that day and wrote his address on the back. "Stay in touch this time."

"I will." She sniffed and sucked in her lips before exhaling hard. "I'll start a letter tomorrow night. On Nazi stationery."

He laughed briefly, and pulled her close for a kiss.

Chapter Forty-Two

Somewhere in France
Tuesday, September 5, 1944

Carol watched until the convoy disappeared from view. Did they have to take Chet away so quickly? He hadn't even finished his breakfast. The trucks were a medical transport, however. They offered the best means of getting Chet to England and the care he needed.

Her shoulders sagged. She wouldn't see him again for months. Maybe a year. The clubmobiles would follow the army into Germany, and who knew how long it would take to sort things out? The Red Cross intended to stay and serve the boys at least until some semblance of a long-term occupation was achieved. Chet might be flying for Pan American Airways long before she made it back home.

She pivoted in place and headed back to the clubmobile. The day's doughnuts weren't going to make themselves. She stirred water into the mix by rote as her thoughts jumped hither and yon.

Maybe she could request a transfer back to England. France now claimed the main focus of the war, but they still had lots of men in England. The airmen who alone had shouldered the war to the continent for so long still needed to know they were appreciated. She could return to a clubmobile visiting the air bases, or maybe work in one of the clubs. With everyone wanting to go where the action was, surely an opening awaited her.

Gloria hustled into *George*. "Make sure you don't leave anything behind. We won't be coming back."

"Oh, bother." Louise turned from the doughnut machine, cleaning rag in hand. "This place is the best we've had. I hate to think what our next accommodation might be like."

"Hmm. Maybe it'll have indoor plumbing and a bathroom." Carol shook dough from her fingers and brushed her hair from her eyes with the back of her hand. "Or no pet rats."

Louise took the bowl of batter and fed it into the machine. "Yeah, I'll go for that. Say, did either of you see the guy with the kitten in his jacket pocket? We should have one. Then we won't have to worry about rats."

"Are you kidding?" Gloria turned from her inspection of their phonograph player. "The rat we saw yesterday would have made mincemeat of a little kitten. Even a full-grown cat would have trouble with jumbo rodents. Besides, imagine all the mischief a cat would do in here."

"It would jump onto the doughnut trays, scattering doughnuts everywhere. After eating some, it would get sick. We'd pull up to a stop, the guys would eagerly gather around, we'd open up, and," Carol clutched her throat, "horrors! What an unappetizing mess. We'd toss the cat out the serving window and the men would grab for their guns to do a little target practice."

Gloria laughed, but Louise threw her rag into the sink. "For crying out loud, Carol. Don't you like cats?"

She shrugged. "They don't like me. I must be allergic to fur. Whenever I'm around them, I have a hard time breathing."

Louise's pique melted away. "That's awful. I love cats."

"I can think of worse things." Carol washed her hands. "Who wants to mix up the next batch?"

Gloria took over. "I just heard that Jean's leaving the *West Virginia*. She's going back to England to get married. Hazel and Doris are in a tiff. Their crew was a solid unit and now they'll have to break in a new girl."

"No different from being rotated around in England, is it?" Carol readied a tray for the doughnuts soon to churn out of the machine.

Gloria paused with her hands buried in the dough. "Are you thinking of leaving?"

"Tempting, but," Carol squared her shoulders, "no. Gotta practice what I preach." She speared her prong through the hole of the first doughnut. "I wonder how long it'll take before Chet reaches the coast."

Gloria shook her head and continued mixing.

By eleven o'clock, they headed out for their first stop. The unit proved to be part of an anti-aircraft brigade. The men swarmed around *President Washington*. Chet's brother was not part of this group, but Carol searched faces anyway, looking for the family resemblance.

"Say, how would you gals like to help out?" A burly sergeant finished his doughnut in two bites and gulped his coffee. "We're testing the muzzle velocity of our gun. You can fire it for us."

Fire one of those huge guns? They hadn't been able to accept the invitation to fire the guns after she'd been manhandled by the obnoxious soldier. These looked the same as Nate Vogel's gun, designed to bring down an airplane. Carol had never even fired a small handgun. She caught her breath. This would be something to write about.

The men clustered about them as they made their way to the exposed gun. One man offered Carol his helmet. Another guided her to the controls. Gloria and Louise flanked her as the sergeant explained the procedure. "When I say fire, depress this."

When he stepped away, Louise whispered, "Should we be doing this?"

A man at the side fiddled with his controls and the gun barrel swiveled up. He nodded to another man who called out, "Fuse range set."

The sergeant yelled, "Fire."

Carol hit the switch.

BOOM.

She shot off the seat and staggered back, stumbling over part of the gun's bracing. She would have fallen had someone not grabbed her. Mirth filled the faces of the men, but if they were laughing, she couldn't hear it. She couldn't hear anything.

Gloria was on her feet, shaking her head and rubbing her ears. Louise still sat, but she clamped her hands to the sides of her head.

One of the men tapped Carol's arm. His lips moved.

"What?"

He stepped back with a big smile, his shoulders shaking. "You don't have to shout."

She read his lips rather than heard his words. "Why didn't you warn us?"

Faint sounds began to register. The sergeant tried to look contrite, but his throaty laugh trickled past her stunned ear drums. "Sorry 'bout that. We're so used to the blast, we don't think about it anymore."

That didn't seem possible. His next words made her forget the ringing in her ears.

"You lobbed that shell a good five miles."

For the first time, she considered implications. "What did it land on?"

He laughed again. "Don't worry. The Germans are out there. They were probably busy getting their lunch and, pow. Everything's blown away."

Carol stared at him. If their guns could reach the Germans, the German guns could reach them and retaliate. "What if there weren't any Germans on the receiving end? What about the French?"

With a careless shrug, he said, "The French should have evacuated. No problem."

A poor French family might return to their humble abode after the fighting moved on and find it blown away. They'd seen plenty of such scenarios in their trek across France, but that didn't mean Carol wanted to be the one responsible for the destruction. She turned away and pressed a hand to her stomach, feeling queasy.

A distant droning brought everyone's head up. Specks crept across the sky at a snail's pace. Carol didn't need to hear the sergeant say, "The heavies."

She'd watched the heavy bombers often enough, but in England, they'd been taking off or landing, low enough to recognize them. Now they were ants on the march to Germany. Shivers chased through her. The drone surged louder, wrapping around her. What must German women feel as they watched the bomber waves converge on their cities?

Her head tipped back to watch the planes pass directly overhead. 'Beautiful' seemed a strange word to ascribe to warplanes, but that's what they were.

Louise had taken her place behind the gun. "Aircraft to aim at. Get that barrel moving around."

The men snapped out of the hypnotic spell cast by the heavies. "Are you crazy? Those are our planes." The man who manipulated the barrel hastened to tug Louise away from the gun. "I think our test is concluded. Thank you, ladies, for your help."

Louise couldn't stop giggling as Carol and Gloria towed her back to the clubmobile and they proceeded to their next stop. They hadn't traveled far before a gun boomed behind them. Louise spared a glance from her driving. "Aw, they've started their test again. Should we be insulted they didn't trust us?"

Carol scribbled an account of the gun test and flyover on the Nazi letterhead balanced on her lap. Potholes made her handwriting atrocious. "Think folks back home would enjoy reading about this? I'll title it 'Red Cross girls lob shells instead of doughnuts at air force.' Think that would get past the censors?"

The closer they got to Belgium, the more stringent the restrictions became. Germans hid in the woods to infiltrate and harass the Allies as they advanced. Undetected land mines made it imperative to stay on marked routes.

The girls pulled into a clearing for their fourth stop of the day. A battalion of engineers happily laid down their tools for a break. Carol reached for a doughnut tray, and headed out to chat with the men. Behind her, Gloria offered a man cream and sugar for his coffee.

"Cream, thanks. If you just stick your finger in the coffee, that'll make it sweet enough."

Carol snickered as she stepped outside. The standard line had grown tiresome. Good thing Gloria was serving instead of Louise. Although after the Belgium, Wisconsin, fiasco, maybe Louise wouldn't dump the coffee over the man's head as she'd threatened.

Before anyone asked her where she was from, she put the question to the men. Georgia, Kansas, Delaware. "I'm from Nebraska," said a young sandy-haired man as he took a doughnut. "Thank you, miss. Sure does feel good to stand up and stretch after crouching down all day."

He took his coffee and doughnut to some trees at the edge of the clearing. Carol watched him tilt his head back and rotate it. He took another step.

Bang. The sandy-haired boy disappeared. A blast of hot air slapped Carol. Something splattered on her. Birds flew out of the trees, squawking their displeasure. Once again, her ears rang. The clearing turned silent for a moment.

Carol stood frozen as a statue. Her eyes riveted on the coffee cup lying broken in two where the boy had been. Around it were bits and pieces of, of...

"Jeepers creepers. *Cyrus.*" The anguished exclamation broke the spell. Men moved about, but Carol barely breathed.

"Let me take that from you, miss." Someone tugged at the tray clenched in her grasp. She dropped her gaze. Her doughnuts were splattered with blood and gore. Something dripped down her cheek. *She* was splattered with blood and gore. Her hands jerked away from the tray, fingers splayed. She wanted to scream, but didn't dare. That something had dripped over her lips.

Gloria was there, turning her toward the clubmobile. "Let's get you cleaned up." A damp cloth sponged her face and hands.

"I'll find some other clothes for her. We need to soak her battle dress." Louise's voice buzzed in her ears, and someone undressed her like a baby. "Put your arm through here, Carol. That's it."

She was sitting at the back door of *George* when a medic arrived. He took her pulse, looked into her eyes. "Shell shock. Typical reaction, especially after the first exposure to battle." A cup was pressed to her lips. "Drink this, little lady. It'll take the edge off."

Her throat convulsed in a swallow. She'd been given something after suffering the burn in the air base mess hall, and it had knocked her out. She pushed away the urge to sleep and looked back. Men collected the bits and pieces. One had climbed a tree and dropped down a ball. The ball was covered with tan hair. Her eyelids slammed down.

"He didn't have a chance. He was just trying to get the kinks out of his neck." Her voice sounded wispy and pitched too high. She wanted to clear her throat, but the cup was back at her lips.

She had wanted to come to Europe and see the war for herself. How foolish could she be? She'd seen it now. A young man on the threshold of adulthood, torn apart because he hadn't paid attention to where he stepped. His last meal, a Red Cross doughnut. An insane desire to laugh infused her. She was losing her mind.

Chapter Forty-Three

Somewhere in France
Tuesday, September 5, 1944

Stretched out in an upper berth litter, Chet could watch the passing scenery from the rear door's window. The convoy's route took them through many towns that had been in the news in the weeks after the invasion. The Germans had been entrenched in these places. Heavy artillery fire had made a shambles of the area. This must have been the same route Carol had traveled. Here a few walls bravely stood. There a chimney leaned precariously. Rubble had been shoved aside to make a narrow, passable lane. Just like she'd described.

The soldier on the stretcher below him moaned continuously. Gripping an overhead bar, Chet peered down. The guy resembled a horror film's mummy, swathed in bandages with holes for the eyes, nose, and mouth. Plaster casts encased both arms. From the humps under the sheet, both feet were in the same shape. Poor guy. He was a wreck.

"He doesn't feel anything. He's unconscious." Someone sat on a chair wedged between the four stretchers. Medic, probably, or maybe a patient.

"If he doesn't feel anything, why's he moaning?"

A lethargic shrug. "His subconscious is aware of pain, but his conscious doesn't feel it."

Jolly joker. Pain was pain, no matter what level. "Can't you give him something so his subconscious doesn't feel it?"

"He's already doped up as much as possible. Any more will kill him."

That might be a blessing. About to ask how the man had been wounded, Chet thought better of it. He'd seen enough planes crash and burn to imagine the worst. He lay back, staring at the ceiling until the brightness outside the window lured his gaze back.

A snort came from the guy opposite him. He jerked awake and groaned. His lips smacked. "Water?"

Apparently, the joker was a medic. He rose, located a canteen at the head of the stretcher, and held it out to the man. The ambulance bounced in a pothole, splashing water in the guy's face. He raised his hand. Only a thumb poked out of the bandages. Chet averted his gaze.

If they were lucky, he'd been told when they set out, they'd reach the beach by nightfall. Luck depended on road conditions, no vehicle breakdowns, and lack of strafing enemy planes. He'd almost welcome a stop so he could sit up for a while. He felt over his head and located a canteen of his own.

The ambulance braked to a quick stop. Joker conferred with the driver and announced, "Truck ahead of us has a flat tire. Hang on. We'll get around them and continue on."

Chet watched the unfortunate truck recede from the rear window. Maybe getting to the beach as quickly as possible was better than a rest break.

The invasion took place three months ago, but the shocking devastation on the shore and surrounding water remained. Chet had seen the invasion fleet from the air. Ships had stretched from England to France, a spine-tingling, awe-inspiring show of force. Here, it looked like they'd lost. His gut twisted at the broken ships jutting out of the water. Like the roads in French towns, the rubble had been shoved aside on the beach. From trucks to tanks, all that equipment had been lost before it got into battle.

And what of the men? The bloodbath had to have been horrific. How could the soldiers have brought themselves to accomplish what they obviously had? Chet craned his neck to look up at the Germans' concrete pillboxes overlooking the beach. Would he have had the courage to run into withering fire?

Was it any different than flying into flak?

A man plopped down on a stack of crates piled alongside the holding area where Chet's stretcher had been placed. He wore an MP armband. A cigarette dangled from his lips and wobbled precariously when he spoke. "Did ya come through Omaha on your way in?"

Chet watched the cigarette, waiting for it to fall from the man's mouth. "No, uh, I'm an aviator. First time on the beach."

"Well, let me tell you something, flyboy. This here beach has been sanitized." He swept an arm toward the waves lapping the shore. "Still a mess, for sure, but all the bodies have been removed. Sometimes another one washes up or, more likely, part of one, but it gets picked up real quick-like. Everything else can wait. It's junk."

"Were you here on D-Day?" Chet's gaze flitted across the beach from wrecked halftracks to burned-out jeeps.

"Nope, I came over the next day. Had to help look for signs of life amongst the dead. Me and another guy picked up a dead man by his arms to pull him outta the water, and his arms came off. We're standing there holding those arms dripping blood and stuff."

Chet hugged his left arm tight against his chest. Not even a twinge of pain came from his shoulder. There, but for the grace of God...

"Just below those waves for a long ways out are all kinds of trucks and barges and tanks and whatnot. Enough to equip a small army. So much loss woulda crippled any other army in the world, but not us." The policeman seemed impressed. "Then there's all the stuff dropped on the beach. We coulda had a swell yard sale and bought a new jeep or two with the profits."

How many men had died here? The guy didn't appear at all concerned about the loss of life. Chet's mouth got away from him. "What kind of stuff?"

"You name it. Lots of Bibles. A ton of cigarettes, all soaked and useless. Toothbrushes, razors, extra socks. Full packs with a bullet hole through 'em. Lots of writing paper and envelopes that the folks back home aren't going to be getting. Even a doggone tennis racket laying on the sand, still good to use. Some poor fool actually thought he'd have time to play tennis."

A little mostly-brown dog sat on the beach near a half-sunk landing craft. At a soldier's approach, the pooch hopped up, its tail wagging furiously, then sagging as the man walked by.

"What's with the dog?"

"All part of the debris." The policeman threw down his cigarette butt and tamped sand over it. "We try to shoo it away, but it stays put, waiting for a dead man."

Chet jerked his head up. "It's been here for three months?"

"Won't leave. We throw it some food now and then."

The last thing he needed was a dog, but that poor creature. Chet snapped his fingers. The dog perked up. He snapped again and wiggled his fingers. The dog trotted over, ears straight up. An indeterminate breed Chet was sure would stay small, he tickled him under the chin. He looked mangy now, but a good bath would set him to rights.

Smoke break over, the policeman headed back up the beach. Orderlies began taking patients down to a landing craft for transfer to the hospital ship. For the moment, no one paid attention to him. A bunch of empty sacks lay on the other side of the stack of crates.

"See those sacks, Omaha? Go get me one." Chet turned the dog in the right direction and pointed. "Fetch."

The dog looked back up at him, its tail unsure whether to wag.

"Fetch a sack, Omaha. Go on."

Tail drooping, the dog wandered over and sniffed the sacks.

"Bring one here, Omaha. Pick one up. That's it. Bring it here."

The dog sniffed again before sinking his teeth in the top sack. Chet stretched as far as he could, snagged the dog's tail, and reeled him in, bringing the sack.

"Good boy, Omaha." Chet ruffled his ears as his tail swished eagerly.

Chet glanced over his shoulder. The orderlies would come for him next. In one fluid motion, he scooped up the mutt and stuffed him into the sack. Oat dust wafted out, making him sneeze. "Stay quiet now, Omaha, or they'll throw you back." Clutching the sack in one hand and the little box of belongings he'd received from Carol and the Chotars, he lay back.

The orderlies grabbed the ends of his stretcher and hoisted him. His unplanned trip to French soil ended.

England lay a mere one hundred fifty miles across the channel, but getting there took all night. Chet eavesdropped on a badly wounded soldier concerned about getting seasick. A nurse couldn't ease his worries. "Remember, soldier, we must stay in the lanes that have been cleared of mines or you'll end up in worse shape."

The armada filling the channel on D-Day hadn't been confined to lanes. Chet shrugged away the thought, patting his sack which occasionally whined.

The nurse stopped at the berth ahead of his. "An airman with a bullet wound. When were you shot down?"

Chet twisted around to see the fellow flier.

"Two days after the invasion." Breathlessness indicated pain. "Been fighting with the Maquis ever since. Tangled with some Jerries couple days ago."

Being off his feet had some benefit. Chet had heard stories of the bold deeds of the French resistance. He wouldn't care to take part in their dangerous activities.

The nurse came to him. "Lieutenant, your sack is wiggling."

"Is it?"

She whisked it away from him before he could react and peered inside. "Oh, how cute." Omaha poked his head out. "Oh, how dirty."

"You'd be too if you had to live on the beach for three months." Chet reached for the dog, but the nurse spun away.

"We can't have such filth around the patients." She marched away, holding Omaha at arm's length.

Hands clenched, Chet watched her disappear. Either she'd bathe the mutt or throw him overboard. He flopped back down. The stretcher poles creaked in their slots. He envisioned them giving way and dumping him on the man below.

He was so tired of being confined in a body that denied him painless, free movement. He was tired of being dependent on others to bring him meals and help him move. How did permanently disabled people deal with their injuries? His wounds were healing. He'd be back to normal soon. But right now, he wanted to get out of his own skin.

Around him lay men clad in tattered uniforms caked with mud and blood. White bandages stood out in stark relief on some. Others wore bandages as filthy as the rest of their clothes and bodies. Nobody had shaved in a while. They all appeared a little shell-shocked. None of them complained.

He didn't belong here. They should have put him with ambulatory patients, not in the bowels of the ship with men straight off the battlefields. His breathing grew ragged. Spots danced before his eyes.

"Lieutenant, take a deep breath." Someone shook his shoulder. "Lieutenant, look at me."

His eyes rolled to the right. A nurse with her hair pulled severely back stood beside him. Wisps of blonde hair had escaped her tight bun to create a halo effect around her. She wasn't an angel though, not the way she slapped his face. "Lieutenant, are you claustrophobic?"

"N-no." Why did he feel woozy? "Need to go outside, need some air."

The nurse laughed under her breath. "Lieutenant, I do believe you are claustrophobic. Now breathe in." She held a surgical mask to his face. "Breathe in slow. That's right. You were hyperventilating. Close your eyes. Relax."

He pushed away the mask. "That other nurse, she took my dog. Did she throw him overboard?"

"No." The denial came instantly, full of dismay. "Do you really think she'd do that?" She patted his arm. "I wondered who that cute little fur ball belonged to. He's had a bath and now he's charming the socks off the mess attendants. You keep breathing slow, deep breaths, and I'll see if we can't move you topside."

Chet sat in a wheelchair on a train platform, waiting to be loaded onto the hospital train. As far as he could tell, everyone was bound for the nearest general hospital that had available beds. He had a different destination in mind.

"Excuse me," he flagged down an orderly. "Does this train go to Braintree? That's where I have to go. The 12th Evacuation Hospital in Braintree, Essex County."

"Sure you do." The orderly grabbed the handles on Chet's wheelchair and pushed him up a ramp. "You'll go where we take you, buddy. From there somebody'll have to come and claim you. Once we know you are who you say you are, your base'll decide where they want you."

Chet dug his fingers into Omaha's clean, fluffy fur. "I was with my brother's unit. He knew who I was. Then I was picked up at my girl's Red Cross base. She knew me."

"Is that so? Well, they ain't here now to recognize you, are they? Rules is rules, buddy. Gotta make sure the Jerries ain't slipping in a ringer."

He secured the chair in place next to a window. At least he didn't grouch about a dog coming aboard.

Chet whispered in the dog's ear. "I'll bet the little blonde nurse put something in my record about being claustrophobic. That's why we're parked by the window. You'll like this better, won't you, Omaha? We can watch the scenery."

Omaha gazed at him with a doggy grin before hopping up to rest his front paws on the window sill and press his nose to the glass.

The miles slid by. Chet spent the time staring out at the gray day and stroking the dog. Anxious thoughts circled his mind like vultures. A lot could happen in three weeks of war. Familiar faces might be gone from the base. His gear would have been packed up and sent home to Grandma and Grandpa. He should send them a telegram. Maybe word had come regarding Paul Braedel's fate. Who would come to recognize him?

He didn't have long to find out. Parked on another train platform, a voice from his recent past hailed him. He looked up into the grinning face of Lowell Hendricks.

"Do you know the penalty for being AWOL?"

Chapter Forty-Four

Verdun, France
September 20, 1944

"Verdun. What's the significance of this place?" Carol stretched after climbing down from *George Washington*. After convoying south from Belgium all day, her muscles protested every move. She leaned over and hugged her knee to her nose. Oh, that felt good.

"Beats me." Louise rubbed her eyes and yawned. "I don't see any chateaus nearby. After that last swanky place in Dinant with running water in the bathrooms and toasty warm bedrooms, I fear we're in for a rude shock here."

They'd come to the headquarters of the 12th Army. The officers treated them to a steak dinner. It tasted divine after two weeks of increasingly unpalatable K-rations. Carol might not mind trading a warm room for meals if they could regularly dine at the army mess. Afterwards, the Red Cross crews were shown to their quarters on the second floor of a stone barracks. Gloria tapped her foot against a tiny stove in the middle of their room. Despite a fire, no heat emanated from it.

"Inferior grade of coal," explained the aide who showed them around. "Don't plan on getting water to boil if you hope to make coffee."

Louise dropped her musette bag on a bed. "Where's the bathroom?"

The aide shuffled his feet. "You'll find the latrine in a tent about a half city block down that-away."

He pointed west.

All three girls chorused, "Half a block?"

Carol shrugged and looked at her friends. "We could use a little exercise."

They headed for the door.

In the morning, Carol joined some of the other girls in the hunt for a laundry. "Don't forget today's password." The same aide materialized as they headed out the door. "It's 'hierarchy.'"

Hazel wrinkled her nose. "What a ridiculous choice of words."

The aide fiddled with his cap. "Krauts have trouble wrapping their tongues around it."

Carol looked up and down the street. "The army's taken over a lot of buildings. Why don't we start at the Hotel de Ville? It's an officers' club now. Maybe someone there can help us."

They passed a fenced compound crowded with men. Catcalls and wolf whistles pierced the air.

Carol's steps faltered. "Why, those are German prisoners."

"Ignore them," Doris hissed. "Show them contempt."

"Oh, no." Hazel rubbed her hands together. "Let's have some fun." She raised her voice. "And here we have examples of the super race. Pretty pathetic, if you ask me."

A girl from the *Liberty Bell* spotted a pair of GIs approaching. "Oh, Hazel. Do you have your camera? Give it to Doris, so she can take our picture." She stopped the soldiers. "May we borrow your rifles?"

She and Hazel grabbed the guns and stood in front of the prisoners, brandishing the weapons as though they were guards.

Carol turned away, and bit back a laugh. "Imagine what would happen if those prisoners could get their hands on you."

One prisoner captured her attention. He looked like Chet, but he couldn't be. Chet was on his way back to England. He noticed her gaze, but she couldn't look away.

"Come on, Carol." Doris tugged her arm. "What are you thinking, ogling a German like that?"

"I'm not. Did you see him? He looked just like Chet." Carol gulped a lungful of air. "He could have been Chet's twin. I know the Vogels are Dutch, but I wonder if they also have German ancestry. That may have been a relative."

"Wouldn't that be crazy?" Hazel handed the rifle back to the grinning soldier. "My grandfather's brother stayed in Germany. I could have not-so-distant cousins fighting for Hitler. Creepy thought."

A shiver raised goose bumps on Carol's arms. As far as she knew, all her ancestors came from France and the British Isles. She glanced back as they started down the road. The look-alike no longer stood at the fence.

A wild idea stopped her. If he spoke English, she could interview him. She couldn't ask political questions. He'd offer expedient answers to garner favor with the Allies. But what if he had relatives in America? How did the Germans feel about their enemy kin? Would her publisher run such an article? She trailed after her friends, weighing the feasibility of getting interviews with enemy prisoners.

A few days later, her plans hadn't progressed any further than watching the aide's eyebrows disappear under his cap when she asked who she'd need to talk to. She jotted down possible questions as they drove in convoy to their assigned units in the 7th Armored Division. Permission might come more readily if she presented a complete interview outline.

By the time they headed back to Verdun, darkness had fallen. Louise strained to see the road in the slits of light furnished by their blacked-out headlights. Recent rains had made a muddy mess of the roads, and more than one pothole threatened them with dental damage.

Suddenly, a terrific crash jarred them, and *George* spun and slid toward the ditch at the side of the road.

"No, no, no!" Louise stomped on the brakes and fought the steering wheel, ramming an elbow into Carol's ribs in the process. *George* shuddered to a stop. "Oh my goodness. Oh my goodness."

Beams from flashlights showed two French vehicles in the ditch. The oncoming truck had fishtailed, sending the trailer it towed directly into the clubmobile. The beams played over *George*, and Gloria's door was wrenched open.

"Are you ladies all right?" inquired an American voice.

Carol released the breath she'd been holding, braced against the dashboard. She inhaled and eased back in the seat. Louise's hands clutched the steering wheel in a white-knuckled grip. Gloria leaned around Carol. "Louise? Are you okay?"

"Y-yes?" Someone opened her door and pried her fingers loose.

The first rescuer helped Gloria and Carol out of the cab. Carol's legs wobbled, and she grabbed hold of the door.

"Good thing we were all squeezed into the front seat." Gloria kept her arms tightly crossed over her chest. "We kept each other from flying around."

"I'm afraid your clubmobile didn't fare so well." The man circled around the front, shining his light on *George*. The entire front end of the clubmobile was ruined. Steam escaped from the damaged radiator. One end of the bumper dragged on the road. A tire was slashed. Louise's side mirror lay shattered. "I do have good news. You're right in front of our ordnance company." His grin looked ghoulish in the dim beam of light. "Just leave it here and we'll have it repaired and ready to go in no time."

The girls spent the next two days serving the ordnance crew while they replaced the front wheel assembly. When their work was complete, the girls applauded.

"*George* has never looked better." Carol patted the new grill.

Gloria shielded her eyes. "We need dark glasses the way he sparkles in the sun."

Louise gleefully bounced in her seat as they headed out. "Boy, they really overhauled the old boy. He handles like a dream."

They were serving a unit near Metz, which the Germans were aggressively defending. Thunderclaps of gunfire rolled through the area, and bursts of artillery fire flashed in the sky. Gloria pointed to an arc of flame. "I think we'd better batten everything down and pull back. This battle's getting too close for comfort."

From the serving window, Louise began collecting cups. "Yeah, we don't want anything happening to *George* after his facelift."

Carol laughed. "Not to mention us."

She grabbed an empty doughnut tray and collected coffee cups from the men.

A shrill whistle grew loud. Around her, men dropped to the ground. She hesitated. What in the world?

Suddenly, a blinding flash. A deafening roar. The weird sensation of flying. An incredible sting of pain.

"Carol, can you hear me?" The voice sounded like Gloria's, but it came from such a distance, or maybe underwater. How odd.

More voices yelled as if though a tunnel.

"Get those women away from here. We don't need more casualties."

"It was just a stray shell, captain."

"We don't know that."

"Carol! I need to stay with her."

"We'll take care of her. Go."

Brutal pain assaulted her when someone touched her. A strangled cry wrenched from her lips. Oblivion rushed at her. She embraced it.

Chapter Forty-Five

Chet studied the faces before him. This was crazy. He wasn't an instructor. Besides, these guys were pilots. He was a navigator. New pilots thought they knew everything and, sure as the sun rises in the east, they wouldn't take kindly to a navigator telling them how to fly.

"I want my pilot to be like a bus driver. You are personally responsible for your eight crewmen passengers. They want a nice, smooth ride." That might be laying it on rather thick, but the hyperbole ought to stick in their craws. "The navigator needs a level platform so his instruments are steady. If you're a throttle jock, bouncing up and down, weaving back and forth, his instruments are going to be jumping all over the place, and he's not going to be able to tell you precisely where you are."

Ten men stared at him. They looked bored. They'd completed their training in the States. Now they were practicing formation flying in England. They thought they were ready for combat. Their first mission would wipe away their complacency.

"Forget your passengers for the moment. You're a truck driver. Your job is to deliver six thousand or so pounds of ordnance to the Germans. That's all your job consists of. Deliver your bombs directly on the target. You need tunnel vision for that. Watch your instruments and ignore what's going on outside."

If the guy in back wasn't yawning, he smirked. He reminded Chet too much of his brother Willard. He focused on someone else. The guy on the left end of the front row started looking a little pale, his eyes growing wider by the minute. Another minute and he'd be sharing his breakfast. Time to ease up. Chet offered a half-hearted shrug.

"Make sure you keep track of your wingmen. You don't want to plant your wingtip into another plane's waist window. The gunners won't like that."

That got a few weak chuckles. Paleface squirmed, glanced at his fellows. His lips twisted in a grin that died before it was born. He'd better be a copilot rather than a pilot slash aircraft commander.

"When you're in the lead, it's easy to keep your dials and needles steady. You won't be flying lead, however. The new crews get the Tail-End Charlie position, where it's easier to find your place in the formation. There you'll want to jockey around to find that perfect spot, especially when the flight leader radios for everyone to tighten up the formation."

Chet resisted the temptation to downplay the difficulties. He'd never tried to hold a B-17 steady in tight quarters. He flapped a hand up and down. "Just remember. This is what your tail is doing when you bounce around. Unless your tail gunner has an iron gut, he's going to have problems. Trust me, on a six- or eight-hour mission, you don't want to be smelling someone's regurgitated breakfast."

If anything, Paleface got whiter.

Afterwards, Chet met Lowell Hendricks outside the Quonset hut classroom. "I think if I'd known I'd be an instructor until I regain flight status, I'd have stayed in France. I don't mind working with navigators, but do pilots really listen to anyone other than pilots?"

Lowell laughed and raised a hand, about to clap him on the back. Instead, he lightly squeezed Chet's shoulder. Chet's use of a cane signaled to everyone to treat him gently.

As they headed for the Officers' Club, Lowell tried to answer his question. "Last year, when the air war really got going, I think there were more hot fly-boy types who flew like fighter pilots, thinking they were great stuff. A lot of them are dead now. Today the mentality is more teamwork orientated. Defeating the Luftwaffe didn't turn out to be the snap everyone expected, so we had to get down to business and figure out a better strategy. At least, that's my impression."

"The Flying Fortress carries a lot of guns, but they don't make it immune to destruction. The change started when the brass finally conceded we need fighter planes to escort us." Chet stopped and faced Lowell. "Aren't you glad we came over after fighter protection was imposed?"

"The Luftwaffe's steadily losing ground, but the flak is worse now. Look what it did to you, although I must say, you're walking mighty fine. Soon you can throw away the cane."

Chet swung the cane up like a sword. "What a relief when the doc announced my femur suffered a simple crack and not a messy break. I was sure those weeks shuffling around would worsen it." He stomped his left foot. Barely a twinge. "All because of a bruised nerve."

"Don't dismiss the trouble that might have caused. My aunt has sciatica pain that makes life miserable for her." Lowell reached for the door, but before he could pull it open, Omaha raced around the corner of the Quonset and barked a doggy greeting, his tail a blur. "I still can't believe you brought back a flea sack. I think if my driver hadn't latched onto that mutt when we came to pick you up at the train station, I would have left it behind."

"No, you wouldn't have. Can't fool me." Chet stooped to ruffle Omaha's fur. The dog washed his hand. Chet gave him a final pat, sending him back toward the motor pool. He wiped his hand on his pant leg. "Truth to tell, I'm glad the ground pounders claimed him. Omaha's sure to have more stability with them than a combat team."

Inside the club, Andy Anderson hailed them. "Hey, Chet, as long as your new crew got a replacement for you, why don't you come back with us? Our new navigator needs a map to find his way to the latrine."

Lowell huffed a laugh. "Green as the grass, he is. He's never prompt with a position report. He relies too much on following the leader, but if we're ever separated from the group, we're going to be in serious trouble."

"What's his name? I'll give him a little one-on-one tutoring."

"Great. I'll go get him." Andy headed for the door.

"Wait a minute." The door swung shut on Chet's protest. He spun to face Lowell. "Right now?"

"No time like the present." This time Lowell did clap him on the back before sauntering to the bar.

Chet huddled with Abner Nelson at a corner table in the club an hour later. Nelson's logbook lay open before Chet, and he paged back and forth. "You haven't been recording anything."

"There's been nothing to record."

Chet bit back the retort that sprang to his lips. He eyed the kid slouched next to him. A hillbilly comic strip character came to mind. The intelligence was there. It just wasn't developed. "There's plenty you should have noted. Every time the group changes course, mark down the new heading and time. Every sighting of enemy flak or fighters, mark the location. If a bomber goes down, record the location, time, its position in the group, whether any chutes appeared. If it's from our squadron, include the pilot's name."

Basic stuff. The interrogators at post-mission debriefings always asked to see his logbook. They should have said something when they saw these blank pages. The squadron navigator or group navigator should have made him aware of the necessity.

Chet straightened up. Someone was watching him. He turned to his right, and surprised the young man leaning forward at the next table, trying to listen in. He wore a navigator's insignia. His shoulder patch placed him in the 535th Squadron.

"What's your logbook like?"

The sudden challenge set the fellow back in his seat. "It, uh, I record flak."

Chet waved him over to take a chair at his table.

"In the navigators briefing before the mission, you're given the route and coordinates. Besides your log, copy the computed headings of each leg of the route on your map, and then when you're in the air, trace your route on your map with time notations. Think ahead. If you have high winds on the way in, will they affect you on the way back? Compute your ETAs. If you realize your estimated time of arrival isn't going to match the briefed ETA, figure out what the wind is doing."

He studied the faces listening to him, and realized that a third navigator straddled a chair behind Li'l Abner to monitor the session. He nodded to the last empty chair at his table and the newcomer scrambled to join them. "What are you fellas going to do if you're flying deep in Germany with ten-tenths cloud coverage below, and you lose two engines? You have to drop out of formation, and you can't follow the leader anymore. Your eight crewmates are depending on you to direct them back to England. What are you going to do?"

Dead silence. All three neophyte navigators looked at the table, out the window, studied their hands. None looked at Chet. They had to have some idea or they wouldn't have gotten out of navigator school. With this level of confidence, though, their crews faced disaster if they ever straggled.

Chet understood the confusion of the rookies. They'd trained in the United States, where checkpoints were more easily identified. In England, and Europe, dense population made recognition difficult. Add in combat, and confidence evaporated.

"Let's start at the beginning. You take off, rendezvous into formation, and head out. What should you be doing?"

The 535th kid piped up. "Keep track of where we are."

"How?"

The kid sucked in a deep breath. "Home in on radio beacons with the radio compass while we're within range of England."

"Good start." They knew something after all. "The radio operator can help you out. He has a remote of your radio compass and a list of the beacon schedules. Those are constantly changed to keep the Germans from utilizing them, but he'll figure out which can be used to get your bearings. Don't hesitate to ask him for position reports. Get him involved."

The pinched look around Li'l Abner's eyes eased. Chet wracked his brain for the name of Lowell's radio operator. Dexter Short. No, Small. Hadn't he utilized his services?

"Okay, you know where you are. What should you be doing now?"

The newcomer jumped in. "Calculate what the wind's doing to us. Headwind, tailwind, or pushing us off course."

Chet clapped three times. Before Newcomer could lean back in his seat, Chet fired one word, "How?"

Li'l Abner had an answer. "Compare our magnetic compass heading with our indicated air speed to our course and speed we're making on the ground."

"Good." Chet nodded once.

"And log it."

"Very good. Don't be afraid to mess up your map. Mark your route from checkpoint to checkpoint. Either that or keep your finger on the map so you don't lose track of the last position."

"Lieutenant." A hand landed heavily on Chet's shoulder. "Put together a crew and take up a plane tomorrow. Give your students some worthwhile practice." Colonel Leber, commander of the bomb group, stood beside him.

"Yes, sir." Chet's stomach shimmied. He should conduct classes in the air? That task belonged to the Group Navigator or at least the Squadron Navigators. He'd flown as lead a few times, but now was grounded without a crew.

Lowell and Andy had gotten him into this, so they could fly the plane. If Dexter Small still served as their radio operator, this would be a fine time to indoctrinate him on helping out Li'l Abner.

He spent the rest of the day in a dither, planning his aerial session. Too bad Paul Braedel no longer served in the 381st Bomb Group, having transferred to Air Transport Command after escaping from Germany while Chet languished in France. They could have brainstormed on what exercises taught them the most at Pan American's Navigation School.

The next morning, he headed for the plane, confident he could sharpen the three trained navigators on their skills. After a month and more of not flying, a little practice wouldn't hurt him any either. He knew a moment of indecision when he climbed aboard and found not three, but six navigators awaiting him. The three had each brought along a friend. Crazy clowns.

"Think Bomby will come back?" Chet lay on his cot, hands linked under his head. The hour was late, but the 532nd Squadron wasn't scheduled to fly the next day.

"He has no choice. He didn't finish his tour of duty." Lowell flipped through a hut mate's collection of records and put Artie Shaw on the Victrola.

"I'm surprised more bombardiers don't end up with shattered eye sockets. I saw Bomby's head bounce on the bomb sight often enough when flak jarred our plane." Chet stretched out full length with no discomfort in his leg. "If I'd been sent home, I would not want to come back."

The Quonset hut door opened and the squadron medical officer entered. He came to the foot of Chet's cot. "Good news, Vogel. Or bad, depending on how you look at it. You are now back on flight status. Report to Colonel Fitzgerald's office at 0800 tomorrow."

His mission complete, the doctor strode out. Chet sat up, staring at the door as it closed behind him. Good news or bad news. Good way to put it. Good in that he would now get on with completing his own tour. Bad, though, because he would once more be back in the war where men would do their level best to kill him.

He lay back down. Despite his exhaustion, sleep didn't come easily that night. The base was on alert for a mission in the morning and, across the field, the ground crews worked on the airplanes slated to fly, probably thirty-seven, their usual contribution. First one or two engines started up, accelerating to a thousand RMP for a five to ten minute warm-up. Then the magnetos, propellers, and full power checks followed. Readying one hundred forty-eight engines took all night. Usually the chorus of Wright Cyclones faded into a drone of white noise, but tonight they grated on Chet like buzz saws.

At the appointed hour, he entered the office of the squadron commanding officer and stood at attention.

"At ease, Captain. Have a seat."

In the process of seating himself, Chet paused and gaped at Colonel Fitzgerald. Captain?

"You're our new Squadron Navigator, and according to the Table of Organization, that entitles you to a captaincy. We put you in for the promotion when you returned from France, having already tabbed you for the job. You'll be flying with Lansing's crew, and we want you to continue working with the new navigators. Congratulations, Captain." He shook Chet's hand and dismissed him.

Outside, the day remained gray and dreary. Chet tugged his collar close around his neck. Captain Chester Vogel, Squadron Navigator. How do you like that? He grinned and headed for the PX to pick up his new insignia. Leader of men. Not bad for a kid whose father didn't expect him to amount to anything.

Chapter Forty-Six

Paris, France
Thursday, September 28, 1944

Squeak, crick. Squeak, crick. The irritating noise penetrated the deep fog that held Carol in its clutch. She dragged in a deep breath. Boy, that hurt. Why should her lungs, or was it her ribs, hurt so much? She tried to shift away from the pain, but it shifted with devilish delight to squeeze her shoulders. It snatched her breath away.

A pungent odor infiltrated the fog. Her nose wrinkled. Definitely not the ink of a newsroom smell. More like a medicinal stench. Pain plus a medicinal stench equaled... Her eyes snapped open. The last vestiges of fog evaporated.

She lay in a hospital. A sack of something hung overhead with tubes snaking down to her arm. A headache proclaimed its presence when she inched her head up to search for the tube's end.

Why was she here? What was wrong with her? Had she been in an accident? Thoughts careened through her mind, ricocheting off her aching skull. She reached a shaky hand up to her forehead. Her fingernails were ragged, dirt pressed into the crescents.

The squeak crick started again, coming closer. The door pushed open and a nurse old enough to be a grandmother poked her head in. "Well, look who's awake at last."

She entered the room, dragging in a metal cart on protesting wheels.

Carol had to clear her throat twice before she could croak, "What happened?"

The nurse poured a cup of water and held it to Carol's lips. "What is the last thing you remember?"

Nothing came to mind. She was a reporter for the *Canton Repository*, she knew that. There'd been a Christmas party. That's right. She wrote for the society page, but wanted to do something different. A memory teased her, but kept to the shadows. "What happened?"

"Do you know what country you're in?"

Country? "Ohio."

The nurse's brow puckered in a frown. "Wait right here. I need to find someone."

She left her cart and hurried off.

Carol didn't have time to ponder long. A doctor strode in, identifiable by his white lab coat and the shiny circle of metal held in place by a band around his head. He pressed his fingers to her wrist. His gravelly voice rumbled out. "What's your name, young lady?"

That was easy. "Carol Jean Doucet."

"Hmm." He flicked a beam of light into her eyes, which didn't help her headache. "How old are you?"

Louise would have said that was none of his business. Who was Louise? She didn't know any Louise. Did she? Carol frowned. Seemed to be a lot she should know, but didn't. The throbbing in her head increased with her efforts to remember. At least she knew the answer to his question. "Twenty-five."

The number held special significance, but that also eluded her.

The doctor stepped back and crossed his arms. "Have you ever traveled abroad?"

The question confused her. First the nurse asked what country she was in, now this. She must be in a foreign country, and yet they spoke English. American English. Her heart picked up its pace, and she pressed a hand to her chest. "What happened to me?"

She heard the hysteria rising in her voice.

Pulling over a chair, the doctor sat down, bringing himself to her level. He picked up her hand, his thumb straying to her wrist. "Do you remember what the world situation is like?"

Carol raked in a breath. Hitler. Pearl Harbor. "War. We're at war."

A smile creased the doctor's face. "Do you know what the Red Cross is doing in the war zones?"

The Red Cross. Again a memory teased her, but slipped away before she could grab it.

The doctor took a clipboard from the nurse. "Do you know anyone named Gloria or Louise?"

Louise again. She must be a friend. Maybe they were in the accident together.

"What about Chet?"

Chet. Finally, an image unfolded. Dark brown hair, brown eyes that sometimes looked green, brilliant smile. *Godspeed, Chet.* They're dropping like flies. "He's in a bomber crew." More than that. She swallowed hard. "He was wounded."

The doctor leaned forward. "Do you know where?"

Now she saw Chet seated on a stool, struggling to his feet. *Careful, honey. I'm damaged goods.* She had seen him. In the field. In France. "Why am I in France?"

Before the doctor could say anything, another scene materialized. A battered truck called *George Washington.* A Red Cross truck. A clubmobile. "Doughnuts." The doctor and nurse both smiled. "We were in an accident." Their smiles faded. "*George* was damaged, I remember. But I wasn't hurt."

"You remember, then, that you were serving with the Red Cross?" The doctor waited for Carol's slight nod before glancing again at his clipboard. "You were near Metz, in eastern France, when a stray artillery shell exploded nearby. The human body doesn't fare too well against one of those, but you're lucky. Good thing you wore a helmet. I understand it sustained quite a gouge. Had that piece of shrapnel hit your head, you wouldn't be here now."

Another image jarred Carol's consciousness. A young soldier walked toward the trees with coffee and doughnut in hand, and blew up. Her stomach cramped, and she squeezed her eyes shut, trying to block out the horrible vision.

The doctor stood and pushed back his chair. "You're in remarkably good shape. I don't know how close the shell landed to you, but vegetation of some sort shielded you and blunted the force of the explosive, slowing down the shrapnel before it reached you." He referred to his clipboard. "You were stitched up at the nearest aid station, and then brought here to Paris. Shouldn't be too long before you can head for home."

With the nurse's assistance, he removed a bandage from her arm.

Carol kept her eyes closed, not wanting to see what they were doing and wishing she didn't have to hear about it either. When his last comment registered, her eyes popped open. "Go home?"

The nurse answered. "You won't be going back to the clubmobiles, dearie. The Red Cross doesn't want to risk further harm. Besides, with winter coming, the lifestyle will be too rigorous for you."

Tugs on her arm suggested stitches being removed. She turned her face away. Good thing she didn't have anything in her stomach. "What day is it?"

"Thursday the twenty-eighth. You arrived here on Tuesday." The nurse brushed Carol's hair off her face. "How are you doing? Would you like a sip of water?"

Long after she was left alone to rest, Carol pondered her situation. The nurse was right. Working in a clubmobile no longer appealed to her. She couldn't imagine living in some of the housing arrangements they'd had in the middle of winter. Even in England, where they ranged from a single home base, the lifestyle sounded arduous.

But did she have to go home? Leaving before the war ended sounded ignominious. She wiggled her toes, shifted her hips, raised both hands. Soreness radiated from a dozen places, but everything worked. She'd heal up and be fine. No need to go home.

Clubmobiles were out. So were the clubs. The few times she ventured into a club in England, the place had been hopping. But she could do hospital work like her old roommate Midge. The recreation they offered couldn't be too strenuous. Playing games, doing crafts, writing letters for the men with hand injuries. She flexed her fingers. No problem.

Or the rest homes. The army had taken over lots of manor houses in England where combat crews could escape from the war for a week. Now there was a sedate job she could handle. All she had to do was convince headquarters. Next time the nurse came by, she'd ask to see someone from the Paris office.

She was massaging her temple when a chaplain stuck his head into the room. "How are you doing?"

"Who said, 'War is hell?'"

The chaplain crossed his arms and raised a finger to tap his chin. "I can think of any number of people who espouse that sentiment."

A smile tugged at her lips. She allowed it to bloom. "I knew the truth of that before, but now I feel it."

"War is the devil's playground, no denying it." He patted her hand. "But don't forget, God is unchanging, no matter the shifting seasons. And this season shall pass, giving way to a time of peace and healing."

London, England
October 9, 1944

Carol found the waiting room at the Red Cross's headquarters and took a seat. Pulling off her gloves, she laid them beside her to avoid twisting them. She shouldn't be so nervous. All they would do was send her home, if they didn't allow her a rest home posting.

Another girl entered the room, and she looked up. "Audrey?"

Her former crewmate had mismatched her coat buttons with their proper holes. The windless day couldn't be faulted for Audrey's unruly hair. No cosmetics adorned her face, usually so carefully made up. Carol had never seen her look so frazzled.

Audrey stopped abruptly. A haunted look flickered over her face as she stared at Carol. Recognition came slowly. "C-Carol? What are you doing here?" Her voice sounded as dull as dirt.

Carol hopped up and guided Audrey to a chair. "Are you all right?" Alarm swirled within her at her friend's listlessness. "Audrey, are you ill?"

Audrey's eyes darted here and there, but they didn't make contact with Carol. "I have to go home." She wound a handkerchief around a finger. Suddenly she turned to Carol with a spark of her old spunk. "Go ahead and say it. You told me so."

"What did I tell you?" Carol didn't like the wild look in Audrey's eyes. She cautiously took her hand and rubbed it between her own. "What's going on?"

"Wally said I have to go home. He doesn't want me serving the airmen anymore. He says I'm flirting with them."

Remembering the tiff they'd had previously over Wally, Carol chose her words carefully. "You set a wedding date, didn't you?"

"We are married." The life drained right out of Audrey.

"You are married?" Carol flinched at the shock audible in her voice. She clamped her teeth together. Of course. Audrey had set the date as the Fourth of July. Three months ago.

"You were right. I should have waited. I didn't know him at all. Right away he started criticizing everything I do. He doesn't want me around the men. I'm supposed to go home and wait for him." Audrey's shoulders hunched and she appeared to cave in on herself.

Carol's thoughts raced. "Has he hurt you?"

"Not with his fists. He just yells. I wonder if his parents are any better."

"Couldn't you stay with your own parents?"

"I wish I could." Audrey straightened up. "I wish I could divorce him and tell him to get lost. But, Carol, I can't. I think I'm pregnant."

She gripped Carol's hand like a lifeline.

Audrey was right. "I told you so" poised on the tip of Carol's tongue. She swallowed the condemnation.

But what in the world could she say to Audrey's announcement? Carol patted her hand. She tried to picture herself in Audrey's place and shuddered. If she remembered right, Audrey and Wally lived on opposite sides of the country. She'd be far from her folks, no friends to welcome her home. Carol released a breath that emptied her lungs. A longer courtship may not have revealed Wally's Jekyll-Hyde character.

Chet popped into her thoughts. He wouldn't be like that. Surely not.

The office door opened and a friendly face peered out. "Carol? The supervisor will see you now."

Audrey roused when Carol pulled free and stood. "Why aren't you in France?"

"I got too close to the war and was wounded. I'm hoping for reassignment." She hesitated. "Good luck, Audrey."

Such lame words.

The supervisor directed Carol to a chair before folding her hands on the desk and studying her. Carol refused to squirm. She held her head high, hoping her smile didn't look artificial.

"So you'd like to stay in Europe with an easy job." This lady would do well at poker. Carol couldn't tell if she was annoyed, scornful, sympathetic, or just plain bored.

"The war's not over, so the job's not done. I still want to serve." If only she could get a peek at her medical report from the Paris office. "The doctor who treated me in Paris said I should avoid physically demanding tasks. I'm healed from my injuries, but he said being in a blast, as I was, is a tremendous shock to the body."

Not by a flicker of an eyelash did her interrogator reveal her thoughts. Carol plowed on. "The doctor told me a lot of people injured in artillery blasts are actually injured more from being knocked down and forcibly coming in contact with the earth or other hard objects, more than being thrown a long distance. I landed in a grassy field with no rocks under me. No shrapnel tore through me like some of the boys suffer."

The statue moved. She pulled over an open file. "It says here you had seventy-six stitches in eight wounds. No lasting effects from any of those cuts?"

Carol hugged herself, unable to stop a shudder. "No, ma'am. And fortunately, I wasn't conscious when they sewed me up."

A smile twitched the supervisor's lips. "Very well. We will have a doctor examine you here, and again in a month or so." She shuffled her papers. "We do have an opening at the Stanbridge Earls rest home. Depending on your physical, you can report there tomorrow. You'll find Rose Armstrong there. She'll provide your on-the-job training."

Carol surged to her feet. "Thank you, ma'am."

Armed with her medical appointment card, she hurried out before the supervisor could change her mind. Audrey no longer waited in the anteroom. Good. With her own prospects glowing, any sympathy she offered might be perceived as gloating by Audrey. She hesitated. It'd be nice to say good-bye, exchange addresses. She glanced at her appointment card. No time. She didn't have addresses for Gloria, Louise, or Irene either. One bright spot remained. In England, she'd have a good chance of seeing Chet again.

Chapter Forty-Seven

London, England
Thursday, October 19, 1944

The squadron flew a mission to Germany, but Chet's crew wasn't assigned to lead. He and Slade, his new copilot, got a twenty-four-hour pass to London. That night, they found their way to the Strand Theater to see *Arsenic and Old Lace*.

As they milled about the lobby, waiting to enter the theater, a voice called out, "Hey, Vogel."

Before Chet could look back, the sergeant in front of him turned around. His father! Everyone else faded from his awareness as he stared at the man who could torment him without even being present. His dad stared back before his eyes drifted down to the shiny new captain's bars and the DFC alongside the Purple Heart. He didn't salute.

Expecting a sarcastic comment, Chet grabbed the initiative. "Hello...Dad." The label sounded foreign on his tongue. "Nate didn't say anything about you being in England."

Dad's brows bounced up. "You've seen Nate?"

Chet nodded. "I went down in France last month. Spent a night with his gun crew."

A hand grabbed his arm. "Hey, Vogel, your lead navigator today is in trouble."

That got Chet's attention. He faced the Squadron Navigator from the 534th. "What happened?"

"Seems the 381st got to the wing rendezvous late. That made the wing late to the division rendezvous. Guess there was quite a mess as planes wandered all over the sky, trying to figure out where they belonged. All the leads have been notified to appear at Wing Headquarters for a review."

Chet narrowed his eyes. "They can't pin this on Zint. He's my whiz kid who's going to take over my job when I finally get to go home."

"You might want to join him at HQ."

"I'll be there." Throughout the exchange, Chet remained acutely aware of his dad's presence, watching, listening. Now the theater doors opened and the crowd surged forward. He lost sight of Dad.

After they settled into seats, Slade asked, "Who was the sergeant?"

"My father."

"Your father?" Slade's eyes bugged so wide, Chet wouldn't have been surprised if they popped out. "When had you last seen him?"

"It's been years." Chet would have left it at that, but his crewmate continued to stare at him. "My grandparents raised me after Mom died." He nodded toward the lobby. "Last I knew, he was a drill sergeant. He made no secret of the fact that he didn't think I'd amount to anything."

Slade eased back in his seat. "If that had been my dad, he'd have squeezed the stuffing out of me, pounded me on the back, and yelled, 'This here's my boy. How've you been, Son?'"

The film began, but Chet couldn't concentrate. His thoughts strayed from his father to Lieutenant Zint and back again. Had Dad been the least bit glad to see him? What had gone wrong with the rendezvous? He'd be glad to get back to base.

The command pilot who led the mission was a colonel. His command navigator was a major. Chet's navigator was a second lieutenant. His own Group Navigator looked dubious, tapping a sheaf of papers first on their side, then on the edge. This debriefing pitted David against Goliath. It was Eschwege all over again.

The colonel spoke first, full of confidence. "We arrived at the rendezvous site on time, but the 381st failed to appear."

Arrogance. Too much arrogance. That led to carelessness. But how to prove it? Chet eyed the Group Navigator. Too bad Major Foster wasn't still here. If this man did lack confidence in Lieutenant Zint, his questioning would portray that lack.

Unless… Chet sat up ramrod straight. He caught the Group Nav's eye. He pointed to himself and mouthed his request. "Let me do the questioning."

A nod and a look of relief. If Chet failed in exonerating Zint, it would be on his head, not the Group Navigator's.

Chet thought fast and prayed for wisdom in his questioning. Zint was innocent. He'd bet a chocolate cake on that. So what mistake did the command navigator make? Could it be a simple miscalculation? Something done so often, it had been glossed over this time? He rose to his feet.

He asked both the command navigator and his whiz kid for the time and place of their last visual check of the ground or pass over a beacon. Then he asked what the wind speed had been. He stepped up to a blackboard and, with all eyes watching, he did the math and plotted their positions on a wall map. Borrowing an E6B computer, he calculated the wind speeds for himself.

"Lieutenant Zint, I figure your ground speed when you arrived at the point of rendezvous to be 158." Chet turned to his Group Navigator. "What did he record in his log?"

"157."

Chet nodded. Close enough. He faced the command navigator. "Major, I'm having trouble with your ground speed. To get to the rendezvous when you said you did, you would have had to have flown into the wind at 550 knots. I don't know of any Flying Fortress that has better than a maximum speed of 325."

The major grabbed his own E6B and twirled the dial. He muttered an expletive under his breath.

Chet grinned. His whiz kid slumped in his chair. The presiding general nodded to Chet, respect in his gaze.

During their drive back to Ridgewell, the Group Navigator said, "Vogel, you did us proud."

Too bad Dad couldn't hear that. He probably left the theater thinking the whiz kid had screwed up because of Chet.

Chapter Forty-Eight

October 28, 1944

Clouds obscured the target. The 532nd Squadron flew as the Low Group leader of the Wing. Chet didn't mind. As a group leader, they shouldered responsibility for eighteen planes, not the fifty-four of the whole wing. Today, he did not envy the men leading the wing. The transportation center in Munster remained hidden by haze.

Chet traced their route on his map. Suddenly his charts blew off his desk. He jerked his head up. A four-inch hole had been punched into the Plexiglas nose, allowing the wind to whistle in. The German gunners had found their altitude.

Memories of a shattered nose window after Cologne chilled him more than the wind. He lowered his goggles to shield his eyes. His map promptly blew away, joining his charts in the passageway. He needed those. Unplugging his oxygen and communication cables, Chet crawled after them.

There they were. Down by the forward escape hatch. He scooped them up. The mission flimsy with the day's codes got away from him. He snatched it out of the swirling air.

Time to get back in the nose and hook up his oxygen cable before he passed out.

An invisible fist slammed him back against the escape hatch. Orange flames leaped out of the nose, licking him from head to toe. Just as suddenly, they disappeared. The rice paper flimsy, meant to be swallowed to avoid falling into enemy hands, disintegrated in his hand. The charts and maps smoldered. So did his clothes. He slapped at them. With no skin exposed, he hadn't been burned.

He needed to get back on oxygen. The nose glowed bright orange. A fire still raged in there. He couldn't go back in and hook up.

The bombardier! He must be dead. What was his name? Chet couldn't remember.

He needed to get the fire extinguisher. One hung on the opposite side of the nose entrance. But he couldn't make himself move. He slumped there, staring at the angry orange glow.

Someone dropped down from the cockpit. Probably the engineer. He grabbed the extinguisher and sprayed it into the nose. His head swiveled as he caught sight of Chet. He dropped the fire extinguisher and removed his own walk-around oxygen bottle, hooking it up to Chet's oxygen mask.

Someone else joined them, bearing more oxygen bottles. The engineer hooked up to one and returned to fire fighting. The other man crouched by Chet. He must be speaking, but Chet couldn't hear him. Only the roar of the engines filled his ears.

The oxygen cleared his head. He shifted. Something was gouging his back. The man hovering over him tugged at his arm and pointed up to the cockpit. He wanted him to move up there. Made sense. He needed to plug into the plane's oxygen system, and hook up to the intercom. He struggled to his feet, still clutching his singed charts.

A second man scrambled down with another fire extinguisher. Before using it, he assisted the engineer in shoving Chet up into the cockpit. Chet sprawled behind the pilot's seat. His helper followed, and soon voices filled his ears.

His helper had plugged in his cables and squatted in front of him. "You all right, sir?"

Sir. How formal. Probably didn't know his name. That's okay. Chet didn't know his name either. He should know the bombardier's name though. He nodded.

The command pilot looked back. He asked, "Vogel, how'd you get out of there?"

"A flak," Chet's voice sounded like he'd just run a mile. He licked his lips and tried again. "A flak hole let the wind blow away my charts out to the escape hatch. I went after them and before I could get back, fire came out." He held out the charts.

Chet's helper took his papers as the pilot said, "Jardine, head on back to the radio. I don't think we should try getting him across the catwalk right now."

His helper, the radio operator, departed. Chet leaned his head back and closed his eyes. He should be doing something, but lethargy held him in a tight grip. He gave up and listened to the voices flooding his headset.

"Fire's out. Melrose is toast." Melrose? The bombardier?

"The left tire dropped slightly from its sheath. Looks like it might be punctured." Had to be the ball gunner. No one else had a view of the bomber's underside.

The firefighters clambered through the hatchway. Chet tucked in his legs to allow them to pass. "Is the deputy navigator guiding us?"

"Yes, the deputy lead took over, and we've dropped back."

"Good. I have no idea where we are." Chet couldn't stop shivering. The wind must be whistling up from the broken nose, although he didn't really feel any colder than usual.

The command pilot was watching him. "Jardine, bring a blanket forward."

Soon Chet lay wrapped in the blanket carried for treating wounded crewmen. It looked like a scratchy old thing that wouldn't be comfortable, but with all his flight clothes on, he didn't feel it. It didn't stop his shivers either. He closed his eyes and let the engine vibrations lull him.

He must have slept. Next thing he knew, the plane was humping and bumping down the runway. That was expected with a flat tire, but why hadn't he been awakened to move to the radio room? They came to a stop and medics pounced on him. In short order, they'd secured him to a stretcher and hauled him out.

In the infirmary, the doctor did a lot of "Hmming." Twice, he tried to blind Chet with his penlight. Twice, he asked Chet to recount the events surrounding the fire. "You keep rolling your head back and forth, and rubbing the back of your neck. Do you remember if you hit your head?"

"I was thrown back when the flak exploded in the nose." He reached a hand back. "Something got me in the ribs. But I didn't get it like Malcore."

"Malcore?"

"The bombardier."

"Ah, yes. Melrose."

Chet's hand massaging his temple stilled. "Melrose? I can't even remember his name."

Lieutenant Colonel Fitzgerald, squadron commanding officer, appeared at his bedside. "How is he?"

"He'll live." The doc talked like Chet wasn't there. "He may or may not have a slight concussion.

A bit of shell shock. He's been harboring a load of guilt over Max Withers' death, and now he's lost another bombardier. I recommend a week at a flak house." He finally turned to Chet. "How would you like to forget about war for a while? Roke Manor is quite a place."

So they thought he was crazy.

Andy brought his mail that evening, including a letter from Carol. About to rip open the envelope, he took a second look at the return address. She must be back in England. He tore off the end and yanked out the letter, scanning the lines.

Forget Roke Manor. He was going to Stanbridge Earls.

Chapter Forty-Nine

Romsey, Hampshire, England
November 7, 1944

Carol closed the front door after bidding farewell to their departing guests and hurried to the fireplace. A roaring fire took the edge off the chill far better than the little gas heaters in Mrs. Lester's house in Saffron Walden. November had never been so damp and cold in Ohio.

Rose Armstrong joined her. "I do believe their week here transformed them. The little copilot certainly is more relaxed. I've never seen a man as shaky as he was his first day here." She referred to a schedule. "The transport taking them to the rail station should return with eight men from the 381st Bomb Group. With the five men still here, that gives us a baker's dozen."

The 381st! Hopefully, someone would be from Chet's squadron and could tell her how he was doing. Back on flying status, he was. His last letter barely mentioned that before he scolded her about being wounded. Hadn't she heard the incoming whistle of the rogue shell? Everyone knew to hit the dirt before it detonated. She smiled. His exasperation reflected his fear for her.

A cold draft swept in from the front hall. Lorna bounded into the room, followed by their five guests. She rubbed her hands briskly before the fire. "We had a lovely bicycle ride in the New Forest, but next time I'll wear gloves."

The officers stayed long enough to drink the hot chocolate brought in by the English butler, Charles. "We're headed back out to the skeet range." One of them grinned. "I feel it in my bones. Today, I'm going to best Smitty."

"Fat chance of that, Blake," Smitty retorted. "The only thing your bones is telling you is it's a good thing you don't have to fire a gun during missions, Mr. Pilot. You couldn't hit the broadside of a Messerschmitt."

This crew squabbled more than any Carol had known during her East Anglia days of clubmobiling. "I'll go out with them and referee."

She retrieved her coat from the cloak room. Charles appeared from nowhere to hold it for her. He never ceased to amaze her with his ability to divine their needs.

On the skeet range, she applauded each clay pigeon that died in a puff of smoke. Smitty had a point. The navigators and bombardiers who manned guns during combat fared better than the pilots.

"Aw, skunked again." Blake watched his pigeon sail away unharmed, his shoulders drooping.

Carol turned around to hide her smile, and spotted the transport pulling in. Time to return to the manor.

She entered through a back door and hurried to join Rose and Lorna at the front door in time to greet the new arrivals. The men entered with their mouths agape at the gigantic proportions of the manor house. Charles always garnered a double take in his butler attire of white shirt, gray waistcoat and trousers, and black hip-length coat. More than once, the Red Cross girls had been asked if they were expected to tip him.

Carol caught her breath. Bringing up the rear was Chet. He didn't gawk at the palatial surroundings. He zeroed in on her. Chills tap-danced up her spine as he strode directly to her and wrapped her in his arms. Lorna gasped, but Carol ignored her as she lay her head on Chet's shoulder. Tears pressed against her eyes, begging for release. Getting caught by the shell explosion was almost worth it to have brought her here.

Pulling away, she searched the faces of his companions. Some looked familiar.

"You remember Lowell and Andy, the pilots from my first crew, don't you?" Chet didn't take his eyes off her, leaving the two to raise their hands in salute. "You're all right now? No lasting effects from your injuries?"

Carol pirouetted in a circle. "Doing fine. I'm leading the lazy life of a lady of the manor. I do go for horseback rides as long as the pace is kept to a sedate walk, or play croquet." She swept her hand around. "These are my new friends, Rose and Lorna."

Introductions were made all around before showing the men to their rooms. Carol grinned as Chet's and his crewmates' jaws dropped when they entered their room. Besides three double beds, enough sofas and chairs graced the room to fill at least two living rooms back home in Ohio. The adjoining bathroom was larger than most average bedrooms. Huge windows offered a panoramic view of the countryside.

"This room is all for us?" Andy dropped his bag on one of the beds. "Or will more be joining us?"

"It's all yours for the whole week," Carol said. "Charles will bring civilian attire for you to wear during the day. You will be expected to wear your uniforms for dinner. You'll be living like British aristocrats who dine formally."

"Whose house is this?" Chet opened the top drawer in the dresser nearest his chosen bed, and dumped in the scant contents of his bag.

"A publisher who still lives on the grounds in a somewhat lesser status. The British government requisitioned the house and turned it over to the Eighth Air Force in a sort of reverse lend lease to keep the American airmen in fit fighting form. The domestic staff is still here."

"Like that butler? What does he do all day, polish the silver?" Lowell pulled back the spread on his bed. "Hey, look at this. We get to sleep between sheets. I didn't know there were any in England." He stretched out on his bed and looked ready to fall asleep. "What's on the agenda for us?"

"As much or as little as you like." Carol picked up Chet's A-2 leather flight jacket from where he'd tossed it on his bed and hung it in the wardrobe. "There's cycling, horses, skeet shooting, fishing, tennis, golf, hiking, lounging, eating." She headed for the door. "Get settled and come on down or take a nap. Dinner's at seven."

Lounging about did not include sleeping in. Charles surprised them the next morning by waking them before dawn. He served them cups of hot chocolate in bed. Chet didn't mind the early wake-up, savoring the drink's soothing slide down his throat. Sure beat hiking through the cold, dark mornings to the mess hall.

Downstairs, they assembled in the huge dining room dominated by a long trestle table. Everything about the room was big—the furniture, the paintings hanging on the walls. And the sideboards! Oh, man. They groaned with fruit juices and coffee, hot and cold cereal, fresh scrambled and fried eggs, bacon and sausages. Chet's mouth watered. No one would guess rationing was in effect. And best of all for him, eating with Carol. She came from the sideboard and set her plate down beside his.

He sipped his orange juice and studied her selections. "Is that all you plan on eating? Toast, one sunny side up, and a bit of oatmeal? Isn't everything as tasty as last night's supper?"

She smiled as she spread her napkin on her lap. "It's all delicious, and that's the problem. With my reduced activity during recovery, I've not only regained the weight I lost dining on K-rations in France, I've packed on extra pounds. Now I'm on a diet."

Chet couldn't hold back a snicker. "That's the first I've heard of that particular problem." He watched Andy load his plate. "Being here is kind of like being a kid in a candy store. So, what do you want to do after breakfast? Walk a mile around the grounds?"

"That sounds good. Too bad the gardens aren't in bloom. Rose says the flowers are glorious."

The other men chose to occupy their morning with golf and cycling. Lorna saw the golfers off. Rose helped the cyclists plan their route. Chet had

Carol to himself. They donned their coats and headed out the door.

Among the topiary on the front lawn, Chet spied an archery target. He flexed his fingers and scooped up the bow and sling of arrows. "Will Charles come running out to shag any wayward arrows?"

Carol laughed, the sound washing over him like tinkling bells. "More likely he'd send a footman."

He took aim and let an arrow fly. It smacked into the straw target midway to the bull's eye. "Ha. Not too shabby, but I'll quit while I'm ahead."

He returned the equipment to the porch and took Carol's arm.

They made their way down a pathway toward the main gate. Carol pointed out a bird soaring high overhead. "After two months away from combat, how did you feel about flying missions again?"

"At first, it was almost a relief after all the inactivity. But getting up in the cold wee hours and then settling into the cramped quarters onboard the airplane, all I could think was, 'Let's get this war over with.' And then there was my last mission." He rushed through his explanation of the fire, his scattered papers, the bombardier. "I have a hard time remembering his name."

He turned to look back at the house surrounded by woods and manicured lawns. Five gables and at least a dozen chimneys. Enough glass for a full-time window washer. "This joint must take a pile of dough for the upkeep."

Carol looked back, too. "I don't think you could manage it on a navigator's salary." She squeezed his hand. "Don't you think not remembering the bombardier's name is a defense mechanism to avoid pain at his loss? Like how you avoid getting to know men other than your crew?"

"Maybe so. Actually, I didn't know him. It was only our second mission together. The doc thinks I'm suffering from battle fatigue."

Some guys had all the luck, flying entire thirty-mission tours without a scratch or a hiccup.

"When we arrived last winter, our commanding officer told us to consider ourselves as dead men. As soon as we accept that, we'd fly better, sleep better, and live longer. When the flak starts flying, my stomach still knots up, but I concentrate on my job." They came to a fork in the path and he waited for Carol to indicate their direction. "I'm glad navigation keeps me busy. If all we encounter is flak and not fighters, our gunners are superfluous. They go through all that for nothing, not firing their guns once."

"A time to die, a time to kill, a time for war, but then a time to heal and a time for peace. A chaplain in the Paris hospital reminded me of that. By this time next year, we'll all be home, don't you think?"

"I hope so. I sure do hope so." He interlaced their fingers. "What do you see yourself doing a year from now? Reporting?"

Carol raised her eyes to his "Maybe, for a little while." Her cheeks pinkened. "I'm ready to move on."

Her voice faltered.

Chet heard what she left unsaid. She was ready to marry and have a family. He bent and touched his lips to hers.

Chapter Fifty

On Sunday, they went horseback riding. Carol led the way up a ridge and reined in her horse. She watched Chet absorb the splendid view.

"Miles and miles, and no destruction. Amazing." He inhaled the crisp air tinted with the scent of evergreen. "Do you regret not seeing more of the continent?"

Carol stroked her horse's neck. "No. I'm glad I went. It was an experience I'll never forget." She surveyed the view. Superimposed on the peaceful tableau, she saw the crumpled French homes. "But after seeing so many ruins, it gets disheartening. Germany's going to end up even worse than France and Belgium, if that's possible. I want to scream at them, 'Why are you doing this?' They can't win. It should be obvious to them."

They guided the horses down a slope and along a stream. "I didn't really think about this while I was with the clubmobile. Too busy, I guess. Now I've had time to reflect. I wrote an article about it, the waste of war, and sent it to the *Repository* the day before you arrived." She shrugged. "I have no idea if they'll publish it."

"Sure they will. The folks back home need to be impressed with what war leaves in its wake." Chet pulled back on his reins so suddenly, his horse snorted in protest. "I forgot to tell you. I saw my father in London."

"Your father?" Carol pulled to a stop. "How'd it go? Was he nice to you?"

"I don't think we exchanged more than a dozen words, and most of them were about Nate. He didn't sneer. If we hadn't been interrupted, I like to think he might have asked how I've been doing."

"Of course he would have. It's plain to see you've turned out very well indeed. If he has any sense at all, he'd be proud of you." Every time she thought of Chet's father, she wanted to knock him on the head.

A hint of a smile tugged at Chet's lips as he nudged his horse to continue. "Thank you, my dear, but I don't expect to ever have more than a relationship of casual acquaintances with him. And that's okay. I realized something. I'm taller than he is now. I no longer look up to him. He's lost his ability to intimidate me like he used to. Maybe it's because I've been doing what the chaplain suggested. On base, we frequently recited the Lord's Prayer. 'Forgive us our debts, as we forgive our debtors.' One day those words really hit me. It may make no difference to Dad, but praying has healed the hurt."

He seemed so pleased. It was a victory of sorts. Carol urged her horse to follow him. She sighed. Maybe Nate would help bridge the gap between them. One thing she could count on. Her father would welcome Chet with open arms.

The evening before the 381st men returned to Ridgewell, they all gathered in the front room. Rose sat at the grand piano and they circled around to sing. It was a common activity, and Carol loved hearing Chet sing, but she wished they could spend their last hours alone together. In the middle of "The White Cliffs of Dover," he tugged her hand and led her out to the library.

He stopped before a window where rain spattered against the glass. Taking both her hands in his, he opened his mouth, then closed it. He brushed his fingers through her hair and grasped her hand again. "I love you, Carol. Will you marry me?"

Her heart skipped a beat. "Chet! Yes. Oh, yes!"

His lips lowered to hers.

"Oh, my goodness. I can't believe it." Lorna stood in the doorway. "I'm supposed to tell you we're going to roast marshmallows in the fireplace and have hot chocolate." She scurried off. In a moment they heard her exclaim, "He popped the question, and she said yes."

Chet rested his forehead against hers. He vibrated with silent laughter. "A town crier. Somehow that's fitting in this throwback-to-days-gone-by house."

She'd have to say goodbye in the morning, but she knew, she *knew*, they would survive this war and go on to a bright new season.

Epilogue

Ridgewell, England
August 28, 1982

Chet shaded his eyes as he gazed across the peaceful tableau. Green fields replaced the crisscrossing concrete runways. The asphalt perimeter track and all the hardstands had vanished. Gone, too, were the tin can Quonset huts and the concrete block control tower.

"If it weren't for the memorial and the museum put up by the locals, you'd never guess what grim business took place here." A light breeze ruffled his hair. He didn't mind. He was pleased he still had hair to ruffle.

"I'm glad we came for the dedication of the memorial. The 381st called this place home for two years. Rafe and I were here for less than a year. That's not a long time in the grand scheme of life." Paul Braedel hunched his shoulders, his hands buried in his pockets. "But that year defined us. Our fathers fought in War World I, we got caught up in the Second World War. I am so glad my two sons did not have to fight."

Rafe Martell stared up into the sky. "I almost expect to see the formation coming back from a mission, hear the roar of the engines, smell the fuel and gunpowder. It's all gone now, but I can still see it."

Chet tilted his head back. It wasn't hard to imagine the long-gone planes flying over. "After Germany surrendered, everyone wanted to go home. We all promised to keep in touch, but we didn't. We bonded fast in the life-and-death struggle, but back in the civilian world, those friendships faded like that." He snapped his fingers.

Paul nodded his agreement. "I'd remember someone at odd times, but by then, his address was obsolete. Other than Rafe, Chet, you're the only one I stayed in contact with, maybe because we met at navigation school before the flak and bullets started flying."

"You flew with different crews. Maybe that had something to do with it." Rafe scooped up ground in a film canister. His granddaughter wanted a souvenir. "I stayed with one crew through combat and internment in Sweden. The other officers and I have remained good friends."

"Living in the same city made it easy for us to get together frequently." Paul slapped his former barracks mate on the back. "Funny thing. We're all members of the Caterpillar Club. Some crews served their whole tour with no one wounded, no major damage. But we all had to bail out. Of course, Chet here, being an over-achiever, also joined the Goldfish Club."

"Believe you me, ditching was a lot better experience than parachuting."

The museum door opened and their wives appeared.

"Are you airmen ready for some coffee and doughnuts?" Carol Vogel wore her Red Cross uniform, her figure as trim as it was thirty-seven years before. Chet hadn't known she'd brought it along. The tray she held wasn't Red Cross issue, but the doughnuts looked like the same dunkers.

Heidi Braedel carried a coffee pot and Jennie Martell had a tray with cups.

"Well, this certainly brings back memories." Paul took a bite of doughnut. "All we need now are some Spam sandwiches."

Chet, Carol, and Rafe groaned.

"At the last reunion, Bomby told me he insists there will always be some Spam in his house. After walking his dog in the winter, a Spam sandwich and cup of cocoa is his favorite snack." Chet savored a bite of doughnut. "There's no understanding some people's tastes."

"Ready to visit the Cambridge cemetery?" Heidi asked.

"Yes." Paul blew out his breath. "I want to see Art Jensen's name on the Tablets of the Missing."

He didn't seem eager. Chet understood. He felt the same about seeing Max Withers' grave.

Many of the 381st men had returned for the dedication, and now a bus took them to the American Cemetery. A long white wall stood engraved with the names of the service people missing in action from that part of the war. There they were. The names of the men of *Sly Buccaneer*, Paul's first crew. He traced a finger over Aubrey Stiles, his pilot, and Quinn McPhee, the copilot. He laid his hand over Art's name and bowed his head. Art had been his friend from childhood.

Turning from the wall, Chet gazed across a sea of white crosses standing at attention in formation, sprinkled here and there with Stars of David. Taking Carol's hand, he headed out unerringly. The others followed and he explained. "Whenever my Pan Am flights brought me to England, I came here for a visit."

He stopped before a cross etched with the name Maxwell Withers. "First chance I had after the war, I went back to France. I needed to see the Chotars and Suzette. They showed me where Max had been buried. He was brought back here. I've always wondered if I had said something about his parachute being cut, if he'd still be alive."

Carol rubbed his back. She knew better than to argue with him.

They wandered through the rows, but ended up back at the wall. Names of other men they'd known brought back long-buried memories.

Rafe sighed. "What would the world have been like if they'd lived?"

Chet turned back to look out over the field of crosses. "We've grown old, but they're still young in my memory. Young and alive. One of my grandkids says I think they're in..." He touched Carol's shoulder. "What did she call it?"

"An alternate universe. Find the portal and you'll find the air base where all the KIAs are still alive and fighting the war, frozen in time."

"Killed in action, but still in action." Paul smiled. "Sounds like she watches 'The Twilight Zone.'"

Carol shook her head in despair. "Or she reads too much science fiction."

"1942." Rafe rubbed a hand across a date on the wall. "Some of these forever-young guys died not knowing how the war would turn out, that we'd win.

"Neither side really wins a war." Chet pulled Carol close to his side. "Both sides lose. One side just loses less than the other."

The sun was sliding down in the western sky, throwing the crosses' shadows in sharp relief. Chet took Carol's hand. "Now we bid farewell again and return to the better world they sacrificed their lives for."

Before heading back to the bus, he saluted the fallen. Paul and Rafe did likewise. Overhead, a flock of birds wheeled across the sky in formation, one bird soaring up and away in solo flight.

Author's Note

Thank you for joining Chet and Carol in their wartime experiences. It was a pleasure to return to Ridgewell and the 381st Bomb Group, first visited in *Friends & Enemies* and again in *No Neutral Ground*. Thank you to my Montreal friend, Nancy St. Cyr, who provided the French translations for the Chotars. If, like me, you don't speak French, here is what Chet heard:

Vers la gauche maintenant. Dépêchez-vous. To your left now. Hurry.

Monsieur, pouvez-vous détacher votre parachute? Monsieur, can you release your parachute?

Il faut couper les cordes du parachute pour le libérer. We have to cut the lines of the parachute to free him.

Buvez monsieur Drink, monsieur.

C'est mieux, n'est-ce pas? That's better, is it not?

Un américain modeste A modest American.

Ma fille est partie chercher le médecin. Reposez-vous maintenant. My daughter has gone for the doctor. Rest now.

And thank you to my critique group members, Connie Cortright, Betty Owens Thomason, Shirley Connolly, and Pat Krugel.

If you're on Pinterest, visit www.pinterest.com/terriwangard to see my board for *Soar Like Eagles* and discover Chet's and Carol's worlds. Visit me at www.terriwangard.com

Discussion Questions

1.   What do you think of Carol's resolve to avoid romantic entanglements? Was it realistic?

2.   Chet's father always belittled him. How does that affect him? Have you been disparaged? How did you handle it?

3.   How do you feel about Sally's situation? What would you have said to her?

4.   Midge was pressured by her mother into applying to the Red Cross. What would you have done in her place?

5.   Chet and Carol don't enjoy Wally's presence in Cambridge. How do you deal with obnoxious people?

6.   When Chet harbors guilt about Max, Suzette tells him we must ask God's forgiveness and put our lost battles behind us. Do you agree? What would you have told him?

7.   Chet's reconciliation with his brother Nate thrilled him. Why do you think he didn't expect to ever have a normal relationship with his father?

8.   Audrey got angry when Carol advised her to wait before marrying Wally. Did Carol have an obligation to urge caution? Could she have handled it better?

9.   Carol felt guilty for being "the other woman" when she learned Ted was married. Since she wasn't interested in a relationship with him, should she have gone for a walk with him in Paris?

37299291R00283

Printed in Great Britain
by Amazon